"You can't tell me what ~~I~~ ~~can~~ can't forgive," I snapped.

"It's my forgiveness. And anyway, it's thanks to you that I have a rest of my life to be worried about, so you'll just have to put up with me not hating you."

Rupert stared at me for a long moment, and then he bowed his head, leaning down until his forehead rested against mine. "How are you like this?" he whispered. "How can you just let this go?"

Other than our foreheads and our hands, Rupert and I weren't actually touching, but it didn't seem to matter. I could feel his warmth across the few inches that separated us, and my whole body was twitching with the sudden urge to wrap myself around him. But then, Rupert was always like this for me. The nearness of him was so overwhelming I hadn't even noticed that he'd trapped me against the sink until I felt the cold metal lip pressing into my lower back. Worse, I couldn't seem to make myself care. All the smart, careful plans I'd made to keep my head on straight and not let myself get burned by him again seemed suddenly pointless. And as his fingers tightened around mine, filling my body with the memory of just how good those fingers could feel, I began to wonder, why was I holding back again?

But just as I pushed up on my toes to bring my lips to his, Rupert's head shot up.

I jumped in surprise, knocking my back painfully against the sink. "What?"

Rupert put a finger to his lips, looking pointedly toward the living room. I nodded, holding my breath as I listened, but I didn't hear anything except the constant rustle of the soypen outside. I was about to push out of his arms and go investigate for myself when I caught the soft but very familiar hiss of a stabilizer. A Paradoxian armor stabilizer, shifting a large amount of weight.

That was all the warning I got before the back door of the house exploded.

By Rachel Bach

Paradox

Fortune's Pawn

Honor's Knight

Heaven's Queen

By Rachel Aaron

The Legend of Eli Monpress

The Spirit Thief

The Spirit Rebellion

The Spirit Eater

The Spirit War

Spirit's End

The Legend of Eli Monpress Volumes I, II & III
(omnibus edition)

HEAVEN'S QUEEN

Paradox Series
Book 3

RACHEL BACH

orbit

www.orbitbooks.net

Orbit
Hachette Book Group
237 Park Avenue, New York, NY 10017
HachetteBookGroup.com

First Edition: April 2014

Orbit is an imprint of Hachette Book Group, Inc. The Orbit name and
logo are trademarks of Little, Brown Book Group Limited.

The Hachette Speakers Bureau provides a wide range of authors for
speaking events. To find out more, go to www.hachettespeakersbureau.com
or call (866) 376-6591.

Library of Congress Cataloging-in-Publication Data
Bach, Rachel.
  Heaven's queen / Rachel Bach. — First edition.
    pages cm. — (Paradox series ; book 3)
  ISBN 978-0-316-22112-2 (trade pbk.)
  I. Title.
  PS3601.A26H43 2014
  813'.6—dc23
                                          2013026335

        10 9 8 7 6 5 4 3 2 1

RRD-C

Printed in the United States of America

For my readers, the wonderful people whose support allows me to work the best job in the world. All my books are for you, but this one especially. Thank you.

PROLOGUE

Commander Brian Caldswell, head of the little-known and terribly named Joint Investigatory Spatial Anomaly Task Force, stood on the bridge of the Republic battle cruiser he'd requisitioned from fleet command an hour ago, staring through the huge observation window at the void beyond, a void that should have been a thriving planet of sixteen billion people, and wondering how everything could have gone so wrong so quickly.

Seven years now they'd been fighting the phantoms. Seven years of working constantly, of never seeing his wife, of missing his daughter grow up. But in those seven years, they'd never failed. They'd never missed an alarm or arrived too late to save whatever colony planet the phantoms had chosen to nest on. Even these last eighteen months, when the phantom attacks had grown so frequent it didn't seem possible to catch them all in time, Caldswell's team had always pulled it off. Always, that was, until yesterday.

"It's pointless to feel guilty."

Caldswell kept himself from jumping just in time, sliding his eyes over to look at his partner. John Brenton was right beside him, his arm almost brushing Caldswell's shoulder, and Caldswell hadn't heard a thing. *Damn creepy symbiont*, he thought with an angry breath. Dr. Strauss wanted to put one of those things in him, too, but that wasn't happening. Caldswell had spent the first fifteen years of his career running slave-freeing missions against those damn lizards—like hell was he going to let the doctor shove one into his brain.

"Even if we'd left the second the gravity alarms went off, the planet would still have been completely destabilized by the time we'd finished the jump," Brenton went on, staring down at the small knot of refugee ships that huddled in the battleship's shadow, the ten thousand people who were all that remained of the Republic core world of Svenya. "The only thing we can do now is make sure it never happens again."

"And how do you suggest we do that?" Caldswell said quietly, glancing over his shoulder.

Behind him, Maat lay on the floor, curled up in a ball under Brenton's coat. Dr. Strauss, the universally renowned plasmex doctor who'd been assigned as Maat's caretaker, was on his knees beside her. He was talking to her in a soft voice, trying to cajole her into getting up, but Maat didn't even seem to hear him. She just lay there, her dark eyes glassy and empty but still afraid. The sight made Caldswell want to pull his hair out, because it meant they were probably going to have to drug her again.

As a powerful plasmex user rescued from the pits of a xith'cal lab, Maat had always been unstable, but they'd never had to drug her until this year. With the added workload from the increase in phantom attacks, though, her fits were rapidly getting out of control. They'd had to drug her nearly unconscious just two days ago, and Caldswell never would have ordered it again so soon, but the moment they'd arrived at Svenya she'd gone into hysterics, nearly killing their entire crew before Brenton managed to get her with the syringe.

She'd screamed herself into unconsciousness, babbling about a god, a monster that spanned the sky. At the time, Caldswell had dismissed it as more of Maat's raving, but that was before he'd heard the phantom they'd come here to hunt had reduced an earth-class planet to rubble in less than a galactic standard day. Now he wasn't so sure she was wrong.

"She's strong," Brenton said earnestly. "She'll snap herself out of this."

"And what if she can't?" Caldswell asked. "What if this thing really is as huge as she claims? Our biggest phantom was, what, fifty feet?"

"Forty-five," Brenton said. "But she handled it."

"And she went to pieces at the sight of this one," Caldswell said, nodding like Brenton had just made his point for him. "Did you see the ships it destroyed? Huge freighters crushed like tin cans. Damn thing must be miles long, and it's *still* out there."

With Maat out of commission, Caldswell had been forced to track the phantom by sending scout ships to fly until they hit the phantom's aura and blacked out. As spotting methods went, it was only slightly less dangerous than randomly shooting the cannons until they scored a hit, but Caldswell had to know if the thing moved. Svenya had been the largest colony in this system by far, but the other planets still had populations in the millions. If the monster made a move toward one of them, Caldswell needed to know. Not that he knew what he'd do if that happened. "Maybe we should try nuking it again?"

Brenton scoffed. "The nukes don't work on the little ones. A phantom this size wouldn't even feel it." He shook his head. "Maat's power is the only thing that can touch them."

"You tell me, then," Caldswell snapped. "There's a monster out there capable of destroying a planet in a day that we can't see, can't track, and can't shoot. Just seeing it was enough to scare our only viable weapon into a coma, and I'm supposed to be sending a message to fleet command right now to report that we've got this under control. So you tell me, John, what do we do?"

"Tell the truth," Brenton said. "Tell them we don't have it under control because something like this *can't* be controlled. Our best bet is to evacuate all the remaining colonies and close off the system. It's never been proven that phantoms can travel faster than light. If we give it enough space, we might never see it again in our lifetime."

"There's also no proof that they *can't* travel faster than light," Caldswell replied. "Seven years and we still don't know jack shit about how they move. We don't even know if this monster is the only one of its kind. The phantom population has been increasing exponentially all year, and we can't even say why or where they're coming from. For all we know, this is the new normal."

The end of humanity, Caldswell thought with a cold clench. He'd always thought the xith'cal were the worst threat to mankind, but the lizards were nothing on this enemy, the monster they couldn't see coming. "We have to do something," he said, turning back to the empty window. "Find some way to wall it in or—"

He cut off as a deep groan rattled through the ship. The noise was more pressure than sound, squeezing his mind in a way Caldswell recognized too well. It was the phantom's scream, but he'd never heard one this deep or this huge. The ship lights flickered in answer before Maat's power neutralized the phantom's aura, and Caldswell let out a long breath.

"It's getting closer," he said as the scream faded, looking back at Maat and her doctor. "Ben! How soon can you wake her up?"

Dr. Strauss looked up at his name and began to shake his head wildly, sending his wispy white-blond hair flying around his paper-pale face. "It would be unwise in the extreme to disrupt her harmony. Her mind is still in trauma from being put under and from whatever she saw. If you bring her up now, the risk of a full-scale psychotic breakdown increases exponentially."

The lights flickered again as he spoke. This time, though, only the low-energy emergency runners came back on, and Caldswell swore under his breath. "Do it," he ordered. "We'll deal with the consequences later."

"We don't even know if she'll be able to do anything," Brenton said, grabbing Caldswell's arm. "Are you really willing to risk damaging her? Our only weapon?"

"If that thing catches us while she's asleep, we're all dead for sure," Caldswell said, plopping himself into the gunnery control seat. Phantoms couldn't be killed by physical objects or energy attacks, but they didn't like them. If he could land a big enough hit, maybe he could buy them some—

The battleship lurched beneath him as something crashed into the port side. Something enormous. Even at low power, the thrusters righted them immediately, but Caldswell had had enough.

"Wake her up!" he shouted, punching the button to authorize live fire on all guns. Before he could shoot, though, a new scream ripped through the bridge, sending a stab of pain right through his head. His first thought was that another phantom had joined the attack, a much smaller one, but then he saw Maat lurch to her feet, her mouth open as she screamed again.

"They're coming!"

As always, Brenton got to her first. "Easy," he whispered, pulling her into his arms. "Who's coming?"

Maat buried her face in Brenton's chest, and Caldswell felt a twinge of guilt. She was nearly twenty now, but when she did that, she looked just like the little girl they'd rescued so long ago. The little girl they should have been protecting, not using like this.

"Who?" Brenton asked again.

Maat's whole body shook with a sob. "The ones who speak in the dark."

Brenton glanced at Caldswell, but the commander just shrugged. Maat said cryptic shit all the time. But before he could try and guess what this particular riddle was about, a flash outside put everything else out of his mind.

Light bloomed in the empty space that had been the colony of Svenya, pushing through the darkness like all of reality was just oil floating on water. Caldswell had never seen anything like it, though he knew enough to guess it must be some kind of hyperspace exit. As for the ships that came through, though, he couldn't guess at all.

They looked like deep-sea fish, their flat bodies marked with gorgeous blues, greens, and purples that glowed with their own light. They dwarfed the battleship Caldswell had requisitioned, but they moved with a grace that belied their hugeness, an effortless, natural motion that he had never seen in any machine. If it wasn't for the fact that he could see obvious doors in their sides and prows, he would have sworn the giant vessels were *alive*. Whatever they were, though, they were beautiful. So beautiful Caldswell could have stared at them forever, but he couldn't, because the final shape that blossomed out of hyperspace stole his attention completely.

If the mystery ships had been huge, this thing was gigantic, as large as any of the xith'cal warships Caldswell had fought—only this, he was sure, was no ship. Unlike the others with their rainbow colors, the last thing to exit hyperspace was as black as the void behind it. Once the hyperspace flash faded, Caldswell could catch only glimpses of its surface in the reflected light of the other ships: a wide, pointed head framed by millions of tendrils; a shiny, shell-black surface; and deep, terrible pits that could have been eyes or mouths or something else he couldn't even imagine. He was still staring at it when the other ships opened fire.

Caldswell grabbed the console on instinct, because from where he was sitting, the beautiful ships seemed to be firing straight at *him*. But the brilliant beams of blue-white fire never hit the Republic battleship. Instead, they struck the invisible mass of the phantom floating between them.

For one terrifying moment, the entire sky was ablaze. For the first time ever, Caldswell saw the whole of the phantom's body as the alien's fire lit it up from within. The thing was even bigger than he'd imagined, and he'd imagined big. Miles, he'd guessed, maybe hundreds of them. Now, with the truth spelled out in fire, all he could think was that he'd been a fool. The phantom's snakelike body stretched from one end of Svenya's dust cloud to the other. It was as big as a planet, bigger even than the enormous black monster commanding the attack, and it wasn't going down quietly.

The creature burned for nearly thirty minutes, thrashing in agony, taking several of the beautiful fishlike ships out in the process. It was only by pure luck that it didn't hit Caldswell's battleship again. But the unknown aliens kept up the attack until, at last, the phantom gave one final shudder and started to disintegrate. That was all Caldswell saw before the alien's fire snuffed out and the phantom's body vanished, invisible once again, though he knew if he could somehow reach out there, he would still feel it falling apart.

All through the attack, Maat hadn't moved. She just stood there clinging to Brenton, her eyes locked on the light show outside. When it finished, she collapsed into a sobbing heap.

Dr. Strauss was at her side at once, helping Brenton move her to the captain's chair. Caldswell was about to go over as well when the voice spoke in his head.

Enemy of our enemy.

The words weren't words exactly, not as he knew them. They were more like impressions, meanings layered together to form something richer than language. For a moment, Caldswell thought he was imagining things, but then Brenton and the doctor snapped their heads up as well, looking around like they'd heard it, too. Meanwhile, Maat began to cry harder.

Outside, the beautiful alien ships were coming toward them with the huge black shape at the center. They moved so fast, there was no chance to run even if Caldswell had wanted to. But he wanted no such thing. He ordered the helmsman to hold course before walking up to the prow of the bridge just as the aliens came to an abrupt halt in front of them, the huge fleet floating like giants over the lone Republic ship.

Who speaks for all?

The words brushed over Caldswell's mind like impatient fingers, demanding to know who was in command. He could see from Brenton's face that he'd felt it as well, but Caldswell was commander here, so he was the one who answered.

"I am."

Any worries that the aliens wouldn't be able to hear him vanished when he felt the presence in his mind focus, the impressions growing louder and clearer, as though the speaker had turned to face him. *Enemy of our enemy*, it said again, only now the words implied kinship and cooperation. *We offer you aid.*

"And we appreciate it," Caldswell replied. "Thank you. We never could have killed that thing on our own."

We know this, the alien said dismissively. *And now you know it as well. You are dead without us.*

Caldswell fought the urge to scowl. "What kind of aid are you offering?"

Protection, the voice said, the word itself a wall. *The universe has been torn open, and the corruption is seeping through. This attack was only the beginning. More are coming.*

"More" was the word Caldswell's brain supplied, but the alien's impression was infinitely larger, an endless flood. "How many more?"

Countless, the voice answered. *More than either of us can fight.*

Caldswell nodded. "So you want to work together."

Amusement trilled through his mind like a swirling feather. *We do not fight unless forced*, it answered. *Violence is a risk we cannot take. We are vital; therefore, we cannot be allowed to end.*

"Is that so?" Caldswell said, folding his arms over his chest. "Then what exactly would we be getting out of this aid if you won't fight?"

Survival, the alien replied, filling the words with the feeling of an open hand. *We are lelgis, those without end, and we offer you our knowledge and the opportunity to save your race. We will show you how to forge the weapon that can kill the ones you know as phantoms, and in return, you will hunt them until we are all safe.* The voice paused, letting this sink in. And then, almost like an afterthought, it added, *We also require an offering.*

"What kind of offering?" Brenton said, making Caldswell jump.

He hadn't realized the others could hear this as well until Brenton spoke, but when he looked back, his partner was glaring murder at the black alien above them. "You seem to be getting the sweet end of this deal while we do all the work."

Without us, you will die, the lelgis said lightly. *You need us, and to aid you, we require the one called Maat.*

"What?" Brenton shouted, but Caldswell put out his hand.

"Explain," he said.

She has the potential to be like us, the lelgis said solemnly, the words heavy with power. *Give her to us, and we will forge her to be the tool that saves this universe.*

Caldswell could feel Brenton's rage building from across the room, so he made sure to speak first. "What would that entail, exactly?"

The enormous black alien moved a little closer. *She will stop the flood in our stead,* it said, offering up the picture of a door closing. *Without a barricade, the corruption will overwhelm us all, and this sad, dead planet will be but the first in an infinite line of tragedies. But with her, we can stop them. A single sacrifice so that all may live.*

Caldswell bit his lip, trying to think this through, to tease out what was really going on. Before he could, though, the alien spoke again. *This offer will be tendered only once, enemy of our enemy. Accept and save your species, refuse and perish.*

"Don't do it, Brian," Brenton said, suddenly beside him. "Don't even think about it. We can't trust them. We don't even know what they are."

"You saw what they killed," Caldswell said. "I'm not saying you're wrong, but without them we'd be dead right now."

"Maat is our only weapon against the phantoms," Brenton said, his voice rising. "You can't just give—"

"Maat is breaking!" Caldswell yelled. "You know that damn well. Even if she wasn't, do you really think we can keep going like we have been over the last few months? Some of us need to sleep,

Brenton, and we can't guard the entire universe with one girl. Not at the rate the phantoms are multiplying. We need a better solution, and if they're offering one, we'd be idiots not to hear it out."

"So you'd just give her over?" Brenton shouted. "Sacrifice her to some alien—"

"Yes!" Caldswell shouted back, jabbing his finger at the floating rocks that had been Svenya. "If it means something like this will never happen again, I'd give them my own daughter!"

Caldswell regretted his words the moment they were out of his mouth, but it was too late. The alien voice was already crooning in his head.

Good, it whispered, petting him with their approval as the aliens turned their fleet around. *Follow.*

"Do it," Caldswell ordered, ignoring Brenton's horrified look. Moments later, the battleship took off after them, following the aliens into the dark.

Once the ship was moving, Caldswell stomped over to Brenton to take Maat from him, but the symbiont wouldn't let go. Maat was trembling in his arms, staring at Caldswell with terrified eyes. "I can see what they want," she whispered, her voice breaking like old glass. "Don't let them take me." Tears appeared in her eyes. "*Please*, Brian, don't do this."

When he didn't answer, she flew into a rage. As Brenton and Dr. Strauss wrestled her back into the chair for sedation, Caldswell slumped into his own seat to watch the lelgis fly. He knew Brenton wouldn't stop fighting him on this. Brenton always took Maat's side, but it didn't matter. Caldswell had made up his mind. If the lelgis could give him the weapon that had burned that monster out of the sky, or any weapon that could reliably kill phantoms on the scale they needed to be killed on, then he would pay any price. He would climb up on the altar with Maat himself if they wanted, so long as they gave him the power to stop the goddamn tragedies.

After all, he thought, slumping down, what were a few more deaths compared to the billions of lives already lost? What was anything, so long as no more planets died? Nothing, he decided. Nothing at all.

Five days later, Maat was given to the lelgis as promised, and at the far corner of the newly restricted zone that had been the Sve-nya System, construction began on the prison that would later be known as Dark Star Station.

CHAPTER

1

I've woken up in a lot of weird places in my life, but coming to in a xith'cal escape pod was pushing it even for me.

I woke with a start, jumping so sharply I would have put a fist through something if I hadn't had the foresight to lock my suit. Fortunately I had, so all I did was bang around a little.

"Welcome back."

I glanced at my cameras to see Rupert smiling over his shoulder at me. In the normal run of things, I would have counted waking up to an attractive man's smile as a plus, but my relationship with Rupert Charkov was a thorny, complicated mess at the moment, so I mumbled a hello and looked away, though not before I noticed that Rupert had shifted out of his symbiont scales and put on clothes while I was asleep.

I'll admit I was a little disappointed I'd missed that. I might have been infected with a crazy plasmex plague and generally confused about my situation, but I wasn't *dead*. At least, not yet, which was in itself nothing short of a miracle considering the events on Reaper's tribe ship and our subsequent crazy escape from the lelgis. But though I'd had one of my best nights ever celebrating not being dead with Rupert back on Caldswell's *Glorious Fool*, a lot had changed since then, so I forced my eyes off Rupert's admittedly lovely back and settled them firmly on my surroundings.

Surprisingly, it turned out to be worth the look.

"Wow," I breathed, craning my neck back. The sky outside the ship's tiny canopy was absolutely *full* of stars all crowded together against a rainbow of color that ranged from deep blue to brilliant pink. The combined light was so bright my cameras darkened to compensate, but even my suit couldn't dim the glare of the giant, golden gas planet we were currently orbiting, its swirling cloud cover shining like a second sun in the reflected light of the twin star system behind us.

"Where are we?" I asked, covering my eyes with my hand.

"The Atlas Emission Nebula," Rupert replied. "Birthplace of stars and, as you might have guessed from the name, a licensed territory of Atlas Industrial."

I whistled. "I know you Terrans give your corporations a lot of freedom, but this is ridiculous." Why would anyone give up a place this beautiful?

Rupert shrugged. "There are plenty who would agree with you, but at the moment the Terran Republic's policy of licensing unused space works in our favor. Every possible terraformable satellite in this sector has been turned into an Atlas cash development, which means we have our choice of places to set down, so long as we do it in the next thirty minutes."

"What happens in the next thirty minutes?"

Rupert turned back to the screen at the front of the ship. "If I'm reading this right, that's when we run out of fuel."

He said this so blithely I almost missed the doom inherent in that statement. "Hold up. You're saying we've got thirty minutes to safely land a xith'cal ship on a Terran colony?" He nodded, and I threw up my hands. "Why don't we just shoot ourselves down and save them the trouble?"

Rupert must have been breathing the xith'cal's poison air for far too long, because he actually laughed at that. "Everything will be fine," he said, pointing at the gas giant below us. "That's Atlas Fifty-Nine. It's got a regular trade route and ten moons we can pick from, any one of which is bound to have communications equipment and a hyperdrive-capable ship we can requisition. We'll be down and back up again before you know it."

I was about to ask where the hell he thought we'd be going since Caldswell—my only guarantee that I wouldn't be immediately tossed in a lab and ground into patties by scientists looking to extract my phantom-killing plasmex virus—was still lost in hyperspace, possibly forever. But I wasn't ready to start up that hill just yet, so I stuck to the more immediate problems.

"Have you been here before?" I asked. "Like, do you have any contacts you could radio not to shoot us?"

"I haven't been here personally, no," Rupert said. "But we've got a Republic military all-access code that will guarantee us safe passage. I just need you to radio it out from your suit, because I can't figure out how to send anything from this." He pointed at the xith'cal ship controls.

I couldn't help smirking at that. "Powered armor comes through again," I said. "But why didn't you wake me before we entered orbit? They could have shot us already."

Rupert flashed me a smile. "You looked like you needed the sleep, and no one puts long-range missiles on a cash colony."

It was a fair point. I pulled up my suit's com with a thought and flipped to an open channel. Since I don't make a habit of getting stranded in ships that don't have communications equipment, I didn't actually have a lot of experience with open-space frequencies. Subsequently, it took quite a bit of fiddling before I figured out how to send a message.

But while my Lady has many strengths, she's not much of a broadcaster, and even after I put all her power into it, my signal was still pretty weak. Fortunately, the com chatter in this sector of space was almost dead silent, which meant even a weak message could get through. I just had to figure out where to send it.

"You were right about having our pick of landings," I said,

looking over the half dozen different colony identifiers my suit was picking up. "I've got a fix on all six Atlas Fifty-Nine moons. Any preference?"

Rupert glanced at something on the complicated screen in front of him. "Whatever's closest would be best, I think."

That didn't sound good. I picked out the strongest of the signals, but as I tried to compose a Mayday that wouldn't be taken for a xith'cal trick, something made me pause. The list of planetary identifiers on my message screen was giving me the strangest sense of déjà vu. This, in turn, was enough to seriously piss me off, because I'd thought I was done with this missing-memory bullshit. But a quick search of my contacts list proved I was overcomplicating things. The call sign looked familiar because it *was*, and my anger vanished as my face broke into a huge smile.

"Oh man," I said, putting in the familiar code. "You are *so* lucky you have me."

I expected Rupert to laugh at that, but all he said was, "I know."

The quick response threw me off balance, and I turned back to my screens before he caught me blushing like an idiot. I wrote my message and sent it off, then crossed my fingers. When we didn't get anything back for several minutes, I started to worry my signal was too weak even in the silence. Before I could work myself into a panic, though, a man's gruff voice sounded in my ear.

"Unidentified xith'cal ship," he said in heavily accented Universal. "I don't usually give warnings, but since you were either kind enough or stupid enough to call in on a Paradoxian ID, I'm giving you ten seconds to explain why I shouldn't shoot you out of the sky."

I'd turned on my external speakers the moment the hail came in so Rupert could hear as well, and the look on his face was priceless when, instead of answering, I pursed my lips and whistled a piercing shriek into the com. It was so loud Rupert actually jumped, but by the time I finished, the man on the other end had changed his tone completely.

"Well met, Blackbird," he said in his native King's Tongue. "How can I help? Are you a xith'cal prisoner?"

"Not hardly," I answered in kind. "Nice to hear your voice, Hicks."

There was a pause, and then the man on the other end burst out laughing. "Deviana Morris, I don't believe it. What the hell are you doing on a xith'cal ship?"

"Trying to get off it," I said, grinning. "Can you get us a safe landing spot? Preferably somewhere that doesn't involve missiles?"

"For you, baby, anything," Hicks cooed. "I'm messaging the tower right now. Give me five minutes and I'll have a beacon for you."

"Copy that," I said. "Thanks, Hicks, see you in a few."

The connection cut off with a *click*, and I looked up to see Rupert glowering at me. "Baby?" he repeated, arching an eyebrow.

I did *not* like the implication in his voice that I needed to explain myself, but since Rupert was the one who was going to be landing us, I did it anyway. "Hicks and I go way back," I said, switching to Universal again. "He was my first squad leader in the Blackbirds before he landed a cushy corp job as head of security on some nowhere colony." I'd thought he was crazy for doing it, too, but Hicks had always liked money more than glory. "Never thought I'd be visiting, though."

Rupert's scowl didn't fade. "And the whistle?"

"Well, we were Blackbirds," I reminded him.

"I never heard a bird make that awful sound."

"You've never heard about Paradoxian blackbirds?" I asked, looking at him sideways. "Black feathers, ten-foot wingspans, teeth like saw blades, hunts in packs?"

Rupert made a face as he turned back to the controls. "From that description, I'm glad I never encountered one."

"What, you didn't think we were named after those sissy Terran birds, did you?" I scoffed. "Please. Blackbirds were the reason no one lived above the snow line until the first Sacred King appeared and gave us back technology. Good-sized flock can pick a grown man down to his skeleton in fifteen seconds, and their *scream...*" I shuddered. "Turn your bones to water. My whistle ain't nothing to the real thing."

"The joys of Paradox," Rupert muttered. "Though I still don't see why we have to go through this man. I could have used my security clearance to get us landing permission."

"Well, now we get the personal touch," I said, though that was only part of it. Honestly, I felt a lot better having an inside man. Hicks was a flirt and a flake of the worst order, but he was still a Blackbird and a Paradoxian, both of which I trusted way more than Rupert's clearances. Especially on a little dirt ball corp planet where it was easy to cover things up. But as I was setting up my com to receive Hicks's landing beacon, I noticed the time stamp on his transmissions.

"Rupert?" I said weakly. "Remember when we first came out of the jump? When you said we lost some time?"

He nodded. "How much did we lose?"

"Eight months, twelve days, five hours," I read off, heart sinking. Eight months galactic was almost a year on Paradox. A whole year gone, just like that. Rupert didn't seem to share my concern, though.

"That's not so bad," he said. "I was braced for far worse, though it does make me worry about Caldswell and the others."

That snapped me out of my self-pity. "Why?"

"The jump from Reaper's tribe ship to here was barely five minutes, and we had the tribe ship's gate to help," he said. "The second jump they made to escape the pursuing lelgis was far more reckless, and much, much longer." He looked up at the star strewn sky. "Dark Star Station is nine hours from here by hyperspace, but on a jump so wild, the time dilation is almost random. They might end up coming out seconds after they went in."

"Or they might come out a thousand years from now," I finished for him. "That would suit Caldswell's terrible luck."

Rupert glanced back at me. "You know, among the Eyes, Cald-swell's actually known for his unusually *good* luck. Though the captain always says that only fools count on being lucky."

I chuckled. "Guess that explains the name of his ship."

Rupert's voice went suddenly serious. "Actually, I believe Caldswell named the *Glorious Fool* after himself. A long time ago, he told me only fools gamble what they can't afford to lose."

"What does that have to do with Caldswell?" I asked. "He's not exactly a reckless gambler."

"I believe the name is meant as a reminder of what not to be," Rupert said quietly.

Not for the first time, I wondered what a man like Caldswell could have gambled and lost that hurt him so badly he'd name his ship after it as a warning. I was still puzzling it over when Hicks called me back with our landing.

———

I'd never been to a cash planet before. The Sacred King had banned them in Paradoxian space, and Terrans didn't bother hiring elite mercs to guard such low-margin operations. Considering what I'd heard, though, I'd always pictured them as barren wastes, hunks of rock stripped of everything valuable by their greedy corporate overlords, so you can imagine my surprise when Atlas 35 Moon E turned out to be actually sort of beautiful.

It was about half the size of Paradox, a bright green and blue ball basking in the intense combined light of the double star and the reflected brilliance of Atlas 35's golden clouds. The place had clearly been terraformed within an inch of its life; there was just no other way continents ended up perfectly square. There were only two seas, both wrapped in rings around the north and south poles, leaving the equator and everything north and south of it for thousands of miles as a huge, flat, uniform tract of arable land covered in a forest so green I had trouble looking at it directly.

As we entered the atmosphere, I realized the brilliant green that covered every inch of the planet's surface wasn't actually forest. Or, rather, it *was* a forest, just not of trees. The green came from rows and rows and rows of soypen. Some genetic monkeying must have been going on, because the stalks were enormous, easily ten times bigger than anything I'd seen back home. Even the smallest ones had truck-sized, neon-green leaves spread wide to catch the bright light that shone from every direction.

Thanks to its pale yellow clouds, Atlas 35's reflected light shone down on the farming moon even brighter than the twin suns did. Even after we'd cleared the reflective upper layers of the atmosphere, the glare was almost unbearable. But when I looked up in disbelief that anywhere could be so bright, I realized I could still see the stars overhead. Even through the hazy atmosphere and the blinding light, the Atlas nebula shone clear through the deep blue sky, creating a star-spangled high noon that would have been amazingly pretty if my visor hadn't had to go almost black to let me look at it without burning my eyes. I was still trying anyway when we reached the coordinates for Hicks's beacon.

Though the planet had looked like nothing but plants and water from the air, Hicks's signal had directed us to a small city. As we got closer, though, I realized "city" was probably the wrong word. There were a lot of buildings, but I didn't see any sign of people. No houses, no shops, no civilian ships, just loading zones, shuttle tracks, and huge packing machines gleaming in the harsh sunlight. No one even came out to gawk as Rupert set us down on one of the huge, open loading areas stacked high with crates of soypen flour, which seemed very odd considering we were landing a xith'cal ship smack-dab in the middle of a Terran colony.

The escape pod set down with a clunk and a shudder it would probably never recover from, but even so, I couldn't help being impressed. The little thing had put in a fine show for what was basically a lifeboat. I could shoot a lizard every day of my life and feel just lovely about it, but damn if they didn't build nice ships. Rupert had just reached up to unlock the canopy when I spotted Hicks jogging toward us across the white paved landing.

At least, I assumed it was Hicks. I couldn't see his face since his visor was blacked against the blinding sun just like mine, but I couldn't believe there'd be anyone else on this dirtball wearing a Count-class suit of Paradoxian armor. I waved to him when he got close, hopping out of the pod just in time to get swept into a bear hug.

"Devi!" Hicks shouted, picking my armored body up and swinging me around without missing a beat. But then, of course, Count armor like his could lift a tank. "By the king, woman, call ahead next time. I almost hit the guns when I saw your lizard can."

"Just working with what I had," I said, wiggling free. "Thanks for guiding us down, and for not shooting. Always a pleasure not to be shot."

"Must be a change of pace for you, certainly," Hicks said, stepping back to look up at Rupert, who was pulling my armor case out of the cockpit. "Who's your friend? Another merc?"

I bit my lip. I didn't actually know how to explain Rupert. Considering he spoke perfect King's Tongue, I could try passing him off as an official from the Royal Office, which wouldn't be too far from the truth. Before I could get a word out, though, Rupert answered for himself in his usual softly accented Universal.

"I am not a mercenary," he said, handing me my case before grabbing his own bag and dropping down seven feet to land neatly beside me on the blinding white cement. "I am Devi's escort."

That stopped Hicks cold. I still couldn't see through his blacked helmet, but I could feel his questioning stare just as a private channel opened to my com. "Is this idiot for real?"

"It's a long story," I said, but before I could explain further, Rupert reached into his bag and pulled out a badge. It wasn't a Royal Warrant, but it must have been serious business, because the moment he opened it, Hicks shut up.

Rupert's smile was polite as always, but I knew him well enough now to catch the smug turn at the edge of his mouth as he closed the badge and tucked it into his jacket pocket. "Mr. Hicks, correct?"

"Captain Hicks," Hicks replied in Universal. At Rupert's raised eyebrow, he added a grudging, "Sir."

Rupert nodded. "I need immediate access to your communications drones. I'm also going to need your fastest hyperdrive-capable ship ready to launch as soon as possible. The Atlas Corporation will be compensated in full for the loss, of course."

"You want a ship?" Hicks said, though from the tone of his voice, you'd have thought Rupert had asked for a unicorn. "Um, sir, this here is a cash colony. We don't have hyperdrive-capable ships."

"Are you kidding?" I asked before Rupert could.

Hicks threw out his arms. "Look around. This entire place is an automated farm. There's like, thirty of us on the whole planet. My job is to run the security drones. Hell, I only put my armor on because I thought you'd need help."

"So you don't have a ship?" Rupert clarified. "Nothing with a hyperdrive?"

Hicks shook his head.

"But," I said, "how do you get off-world?"

"On the freighter," Hicks replied, pointing at the wall of shipping containers behind us. "See those crates? Corporate sends a continent freighter around to pick them up every month."

I blinked. "Continent freighter?"

"An industrial ship too large to enter orbit," Rupert said. "Usually loaded by space elevator. The corps use them for planetary scale transport."

"Basically a giant moving space station," Hicks finished. "Only it holds cargo instead of people. The automated harvesters pick the soypen and load it onto the trains, which ship the beans here from all over the planet. Every month, the freighter comes and picks up the harvest. At that point, if you want to get off-planet, you just go up with the produce. The freighter makes a few more stops after us, and then it uses its internal gate to jump back to the Atlas distribution facility in the core worlds. Once you're there, you can get a flight anywhere you want."

"Hold on," I said. "So this freighter has a gate *inside* itself?"

Hicks nodded. "Told you it was big."

"How long until the next freighter arrives?" Rupert said.

"'Bout two weeks galactic," Hicks said with a shrug. "Give or take a week."

Rupert did not look happy about that. "Can't you signal it here now?"

"*I* can't," Hicks said. "I'm just security. The freighter's route is determined by corporate, but I could get you the contact info for Atlas Industrial Farming Division."

Rupert turned away, and I would have sworn he cursed under his breath. Still, he was all politeness when he turned back around. "That won't be necessary, Captain Hicks. We don't have time to cut through corporate red tape. I'll be putting in for our own pickup, which means I'll still need to use your communications drone, but now I'll also require lodging and supplies for myself and Ms. Morris until our ship arrives."

Hicks sighed. "Well, about that. We don't exactly have a hotel here. I'd offer to let you stay with me, but I'm married now and I don't think my wife would like it."

"*You* got married?" I scoffed. "Woman must be nuts."

Hicks chuckled, and then he snapped his fingers. "I know! You can stay at the colony manager's house. It's a nice little place, and he's been off-world all year."

"Fine," Rupert said, though I could tell he was starting to get very annoyed. "And the communications drones?"

"Right over there," Hicks said, pointing across the landing zone at something that looked more like a jury-rigged water tower than a communications facility. "Our com guy's an antisocial bastard and prefers to run things from the southern hemisphere, but just flash your badge at the camera and he should give you full access. Meanwhile, Devi and I'll bring the car around."

Rupert nodded, and then, before I could even think about dodging, he leaned in and pressed a kiss to the side of my helmet. "I won't be long."

When I turned to glower at him, Rupert was already jogging away at a brisk but still acceptably human pace across the blinding expanse of sunny cement, his bag hooked over one shoulder. Hicks watched him go, whistling softly. "God and king, Devi, you're slumming with Terrans now?"

"Shut up," I muttered, suddenly furious, both at Rupert for setting me up like that and at myself for kind of liking it. "Let's get out of the sun."

"How the mighty have fallen," Hicks said, motioning for me to follow him.

By the time we'd finished crossing the two hundred feet of blinding white cement to the garage at the landing's edge, I was good and sick of this bright, sunny place, beautiful day stars or no. Hicks, on the other hand, seemed far more at ease now that Rupert wasn't around, and he showed it by talking nonstop about the life he'd built here. By the time we got inside, I'd heard all about the crazy money he was making and how he'd married the lady who supervised the automated soypen trains.

"Honestly, if it wasn't for her, I'd have invited you to stay with me instead of sticking you out in the manager's place," Hicks said as we entered the blissful dark of the shaded garage. "But I'd rather deal with him than my wife. She worries I only married her because there are only five women on the whole planet."

"Did you?" Because that was totally something Hicks would do.

"Sort of," he admitted, taking off his helmet. My first sight of his face shocked me a bit, mostly because he looked so much older than I remembered. Apparently, the year I'd lost had been a doozy. "I also might have told her a bit about you."

I rolled my eyes. Hicks and I had slept together once or twice while we'd been out on assignment. It was good fun at the time, but he'd gotten on my nerves after a while, mostly because he did stupid shit like this. "Why would you tell your wife something like that?"

He shrugged and walked over to a truck that looked like a cross between a tank and a tractor. "She asked."

I decided it was time to change the subject. We spent the ride over to the communications tower talking about the planet's crazy sunshine. Apparently, with two suns and the bright gas giant of Atlas 35 acting like a mirror, the colony never actually got dark. The closest thing they had were two hours of dusk out of every forty.

"How the hell do you live out here?" I asked. "Nothing to do, no night, and no way off. I'd go crazy."

"You get used to it," Hicks said, slowing down as we approached the tower where Rupert was already waiting for us, standing in the sliver of shade provided by a tiny metal overhang. "Devi," Hicks said, dropping his voice to a whisper even though we were talking through our suits. "Are you *really* okay? I don't know who that Terran is, but—"

"I've got it covered," I said, cutting him off. "This is me we're talking about, remember?"

Hicks shot me a look. "That's what I'm afraid of. I mean, you don't exactly have the best record when it comes to staying out of trouble."

I couldn't help laughing at that. "Thanks for the sentiment," I said as we rolled to a stop. "But everything's fine. I just want to get to wherever you're taking us so I can get some real sleep. You would not believe the week I've had."

Hicks shot me a sideways look, but with Rupert climbing into the backseat, he didn't press. We drove in silence after that, speeding through the huge, empty streets of the loading facility. I hadn't fully appreciated just how big the place was from the air, but it took us nearly fifteen minutes to get away from the buildings and into the fields. Once we did, though, soypen was all I saw.

At first it was kind of neat to be surrounded by enormous versions of plants I was used to seeing in shoulder-high rows, but soon it just got confusing. The fields were laid out for automated harvesters running on a maximum-efficiency pattern, not for human naviga-tion. There were no signs either, and by the fifth turn, I was com-pletely lost. Fortunately, Hicks seemed to know the way by heart, or at least his suit did, because half an hour later he slowed down and turned us off the dirt road onto a paved drive that stopped abruptly at a wide front porch.

Even though we were only a few feet off the main harvester cor-ridor, the manager's house had the feeling of being buried deep in the forest. The cinderblock construction and boxy design should have made the two-story structure look cheap, but the little house was painted a very soothing shade of deep green that blended into the leafy shadows of the soypen stalks. The soldier in me didn't like that the fat waxy leaves pressed right up to the windows, provid-ing excellent cover for anyone who might try and sneak up on us, but the rest of me thought the sheltered house was charming, like a bird's nest hidden in tall grass.

As soon as the car stopped, Hicks hopped out and did something to the keypad by the door that turned all the lights green. "There you go," he said, putting up his visor as he turned back around to face us. "There should be plenty of food in the deep freeze and there's a satellite uplink on the roof that'll keep you connected to the planet's com system. I live about thirty minutes down the road, so just call if you need anything."

"Thanks, Hicks," I said, lifting my own visor to give him a grin. "You're a lifesaver."

He winked at me and hopped back into his truck. He didn't salute Rupert as he left, but I don't think Rupert noticed. He was too busy opening up the house.

Stepping inside the manager's place felt a bit like breaking into someone's summer home. Pictures of a family I'd never seen smiled down at me from every wall, and a stranger's coats hung on the pegs by the door. The towering soypen kept the place nice and shady, so at least it wasn't baking after being shut up for so long, but everything was dusty from disuse.

Even though it was obvious no one had been here in months, I hesitated before going over to the corner to plug my armor case into the house's power grid. With all the stuff around us, it was too easy to imagine the manager storming down the stairs at any second, demanding to know what we were doing in his living room. Rupert, however, didn't seem discomforted in the least. He was already checking out the small kitchen, opening cabinets and peering into the chest freezer like he owned the place. In his mind, at least, we were here to stay.

I shed my suit and locked her in her case to repair and recharge. I didn't have my gun cases, so I had to hook Mia directly into the wall to charge up. I set Sasha right beside her, nesting my guns together with their handles out so I could grab them quickly if I needed to. But while my equipment was easily taken care of, I was another matter.

I was still dressed in the military-issue underarmor pants and tank top from the Paradoxian embassy, and though I thanked the king Rupert had had the presence of mind to grab my armor case instead of my duffel, the fact remained that I had no clothes other than the filthy set I was wearing. I needed a change and a shower in the worst way, but while I was sure this place had an autowash around somewhere, I wasn't ready to sit around naked waiting for my laundry. I was pondering what to do about it when Rupert walked back into the living room and placed his bag on the table. When he unzipped it to dig out his gun, I saw he had several spare shirts in there on top of what looked like an entire spare suit, which only made sense when you considered how he ripped through them.

"Hey," I said, walking over. "Can I borrow some clothes? I'm going to take a shower."

Rupert, who'd just sat down on the couch, looked up at me like I'd stung him. "Of course," he said after a short pause. "Help yourself."

I smiled my thanks and snagged one of his shirts, then walked upstairs to find the bathroom.

Like everything else in the house, the bathroom was dusty from disuse. I found soap and shampoo in the cabinet, and though the water here was so soft it was almost slimy, that didn't stop me from luxuriating in the first real, not-on-a-ship-or-in-a-military-bunker shower I'd had since the night I'd spent in Anthony's apartment back on Paradox. By the time the hot water started to go tepid, I was so relaxed I was nearly asleep on my feet. Considering my life over the last few days, I was pretty sure the strange calm was some kind of shock, but I was okay with that for now, especially since I hadn't seen a single phantom since I'd taken off my helmet. Mostly, though, I was just tired, like I hadn't slept in a year, and it was all I could do to keep my eyes open as I climbed out of the shower and toweled off.

When I was more or less dry, I shoved the towel and my filthy clothes into the autowash canister in the corner and put on Rupert's button-up shirt. Thanks to our height difference, the hem went almost to my knees, well long enough to be decent. The long sleeves swallowed my hands, but once I rolled them up, I got along okay.

My hair was another story. Thanks to the slimy water and harsh soap, the brown mass on my head was looking more like tree roots than anything that should grow on a human. It needed a good brushing and some real shampoo, but I didn't have either. I was too tired to care much in any case, so I just let it be, swearing for the thousandth time to cut the whole mess off the next chance I got.

It was a toothless threat. Obnoxious as it could be, my long hair was the only thing that balanced out my baby face, and even in full armor with guns drawn, no one took a woman with short fluffy hair who looked like a sixteen-year-old seriously. But the thought made me feel better all the same as I padded barefoot back down the stairs to ask Rupert what we were going to do next.

My exhaustion must have been even worse than I thought, because by the time I made it to the first floor, I felt almost dizzy.

Fortunately, Rupert was still sitting on the couch where I'd left him. He'd arranged all his things neatly on the table while I'd been washing, though I was pretty sure the tablet in his hands was a new addition.

"Where'd you get that?"

"I requisitioned it from the communications tower," Rupert said, glaring at the screen. "And it's a piece of garbage. But at least this way I can monitor the incoming transmissions."

He turned around to say something else, but the moment his face came up, his scowl fell away. Rupert was usually pretty good at hiding his expressions, but I must have caught him by surprise, because he looked dumbstruck, blatantly staring at me before he seemed to remember himself.

"You look very nice," he said softly, giving me a slow, warm smile.

I looked like a drowned dock rat in a stolen shirt, but I already knew firsthand that Rupert didn't see the truth when it came to me. I also knew that I didn't have the energy to handle how happy that smile made the deep, stubborn part of me that couldn't seem to understand that Rupert was a risk I was *not* taking again. I didn't have the energy left to do anything, actually.

The exhaustion I'd felt in the shower had multiplied exponentially with every minute I'd spent upright. It was so bad now I was actually swaying on my feet. As much as I wanted to talk strategy with Rupert before passing out, my body clearly had other more pressing priorities, and so, mumbling something about bed, I turned away from Rupert and started back up the stairs. I made it about halfway before Rupert caught me.

I have to admit, I didn't protest too hard when he picked me up. If I'd felt better, I would have told him to keep his hands to himself, but I didn't feel better. I felt terrible, and I was ready to take my not walking where I found it. I didn't even grumble when Rupert carried me into the green shaded bedroom and laid me down on a couch under the windows that smelled strongly of dust and soypen.

I think he must have made the bed after that. I heard the sound of cloth rustling before Rupert scooped me up again only to set me down seconds later on a much softer, smoother surface that smelled of closet. The last thing I felt was the soft brush of his lips on my cheek before I passed out, falling into a deep and mercifully dreamless sleep between one breath and the next.

―――――

I woke up slowly, blinking in the soft light. It had been so long since I'd woken up to real sunlight instead of an alarm, an emergency, or ship lights coming on for day cycle that I didn't recognize it at first. I did, however, recognize the almost invisible shape floating like a dust mote in the sunbeam.

A phantom was hanging in the air not a foot from the edge of the bed. It was slightly bigger than the ones I usually saw, with a bulbous body about the size of my fist and three long feelers attached to what I could only guess was its head. The feelers were hanging limply when I opened my eyes, but then, almost like the phantom knew I'd woken up, the little tentacles started to move.

I sighed, waiting for the little glowing bug to scoot away, but it didn't. The phantom stayed right where it was, waving its three little appendages with increasing speed, almost like it was trying to get my attention. The behavior was so odd, I reached for it without thinking, stretching my fingers out to meet the glowing tendrils.

I'd barely moved my arm before the phantom bolted through the window, its frosted glass body vanishing instantly into the bright sunlight outside. I stared after it for a moment, and then reached up to rub my eyes. I was contemplating rolling over when a soft, warm, accented voice spoke right beside me.

"Good afternoon."

I must have jumped a foot off the mattress. I landed hard a second later, flipping onto my side to see Rupert leaning over the bed with a sheepish smile. "Sorry."

"Don't *do* that," I snapped, collapsing back into bed. I was still trying to get my jacked-up heart rate back down to normal when I realized there was something odd about our arrangement.

The bedroom couch, the one that had been pushed up under the window, was now right beside the mattress, its green upholstery well dusted and covered in a neat spread of electronics. Apparently, Rupert had set up shop. In addition to the com receiver and the ledger he'd requisitioned, he'd also laid out his gun and his stack of leather badges in a grid beside him for easy access. There was a notebook on the nightstand at his elbow, and his bag was tucked away behind his feet. He even had a mug of that bitter black stuff Terrans like to drink in his hand. Coffee, I thought it was called.

"Couldn't get a good signal downstairs?" I asked, arching an eyebrow at his setup.

Rupert shrugged and sat back, sipping his drink. "The signal was fine," he replied a little too casually. "But I liked it better up here."

From anyone else, I would have called bullshit on that, but Rupert did look quite content. He was sitting on the couch in his socks with his shirtsleeves rolled up and his black hair down and loose around his shoulders. It was the most casual I'd ever seen him other than the night I'd shown up at his bunk. Unfortunately, that memory combined with our present intimate arrangement sent my mind running to all kinds of places it wasn't supposed to go, and I had to look away to force it back on track. "How long was I asleep?"

"Almost eighteen hours."

My mouth fell open. "*Eighteen hours?*"

"More or less," he said, putting down his mug. "I was going to wake you earlier, but you looked so peaceful."

I swore and sat up, swinging my legs over the edge of the mattress.

"Where are you going?" he asked as I stood up with a wobble.

"Bathroom," I replied, stumbling toward the hall.

Thankfully, the stiffness in my limbs was temporary. By the time

I made it to the bathroom, I was walking more or less normally. I felt a lot better, too, which I damn well should have, considering how long I'd passed out. I finished my business and splashed some water on my face until I felt more or less myself, and then looked around for my clothes.

I found them stacked on top of the autowash, cleaned and neatly folded. Rupert's pants and shirt, also freshly washed, had been hung on the wall hook with military precision, which almost made me laugh. Not that I didn't appreciate Rupert's need for order, but who ever heard of a supersoldier neat freak?

I grabbed my clothes and changed quickly, pulling on the thin, drab underarmor pants and tank top the embassy had given me. It wasn't much, but getting back into combat wear made me feel more like myself. To be polite, I put the shirt Rupert had given me in the autowash, starting the cycle even though I was only washing one thing. Once it was going, I headed out to find Rupert, because now that we were alone and I wasn't passing out on my feet, it was time to talk about what we did from here.

He wasn't in the bedroom when I got back. His couch was cleared off, too, so I headed downstairs. The living room was also empty, and I was starting to get a little worried when Rupert stuck his head out of the kitchen. "You're dressed."

He sounded so disappointed I couldn't help smiling. "Yeah, well, no offense to your shirt, but I prefer clothes that fit."

"I thought it fit you very well," Rupert said, his voice low and warm in a way that went straight through me. "Are you hungry?"

The moment he mentioned food, my stomach rumbled. He smiled at the sound and waved for me to follow him. I did, walking through the narrow door into the small kitchen to find Rupert stirring a pot of something that smelled like a cross between chicken soup and heaven.

"What's that?" I asked, sitting down at the little table under a window that looked out into the forest of dense soypen stems behind the house.

"Something to make you feel better," he said, ladling liquid from the pot into a heavy bowl, which he then placed in front of me. The soup looked as good as it smelled, a clear golden broth filled with white meat, bright green vegetables, and fat little dumplings resting at the bottom.

Mouth watering, I grabbed the spoon he held out for me and dug in. Unsurprisingly, considering who had cooked it, it tasted amazing. I made sure to tell him so, but Rupert just waved his hand.

"Salt and protein are good for helping plasmex users recover when they push too far," he explained, sitting down across the table from me. "We give it to the daughters when they overexert themselves. You're not a plasmex user, of course, but considering the events leading up to your collapse, I thought it couldn't hurt."

I paused, spoon halfway to my mouth. I hadn't even considered that my weird exhaustion might have been related to the black stuff. I was, however, slightly horrified by the thought of Rupert feeding me the same thing he gave the girls he shot. "You made this for the daughters?"

"No," Rupert said. "I gave them broth. You're the only person I make dumplings for."

I couldn't decide if that was sweet or depressing. "What did I miss?" I asked as I resumed eating.

"Not much," Rupert said, leaning back in his chair. "The pickup I put in for hasn't replied yet, and I don't have any word from Caldswell, though that's to be expected."

Right, since he was probably lost in hyperspace forever. "Gotta say, I'm surprised we're not up to our necks in Eyes yet. I thought you guys had instant everything."

"We do," Rupert said. "But I didn't request a retrieval from the Eyes."

I frowned. "Why not?"

Rupert's face turned suddenly serious. "Not all Eyes are as flexible as Caldswell," he explained. "If I followed protocol and alerted command without him present to ensure the deal you made was upheld, you'd be in a lab by tomorrow."

That thought soured my stomach. I'd gotten so used to being hauled around like a glorified test tube I'd forgotten I'd actually been dealing with the moderate Eyes who were willing to work with me. "But if we can't go to the Eyes, who's left? What do we do?"

"For now, we lie low," Rupert said. "Considering the events on the tribe ship, headquarters most likely believes we're dead. Until Caldswell reemerges, it's better to let them keep thinking that. Once the captain comes back, we can return to the original plan of finding a safe way to extract and use your virus."

I looked down at my soup, poking the soft dumplings at the bottom with the tip of my spoon. I hadn't actually told Rupert the whole truth about the virus yet. He'd seen me use it to call the lelgis on the tribe ship, but he didn't know that they found me every time I touched a phantom whether I wanted them to or not, which was kind of a deal breaker since their entire race wanted me dead. He also didn't know that the virus flared up whenever I got mad, which I probably should clue him in on since controlling my temper wasn't exactly one of my strengths. But when I opened my mouth to bring him up to speed, I ended up taking a bite of soup instead.

Coward, I thought as I swallowed. Whatever emotional problems I was having with Rupert, he still deserved to know the danger I was putting him in, but I couldn't get the words out. Not because I was worried he'd use the knowledge against me or anything so suitably cynical. The truth was far more petty. I didn't want to tell Rupert about the virus because I didn't want him knowing just how messed up I was.

"Devi?"

I looked up to see Rupert watching me, his eyes soft and warm. "I meant what I said before," he said quietly, reaching out to put his hand over mine. "I'm on your side now. Whatever you want to do, I'll be with you, and I won't let the Eyes do anything to you against your will. I swear it."

His concern was making me feel even worse, and I quickly changed the subject. "So," I said, taking another bite of soup. "If you didn't call the Eyes, then who are we getting a pickup from?"

I don't think I fooled him. Rupert was always annoyingly perceptive, but he accepted my deflection with a shrug and played along. "I used my general security clearance to request an evac from the Terran Republic Starfleet."

"Won't that alert the Eyes?"

Rupert flashed me a confident smile. "No. I called it in using my Republic Starfleet Λ-Level Anonymous Agent Special Clearance."

I stared at him blankly. "Your what?"

"It's the Terran equivalent of a Royal Warrant," he explained. "It's meant to let field agents get whatever they want anywhere in Terran space without having to risk their cover. Even if the Republic investigates, I'll just show up as one of the hundreds of classified agents they have in the field at any given time. And with so many government agencies keeping secrets from each other, it's nearly impossible to figure out who belongs to whom."

"You mean you're hiding from the Eyes in the Terran's own bureaucracy?"

Rupert nodded. "More or less."

I'd always known Rupert was sly, but using the Terran's own convoluted government structure as cover while still getting all the perks of rank was pretty damn beautiful. "So once Terran Starfleet gets their act together and comes to pick us up, where do we go? Do we just stay on the run and wait for Caldswell or what?"

"The more we move, the more likely it is the Eyes will find out we're not dead," Rupert said. "There's also no way of knowing when or if Caldswell will come back, or how long your virus will remain stable, so I thought we could try another option."

I almost choked on my soup. "There's another option?"

Rupert nodded. "I know of a doctor. He's a plasmex specialist. He worked with Maat in the early days, but he cut ties with us several years ago."

"Like Brenton?"

"No, he was never an Eye," Rupert said. "And he doesn't attack the daughter teams. Quite the opposite—he stays as detached from us as possible. It's a bit of a long shot. I don't know if he'll even agree to see you, but he's probably the only human in the universe outside of Dark Star Station who might know what to do with your virus."

I wasn't a big fan of doctors, but I was open to anything at this point that didn't end with me being dragged into a lab with a bag over my head. "Sounds worth a try," I said. "So we're just waiting for the evac, then?"

"That or the freighter," Rupert said with a sigh. "Not much else we can do under present circumstances."

I glanced around at the comfortable little kitchen. "I guess there are worse places to be stranded."

"I'd be hard pressed to think of a better one," he replied, smiling wide.

I swallowed. He was doing it again, looking at me like I was the only thing in the universe. Back before everything had gone wrong, I'd reveled in that look. Now I couldn't even meet his eyes.

Fortunately, the soup made an excellent distraction. The dumplings were especially good, little folded dough balls that somehow managed to be both chewy and soft. But there was something about the flavor that bothered me. I was too distracted and hungry to put my finger on it during the first bowl, but by the time I'd worked my way to the bottom of the second, I'd slowed down enough to recognize the strange, wistful feeling tugging on my mind as nostalgia.

The delicious taste coupled with the warmth of the soup in my stomach had stirred up a deep, complex mix of homesickness and comfort, which was strange, because I was sure I'd never eaten a soup like this before. But it wasn't until I spooned the final dumpling into my mouth that I realized the truth. I couldn't remember eating the soup before because I hadn't. The warm nostalgia wasn't mine; it was Rupert's, and it came with a memory.

This one was softer than the others, floating to the top of my mind like a warm bubble rather than shoving its way to the front. In it, a large woman with steel-gray hair and deep wrinkles sat at a wooden table kneading golden dough with sharp punches from her gnarled hands. Behind her on the stove, a pot of soup was cooking, filling the whole house with that same familiar, delicious smell.

As always with Rupert's memories, the vision vanished quickly, leaving only a strange feeling of warmth mixed with loss so strong I had to blink a few times to keep from tearing up. I finished the dregs of my second bowl in silence and then walked over to the little sink. "Thank you for the soup," I said, keeping my voice light as I washed out my bowl. "It was your grandmother's recipe, wasn't it?"

I had my back to him, but it didn't matter. I *heard* Rupert go still. It wasn't even a sound, just a deepening of the silence, like I was suddenly alone in the room. It was so alarming, I looked over my shoulder to make sure he hadn't vanished in a poof of smoke only to find Rupert staring at me like he'd seen a ghost.

When he saw me looking, Rupert dropped his eyes. "How many of my memories did you get?"

The question caught me by surprise. I'd gotten so used to having him in my head, I'd forgotten I hadn't actually discussed this with him yet. "I'm not sure," I said with a shrug. "They're not my memories, so I can't just reach for them and count. They only come up when they're triggered by something, like the taste of the soup."

I kept my voice casual, trying to show him this was no big deal, but Rupert was still deathly silent, so I decided to move the conversation in a happier direction. "Tell me about your grandmother," I said, turning around to put my bowl on the rack to dry. "She looked nice, and she was obviously a good cook. Did she teach you to make anything else?"

I paused, waiting for him to answer. When he didn't, I looked over... and almost jumped out of my skin. I hadn't even heard him move, but Rupert was suddenly right next to me. "Goddammit, Rupert," I snapped, smacking him on the arm. "Don't *do* that!"

"Sorry," he said quietly, but he didn't step back.

"Just give me some warning next time," I scolded him. "Make a noise or something."

Rupert shook his head. "No, it's..." He trailed off with a frustrated sigh. "I'm sorry for everything, but the memories especially. I would have kept them from you if I could, but the daughters can't return memories without guidance, and whenever you go into someone's mind, especially someone you care about and share a history with, you can't help leaving things behind."

I sighed as well. "It's okay. I already forgave you, remember?"

"It's not okay," he said. "You shouldn't be burdened with my past. It's not a good place. You shouldn't have to see that."

His voice changed as he spoke, growing thinner and quieter just as it had when he'd told me the truth of what he'd done as an Eye. That in turn made me remember what he'd said before he'd taken my memories the first time, when he'd pulled me out from under the trauma shell to confess that he loved me even though he knew he didn't deserve to, that he wasn't worthy of my affection. Now as then, the idea made me angry, so much so that I had to take a deep breath to make sure I didn't accidentally trigger the virus. Because while I might not be able to make the call just yet on what exactly Rupert was to me, it was still my call to make. No one decided who was worthy of me except myself.

I reached down and grabbed Rupert's hands. He jumped a little at the sudden contact, but I held on tight, glaring at him until he met my eyes. "Listen," I said when I was sure I had his attention. "If I say it's okay, it's okay. You did what you did to save my life, and I'll take bad memories over a grave any day. So stop apologizing, because there's nothing left to forgive. Understand?"

"No," Rupert said sharply. "Devi, those memories will stay with you for the rest of your life. You might not have even seen the worst yet, so you can't just forgive—"

"You can't tell me what I can and can't forgive," I snapped. "It's my forgiveness. And anyway, it's thanks to you that I have a rest of my life to be worried about, so you'll just have to put up with me not hating you."

Rupert stared at me for a long moment, and then he bowed his head, leaning down until his forehead rested against mine. "How are you like this?" he whispered. "How can you just let this go?"

I took a deep breath. Other than our foreheads and our hands, Rupert and I weren't actually touching, but it didn't seem to matter. I could feel his warmth across the few inches that separated us, and my whole body was twitching with the sudden urge to wrap myself around him. But then, Rupert was always like this for me. The nearness of him was so overwhelming I hadn't even noticed that he'd trapped me against the sink until I felt the cold metal lip pressing into my lower back. Worse, I couldn't seem to make myself care. All the smart, careful plans I'd made to keep my head on straight and not let myself get burned by him again seemed suddenly pointless. And as his fingers tightened around mine, filling my body with the memory of just how good those fingers could feel, I began to wonder, why was I holding back again?

But just as I pushed up on my toes to bring my lips to his, Rupert's head shot up.

I jumped in surprise, knocking my back painfully against the sink. "What?"

Rupert put a finger to his lips, looking pointedly toward the living room. I nodded, holding my breath as I listened, but I didn't hear anything except the constant rustle of the soypen outside. I was about to push out of his arms and go investigate for myself when I caught the soft but very familiar hiss of a stabilizer. A Paradoxian armor stabilizer, shifting a large amount of weight.

That was all the warning I got before the back door of the house exploded.

CHAPTER

2

I ducked on instinct, covering my face with my hands, but with Rupert curled over my body, the hail of wood didn't even touch me. He was up again a second later, turning around so that I was caught behind him. When I tried to wiggle out, he pinned me in place with his arm, forcing me to look over his shoulder as the soldiers walked in.

Considering the long list of people looking for us, I was expecting symbionts, or maybe Terrans. I should have trusted my ears, though, because the suits that came in to flank us were clearly Paradoxian. There were three that I could see, one at the back door, his foot still coming down from the kick that had splintered it, and two more who'd busted in through the front and were now moving to block the door to the living room.

I swore, shoving at Rupert in a futile attempt to break free, not that it would have done me any good. There were now two suits of Knight-class armor between me and my Lady, still charging in her box in the corner of the living room. I didn't have a gun or thermite; I didn't even have shoes on. The best I could manage was a kitchen knife, which wouldn't even scratch Paradoxian plating, especially not these suits.

The soldier's armor was painted in the red and silver of the Paradoxian Home Guard, which meant this was the king's business. Considering he'd handed me over to the Eyes like a present, I could guess well enough what that business was. You can imagine my shock, then, when the soldier wearing officer's colors stopped short, lowering his gun.

"Devi?"

I knew that voice, but I still didn't quite believe it until the officer flicked up his visor to reveal a familiar, and very pissed off, face.

"Anthony?" I said, leaning into Rupert's back as I tried to get a better view. "What are you doing here?"

"What am I..." Anthony faded off into a sputter. "What the *hell* is going on?" he shouted, pointing at Rupert with his gun. "Who's he?"

I felt Rupert go stiff, but it was too late. I'd already hopped up on the sink and slid sideways, jumping down on the other side, out of his grasp. Anthony started forward to meet me, but Rupert cut him off at once, though he didn't try to pin me again. Good thing, too, because I was in no mood for gallantry. Especially not when the man he was trying to protect me from had been my friend and lover for over seven years.

"He's with me," I said. "Now, why are you here?"

Anthony shot Rupert a nasty look before turning back to me. "I'm here for *you*. I got an emergency message from a Blackbird that you'd showed up here with some Terran, and I came as fast as I could."

I gaped at him. "Why would you—"

"I thought you were *dead!*" Anthony shouted. "Goddammit, Devi, you send me that letter, then you brush me off, and then, before I can come pick you up, the whole universe goes nuts because Reaper's laid siege to Montblanc on your account. And then the lizards get slagged by the damn lelgis and no one knows why and you're gone for a year and *what the hell was I supposed to think?*"

I snapped my mouth shut. All of this had happened so recently for me I hadn't actually stopped to consider what it must have looked like from the outside. Now that Anthony spelled it out for me, though, it did sound pretty bad.

"I wouldn't even know you were alive if Hicks hadn't tipped me off," Anthony continued. "I almost didn't believe him, but I was so desperate I came anyway. I flew all the way out to this dust speck on a *hope*, and when I finally find you, you're shacking up with a goddamn *Terran!*"

"Rupert has nothing to do with this," I said pointedly. "Look, I'm sorry—"

"Oh, that's his name?" Anthony said, cutting me off with a nasty sneer. "So you have time to play house with him but you don't even think of sending a note back home to let the people who've been worrying about you know you're alive?"

"It's not like that!" I shouted.

"I don't care what it's like," Anthony said. "You're coming home. Right now. You can tell me the rest on the flight back to Paradox."

That was the last straw. Anthony might be a captain, but I was not his soldier, and he did *not* give me orders. I was about to tell him as much when Rupert stepped in front of me.

"That's enough of that," he said in King's Tongue. "Ms. Morris is not going anywhere."

The words rolled out with the same smooth, authoritative, high-class Kingston accent he'd used back at the embassy. Unfortunately, it didn't work as well this time.

"You shut up," Anthony snapped, getting in Rupert's face. Normally, that would have been hard since Anthony wasn't much taller than I was. In his armor, though, he and Rupert were at eye level. "I don't know who you think you are, asshole," he snarled. "But you don't dictate to me. This farce is over. She's going home with me, so back off."

Since Rupert had his back to me, I couldn't see his expression, but it didn't matter. I could practically feel the cold little smile that must have been on his face as he reached into his back pocket and pulled out what looked like a thin, leather wallet. "No," he said, flipping open his Royal Warrant. "She's not."

Anthony's eyes went wide. "What the hell is this?"

"Thank you for coming all the way out here, Captain," Rupert went on as though Anthony hadn't spoken. "You've saved us a great deal of trouble. Now, under the authority of the Sacred King, I'll be requisitioning your ship. You may give me your authorization codes now."

The blood drained from Anthony's face as Rupert spoke, leaving him chalk white. The two soldiers he'd brought with him were also looking spooked, and I didn't blame them. Royal Warrants were serious business, as good as the king's own command. Seeing that, I fully expected Anthony to back off and bow out like a captain should, but he did no such thing. Though he was pale as death, he held his ground, glaring at Rupert with more hate than I'd known he could muster. "I don't think so, pal."

"Sir!" one of his officers said, just as I yelled, "Anthony!" But it was Rupert's voice that cut through everything else as he said, "Shut down."

Anthony's guards froze as their armor locked up, and I flinched in sympathy. But while his men were frozen, Anthony's armor stayed online, and he gave Rupert a bone-chilling smirk as he recited, "Override One. Voice Authorization: Captain Anthony Pierce, Home Guard Unit Nine, Kingston Division."

As soon as the words were out of his mouth, the soldiers' suits came back online. Not a second later, both of them had their guns trained on Rupert, and Anthony, standing between them, was grinning like a gladiator standing over his fallen opponent.

"Nice try," he said, lifting his own cannon of an anti-armor pistol, the one I'd helped him pick out three years ago. "But that trick doesn't work on the king's Home Guard. Not that you have any right to that Warrant in the first place, you Terran piece of shit."

"Anthony!" I shouted, horrified. "Are you insane? You can't just ignore a Warrant! It's blasphemy! They'll hang you!" I paused to let that sink in, but Anthony wasn't even looking at me. "Back the hell off!" I shouted, shoving out from behind Rupert. "So help me, I will report your ass if you don't stand down!"

"Report me to whom?" Anthony said, never taking his eyes off Rupert. "This isn't the king's space, Devi. It's a little cash colony in the middle of nowhere, and the chief of security is a loyal Paradoxian who values the goodwill of a Home Guard captain far more than some Terran agent's hide." He lifted his arm, aiming his gun at Rupert's head. "I could shoot him right here and no one would ever know."

Even knowing normal guns couldn't really hurt him, Rupert looked remarkably calm for someone who had three giant anti-armor pistols pointed at his face. He just folded his Warrant and slipped it back into his pocket before shooting Anthony an indulgent smile. "Last chance not to make a mistake, Captain."

His face was all sincerity, but the quiet anger in Rupert's voice made me wince. I was used to him being cold, but Rupert pissed was something new. I opened my mouth to tell Anthony he didn't know what he was messing with, but before I could get a word out, Anthony said, "Kill him."

After that, everything happened at once.

The soldiers fired first, but they were still miles too slow. Rupert was moving the moment Anthony spoke, and it was only because I was used to symbiont speed that I looked fast enough to see what he did.

He sidestepped both shots, coming up directly beside the soldier on Anthony's left. The boom of the gunfire was still ringing in my ears when Rupert's arm reached out to grab the man's shoulder. After that, all I saw was a flash of black before Rupert's claws ripped the man's suit straight down the side.

The soldier fell with a surprised yelp, using the last of his busted stabilizers to try and grab his attacker, but Rupert was already gone. He slipped around Anthony like water, coming up behind the soldier who'd come in the back door. The man was still trying to turn around in a last-ditch effort to land a shot when Rupert lashed out, ripping out the back of the man's suit from the base of his helmet to the motor at the small of his back.

Rupert must have fought armor before, because that was a pro shot. The soldier didn't even have time to squeeze the trigger before his suit went black. By that point, though, Rupert was back to where he'd started, standing in front of Anthony with his hands perfectly normal again as both soldiers toppled over.

Anthony's eyes went wide as the armor crashed to the kitchen's plastic floor, but he didn't fire again. That struck me as odd, because the Anthony I knew would have been emptying his clip into Rupert's chest by this point. But other than that first missed shot, Anthony hadn't used his gun at all. He was just staring at Rupert like he was seeing him for the first time, and then he tossed his gun away.

"It's you," he said, reaching up to grab the handle that was sticking out over his left shoulder. "*You're* the one she was talking about!"

I always knew the letter I'd sent Anthony about symbionts would come back to bite me in the ass, but I don't think I could have foreseen it playing out like this. Rupert glanced at me in surprise, but before I could say anything, Anthony pulled a thermite sword off his back and fired the blade. I jerked back, temporarily blinded as the kitchen lit up with white fire. By the time my eyes had recovered, Anthony was swinging for Rupert's head.

Rupert dodged easily, but I didn't hang around to watch. I was already scrambling to find a weapon, *any* weapon, because with that move Anthony had just taken this fight to a new level. I hadn't actually been worried about Rupert getting shot, but that thermite blade was another matter. I still didn't think Anthony could take Rupert in a straight-up fight, thermite or no, but neither Anthony nor Rupert looked like they were going to back down, which meant unless I did something soon, one of them was going to end up dead. Probably Anthony, which I couldn't allow, because even though he was being a dick about it, he'd come here for my sake, and I couldn't let him get killed for that.

Unfortunately, my options were limited. Both soldiers and Anthony had dropped their guns, but they were all serious armor-rated pistols that kicked even harder than my Sasha. I'd be lucky to hit anything firing one barehanded, and I didn't even want to think about what it would do to my arm. Also, the rapidly escalating fight was quickly forcing me into the corner of the kitchen, cutting me off from the living room where my armor lay tantalizingly out of reach. I was about to try jumping out the window and going around that way when I saw Rupert's disrupter pistol sitting on the kitchen counter.

I lunged for the gun, my fingers closing on the smooth pearl handle. As before, the weight surprised me. It felt more like I was holding a lead model of a gun than an actual working weapon. But it was what I had, so I picked it up and whirled around to find my shot.

I'd only looked away for a few seconds, but that was enough for the fight to turn ugly. Rupert was a symbiont, but Anthony was a captain. His suit was as nice as my own Lady, and it was keeping pace with Rupert's lightning-fast dodges. Anthony was no slouch either, his skills still top-notch despite his years behind a desk. Plus, he was pissed, and every time Rupert dodged, he only got angrier. He was going for Rupert's legs when I came around, and though Rupert dodged with room to spare, Anthony changed direction instantly, pivoting on his heel to follow Rupert's retreat.

For Rupert's part, he seemed to be trying to get Anthony into a submission hold, which was probably the only reason Anthony was still alive. If Rupert had been serious, I'm pretty sure Anthony's head would have been off before he'd pulled his blade. But while Rupert clearly didn't want to kill Anthony, I could tell from his scowl that the effort to keep him alive was quickly becoming more trouble than it was worth, especially when he ducked a fraction too slow, allowing Anthony's thermite to singe the tips of his hair.

Between Anthony's suit and Rupert's speed, there was no way I could take time to line up a shot without my targeting system. Even with my computers, I'd probably have been too slow. But I've never needed a computer to shoot straight, so I took a deep breath and watched the fight, trusting my instincts until, in a flash, I saw my opening.

I fired before I could think, squeezing the trigger on reflex. I braced for the kick a second later, but it never came. The disrupter pistol didn't even twitch in my hands. What it did was get fantastically hot, singeing my hand so fast I couldn't have dropped it if I'd wanted to. But though the pain was intense, I was too distracted to care, because a second after I fired, Anthony's thermite sword exploded.

Ignited thermite was a finicky thing. There was almost nothing you couldn't slice with the stuff, which was why I loved it, but its power was also its weakness. In order to keep that crazy cutting edge, the thermite had to maintain an even temperature: too cold and it went brittle, too hot and it got unstable. But I remembered from Rashid that a disrupter pistol was a heat weapon, and though I'd known it wouldn't do shit against Anthony's suit, his thermite blade was another matter entirely. One shot of extreme heat was all it took to shatter it completely.

Both Anthony and Rupert jumped back at the blast, and I took my opening, elbowing my way between them before the smoke had a chance to clear. "Show's over," I snarled, putting my hands on their chests so that I was a brace between them. "Anthony, back the hell off. Rupert, stand down."

Rupert obeyed at once, stepping back. Anthony, however, got right in my face. "What the hell are you doing?" he shouted. "Get out of here!"

"No," I said, whirling to face him. "I don't take orders from you. But if you want to fight someone, fight me. I'm the one you came out here for."

Anthony's face went scarlet and he leaned in, looming over me. But though he was dressed in several hundred pounds of advanced Paradoxian engineering and I didn't even have a proper shirt on, I held my ground, glaring straight into his eyes like I was just waiting for him to give me an excuse.

Stupid as it seems sometimes, dominance is an animal game, and it was one I played very well. I'd learned a long time ago that it doesn't matter if the other person can technically kick your ass all day long so long as you can make them doubt. I had an edge with Anthony, too, because we had history together. He knew exactly what I was capable of in armor and out, and though he had every advantage in our current situation, he was the one who dropped his eyes and backed away, retreating toward the door. I would have glared him right out of the room if Rupert hadn't chosen that moment to butt in.

"I believe this is over, Captain Pierce," he said calmly, speaking Universal now, like he was putting the whole situation back on his terms. "You will remove yourself and your men from this house. We'll be out in fifteen minutes. Have your ship ready for us by then and I won't report your insubordination."

Anthony blinked at Rupert's voice like a man waking up from a spell, and then his mouth pulled up in a sneer. Whatever he was about to say, though, he didn't get a chance, because Rupert cut him off. "You're very young to be a captain in the Home Guard," he said, his voice smooth and sharp as a knife. "I would hate to ruin such a promising career."

Anthony looked so livid I thought he was going to try another swing. But pissed as he was, he was still a soldier, and he knew when he was beaten. He threw his broken sword on the ground with a curse and stepped back, putting his hands up in surrender.

"Thank you, Captain," Rupert said, sliding his arms around my waist from behind. "We are much obliged."

The words were unfailingly polite, but Rupert's message was aggressive and clear, especially when he leaned down to press a kiss against my hair, keeping his eyes on Anthony the whole time. I wanted nothing more than to plant an elbow in his stomach for goading the poor man with such a blatant display, but it was important to present a unified front until the enemy was fully routed. Also, it would have killed my elbow.

I did pull out of Rupert's hold, though, stomping toward the living room door. I stopped when I was right next to Anthony. "We need to talk," I said, glancing pointedly over my shoulder at Rupert. "Alone. Give me a moment and I'll meet you outside."

Anthony didn't look happy, Rupert even less so, but neither of them dictated to me, so I didn't stick around to hear their opinions. I just stepped over Anthony's downed guard and stomped up the stairs to the bathroom, slamming the door behind me.

———

My hands were pitch-black by the time I reached the sink.

The sight of the virus I'd pulled up with my rage only made me angrier, because I didn't *want* to calm down. If anything deserved my anger, it was this shit. Anthony barging in and ordering me around like I was one of his Home Guard rookies was bad enough, but Rupert's little possessive display was the absolute last straw. He might be the one with the authority, he might even be on my side like he claimed, but neither of those gave him the right to call the shots with my life.

But as much as I wanted to be furious, *deserved* to be furious, I couldn't be, because the black stuff was spreading before my eyes. It was over my elbows now, working its way up my biceps toward the edge of my tank top. But while the stuff wasn't spreading nearly as fast as it had back on the xith'cal ship, it wasn't stopping either, which meant I needed to get a goddamn grip before I *died in a bathroom* from my own stupidity.

With that grim resolution, I sat down on the edge of the tub and held my stained arms out in front of me. The sight got my fear going nicely, and the resulting chill helped me rein in my temper. Even so, it took an embarrassingly long time before I calmed down enough to stop the virus's spread, halting the black stuff just before it crested my shoulders.

I let out a frustrated breath. Forget the lelgis, *this* was going to be the death of me. It'd be fitting, too. My mother had always said my temper would get me killed. Of course, she'd been talking about picking fights with bigger kids, but the idea still stood, and I hated it. From my earliest memories, my rage had been my ally, my power, the strength I could draw on when everything else was gone. Now it was working against me, and I felt like I'd just gotten stabbed in the back by my lifelong partner.

That thought made me angry all over again, sending the black stuff over my shoulders before I could stop it again. By this point, my resentment over the whole situation was so deep I was shaking. It was just so unfair. I couldn't even be angry that I couldn't be angry. The goddamn virus had me by the throat, and unless I either got rid of it or learned to control it, I'd be its slave forever.

Strange as it sounded, that was the thought that actually gave me hope. If there was one thing rooted more deeply in me than my temper, it was my autonomy. I obeyed two authorities: my officers and my king. I was a loyal subject and a good soldier, but I was no one's slave, and like hell was I going to let this virus make me one. It was just like what my first armor coach had said back home when she'd taught us how to use our suits' engines: if you don't control the power, it ends up controlling you. I'd mastered my armor that same year, and I would master this, too.

With that, I turned my focus inward, concentrating as hard as I could—not on controlling my anger, but on mastering my response. I could beat this. I *would* beat this. This virus was my prisoner, not the other way around. And as that resolution settled into my bones, the tingling in my arms began to fade.

I looked down to see the mark receding, the blackness vanishing from my skin like an ink spill in reverse. When the final traces disappeared from my fingers, I stood up, grinning like a madwoman as I shook my hands to get rid of the last of the pins and needles.

Considering how close I'd just come to dying, you'd have thought I'd be feeling pretty depressed about all this. But now that it was over, this incident actually made me more positive about the virus than I'd been since Maat had first predicted I'd kill myself through my own lack of control. I hadn't been able to make much of an argument at the time because she'd been pretty much right. Now, though, things were different.

It had taken me far too long and way too much thinking, but the fact remained that I'd turned that black shit around, and I'd done it without cheating and finding a new outlet for my anger or getting distracted away from my rage. I'd beaten it back all by myself, on my own power, and if I could do it once, I could do it again. All it would take was practice, dedication, and work, and unlike plasmex, those were all things I understood just fine.

But though I was riding high on my victory, I had a bigger challenge coming. Namely, I had to go back downstairs and confront Anthony without turning myself inky again. I actually considered chickening out and skipping it, but even though I hadn't asked him to, the truth was that Anthony had come all this way out of care for me. He didn't deserve my obedience, but he did deserve an explanation, and like hell was I going to cheat him out of one because I was scared of my virus.

With this in mind, I spent the two minutes it took to clean and bandage the hand I'd burned on Rupert's disrupter pistol trying to see things from Anthony's perspective.

It wasn't as hard as you'd think. Despite our present situation, Anthony was one of my oldest and dearest friends. Not counting the time I'd lost in hyperspace, we'd been seeing each other regularly since my second year in the army, which meant he was probably the closest thing I'd ever had to an actual boyfriend. We'd never put a name on our arrangement, and we'd both taken plenty of other lovers, but he'd always been the first person I called when I came home. Seeing that, I could understand why—after thinking I was dead for months and then flying all the way out here on a rumor that I might not be—finding me almost kissing another man would have sent Anthony over the edge. Not that it excused him attacking Rupert or ignoring the king's Warrant, but I could at least see where he was coming from. That understanding helped me maintain my cool as I tied the bandage tight around my hand and walked out of the bathroom to face the music.

I didn't see anyone when I went downstairs. I did notice that Rupert had cleaned out the house, though. The bedroom was stripped and the kitchen was spotless, everything put back in its place. A little looking turned up Anthony's guards standing out front, staring down the road toward their ship.

Now that I saw it, I couldn't believe I hadn't heard the thing set down. Anthony had landed his damn cruiser not five hundred feet from our house, crushing a huge swath of soypen in the process. Hicks was out there as well, staring at the ruined plants in dismay, probably because they'd be coming out of his paycheck. Of course, considering he'd been the one who tipped Anthony off, I wasn't feeling particularly sympathetic to his plight. But for all the ruckus, I didn't see Rupert or Anthony anywhere, and for a moment I was half afraid they were off finishing their duel where I couldn't stop them. Before I could get too worried, though, I spotted Anthony stalking back and forth through the dense soypen forest behind the house.

He must have been listening for my footsteps, because he turned around the second I walked through the broken back door. He had his helmet off, so there was nothing to hide the betrayal on his face as I joined him. I refused to let that disturb my hard-won calm, though. I walked right up to him cool as you please, folding my arms over my chest as I tilted my head back to meet his eyes.

When it was clear I wasn't going to speak first, Anthony sighed, running a gloved hand through his dark brown hair. "I didn't think you'd show."

"I said I would," I replied, leaning against the smooth trunk of the nearest soypen.

"And do you have anything else to say?" Anthony snapped. "Anything at all for me after I came all this way?"

"I didn't ask—"

"Don't give me that bullshit," he growled. "Do you have any idea what I've been through?"

I put up my hand. "Stop. Just stop a second and listen."

He shut his mouth with an angry huff. When it stayed closed, I continued. "I'm sorry I worried you," I said in a measured voice. "I didn't mean to disappear for so long. We had to do a wild jump to escape Reaper's ship and we lost time in hyperspace as a result. We actually just got out not thirty hours ago, and I spent most of those asleep. That said, I'm still sorry I scared you. I hope you know I'd never do anything like that on purpose."

"I do know…" Anthony said, but his voice trailed off as he glanced through the soypen in the direction of his ship. "What's going on, Devi? Why are you out here, of all places, and with a symbiont? And what the hell did you do to piss off Reaper so bad he'd siege a core world to get you?"

I grinned. "Made the news, did I?"

Anthony snorted. "More like dominated it. That picture he put up of you was everywhere. Reaper was as aggressive as they come, but even he stayed away from the major colonies. And then, out of nowhere, he comes in with a full siege, demanding you as payment. So when he vanished ten minutes later, everyone presumed he got you."

He looked at me, and I nodded. "Yeah, he got me."

"Did you really give yourself up to save Montblanc?"

I made a face, because the truth was exactly opposite. We'd been trying to get *away* from Montblanc under Caldswell's orders when Reaper caught us. But I couldn't tell Anthony that, so all I said was, "More or less."

"It was all anyone talked about for weeks," he said. "There was talk about going to war with Reaper for real, not just skirmishes. Before the Republic could vote on it, though, they found the burned ships."

I knew where this was going, but I asked anyway. "Burned?"

Anthony nodded. "The Terrans tried to keep it secret, but we've got good intel that the lelgis burned every one of Reaper's ships to a cinder. We also know they're the ones who burned Stoneclaw's ships, meaning the squids have now taken out two of the three known xith'cal tribes."

"What about the Bloodtooth?" I asked. The Bloodtooth tribe was the one I'd dealt with the least since they were on the opposite edge of the galaxy and mostly preyed on the Aeon Sevalis, but they were rumored to be absolutely awful, even for xith'cal.

"In retreat," Anthony said. "They ran for the Waste Belt soon as word got out, though they won't stay there long. Not even the lelgis can keep the xith'cal from making a play with such prime hunting grounds up for grabs."

That would be nasty business once it started, but still, the loss of two tribes was an enormous blow to the xith'cal. It was a different universe, a safer one, and I'd helped make it that way. I'd killed Reaper, the ancient enemy, and his whole tribe with him. Now that I actually thought about it, I realized this meant I'd probably killed more xith'cal than all of Terran Starfleet put together. Not that I could explain that to Anthony without getting into the virus, but if I ever did get to take credit, I'd be a war hero for sure. The king might even knight me, assuming I survived to claim the honor.

"But I didn't come here to talk about the news," Anthony said, scowling again. "And you still haven't answered my question. What's going on? Really?"

Now it was my turn to sigh. "It's complicated. I can't explain right now."

"Why not?" Anthony demanded. "Does it have to do with that damn Warrant of his?"

I glowered at him. "If it did, do you think I'd tell you?"

"Don't you dare try and brush me off," Anthony said, stepping closer. "Not after I came all the way out here. Do you have any idea what the last few months have been like for me? I was the one who told you about Caldswell. It was my fault you were on that death trap of a ship to begin with, and now you're wrapped up with a symbiont and Reaper and god knows what else."

"I think you're taking a little too much credit," I said. "You gave me the tip, sure, but I made the decision to go. Everything I've done has been my own choice, not yours."

"I went to your damn *funeral*," Anthony said, his voice rising. "Full honors service—I made sure of it. And while your mother was sobbing over your empty casket, all I could think was that I should have prevented it. I had trackers going for Caldswell's ship as soon as I got your letter. I saw you put down in Wuxia. I could have gone for you then, taken you away, but I didn't want to push you. I thought you'd reach out to me on your own when things got bad. But you never did."

His voice was so bitter I winced, but Anthony wasn't done. "After Montblanc, I put out word to every person you might possibly contact," he said, stepping closer. "The Blackbirds, our army friends, *everyone*, offering a reward for any information about you. We knew you'd left the embassy, but no one had seen you leave the planet, so I had hope you might still be alive."

He was right in front of me now, so close I could feel the soft brush of his breath on my cheek. The invasion of my personal space had me bristling, but I didn't dare push him away. I'd never seen Anthony this worked up before.

"I had to believe there was still a chance to find you," he whispered, leaning down and in until we were nose to nose. "I couldn't accept that you were gone. Not before I told you."

"Told me what?" I whispered back.

I saw his lips quirk in a smile right before he pressed them to mine. "That I love you."

I jerked back, staring at him like he'd lost his damn mind. "Are you kidding?"

Okay, maybe that wasn't the best response to a confession, but Anthony had caught me completely off guard.

"Oh, come on," he said, straightening up again. "This can't be a surprise. I've loved you for years. You have to know that."

"N-no, I don't!" I sputtered. "What about all your other girl-friends? You almost married that one girl from Summerland. How could you do that and claim you love me?"

Anthony at least had the decency to look embarrassed. "I was trying to make you jealous," he admitted. "Those other girls didn't mean a thing to me, no more than all your one-night stands meant to you. I was the only one you came back to year after year. I thought if I was always there for you, you'd see that eventually."

"And you never thought you should clue me in?"

Anthony reached out, running his gloved fingers gently down my jaw. "I know you," he said. "If I'd told you the truth, you would have run. Hell, the one time I suggested you move in, you hopped on Caldswell's cursed ship and never came back."

I swore under my breath. Couldn't argue with that.

"Devi," Anthony whispered, leaning in close again. "It's not too late. I don't know what business that symbiont has you wrapped up in, but you don't have to go with him."

"Where else would I go?"

"Home," Anthony said sharply. "With me, where you belong. He's on my ship right now, but I've still got the codes. I can detonate the entire missile complement from here if—"

I sighed. "Anthony, he's not holding me prisoner, and I'm not letting you kill him. Look, I know you're trying to protect me, but I don't need it."

"Don't need..." Anthony trailed off, eyes wide. "Devi, you got taken by a xith'cal tribe lord and then vanished for eight months without a trace—"

"I was in hyperspace!" I cried.

"—only to turn up again with a symbiont," Anthony said over me, his voice getting angrier with every word. "*Sleeping* with a symbiont, and you say you don't need me to bring you back to your senses?"

"We're not sleeping together!" At least, not recently. "And even if we were, that's none of your damn business!"

"Of course it's my business!" Anthony shouted. "Did you completely miss the part of my letter where I told you that symbionts are alien killing machines?"

"Rupert isn't like that!" I shouted back. My hold on my temper was starting to crumble now, but I was just so sick of people who didn't know shit taking cracks at Rupert. "He's a good man who's saved my life more times than I can count."

"Listen to yourself," Anthony said. "You sound like you're in love with that monster!"

"That's none of your business either," I said coldly. I couldn't sort out my feelings for Rupert myself right now, like hell was I discussing them with Anthony. "And he's *not* a monster."

"He ripped apart two suits of military-grade Knight's armor with his bare hands!" Anthony cried. "What else do you need?"

"And what part of 'none of your business' don't you understand?"

"It *is* my business!" Anthony roared. "I love you! And even if you don't feel the same way, I don't want to see you get hurt, which is exactly what's going to happen if you stay with him!"

"I don't have to listen to this," I said, pushing off the soypen to go back to the house.

I'd made it less than a foot before Anthony grabbed my arm. "I did some more digging into symbionts after I sent that letter," he growled, tightening his grip. "Do you know why the Republic banned them?"

"I already know all about the instability," I said, trying to pry his hand off me.

"Instability doesn't begin to describe it," Anthony said. "The symbiont part of them is made from the xith'cal, but it's more than just scales and hopped-up regeneration. The alien also gives them the xith'cal's bloodlust. There are reports of symbiont soldiers going crazy, even *eating* their comrades. They're monsters in the truest sense, and you want me to just stand back and let you fly off with one like he's your goddamn boyfriend?"

"Yes!" I shouted, finally breaking free. "Because like it or not, you don't control me or my life! Look, I'm sorry I worried you and I'm sorry I got you involved, but this really is none of your concern, Anthony."

"Damn you, Devi!" Anthony cried. "Does it not even occur to you that there are people who care about you? Who've already had to deal with your death once and don't want to do it again? I don't know what mission you think you're on, but it cannot possibly be more important than your life."

He reached out again, grabbing my hand, but his grip was gentle this time. "Whatever trouble you're in, we can deal with it," he said, softly now. "I'm captain of the entire Ninth District of Kingston now. I've got contacts all the way up the Royal Office. I can get you anything you need. Just don't vanish again. Don't go with him. That man is a Terran and a symbiont. He doesn't understand you. I do. I can protect you, Devi, so come home. Come home to Paradox where you belong. Come home with me." He lifted my hand, pressing my knuckles to his lips. "Please."

That whispered *please* was the closest I'd ever heard proud Anthony Pierce come to begging, and part of me was surprisingly touched. Because I liked Anthony, I really did. It was the reason I'd stuck with him as long as I had. But for all that, I didn't love him, and now I was sure I never could. Any man who thought I wanted protection or that I had nothing I valued more than my life didn't understand me at all.

"I'm sorry, Anthony," I said, pulling my hand away. "I can't."

Anthony shut his eyes, his fingers slowly closing over the empty space where mine had been. "Can you at least tell me why?"

"No," I said. "But I can tell you I'm not being forced, and I'm not doing any of this for Rupert. Whatever you might think, we're not here because we ran away together. We're only stuck on this planet by accident, and now that we've got a ship, we're getting back to work. I can't tell you what we're doing, but believe me when I say it's important, and that I'm doing it of my own choice."

Anthony opened his eyes to glare at me. "And I suppose *he* helped you make that choice?"

"Yes, he did," I said. "But if you think there's a man anywhere who can make me do anything I don't want to do, you haven't been paying attention."

Anthony didn't say anything after that. He just stood there, fists clenched tight. Since there was apparently nothing left to discuss, I turned and started back to the house. I'd made it two steps when I heard his voice behind me.

"You turn your back on me," he said softly. "You walk away now, Deviana Morris, and we are through. I risked more than you can know to come save you today, but if you throw that back in my face, I will leave you to your damn monster."

"You don't leave me anywhere," I said, turning to face him again. "I got this far on my own. I'll finish the same way." And though I knew it was petty, after that display, I couldn't help adding, "Besides, considering we've got your ship, I'd say you're the one getting left." I turned, waving over my shoulder. "Enjoy your stay in the soypen, Captain Pierce."

"Devi!" he shouted, but if I looked back, I'd punch him, so I didn't. I marched into the house, grabbed my armor and my guns, and kept going, blowing past Anthony's guards on the porch. Neither of them tried to stop me as I stomped out over the crushed soypen stalks toward the ship.

As a captain in the Home Guard, Anthony had access to a wide variety of top-line hardware, and the cruiser he'd flown here was no exception. The five-man ship was new and shiny, though, being Paradoxian, it was three times the size of a similarly outfitted Terran model with less than half the features. I'm as loyal a servant to the king as you'll ever find, but even I could admit the Terrans had us stomped on shipbuilding. Still, it was nice for a Paradoxian rig, and there was something nostalgic about the absurdly thick armor plating that was stuck everywhere.

Unfortunately, there were phantoms, too. I hadn't seen any of the little buggers other than the one that had been waiting for me when I'd woken up, but for some reason, Anthony's ship was full of them. My best guess was that the bright light outside had made them harder to see, which meant I just noticed more in the shady ship. I didn't know if that was actually the case, but it was far preferable to my first paranoid impulse, which was that they were following me. That was stupid, of course, and I made a great point of ignoring the phantoms as I lugged my armor case down the ship's narrow hall toward the bridge.

Spoiled as I'd gotten during my years working in the Republic, once thing I had missed about flying Paradoxian was the armor-ready rack located at the back of every ship's bridge. As expected, Anthony's was fully outfitted with top-end hookups and chem tanks full of everything a suit of powered armor could need. My suit was still sitting pretty from my stay at the Montblanc embassy, but I wasn't about to miss a chance to top off, especially since my adventures on Reaper's ship had depleted my air purifiers, so I hooked my case in to refill before going to look for Rupert.

I found him up front in the pilot's chair, scowling through the colorful cloud of stars the projected navigation map had thrown up around him. I sank down in the gunner's seat beside him, careful not to touch anything. I was looking for a safe place to rest my elbows on the chair's touch-screen arms when Rupert said, "Hicks asked me to tell you he was sorry."

I blinked. "What?"

"Hicks wanted me to tell you he was sorry he tipped off Captain Pierce," Rupert repeated, turning off the star maps. "He'd heard something about Montblanc but he didn't know the full story or that you'd been declared dead, and when he saw me, he was worried you were in trouble. But now he sees that you didn't need help, and he wanted you to know he was sorry for interfering."

It was nice to know Hicks hadn't turned me in for the money. Still... "Why did he tell *you?*"

"Given that you were chewing out a Home Guard captain at the time, I think he decided I was the safer option," Rupert said, tapping his console. "He left immediately after."

I arched an eyebrow. Rupert didn't look like the safer option to me. Actually, sitting hunched over in the pilot's console with his face set in that deadly scowl, he looked downright dangerous, and extremely un-Rupert-like.

"Hey," I said. "Are you—"

I was cut off by the boom of the thrusters as Rupert fired the engine. "Strap in," he said, buckling his own harness. "Lift off in thirty seconds."

I glared at him as I lashed myself in, but I didn't want to yell over the engines, so I sat back to wait. I caught one last glimpse of Anthony stepping out to join his officers on the front porch before Rupert jumped us into the air. After that, all I saw was green as we lifted out of the soypen field and into the blazing light of the gas giant and the two suns hanging in the star-spangled blue sky.

Rupert turned as soon as we cleared orbit, putting the light at our tail as he angled the ship toward the nebula's outer edge. "We've got two hours before we hit the Atlas continent freighter," he said, tapping numbers into the autonav system. "From there, we'll use its gate to jump to Kessel."

"Kessel?" I said with a snort. "That's a pirate haven. Why the hell would we go there?"

"Because if Captain Pierce knows you're alive, everyone else does, too," Rupert replied. "If we want to avoid the Eyes, we'll need to switch this ship for something less obvious, and unlike legitimate shipyards, pirates don't ask questions."

I pursed my lips. I hadn't considered that angle yet, but he was right as usual. Even if Anthony hadn't told anyone before he left, he sure as hell was going to light things up now. "Do you think the Eyes will try to jump us?"

"Without a doubt," Rupert said, locking the autonav on course. "Commander Martin is the Eye's current head officer. He was the one who sent Caldswell and me to Montblanc to collect you after our office on Paradox forwarded Baron Kells's write-up of your report. Once word gets out that you're not dead, I'm sure the order to bring you in will be reinstated, and having lost you once already, I don't think they'll be taking any chances."

I did not like the sound of that. Still, it wasn't like Rupert and I were a soft target, and we had a head start. I just hoped Rupert's mystery plasmex doctor didn't turn out to be a disaster like Brenton's xith'cal, because if this failed, I didn't have another plan B. I turned to tell Rupert my worries, but he wasn't even looking at me. He was sitting on the edge of his seat, scowling at the navigation console like he wanted to smash it to pieces.

I rolled my eyes and leaned back in my chair. "Spit it out."

Rupert looked at me like he didn't understand, and I crossed my arms over my chest. "If you're pissed at me, just say so. You sitting there taking it out on the ship doesn't help anything."

Rupert glanced at the console in surprise, like he was seeing it for the first time. "Sorry," he said softly.

"Why are you apologizing?" I snapped. "I asked you to tell me why you were mad, not apologize for it."

"I'm not angry."

My look must have told him what I thought of that, because Rupert covered his face with a frustrated sigh. "Fine," he said. "I'm angry. I'm angry we have to be on the run again so soon. I'd hoped for more time, but then that man came in and ruined it."

Considering what Rupert and I had been doing—or rather, almost doing—when Anthony busted in, I didn't have to ask what the "it" was. Honestly, though, I was kind of glad Anthony had broken that up. I'd been very close to just saying screw it and jumping Rupert right there in the kitchen, which would have been a monumentally bad idea. Casual hookups were one thing, but adding sex to the confusing emotional minefield that lay between Rupert and me was asking for a disaster I did not have the resources to handle. Especially not when I found it so unexpectedly gratifying that Rupert, Mr. Iceberg, had gotten this upset over *me*. I was busily reminding myself of all the reasons why being happy over his attention was a *very bad thing* when Rupert dropped the real bomb.

"I'm also upset that you've been hiding the virus from me."

I jerked around to see him glaring at me. "I saw your hands as you were going upstairs," he said. "You had another attack after the kitchen. That was why you went and hid in the bathroom, wasn't it?"

I briefly considered lying, but there wasn't really a point now. "Yes," I said. "But I've got it under control, so you don't have to worry."

Rupert's jaw tightened, and I suddenly got the feeling that the anger I was seeing was only the tip of the mountain. "And what part exactly shouldn't I worry about?" he asked. "The part where you're having flare-ups of a virus that could kill off every living thing around you, or the part where you're hiding it, thus preventing me from doing anything to help?"

"It's not like you could do something," I said, suddenly defensive. "It's my virus, okay? I've got it under control."

"That's just it," Rupert said, his voice creeping up. "I don't think you do, because I don't think something like this *can* be controlled. Not reliably." He stopped and took a deep breath. "I know you don't trust me, Devi, and I don't blame you for that, but you can't keep trying to handle everything by yourself."

"I have to," I said. "I didn't ask to get this virus, but it's mine now. I'm the only one who can use it, and it's my duty to make sure I do the most good I can."

"But you don't have to do it alone," Rupert said. "No one's doubting your courage or your honor, but there's a difference between being brave and being reckless. You always charge blindly forward, throwing your life around like it's meaningless, but it *isn't*."

"I do what I have to do," I snapped. "If I'd sat around worrying about my hide in Reaper's arena, we'd all be dead. Instead, we're alive, Reaper's fleet is gone, and we have another chance to actually do some good."

"It's pure luck you didn't die," Rupert said.

"If I was afraid of dying, I couldn't do half the shit I do," I told him. "But I'm not, and if you're going to try and tell me I should be, you can forget it."

That was probably a step too far, but I didn't care. I was so sick of men trying to protect me. "I can handle myself," I said. "I've been handling myself in combat for nine damn years, and I will *not* let you hold me back now."

"I'm not trying to hold you back!" Rupert shouted, and then he stopped, taking a deep breath. "I don't want to control you," he said, his voice quieter but no less intense. "But I do worry about you, Devi."

"I never asked you to."

"That makes no difference," Rupert said. "I've worried about you constantly from the moment we met." He glared at me. "You are, without question, the single most stressful person I've ever encountered."

I glared back at him. "So why are you still here, then?"

"Because I love you," Rupert snapped. "And even though you drive me mad with worry, I wouldn't change a thing. I can't, anyway. Anyone who thinks they can push you around is either stupid or crazy."

I was perversely flattered by that statement, but Rupert wasn't finished.

"I've made peace with the fact that I can't make you stop charging in recklessly or treating your life like something that can be thrown away," he said, reaching out to take my bandaged hand. "But I see no reason for you to take everything on yourself."

He turned my hand over in his, gently stroking my burned palm with his thumb. "Let me help you," he whispered, leaning down to kiss my fingers. "Do it out of pity for a worry-prone man who goes out of his mind when you're not with him. Just please, for my sake, let me be of service. Let me help you."

The feel of his lips sent a chill through me, because this was the second time today that a man had kissed my fingers and asked for something. Unlike Anthony's, though, Rupert's plea got through to me, because he wasn't asking for something I couldn't give. Where Anthony had demanded I come home and come to my senses, Rupert had admitted he had no control over my decisions and was simply asking for the chance to help. In those few words, he'd proven he understood me better than my lover of seven years, and after so long fighting alone in unknown territory, the idea of having someone at my back who just wanted to support me, even if he didn't agree, sounded very nice indeed.

No sooner had that thought formed than the rest of me started to balk. What was I, stupid? Charkov had *betrayed* me. I'd sworn never to trust him again not two days ago, and now I was seriously considering teaming up? But the old arguments didn't hold the water they used to, because a lot had changed since I'd fought him in the clearing.

I don't normally put much truck in apologies, but Rupert's had been pretty good, and he'd stuck by my side through some pretty scary shit ever since. It wasn't enough to balance out what he'd done, but the more I learned about what was really going on with the universe and my growing place in it thanks to the black rot hiding under my skin, the more I realized I couldn't afford absolute choices like never trusting again. Life wasn't that simple anymore, and as I looked down at Rupert, who was still bent over my hand like he was scared to let me go, I decided it was time to try something new.

"I have a crazy idea," I said quietly. "What do you think about starting over?"

I felt Rupert's breath catch as he looked up. "Starting over?"

"Between all the lies and the lifesaving, our balance sheet is pretty tangled," I said with a shrug. "Frankly, I'm sick of trying to figure it out. So what do you say we just wipe the whole thing clean and start fresh?"

Rupert released my hand at last. "I'd like that," he said softly. "More than anything."

"Good," I replied. "Here's my offer. If you really want to help me, then we have to start acting like a team. No more secrets, no more lying, no more of that 'keeping things from me for my own good' bullshit. Clean slate from here out. And if you betray me again, I will shoot you in the head for real this time."

It's a sign of how messed up our history was that Rupert smiled at that last bit. "That sounds more than fair, but does this no secrets promise cut both ways?"

I spread my arms. "What do you want to know?"

Rupert swiveled his chair all the way around so he was facing me. "Let's start with the virus."

I was afraid that was where this was headed, but I'd been the one who'd suggested this, and if Rupert was going to be throwing all in with me, he deserved to know what he was risking. So, with a deep breath, I told him. All of it. I told him about Maat and the phantoms and killing the daughter on Reaper's ship and how the virus came up when I got angry. He looked pretty shocked and worried when I mentioned Maat, but he didn't try to stop me. I don't know if he could have. I hadn't meant to say so much, but once the story started, it came out like a flood. I even told him the weird stuff with the lelgis, which I hadn't meant to tell anyone, but the words just tumbled out, and I had no choice but to let them go until I was empty.

By the time I finished, I was braced for the worst, but Rupert's face was thoughtful. "Maat contacting you directly does explain how you knew so much about her," he said, looking up at me in concern. "She's crazy, you know."

"Oh, I know," I said bitterly. "Why do you think I feel so sorry for her?"

"I should have guessed the virus was triggered by anger," Rupert continued. "Plasmex is always tied to emotion at first, before training decouples it. It makes sense that the virus would be, too." He thought about it a moment, and then he shrugged. "We'll just have to be careful to keep you calm."

"Hold up," I said. "How can you be so accepting about this? Aren't you afraid I'll get pissed and kill you?"

Rupert actually had the nerve to laugh at that. "That's a risk with or without the virus. But you're worth it."

I stared at him, disbelieving, but Rupert had already turned back to the flight console. He squinted at the autonav's projected screen, then sighed and dropped his head, rubbing his eyes.

"What?" I asked, suddenly alarmed.

"Just tired," Rupert replied, his voice slightly off. Before I could put a finger on how, though, it was gone, replaced by Rupert's usual business tone as he pointed at the bridge window. "There's our jump."

I turned to look, but we were still deep in the Atlas Nebula, which meant the sky was packed. There were so many lights and rocks and bits of space debris flying around, it took me several moments to realize the huge, irregular black shape in front of us wasn't another asteroid like I'd assumed. It was a ship.

"Damn that thing is big," I said. "And ugly."

"Ships that never have to enter the atmosphere can be ungainly," Rupert admitted.

"Ungainly" didn't begin to cover it. The continent freighter was nothing on a tribe ship, but it was still the largest human vessel I'd ever seen. It looked absurd, too, like a giant, crumpled up ball of foil with a string dangling below it. The space elevator, I guessed. I shook my head and looked over at Rupert to ask what we did now, but he was rubbing his eyes again, grinding them with the heels of his hands.

"Are you sure you're okay?"

"I'm fine," Rupert said. "But once we get into the jump, I'm going to have to sleep."

He said this with the same gravity you'd use to announce you were dying of radiation poisoning, and I gave him a suspicious look. "Is sleep a big deal for symbionts or something?"

"It can be," Rupert said. "I'll explain once we get in hyperspace."

Considering how cryptic that sounded, I would have preferred he explained now. Rupert was already hailing the freighter, though, so I sat back to wait. After all, we were working together now. I could extend him the benefit of the doubt for a few minutes. It was a simple decision, a tiny bit of trust, but it settled in my mind like a long-pulled joint finally popping back into place, and for the first time since Rupert had turned away from me in the rain so long ago, I started to wonder if maybe things could be okay between us again.

That was a dangerous hope to cultivate, though, so I pushed it out of my head, staring out at the endless stars instead and wondering what happened when a symbiont went to sleep.

CHAPTER
3

Despite being the only ship in the sector, it took an absurdly long time for the continent freighter to answer our hail and even longer to clear the jump. The worker who picked up the com didn't even know how to turn on the jump computer, and Rupert had to sweet-talk him into waking up his superior before we could even start negotiations. Since we were in Anthony's ship using his codes, the freighter's Terran crew was predisposed to dislike us, but as soon as Rupert had someone of authority on, he had the man eating out of his hand in minutes.

It was a surreal conversation to listen to, both because I hadn't actually realized just how much Rupert could turn the charm on and off until I watched him turn it to the max and because he'd shed his normal accent, switching over to something I could only call "well-educated Paradoxian noble trying to sound Terran," which was an accent I didn't even know existed until he pulled it out. The combination worked like gangbusters, though. By the time the jump gate was up and ready to accept Rupert's coordinates, we had the whole crew on the com chatting like Rupert was an old friend, and not a one of them seemed concerned that a Paradoxian officer was using their freighter's gate to jump to a pirate haven.

It was a disgracefully unprofessional display, and if they'd been a Paradoxian outfit, I would have reported the lot of them. However, since we were benefiting, I tried my best to look the other way.

But when they started shouting corporate security passcodes back and forth to each other *while the com was still on,* I couldn't keep my mouth shut any longer.

"That's it," I muttered angrily in King's Tongue. "I'm filing a complaint with Republic Starfleet. No wonder the Terran Republic is crawling with pirates. These corporate slackers are a disgrace! You'd never see behavior like this in the king's space."

"Good thing we're not in the king's space, then," Rupert replied in the same language, giving me a wink as he started up the hyper-drive coil.

I rolled my eyes, irrationally irritated. It was his accent, I decided. When he spoke King's Tongue like that, it made me feel like I was flying with a noble, which was always an obnoxious experience. Not that I'd had much experience flying with nobles, thank the king, but hearing Rupert talk like one reminded me of a question I'd been meaning to ask him.

"If you spoke the king's language so well all this time, why didn't you use it with me before?" I said, wrinkling my nose at him. "It would have made talking so much easier." Especially while drunk. Universal verbs were murder when you were sloshed.

"I was under orders not to," Rupert said, lips curling into a sly smile. "And if we hadn't been speaking Universal, I wouldn't have gotten to enjoy your charming accent."

My accent was a lot of things, but charming *definitely* wasn't one of them. Before I could call bullshit, though, the jump flash washed over us, and the whole ship bucked sideways. I scrambled with a yelp, clinging to the chair. Quick as it came, the bump was over, and the stillness of hyperspace descended on the ship as the universe vanished, replaced by a flat, purple wall.

"Nice entrance," I said, righting myself.

"Sorry," Rupert replied. "I was an Eye, not a hyperspace pilot."

The words were clearly meant as a joke, but his voice sounded oddly strained. When I looked up to see why, he was leaning back in his chair with his eyes shut, breathing in soft, shallow pants. He'd looked tired before, but now he looked exhausted, and the sight made something in me clench.

I ignored the feeling and stood up, my face all business as I grabbed his arm. "Come on, let's get you to bed."

Rupert's lips quirked, but he let me help him up without comment. He wobbled a bit when he reached his feet, shaking his head like he was trying to clear it while I watched with growing trepidation.

"When was the last time you slept, anyway?" I asked, covertly sliding an arm around his waist to steady him before he pitched over.

He frowned, thinking. "Seven days."

I froze. "Seven *days*?"

"Symbionts don't need as much sleep as normal people," he explained as we walked toward the rear of the ship.

That certainly explained a few things about the operation of the *Glorious Fool*. "So you haven't slept since before you came to get me at the embassy?"

"I haven't slept since before we restored your memories," Rupert said, pulling away from me when we reached the door to what had been Anthony's bunk. "There was too much to do."

He said this so casually I wanted to strangle him. "So you just pushed yourself to the point of exhaustion?" I snapped. "Why didn't you sleep at the house?"

"I didn't want to leave you alone and unconscious in a strange place," he said. "And sleep is...not a pleasant experience for a symbiont. I didn't want to wake you up."

This was the second time he'd mentioned that, more than enough for me to get the hint. "Okay," I said slowly. "So what should I expect?"

"Hopefully nothing," Rupert said, opening the door to reveal a small officer's room with a single, narrow bunk. "But just to be safe, I'm going to lock myself in." He tapped the officer's key lock just inside the door as he spoke, sliding it up to the highest security level. "We've got six hours in jump. The exit alarm will wake me if I don't wake up on my own before that, but no matter what, don't try to open this door. Whatever you hear, whatever I do, just leave it locked."

I gave him a sideways look. "What will you be doing? Clawing at the walls?"

"Maybe," he admitted, leaning on the door frame. "The nightmares can be intense, but I'm usually a quiet sleeper. I don't think anything will happen, but I'm not going to take any chances. Just promise me you won't open the door."

I started to point out that the officer's door locked from the inside, but he looked so earnest and exhausted, all I ended up doing was nodding.

Rupert reached out to close the door, and for a crazy moment, my hand came up to stop him. I caught it just in time, folding it behind my back instead. "Sweet dreams," I said.

He smiled at me. "Good night, Devi." And then the door closed. A second later, I heard the heavy lock click into place, leaving me alone.

I stood in the hallway for a while after, ears straining, but I didn't hear a thing except for the low hum of the engine. He'd probably fallen right asleep, I thought, which made me feel strangely tender. Poor man had been driving himself so hard. He deserved some rest. I probably should have slept as well, but after my eighteen-hour power nap I wasn't tired in the least, so I wandered up to the bridge instead.

I flopped into the captain's cushy chair and pulled up the ship's information interface with the vague idea of catching up on the eight months I'd lost, but the military cruiser was all business. Everything interesting was hidden behind security walls, and there was nothing in the way of entertainment in the ship's memory unless I wanted to watch Home Guard training videos. There were a few basic news feeds available in the public memory—royal announcements, galactic events, that sort of thing—but I couldn't concentrate enough to read them. My mind kept slipping back to Rupert.

He'd just looked so worried, I thought, tapping absently through the ship's interface. Worried and exhausted. It had been easy to ignore while I'd made up my mind to hate him forever, but now that we'd wiped the slate clean, I could hardly miss how he'd pushed himself to the limit for my sake. Not that I'd asked him to, of course, but even so, I was touched. Not many people would do something like that for me, the *actual* me, not Devi Morris, Virus Container. But Rupert had, and now I was more confused than ever.

I'd sworn I'd never be *that girl*, the one who claimed she was done with a guy only to come crawling back a few days later. But apparently all it took was a little groveling, some overtime, and a pot of homemade soup and I was ready to forgive and forget. Even now, I was more disappointed than I wanted to admit that Anthony had interrupted us in the kitchen. I was especially grumpy that I hadn't kissed Rupert good night before he'd locked himself in, which was just embarrassing. We'd agreed to a clean slate, not a step back in time. What the hell was wrong with me?

I leaned back in the captain's chair, digging the heels of my palms into my eyes with a frustrated groan. It was just lust, I reasoned. Brushes with death always left me vulnerable and needy, and death and I had been best friends lately. Add in my well-documented weakness for Rupert and our physical proximity and it was no wonder I was having these idiotic impulses. But lust didn't explain the way his smile made my stomach flip-flop, or the way my whole body lit up every time he said he loved me, or how happy I'd felt when I'd learned he worried about me, or how much I worried about him, or—

To hell with this. I shot out of the chair and marched down the hall to the tiny mess at the rear of the ship. Kicking open the dry goods cabinet, I crouched down and dug through the crates of ration bars until I found the chocolate ones. I ripped off the plastic wrap and shoved the whole thing into my mouth, chewing angrily as I paced the small space and forced myself to face facts like a professional.

Smart or not, embarrassing or not, the truth was that I still had feelings for Rupert. In my defense, though, what was not to love? He was handsome, thoughtful, a fantastic fighter who respected my abilities, a good cook, and a great kisser. He was also a sly operative, something I deeply respected because I was anything but, and he was so, so loving. Love was what had made his betrayal sting so badly to begin with, but once he'd explained his reasons, even that was something I could understand. It didn't hurt that he'd gone above and beyond trying to make up for it, either. I mean, Rupert had chosen me over the *entire universe*. Even if I didn't trust him, how could I not be touched?

So there it was, then. I loved him. I wasn't sure about the rest, but that much I could no longer deny. I loved Rupert, had always loved him really, and it didn't matter for squat, because I was going to die.

I chewed sullenly, forcing myself to swallow the ration that suddenly tasted more like coal dust than chocolate. I was going to die. That wasn't just pessimism, either. Any way you cut it, my life was a done deal. If the lelgis didn't get me, the virus would. Even if Rupert's mystery doctor knew exactly what to do, even if we popped out of hyperspace to find Caldswell waiting to keep all his promises and proclaim me the hero who saved the daughters and ended the war with the phantoms, the likelihood of me getting out of this alive was practically null. And even if I did, it wasn't like the Eyes would let me escape, not with what I knew.

I stopped pacing, sinking to the floor with my head in my hands. It was that or cry, which I was *definitely* not going to do. I couldn't even explain why I was suddenly so upset. To die gloriously for a greater cause was a blessing, an honor. Even if I failed to find a use for the virus and couldn't save the daughters from their slavery, at least I'd kept it out of Reaper's hands. That alone was enough to earn me a spot in the Warrior's Heaven five times over, so why wasn't I happy? Why did I feel this stupid sense of loss?

This was exactly why I should have stuck by my resolve, I thought with a growl. *This* was the real reason I should have just told my lust to shove it and kept the hell away from Rupert. Because at the time in my life when I needed to be strongest, he made me weak. He made me want to live, to reach for a future that I couldn't have, shouldn't want, and wouldn't get, and the more I thought about how stupid and unfair that was, the angrier I got.

That wouldn't do at all. We were only twenty minutes into the jump. If I spent the rest of it stewing like this, my virus would kill us both before we got to Kessel. What I needed was a distraction, something to keep me too busy to rage about the hopeless tragedy my life seemed to be turning into. A pirate attack would have been perfect, but there was no hope of that in hyperspace. So, with nothing else on offer, I decided it was time to do what I usually did when I was feeling trapped, upset, and anxious. I decided it was time for a drink.

Alcohol was forbidden on royal fleet ships, but Anthony had never paid much mind to rules he didn't like. Sure enough, a little hunting turned up a bottle of whiskey tucked away in the tiny freezer behind the medical ice packs. It was a good Paradoxian label, too, not as smooth as the Terran blends, but it tasted like home.

Four swallows later, I decided this was the best decision I'd made all day. True, I was still going to die and lose the only man I'd ever loved before I'd even gotten him, but at least I didn't have to be sober for it. Part of me knew that didn't make any sense at all, but the rest of me was buzzed and ready to tell all the problems I couldn't do shit about to go to hell with my compliments.

I put the whiskey back in the freezer and sauntered up to the bridge to check out those training videos. The Home Guard always got the newest, coolest stuff, and between my time on the *Fool* and the eight months I'd lost, I was criminally out of date on my armor knowledge, which meant I might actually learn something. I was just about to flop into the captain's chair and pull up the video list to see if there was anything promising when I discovered I had an audience.

The little phantoms I'd seen floating around when I'd first gotten on the ship were now sitting in a line on the edge of the flight console like birds on a wire, if birds were semi-transparent and came in shapes ranging from small spider with too many legs to fist-sized blob. There were seven of them, all sitting perfectly still, and though no two were alike and all seemed to be lacking eyeballs, I got the distinct impression they were staring at me. This would have been creepy sober. Drunk, it just pissed me off.

"Scram," I said, waving my arm at them.

I didn't expect it to work. I wasn't close enough to send them running, which was the only time the phantoms seemed to notice I existed. If anything, I expected the little critters to break their line and float away. Instead, they moved closer together, waving their little appendages like they were trying to get my attention.

I arched an eyebrow and hauled myself up out of the chair, walking forward until I was standing directly behind the pilot's seat. This put the glowing bugs right on the edge of what I'd begun to think of as my phantom panic zone. But though I was dangerously close, they didn't run. They just waved harder.

I looked around the bridge, but there was nothing to see. I was alone in hyperspace with no witnesses to judge my weirdness, and so I decided to take a risk. I cleared my throat and leaned down, fixing my eyes on the largest phantom, a strange, foot-long glowing critter that looked like what might happen if a lobster and a centipede got stuck together. Then, feeling like a right idiot, I whispered, "I see you."

I held my breath, waiting for a response, but the phantoms just kept waving like I hadn't said anything.

"I see you," I said again, louder. "What do you want?"

Nothing.

I rolled my eyes and stepped back, more angry with myself for expecting an answer than with the phantoms for not giving me one.

I gave them the finger before sweeping my hand over the console, sending them flying. As usual, they scattered like frightened mice, but they didn't leave the bridge. Instead, they regrouped on the headrest of the captain's chair and resumed waving, leaning into each other like gossiping monkeys.

"Oh no you don't," I snarled, marching back to the chair. "That's where I sit. Take your crazy somewhere else, glowworms. We're full up here."

The phantoms scattered again when I sat down, but like before, they didn't leave. Instead, they went back to the flight console and started gesturing even more frantically, like they were desperately trying to tell me something.

"Go tell it to Maat," I drawled as I brought up the training menu.

Sadly, there were no new armor titles, but there was a whole series about the new Maraday line of sniper rifles. I'd never been interested in sniping, but seeing Rashid in action had changed my tune. I hit the first training session and put my feet up on the console, which was both comfortable and blocked my view of the phantoms. Out of sight, out of mind, and as the video started, I put the crazy glowing bugs firmly out of mine.

Unfortunately, they didn't stay there. I watched ten videos over the next four hours, and by the time I was sober, I had a shopping list as long as my arm just in case I lived long enough to upgrade my equipment. This should have put me in a much better mood, but I was on permanent buzzkill because the goddamn phantoms still hadn't moved, and they hadn't stopped waving at me.

"God and king, would you just *go away?*" I groaned, dropping my feet to glare at them. "What do you want from me?"

They didn't answer, of course, but I'd had enough. I switched off the monitor and stood up, stretching the last few hours out of my joints. I was about to evacuate to the kitchen again to see if there was anything more appetizing on offer than ration bars when a piercing scream ripped through the ship.

I dropped into a protective crouch before I realized I'd moved, hands going for the gun that wasn't there. My first instinct said it was a phantom scream, and I glanced at the little bugs. Was this what they'd been trying to warn me about? But when the scream came again, I knew it was a real sound, not that awful stabbing pain in my skull. Not a phantom, then, but it still didn't sound human.

It had to be Rupert, I reasoned at last, standing up. He was the only other thing on the ship besides myself and the phantoms. Now that I knew what I was hearing, I could actually recognize his voice, barely. By this point, the screams were nearly constant, and each one was horrifying, a barely human sound of rage and pain that made me want to run to Rupert's room and wake him up, anything to make it stop.

But I didn't. Rupert had told me to stay away, and that was exactly what I planned to do. I wasn't about to be the idiot who got herself killed ignoring basic safety instructions because she couldn't take the noise. So even though the screams seemed to be getting worse by the second, I climbed back into the captain's chair and stayed put, covering my ears with my hands as I waited for it to end.

Three minutes later, the screams showed no sign of stopping, and I was wondering how the hell Rupert had slept on the *Fool*. There was no way I could have missed such a horrible racket even a deck up. Of course, he'd said he was normally quiet, so maybe this was a fluke? I prayed that it was. Whatever could pull that sort of sound out of a person wasn't the sort of thing I'd wish on my worst enemy.

At last, after nearly ten minutes of howling, Rupert's screams faded to whimpers. I slumped into the captain's chair, flexing my shoulders as I tried in vain to relax my muscles. My body was tight as a clenched fist, leaving me feeling like I'd just gotten the bad end of a drunken brawl, and I'd only been listening. I couldn't imagine how Rupert must feel.

Fortunately, we had only forty minutes left to go in the jump. His whimpering died out a few minutes after the screaming, which I took as a good sign. I was debating whether to go knock on his door when I heard the lock click open.

I jumped out of the chair. "Hey!" I called, running across the bridge to the hall. "Are you okay? That sounded horri—"

I stopped short, words dying. Rupert was standing in the door of the officer's bunk, and the second I saw him, I knew something was wrong. It wasn't that he was covered in scales or anything like that. He actually looked perfectly normal, dressed and steady on his feet, but though he was staring straight ahead at the opposite wall, his eyes were empty, like there was nothing behind them at all.

Not making a sound, not even daring to breathe, I took a step back. My suit was still in her case hooked into the charging rack at the back of the bridge, but my guns were lashed on top. I could almost see them from where I was standing. All I'd have to do was step back out of the hall and dive to the left. One step, that was all I needed, but the moment my foot left the floor, Rupert's head snapped toward it. That was all the warning I got before he slammed into me.

With my suit, prepared, I could keep up with Rupert's speed. Unarmored, I didn't have a prayer. I barely had time to gasp before Rupert's hand wrapped around my throat like a metal vise. This close, I could see his eyes weren't actually empty. They were vicious and mad, like Maat's could be, with absolutely nothing of Rupert in them at all, and I knew right then that if I was going to survive the next few seconds, I had to fight for real.

After that, my battle instincts kicked in with a vengeance, clearing my mind and banishing my panic. All at once, there was no more fear, no more Rupert either. Just me, my survival, and the obstacle that stood in my way.

I lurched forward, pushing off the wall behind me and lifting my leg to slam my heel directly into his knee. Symbionts are tough, but their physiology is still basically human, and a kick to the joint still hurts. I couldn't get enough power to break it, but my kick made him stumble, which loosened his hand on my neck enough for me to tear away.

I dove the second I was free. Rupert's charge had knocked us back onto the bridge, which meant the charging racks were directly to my left. I landed hard on my stomach right under my armor case, and my arm shot up instinctively, grabbing Mia off the top.

My plasma shotgun weighs sixty-three pounds, far too heavy to use unarmored. Stuck in fight or flight as I was, though, I didn't even feel it. I snatched my gun to my chest and flipped over, hitting the charge as I brought her barrel up. I didn't have time to aim, barely had time to get the damn muzzle pointed the right direction before Mia's whistle hit the ready note. The instant I heard it, I pulled the trigger.

Fortunately for me, plasma shotguns don't require much aiming. Just pointing Mia in the right direction was enough to send a blast of burning plasma directly into Rupert's chest, and not a second too soon. By the time I'd flipped over, he'd been almost on top of me. The blast knocked him right off again, making him yelp in pain as he flew backward to land flat on his back a few feet away, his chest smoking.

I was on my feet again by the time he hit with Mia cocked and singing against my shoulder, ready for another shot, but I didn't take it. Rupert's cry just now had sounded like himself, and so I waited, gun ready, to see what he'd do.

It took a while. The blast must have knocked his breath out, because Rupert lay still for several seconds. Finally, he sat up with a groan, looking down in confusion at the smoldering hole in his shirt. The burned skin beneath was already healing, which made me feel better about shooting him. But as I was lowering my gun to ask him what the hell had just happened, Rupert looked up, and the horrified expression on his face almost made my heart break.

"Devi," he whispered. "What..." The word faded out as his eyes went even wider. "Did I do that to your neck?"

I'd been so caught up in the fight, I hadn't even realized I was hurt until he said something. Now, like it had just been waiting for its cue, my whole throat exploded in pain. I could actually feel the imprint of his hand around my neck still, as well as the massive throbbing that was always a sign you're going to bruise all to hell. Worse, the unexpected pain sent me into a coughing fit, which in turn sent me to the floor, clutching my throat as I tried to breathe through the pain.

Rupert was at my side in an instant. He left again a second later only to come right back, this time with a first-aid kit. He was talking the whole time, and though his tone told me the words were meant to be calming, I couldn't make them out. At first I thought this was because I just couldn't get enough attention away from my throat to make sense of what he was saying, but a few words later I realized I couldn't understand Rupert because he wasn't speaking Universal. But it wasn't until he pulled me into his lap, pressing me painfully tight against his shaking body, that I realized Rupert, the eternally calm operative, the cold killer, was in a full-blown panic.

"I'm sorry," he whispered, finally switching back to Universal as he hurriedly wrapped a cold pack bandage around my neck. "I'm sorry. I'm so so so sorry, Devi. Hold on. I don't—"

"Rupert," I croaked out, reaching up to grab his jaw with my hand, forcing him to stop and look at me. "Shut up."

It wasn't the most eloquent sentiment, but my throat hurt so badly I couldn't get out anything better. Even those few words had brought tears to my eyes, but I couldn't bear to see Rupert so upset, especially since I was fine. Well, not fine exactly since my neck hurt like a bitch, but I wasn't at death's door by any stretch, which was what you'd have thought given how Rupert was acting.

Fortunately, the words did the trick. Rupert's babbling cut off like a switch. From then on he worked in silence, swaddling my neck in the icy comfort of the cold pack bandage before injecting me with a painkiller followed by something to bring down the swelling.

The painkiller didn't do shit for me, of course, but the anti-swelling agent worked like a charm. The pressure in my neck began to go down almost immediately, and a few minutes later I was able to breathe more or less normally. "Thank you," I said, sitting up in his lap. "Now, what the hell was that?"

Rupert didn't answer. When I glanced up to see why, he wasn't looking at me. Instead, his head was lowered, his face buried in the tangled mess of my hair. Pressed against him as I was, I could feel his body like metal beneath me.

That made me pause. Hugging Rupert had always been a bit like hugging a rock, but this was different. There was no give in his muscles at all, like his whole body was tensed to bolt. He was like a fist clenched tight, but it wasn't until he started to pull away that I realized what was really going on.

"Oh no you don't," I said, leaning back until he had no choice but to face me. Rupert's face was blank when it came into view, but I wasn't fooled for a second. "Don't you dare shut me out," I snapped, pointing my finger right at his nose. "We had a deal. No secrets. Now tell me what happened."

I knew Rupert was really upset because his calm mask crumbled almost instantly, giving way to a look that was caught somewhere between terror and pleading. "I'm not sure I can."

"Try me," I said with a coaxing smile.

Rupert sighed and closed his eyes. "It's the symbiont," he said softly. "It's more than just nightmares. The symbiont is another entity that shares your mind."

"Does it talk to you or something?"

He shook his head. "It's not... intelligent. Symbionts were originally created by the xith'cal to empower their warriors. Republic scientists stole the technique over a century ago, but even once they'd adapted the implant to work in humans, it still had xith'cal instincts inside it. Specifically, the host body inherits the xith'cal bloodlust."

Anthony had said something to that effect. He'd also said something about symbionts eating people, but Rupert wasn't finished.

"Normally the bloodlust is kept in check by the tribe leader," Rupert said. "But symbionts aren't part of a tribe, so we have to control it on our own. Those who can't learn to control the will to kill are put down."

"But you can control it, clearly," I said. "So what went wrong?"

Rupert bit his lip, thinking. "Controlling the symbiont isn't like controlling your muscles," he said at last. "It's more like keeping a mad dog on a leash. So long as your hold is good, everything stays under control. But if your grip slips, the dog gets free and runs wild." He reached up to run a hand over his face, rubbing his eyes. "I've held mine for so long it's second nature. I haven't lost control since the very beginning, but I can't hold on when I'm asleep."

"I get it," I said. "That's why you locked yourself in, so your symbiont wouldn't go joyriding while you were asleep." I glared at him. "You know, I wish you'd just told me this earlier. If I'd had some warning your alien was going to go nuts, I would have lashed you down and waited in my suit."

"I still haven't told you everything," he said quietly.

I motioned for him to go ahead, but Rupert seemed to have run out of steam. He just sat there, avoiding my eyes, and I got the sinking feeling that this was going to be bad.

"I told you the symbiont isn't intelligent," he said at last. "But it does have a will of sorts. It wants to kill, and it gets frustrated when it can't. That anger gets reflected back on its host, and if the host keeps refusing to give up control, the symbiont begins to hate."

I grimaced. "I guess yours must hate you a lot, then?"

Rupert closed his eyes. "Yes," he said quietly. "It hates me very much. But it wasn't a problem until recently, because I never gave it an opening. Now, however, the situation has changed."

My sinking feeling got worse. "Changed how?"

"The symbiont is part of me," Rupert said, lifting his eyes to mine at last. "It knows what I know. That's why it's so dangerous for people with symbionts to get attached. It gives the symbiont a target, a way to hurt their host and take out their hatred. I thought if I locked the door, you'd be safe. The symbiont isn't supposed to be able to operate complex systems like code locks. But I underestimated it, and you paid the price." He closed his eyes. "It could have killed you. It could have ripped you to pieces and I wouldn't even have known until I woke up and saw—"

"Stop," I said sharply, making his eyes pop open again. "Stop right there and listen. I don't care what *could* have happened. It didn't, and this wasn't your fault."

"It was," Rupert said, eyes narrowing. "Whose handprint do you think that is?"

I set my jaw stubbornly. "I refuse to hold you accountable for things your symbiont did while you were asleep."

"It doesn't matter. I *am* accountable!" Rupert said, his voice rising. He stopped after that, like his anger surprised him, and took a deep breath. "Caldswell was right," he said, calmly now. "No matter how good you think your control is, it always ends the same way."

"Don't you dare bring Caldswell into this," I growled. "He has nothing to do with it."

"He does," Rupert said, leaning back to give me an appraising look. "Did Brenton tell you how Caldswell lost his position as head of the Eyes?"

I shook my head.

"It was his symbiont," Rupert said. "He put off the implantation as long as possible, but in the end he had to get one to survive Maat's rages. Despite his worries, he adapted very well, making one of the best transitions on record, and he used this to argue that he should be allowed to continue visiting his family."

I blinked. "Wait, Caldswell has a family? Why couldn't he visit them?"

"A wife and a daughter," Rupert said. "And he couldn't visit them because Terran military law prohibits symbionts from having relationships with nonsymbionts for reasons you now understand. But Caldswell refused to give up. His control was the best around, he said, and he was the commander. No one wanted to argue with him, so he went home as soon as they released him from observation."

As Rupert spoke, the hairs on the back of my neck stood up. I could guess where this was going, but I didn't stop Rupert from telling me.

"Caldswell loved his wife and daughter deeply," he said quietly. "He told them the risks, locked himself away whenever he needed to sleep during his visits home, and for a year, everything was fine. Then, one night, there was a power outage at his farm. The blackout caused the two maglocks on his door to malfunction, leaving only the dead bolt. His symbiont kicked out the lock and murdered his family before Caldswell could wake up. When he opened his eyes at last, he was eating his wife's arm."

I pressed a hand to my mouth, fighting not to gag. I'd known something awful must have happened to make Caldswell so bitter, but the truth was even worse than I could have imagined. "What happened after that?" I asked when I got my voice back. "How did he cope?"

"He didn't," Rupert said. "Caldswell went AWOL, vanished for two years without a trace. Fleet command put in temporary commanders while he was gone, but none of them could handle Brenton, who took Caldswell's desertion very badly."

My disbelief must have been clear on my face, because Rupert explained, "They used to be very close. The two of them were Maat's original Eyes, back before the daughters when she could actually travel and take on phantoms herself. When Caldswell finally came back, Brenton tried to get him reinstated as commander, but fleet command wouldn't have it. They wanted to court-martial him, but Caldswell's experience was too valuable, so they demoted him to field commander. He's been there ever since, running things for the rotating roster of commanding officers that Starfleet keeps installing. Commander Martin is our seventh commander since Caldswell's demotion."

"Why did Caldswell return?" I asked, because I didn't think I would have ever come back after that.

Rupert sighed. "Because defeating the phantoms has been Caldswell's purpose from the very beginning. He told me once that if he gave that up, he'd have nothing. He also came back because he didn't want anyone else repeating his mistake. He tells the story of his family's death to every candidate before they agree to the symbiont implantation. Fleet command tries to stop him because he scares away half of the applicants, but he always gets his way in the end. He might not be the head of the Eyes anymore, but very few people will say no to Commander Caldswell."

"It didn't scare you away."

"I never thought I'd have someone to kill," Rupert said sadly. "Now I've made the same mistake Caldswell did."

"Except I'm still alive," I pointed out. "You didn't kill me."

"But I will." His voice sounded so tired now. Defeated, I realized with a chill. "So long as I care about you, my symbiont will see you as a target and try to kill you any chance it gets." He reached out as he spoke, running his fingers gently through my hair. "I knew that, but I selfishly stayed by you. I wanted to be with you so badly I convinced myself I could manage the risk, and it nearly got you killed. I can't put you in that situation again."

My chest tightened with every word. I could see where this was going, just like I could see the resolve in Rupert's eyes when he dropped his hand. He was going to leave. "No," I said.

Rupert sighed. "Devi…"

"No," I said again, louder this time. I might have just been brooding over how Rupert poisoned my resolve and made me weak, but like hell was I going to let him run out on me. Especially not over a problem that could be solved with some metal cables and a sturdy bed bolted to a bulkhead. "You are *not* leaving."

Rupert's eyes widened at my vehemence, and for a moment, he looked almost hopeful. But the spark died as quickly as it flared. "I have to," he said, gently removing me from his lap as he stood. "I put you in danger just by—"

"The only way you put me in danger was by not telling me this shit earlier!" I yelled, ignoring the pain in my throat as I shot to my feet as well. "If you want to beat yourself up over something, beat yourself up over that, but like hell am I letting you abandon me out of some stupid, chivalrous, self-punishing sense of guilt."

"It's not—" He cut off, gritting his teeth. "I am *trying* to protect you."

"Well don't," I snapped, pointing at my neck. "You think this frightens me? This is nothing. I've done worse to myself by accident while drunk. I'm not scared of you, and I'm not scared of your symbiont!"

Rupert's eyes flashed with anger. "You should be."

"Why, because it wants to kill me?" I shouted, standing on my toes so I could yell in his face. "Tell it to take a goddamn number!"

"This is not open for argument," he said fiercely. "I have to do this, Devi."

"Why?" I snarled.

"Because I can't lose you!" Rupert shouted. His voice cracked on the words, but it wasn't until he wrapped me so tight in his arms I could barely breathe that I realized Rupert's panic hadn't actually gone away yet.

"I can't lose you," he whispered into my shoulder, his accent thicker than I'd ever heard it. "If I killed you, I can't even think what I would do. I don't want to leave, but I can't do this again. I can't risk you."

I sighed against him, snuggling into his chest. I knew this was counterproductive. I should stay mad at him, use anger to widen the distance between us for my own protection, but I couldn't. Forget weak, I practically melted against him, wrapping my arms around his neck to slide my fingers through the silky fall of his long black hair.

He froze when I touched him, holding so still I could feel his frantic heartbeat thrumming like a drum against my skin. He was so scared, I realized, deadly terrified, and all for me. And as I listened to the pounding of his hectic pulse, it occurred to me for the first time that I was an even greater weakness for Rupert than he was for me.

That realization sent a crushing wave of tenderness through me, and I knew I'd just lost another inch in my fight not to get pulled any further into this doomed relationship. Unfortunately, I didn't have time to care. I still had to talk Rupert down before he gave himself a heart attack.

"You're right," I said solemnly, locking my fingers at his nape. "This *won't* be happening again, because I know what to expect now. The next time you go to sleep, we'll chain you up and let your symbiont thrash all it wants. I'll wear my suit just in case, and if it tries to take me out again, I'll give it some new instincts about not messing with Paradoxians. But under no circumstances will I let you leave."

Rupert opened his mouth to protest, but I cut him off. "You want to protect me?" I said sharply. "Then stay here and help me see this through. *That's* what I need from you, not some self-sacrificing bull about leaving me for my own safety. You were the one who promised I wouldn't have to do this alone, right? So prove it. Stay with me." I tilted my head back, smiling up at him. "Please."

Rupert took a deep breath. "Are you sure you want me to?"

"What kind of question is that?" I asked, giving him a skeptical look. "You put yourself on my team, remember? Like hell am I letting you off the hook."

Rupert didn't seem to have an answer for that. He just stood there, looking at me with some strong emotion I couldn't name, and then he hugged me tight, pressing me into his chest. He didn't say anything, didn't make a sound, but I could feel him shaking harder than ever, his fingers digging into my back until I tensed.

"Sorry," he whispered, loosening his hold at once.

"It's okay," I said softly, locking my arms around his chest before he could pull away. When he stopped trying, I pressed my face against his ruined shirt, which still smelled like burning plasma. "It's okay, Rupert."

I'm not sure how long we stayed like that. It felt like hours, but it couldn't have been more than ten minutes before the soft tone of the hyperspace exit alarm pulled us apart. Rupert let me go reluctantly, trailing his fingers down my arms like he wanted to keep touching me for as long as possible.

He still looked like hell, though. "Would you like me to get you a drink or something?" I asked softly. "Anthony stashed some whiskey in the freezer."

Rupert shook his head. "Symbiont metabolism is incompatible with alcohol. We digest it before it can do anything."

I arched an eyebrow. "So if you can't get drunk, what were you doing that night in the lounge?"

He sighed as he walked toward the pilot's seat. "Trying very, very hard."

Inappropriate as it was, that made me giggle. I was just walking up to take my own seat when he suddenly said, "Thank you."

"For what?" I asked. "Not taking your bullshit? 'Cause I do that free of charge."

Rupert must have been feeling better, because that got a laugh out of him. "Thank you for drinking with me that night and for not letting me go now," he said as I sat down. "Thank you for not hating me."

Maybe I'd hit my head at some point during our fight, because when I got that sudden feeling like my heart was too big for my chest, it didn't bother me at all. "My pleasure," I said, shooting him a smile.

He smiled back. A real, wide, honest-to-god smile that went straight to my head and left me stupid and breathless. Sacred King, I thought as I fumbled with my harness, I'd forgotten how good he looked when he did that. He was still doing it, too, the bastard, smiling to himself as he worked the controls. Even when it wasn't directed at me, the warm turn of his lips made my stomach do all kinds of acrobatics.

Get a grip, idiot, I snarled at myself when I finally managed to tear my eyes away. What part of 'Nothing could come of this' didn't I understand? I had a job to do, one that a lot of good people had sacrificed for. The whole universe could be riding on my virus, and if I let myself get distracted away from that because of a stupid man and his stupid smile, then I was the most selfish, awful, empty-headed idiot of a merc girl ever to put on a suit.

Properly chastised, I turned away from Rupert and began trying to rebuild my walls. I was so busy listing all the ways the events of the last half hour were *never happening again*, I didn't even realize the line of phantoms that had been tormenting me for the last four hours had vanished until the jump flash started washing over the ship.

I twisted around in the chair, positive they must have just moved off while I wasn't looking, but I didn't catch so much as a glimmer. I was still looking when the jump flash faded, leaving us floating high above a small, cold world.

That made me forget about the phantoms real quick. "God and king," I grumbled, leaning forward to get a better view of Kessel's icy mountains, which looked just as cold and miserable as I remembered. "Never thought I'd be back at this dump."

"You've been here before?" Rupert asked, surprised.

"Of course," I said. "I'm a merc. Kessel is a lawless pirate haven. When pirates steal something valuable from people they shouldn't, we get hired to steal it back." And make an example of the thief, which was my favorite part of Kessel missions. "I took my team here to retrieve a shipment not six months ago, right before I quit the Blackbirds. Well, fourteen months ago, counting the eight we lost, but you get the idea."

"Good," Rupert said. "So you know how to find a reputable doctor, then."

"On Kessel?" I said with a snort. "No such thing. We don't need a doctor, anyway. I'm fine."

Rupert shot me a cutting glare that had me throwing up my hands. "No," I said. "Did you not listen to what I just said? It's a *pirate haven*. If I go into a clinic down there, I'll probably come out short half my organs."

"Your neck needs more than I can do with first aid," Rupert said, crossing his arms. "You're going."

I crossed my arms back. "I am not."

When Rupert gave me an implacable look, I arched an eyebrow, daring him. But Rupert could be as stubborn as I was when he put his mind to it, and I could almost see him digging for a long fight as he put the ship on auto and turned his chair to face me. I didn't care. I'd do an arena fight naked before I set a toe inside a Kessel medhack's lair. But Rupert clearly wasn't going to see reason easily, so I settled in for the long haul, pressing my back deep into the hard chair as we both began to push.

CHAPTER

4

I caved after only twenty minutes.

Not from any lack of dedication on my part. I would have kept going until the king came to take me home, but the anti-inflammatory shot Rupert had given me had started to wear off halfway through, and the fact that I was having trouble speaking through the swelling was fatally undermining my "I don't need a doctor" argument. Even if I'd been perfectly fine, I don't think I could have won. I might have convinced Rupert not to run off in a guilt-induced panic, but I could tell he still blamed himself for what had happened. He was going to get me to a doctor if he had to carry me kicking and screaming, and since we both knew he was perfectly capable of doing just that, it was probably better for everyone that I quit while I was ahead.

He gave me another anti-inflammatory shot to tide me over until we landed, prepping my arm so gently and expertly I didn't even notice the needle until it was over. And weird as it sounded, I kind of liked that. I might have flat out hated the idea of getting my neck anywhere near the sort of unlicensed quack who'd set up shop on Kessel, but I had to admit it was nice to have someone who cared enough to take care of me even when I fought them. So nice, in fact, that I didn't even feel too put out that I'd lost the argument—that was, until Rupert told me I couldn't wear my armor.

"Are you out of your damn mind?" I cried, stabbing my finger against the ship's window at the planet below. From orbit, Kessel looked a dirty snowball filled with bits of metal and rock, and this was the scenic distance. "That is a *pirate haven* that I used to *raid*. If I go down without my suit, I will be *dead*."

"Unless you did that raiding with your helmet off, your chances of being recognized and attacked are actually lower without your suit," Rupert calmly pointed out. "And it's not like I'm asking you to go unarmed. You'll have a gun and I'll be with you the whole time. You'll be perfectly safe."

"I'll be perfectly shot," I snapped.

Rupert arched a skeptical eyebrow, and I stopped for a deep breath. "Listen," I said, striving to match his calm. "You're talking about landing a Paradoxian military ship in an enemy starport and then walking out barefaced. That's like tying a bow made of bacon onto a pig and then throwing it into a shark-infested sea. They'll shoot us and steal our ship just on principle."

"Devi, if you go out there wearing your armor, you might as well throw a party to announce your presence here. I am completely confident in your ability to hold your own against a few pirates with or without your Lady, but I am far less sure of our odds for dodging the Eyes once they hear you're on Kessel."

"Eyes are not going to listen to pirate gossip about a supposedly dead merc," I reminded him.

"Once your Anthony reports back to the Home Office that you're alive, which he probably already has, they'll listen to everything," Rupert said. "Trust me, this way is much safer."

I crossed my arms and glowered out the window. I couldn't even say what I was angrier about—that I was going to a doctor on Kessel or that I'd be doing it unarmored. But pissed as I was, even I'm not stubborn enough to ignore sense when it's spoken. Didn't mean I had to like it, though.

"Fine," I snarled. "But I'm bringing my case and weapons with me. First sign of trouble, I'm rolling everything I have."

"Compromise accepted," Rupert said, turning back to the flight controls. "Was that so hard?"

I glowered at him. "I think I liked you better when you were desperate for my forgiveness."

"Really?" Rupert said as he began our descent. "I think you like someone who will stand up to you."

I didn't even dignify that with a response, focusing on the view outside as we entered Kessel's cloud cover.

The trip down was a hairy one. A former corporate mining colony, Kessel had fallen on hard times when the minerals ran out. Its icy surface was littered with the husks of old extractors and huge, open pit mines filled with toxic yellow ice. There were underground mines, too, thousands of miles of abandoned tunnels that ran under the planet's rocky exterior like termite tracks under bark. Combine that with Kessel's isolated location far from the core worlds and a shoddy jump gate that tended to "malfunction" whenever the Republic Enforcers needed to use it and you had smuggler heaven.

We were headed for Kessel's only real starport, located at the center of its only major city, the aptly named Port One. This wouldn't have been a big deal on most planets, but Kessel's mountainous terrain vastly limited the approach options, which meant that all incoming planetary traffic ended up funneled into a single flight path, and since pirate havens don't bother with official flight towers or landing regulations, we were dodging ships the whole way down.

In addition to its starport, Port One had also been the central processing facility for Kessel's mineral wealth. From the sky, you could still see the outlines of the huge factories and warehouse complexes under the crust of caked-on black ice and makeshift repairs. Since it was so cold, most of the planet's population stayed underground all year long, but judging by how packed the starport was, Kessel was doing good business. There had to be a hundred ships parked on the dock where Rupert set us down, and every single one of them was old, dented, and armed to the teeth without a serial number in sight. They might as well have just spray painted PIRATE on the side and called it a day.

Since I wasn't going to be wearing my armor like I'd expected to, my lack of shoes was now a problem. Rupert wasn't much better. Dress shoes and a suit look nice on a ship, but they weren't much good in the snow. If we were going to make it ten feet without freezing, we needed new clothes.

Fortunately, the Home Guard flies prepared for anything. The ready closet at the rear of our ship was stocked with gear for all kinds of weather. I found a thermal shirt and cargo pants to go over my tank top and leggings from the embassy and a pair of general-issue combat boots that, while two sizes too big, were better than nothing. But while I looked like a kid playing dress-up in my over-sized clothes, Rupert looked amazing.

After months of conservative white button-ups, old-fashioned suits, and black alien scales, seeing him in combat gear was something of a revelation. He'd always been easy on the eyes, but seeing his broad shoulders and long limbs defined by the thin, clingy, black fabric of a long-sleeved Paradoxian underarmor shirt was almost indecent. He'd traded out his slacks and dress shoes for gray fatigues and tall combat boots like the ones I wore, except that he wore his *much* better.

He wore everything better, I thought with a sigh. Even before I'd gone off to the army, I'd always had an appreciation for guys in military wear. Combine that with my appreciation of Rupert, and I decided it would be much safer if I just focused on finding us some coats.

While I searched through the gear trunks, Rupert grabbed a black surplus duffel and headed for the mess. By the time I'd dug up two dark gray and red snow jackets, he'd packed the large bag full of prepackaged rations, the ship's first-aid kit, and extra ammo for the standard-issue sidearm pistol he now wore at his hip. I'd grabbed one for myself as well, a sleek little Maraday S Class Automatic that was no bigger than my hand but still capable of punching a hole through most light-armored suits if you knew where to aim. It wasn't a patch on any of my girls, but for a standard-grade gun, it wasn't half bad. Home Guard always got the best stuff.

Loading up on Anthony's gear made me feel a little guilty, but considering where we were, I reasoned it was just going to get stolen anyway, and it wasn't like we'd be coming back. I had no doubt Rupert was right when he said Anthony would report that I was alive. The Paradoxian army would be combing the galaxy for this ship soon, if they weren't already. If we wanted to stay free and clear, we had to ditch it, but I'll admit I felt a pang as Rupert lowered the ramp. This ship was the closest I'd been to home in a long time now. Abandoning it unprotected in a pirate haven, especially when we had no ship to replace it, felt both reckless and blasphemous.

"Blasphemous?" Rupert asked, raising his voice over the wind.

I nodded, trying not to slip as I lugged my armor case down the rapidly icing ramp. "Home Guard ships are the Sacred King's own property. Leaving it here for pirates to pick over seems wrong." I glanced up at the ship's prow where the Home Guard crest and serial were proudly displayed. "Are you sure you can find us another ride?"

"Sure as I can be," Rupert said, strapping both bags over his chest so his gloved hands were free to help me step down into the crust of dirty ice that covered the starport's landing deck. "Come on, let's go."

I nodded, lugging my armor case onto my back as we hurried toward the exit.

Kessel's lone starport was guarded on all sides by five-story windbreaks to protect landing ships from being blow off course and possibly into mountains. Once we stepped outside, though, the wind hit us like a train, pushing me sideways into Rupert. He grabbed my arm after that, steadying me down the huge loading ramp to the covered road that had once been a railway between the starport and the mineral processing factory just across the valley. Now the rails had been paved over and huge pieces of sheet metal had been welded between the warehouses that flanked the path on either side, creating a covered corridor that was packed to the rafters with people.

The man-made cave was actually brighter than the cloudy day outside thanks to the glowing signs on the shops, carts, and kiosks that crowded into every possible nook of the sheltered street. The old ore warehouses had been sliced up into hundreds of shops offering anything you could want of the mostly legal variety. I knew from experience that the real goods were kept underground in the smuggler's market, but on the surface at least, Kessel flirted with propriety. It was still a dive, though, as evidenced by the fact that we had to walk two blocks before we saw an establishment that wasn't a bar, a pawnshop, a strip club, or a brothel.

I'd told Rupert that if we were going to find a doctor who was even remotely close to decent, it would be up here in the relatively legal aboveground. The crowds by the starport had been too thick to do anything except push through, but once we'd walked far enough to clear the crush, Rupert stopped and pulled out his handset, keeping one hand wrapped tightly around my elbow while he browsed the planet's commerce grid with the other, his dark brows pulled in a scowl.

Normally I would have resented his grip on me and the control it implied, but at the moment I was glad to have him. Unarmored and wearing oversized clothes that made me look like a runaway teenager, I wasn't exactly an imposing figure, a dangerous disadvantage on a planet where everyone was armed and abduction in the street was met with little more than annoyed looks. But with Rupert beside me, I didn't even have to worry about it. Between the new military clothes and the scowl, his normal casual lethality had been turned up by a factor of ten. Add in his towering height and obvious comfort with the gun on his hip, and the crowd parted around us like water around a rock without him having to lift a finger. It wasn't as nice as parting the crowds myself, but it was nice all the same.

After five minutes of reading through listings, Rupert told me an address and we started walking. Two blocks later, we turned off the main road onto another, much narrower covered street that looked like it had once been a wind gap between warehouses. There was barely enough room for both of us to walk side by side, and the wind channeling between the buildings was so intense I had to brace to keep from being blown over. Fortunately, we didn't have to go far. I'd already spotted the clinic sign shining red like a warning, and my feet slowed down of their own accord.

"Devi," Rupert warned.

"Oh, come on," I pleaded, eyes wide. "There's a freaking chop shop right next door."

But Rupert would not listen to reason, and a minute later, we were walking through the clinic's heavy door.

The best thing I could say about the tiny waiting room we stepped into was that it was clean. Like all the other shops that had taken over the old warehouses, this one had walls made from what looked like stolen metal sheets welded together, but at least these were painted a spotless beige. The door had barely closed behind us when a formidable, middle-aged woman with graying, tight-curled hair hidden under a threadbare shawl pushed through the curtains that separated the entry from the rest of the clinic.

She stepped up to the counter with a sour look, like having customers was a burden she could have done without. "Welcome," she said in a voice that was anything but. "What do you want?"

Her Universal was so accented I could barely understand her, but Rupert's face broke into a smile as he pushed back his hood and began speaking another language to her. I had no idea what he was speaking, other than it wasn't the same language I'd heard him use when he'd panicked back on the ship. Whatever it was, the sour woman's face lit up like a sunbeam the second she heard it. From that point on, she was eating out of Rupert's palm, though I still got the stink eye. After a few minutes of happy chatter, they seemed to strike a deal, and the woman vanished into the rear of the shop while Rupert walked back over to me.

"What was that about?" I asked, arching an eyebrow. "Greasing the wheels?"

Rupert's smile turned sly. "In a manner of speaking. They weren't going to take you since we don't have cash on hand, but I convinced her otherwise."

"You got us credit on Kessel?" I said, astonished. "What did you do, agree to marry into her family?"

"Hearing your home language in a strange place can be very comforting," Rupert replied sagely. "Comfort brings trust, and trust gets us what we need."

I snorted. "How many languages do you speak, anyway?"

"Ten," Rupert said. At my incredulous look, he explained, "It was useful in my line of work, and I had a long time to learn. Also, they get easier as you go."

The woman came back in then, giving Rupert an adoring look before waving at me to follow her. I sighed. There went any hope that I was getting out of this. "Are you coming with me?"

Rupert shook his head. "I have to go solve our funds problem. I shouldn't be long, but if I'm not back before you're done, wait for me here."

I wanted to ask him what he meant by that, but I couldn't with the woman standing right there, so all I said was, "Be careful."

Rupert smiled and ducked down, pressing a quick kiss to my cheek before I could react. "Don't give the doctor a hard time," he said as he walked toward the door.

I scowled after him, cheeks heating, but he was already gone. Behind me, the woman cleared her throat impatiently. I glared at her over my shoulder, and then I grabbed my armor and started my gallows march, grumbling a string of curses in my own native language as I followed her into the back.

———

I wish I could say it wasn't as bad as I'd feared, but that would be a lie. The doctor turned out to be the sister of the lady up front, and she looked exactly like you'd expect a Kessel medhack to, complete with old bloodstains on the front of her dingy medical apron. My only comfort was that at least she didn't bother me with stupid questions about how I'd ended up with a handprint on my neck as she strapped me to the table.

I don't do well with being tied up in general, but being lashed down on my back while a stranger ran a tissue repair wand over my exposed throat was a special kind of hell for me. The doctor had given me a shot for the pain even though I'd tried to tell her not to bother because it wouldn't do crap. She must have mixed in some serious black market drugs, though, because even though it took over two hours to repair all the broken blood vessels, I only remembered about ten minutes of it. Before I knew it, the doctor and her sister were helping me sit up on the table and telling me not to move because I might feel dizzy.

I felt like I was going to hurl, but it passed quickly. My neck, on the other hand, felt great. When the nurse sister handed me a mirror, I saw my throat was whole and perfect, without even the shadow of a bruise. I still wasn't sure the improvement was worth baring my neck to strangers, but at least Rupert would stop pitching a fit now.

After his cryptic remarks earlier, I fully expected to have to wait. But when I walked into the waiting room, Rupert was already there, sitting on the worn couch with his bags beside him. His eyes went straight to my neck, and though his face revealed nothing, his chest moved in a relieved breath.

While I waited by the door, Rupert paid the nurse in cash. That alone would have been noteworthy. Paper money was a relic. I didn't even know they were still printing the stuff. But what really got me was that Rupert was handing her a *lot* of cash, enough to make me gape. I didn't dare ask him about it in the clinic, but as soon as we were outside, I grabbed him and pulled him into the darkened doorway of a closed shop, crowding up against him to get out of the howling wind. "How much money did you give her?"

"Double fee plus tip," Rupert answered without missing a beat, reaching up to tug my coat away from my healed neck with a gentle gloved finger. "I trusted them with something very important, and they clearly did an excellent job." His voice grew tender. "I'd have paid much more to see you whole again."

I smacked his hand away. "You can't go throwing money around like that here! You're going to get us targeted."

Rupert gave me a skeptical look. "I'm pretty sure we can handle any would-be muggers."

He had a point, but still. "We don't have the money to waste. We still have to buy a ship off this rock, remember?"

"Actually," Rupert said, lips curling as he reached down and unzipped the bag hanging from his shoulder, "I think we're settled at present."

My eyes went wide. The duffel bag Rupert had taken from Anthony's ship was absolutely stuffed with cash. It was more paper money than I'd ever seen in one place. All Republic Script, too, no colony notes, and every bill had a four-digit number at the corner.

"Holy shit," I whispered. "Did you rob a bank or something?"

"Of course not," Rupert said, giving me a handful of cash before zipping the bag shut again. "I pawned my Royal Warrant."

I was too busy shoving the money into my coat before someone saw it to process what he said. When I did, though, I went ballistic. "You *what*?!"

My shout drew looks from passersby, and I dropped my voice to a hiss. "You sold a *Royal Warrant*? Are you *crazy*?" It would have been safer to rob a bank. At least then we'd only have the local authorities to deal with. They sent Devastators after people who abused Warrants.

"It was the best option available," Rupert said patiently. "We don't have King Stephen's backing anymore, and the Royal Office tracks Warrants very closely. Using it from this point on would be asking to get caught."

"Did you tell that to the guy you sold it to?"

Rupert's smile turned sly. "Why do you think I asked to be paid in untraceable cash?"

I leaned forward with a groan, burying my face in Rupert's coat. Not only had he sold the king's trust, but the criminal he'd sold it to was going to get busted by the team sent to nab us as soon as he used it. My only consolation was that the pirate probably wouldn't survive long enough to take his revenge. But while I had to admit it was a clever plan that neatly solved our current problem, I couldn't shake the feeling that by accepting Rupert's money, I was being complicit in high treason.

"I'm going to hell for this," I moaned.

"Devi," Rupert said softly, prying me up. "Listen to me. I was entrusted with that Warrant when the king signed you over to my protection, and that's exactly what I'm doing. If you free the daughters and stop the phantoms, everyone benefits, including Paradox. I'm sure the king will forgive a little creative license with his Warrant in exchange for such an obvious greater good."

When he put it that way, I guessed he was right. But still. "It's a mortal offense."

"For me," Rupert said with a smile. "I sold the Warrant. I'd have done as much for the Eyes before, and I'd do far worse for you."

"Well don't," I snapped. Rupert was a Terran, he didn't understand. Even if the king did buy the greater-good angle, Rupert would still hang for it. The sainted king could be merciful, but he could never be lenient. "I know you love me and what's done is done, but this is too much. You can't just—"

I cut off when Rupert's hand found my cheek, tilting my head up so that I had to look at him. "Love is only part of it," he said softly.

Before I could ask what he meant, Rupert leaned down, pushing my hood back just enough to whisper in my ear. The position made me stiffen. Other than the fact that we were standing, this was exactly how we'd been when he'd first whispered he loved me back on the *Fool*, right before he'd taken my memories. That time, his voice had been despairing, desperate. Now it hummed with pride and determination.

"You are doing things I could only dream of," he said quietly. "I used to think keeping what happened to me from happening to anyone else was the most important thing. But even at the beginning, even when I was a perfect loyal Eye, I knew we were doing the right thing the wrong way. I knew that what we did to the daughters was unforgivable, but I thought it was the only way, a necessary evil to achieve a greater good. It wasn't until you appeared and demanded that *everything* be right that I began to imagine it could be."

He leaned in a little closer, and I felt his smile against the curve of my ear. "Seeing you put that gun to your head nearly gave me a heart attack," he admitted. "But at the same time, I never loved you more. From the moment you found out the truth, you've been fighting for everything I always knew I should but was too afraid to reach for before I met you. That's how I know you're the only one who can stop the abuse we perpetrated over seventy years of well-intentioned cruelty. Not because of the virus, but because you are too stubborn and proud to settle for anything less."

I started to say something, but then he pressed a soft kiss against the curl of hair tucked behind my ear, making my heart pound. "*That* is why I love you, brave girl," he whispered. "Because I know without a doubt that your path is the right one, and now that you've given me the courage to walk it with you, no one, not the Eyes or Caldswell or the Sacred King himself, will ever put me from it. Or from you, Devi Morris"—he smiled wide against my hair—"the one who gave me back my life."

I closed my eyes tight as he finished, fighting for control. Why did he always have to be so intense? When he said things like that with his heart in his throat, how could I not believe him? Trust him? How was I supposed to remember that he was my weakness when everything he said made me feel like he was my partner, and he was going to fight beside me whether I liked it or not?

But when I opened my eyes to tell him that I'd take the damn money, so would he please step away and stop undermining my resolve to not fall head over heels for him like a ninny, a flash of light caught my eye. I was so jumpy I looked, even though I already knew what it was. With that pale glow, it could only be a phantom. But when I glanced over at the busy street, it wasn't a phantom. It was a girl.

Maat was standing in the frozen alley not five feet away from me. She looked just like she always did, straight dark hair cut flat above her shoulders, her small, thin body wrapped in a white medical gown that didn't even twitch in the icy wind, because she wasn't really here. The crowd in the street passed right through her like she was a projection, but the fear in her eyes was as real and cold as the snow-crusted wall at my back.

When her lips opened, I winced, bracing for her voice in my head, but nothing came. Maat's mouth was moving, her expression frantic, but I couldn't hear a thing. All I could do was stare as her lips made the same shape over and over. By the time I realized what word she was trying to say, it was almost too late.

Run, Maat mouthed at me, her eyes terrified. *Run!*

"Devi?" Rupert asked, pulling back. "What's wrong?"

I grabbed his arm so hard my fingers hurt. "Run."

The word was little more than air by the time I got it out, but Rupert didn't make me repeat it, and he didn't hesitate. He ran, grabbing my hand and dragging me after him as he darted into the main street, shoving people over to clear a path just as a man in a black suit appeared in the shop directly across from where we'd been hiding from the wind, his arm already shooting out to grab me.

The man's fingers came so close I felt them brush against my coat. But fast as he was, he was too late. Rupert and I were already charging down the crowded street, running full tilt toward the bustling center of Kessel. I heard angry shouts followed by pained yelps as the man barreled out of the alley after us, but I didn't dare look back. I kept my eyes on Rupert as he yanked us around a corner and down the ramp leading into the city's underground.

The upper roads of Kessel were covered, giving the illusion of being closed in, but the underground was the real thing. Down below the surface where the old corp had dug in to keep their machinery from freezing, the now empty factory floors had been taken over by the new industry of Kessel. While the more legitimate businesses huddled together on the frozen surface, the smuggling and fencing and arms dealing that actually kept the planet's economy ticking thrived in the comparative warm and sheltered comfort of the old ore refineries. This meant that unlike the upper roads, I'd actually been to this part of the city enough times to know where I was going.

When Rupert and I reached the bottom of the icy cement ramp, I let go of his hand and turned left. Rupert adjusted instantly, turning on a pin to follow my lead into the stadium-sized cavern that sheltered Kessel's main underground market, a maze-like bazaar of tents and tables stacked with all the illicit delights money could buy. Banners advertising everything from sex to counterfeit armor to organ sales fluttered from the ceiling, their colors faded from the sunlight streaming in through the ground-level windows set thirty feet up on the walls.

If we'd had a normal crash team after us, I would have run through the merchant stands since no merc would be dumb enough to pull a gun in this place. But I didn't need Maat or the man's black suit to tell me our pursuers were Eyes, and they wouldn't bother with guns. They'd take us down in the middle of a crowd just as fast as they would in an empty alley, which meant our only hope was to lose them. Fortunately, Port One's underground was an excellent place to get lost.

My armor case was slowing me down, so I handed it to Rupert as we ran along the bazaar's outer edge toward the huge tunnel that led to the Pipes, Kessel's underground residential district. The Pipes were exactly what they sounded like, a huge network of pipes that brought up hot steam from below the planet's crust to power the generators that had once run the factories and now ran the town. This steam meant the Pipes were also the warmest place on Kessel, and the entire population of the city had built their homes huddled around them like cats around a heater.

I could feel the heat coming over me like a blanket as we ran down the echoing cement tunnel. By the time we reached the Pipes themselves, I was sweating buckets under my heavy coat, but I didn't dare stop to take it off as I dodged the line of people waiting for the elevator to the lower levels and ran instead for a worn metal ladder leading down.

Originally, this whole area had been a tank big enough to hold the small ocean of water needed to blast usable chemicals out of ore on a planetary scale. The steam pipes had run through the middle, heating the water on their way to the generators above. Now, all that water had been drained away and replaced with a honeycomb of ramshackle housing and repurposed shipping containers held together by chains, beams, and metal ramps stolen from the mines, creating a half-mile-long, hundred-foot-wide, cylindrical shanty-town going straight down.

There was no way I could navigate the Pipes properly without my suit's maps, so I just focused on getting as lost as I could, sliding down the ladder and hopping into the maze of corrugated metal alleys below. Even encumbered by my armor case and his bags, Rupert was right behind me, his eyes flicking around to take care-ful note of his surroundings as I led us down, down, down until we reached the very bottom.

The base of the old tank was black as pitch. Other than the faint orange glow of the low-energy lights someone had been kind enough to string along the edges and the occasional shaft of light that made it down from the floors above, there was nothing. Since this was where the pipes first left the ground, it was also hot as sin and so humid I could feel the air in my mouth, but worst of all was the smell. Garbage and other refuse from the floors above found its final home down here, and the stench was enough to curl my hair.

"What is this place?" Rupert said, covering his mouth.

"My old commander used to call it Money Town," I said. "Nine times out of ten, if we were after someone on Kessel, this was where they were hiding. No better place for it, either." I pointed at our feet. It was hard to tell in the dark, but the huge, grime-covered metal walkway under our feet was actually the now empty water pipe that had once filled the tank. "This pipe goes twenty miles to the sea, so you've got warmth, food up top, and a built-in bolt hole."

I couldn't see Rupert's face very well in the dark, but I could hear the horror in his voice. "And you want to hide here?"

"Hell no, this place is disgusting," I said, grabbing my armor case from him. "We're just going to lie low for an hour while I scan the channels and try to figure out what the Eyes are doing."

"Is that why you ran?" Rupert said, going tense. "You saw an Eye?"

"You didn't?" I asked, hauling my case over to a spot where several smaller pipes running down from the floor above passed right next to our huge one, creating a sheltered place to change.

Rupert shook his head. "You said run, so I did."

I couldn't help smiling at his blind trust. The man really would follow me anywhere. "Well, he wasn't wearing a name tag, but he was grabbing for me fast as crap and Maat was there, so it wasn't hard to put two and two together."

He scowled as I spoke. "If you saw her, then there's a daughter on-planet already."

"Why do you think I'm hustling?" I said, tearing off my coat and boots. I should have removed the rest as well, but it would have taken too long to peel off my heavy pants and thermal shirt, and I wasn't going another second without my armor. "How many Eyes do you think we're dealing with?"

Rupert caught my coat when I tossed it, saving it from hitting the hideous, grime-covered floor. He folded it over his arm without looking, his face grave as he considered my question. "At least four," he said at last. "That's all the teams that would be in range to respond to Kessel so quickly. There could be more, though I'm not sure how many on such short notice. In any case, they'll have already shut down the starport for sure, which means we need to find another way off-world as soon as possible."

"I know, I know," I said, popping the locks on my armor case. "But I'm pretty sure we're safe for now. Not many off-worlders know about this place. We can hole up here until—"

I cut off sharp, listening. I couldn't even say what I'd heard, but my brain had suddenly gone on high alert. A second later, I heard it again, a faint vibration in the metal pipes behind me, almost like someone was climbing down.

I realized the truth too late. By the time I looked up, the symbiont had already landed on top of me, sliding off the filthy, dirt-covered pipes above us to land feetfirst on my shoulders. The impact sent me to the ground, knocking the breath from my lungs and banging my ribs hard against the metal pipe below. I didn't even feel it. I was too busy trying to get away, rolling and kicking in an attempt to dislodge the symbiont's weight from my back.

Fat lot of good it did. I couldn't even budge the bastard. I also couldn't see him, positioned as we were, which was why it never crossed my mind that the lead weight on my back wasn't the man who'd made a grab for me in the alley until a cold, female voice spoke just above my head.

"Nice to see you alive, Charkov."

I stopped struggling, gritting my teeth against the sudden flash of rage. I recognized that voice. It was the bitch from the bunker on Io5, the wiry, dark-haired one who'd helped Caldswell convince Rupert he was shooting me.

"Maria Natalia," Rupert said calmly. "What are you doing?"

"Following orders," Eye Natalia said, her voice scornful. "Something you seem to be having trouble with."

"Get the hell off me!" I shouted, craning my head from side to side as I tried to find a way to glare at her. "Rupert! Kick her!"

"Be quiet, Morris."

I went still. Rupert's voice was cold and sharp as an iced knife. He wasn't even looking at me anymore. He was watching the woman on my back, and his face was the killer's cold mask I'd seen on the *Fool*'s bridge. The sight was enough to make me cringe, and I wasn't alone. The woman on my back went perfectly still, holding her breath, and that was when I realized that this wasn't just more of Rupert's coldness. This was the face of Eye Charkov, the cold killer.

"You are interfering, Maria," Rupert said, his voice soft as frost. "I didn't keep her alive all this time just so you could damage her now. If you wanted to take her in, all you had to do was ask."

As he spoke, the tiny part of me that was still waiting for Rupert to sell me out clenched up in a knot. Two days ago, that tension would have been enough to send me into a bitter rage, roaring about betrayal. Now, no rage came, and no one was more surprised by that than I was. But as I lay there, helpless, staring up at Rupert's cold mask, I realized why.

The tiny voice of doubt, the one screaming that he'd just thrown me to the wolves again, was no longer the voice I believed. Instead, I heard his voice whispering in my ear that I'd given him back his life. I thought of how he'd followed me into Reaper's arena, of the faith he'd showed me at every opportunity since he'd given me his gun and told me where to shoot back on Montblanc. Every one of those memories was a barrier against doubt, and even though my guns were almost in reach, my armor case a tantalizing half foot away, I stayed perfectly still, trusting Rupert like I'd never trusted anyone in my life as I forced myself to lie beneath my enemy's boot and wait.

But while my crisis of trust over Rupert had resolved itself quickly, Eye Natalia seemed to be struggling. I felt her lean forward on my shoulder blades, like she was trying to study him. Then her weight shifted as she slipped a hand behind her, and I felt the unmistakable brush of a gun muzzle against the small of my back.

"If you were keeping her for us, why didn't you call in?" Natalia said suspiciously, her grip tightening on the disrupter pistol I now knew she'd been hiding. "We had a report that you'd gone rogue and stolen a ship."

"We had an issue with the woman's ex-lover," Rupert said, his voice cold and dry, calmly relaying facts. "She can't be near anything that upsets her, so I had to remove her from the situation. I thought Commander Martin would appreciate me not killing a Home Guard captain, but if I'd known such a thing would be enough to cast doubt on me, I would have brought you his body."

His disdain was chilling even through hot, humid air, and Natalia began to quiver. "Well, sir," she said softly. "You have been acting erratically. After Io5—"

"I proved what I was willing to do on Io5," Rupert said, casually hooking his thumbs through the belt loops of his cargo pants like none of this mattered to him. "I passed my test. Now get off my target before you undo all the work I've put in convincing her we're not monsters, and we'll go up together to call for a proper pickup. I don't know about you, but I'd like to get out of this pit."

That sounded good to me, but Natalia clearly wasn't buying. "If you wanted a pickup, why did you run?"

"Because my target ran," Rupert answered testily. "I didn't know she was running from you. She has a lot of enemies on Kessel. "

"Then why did you take her here at all?" Natalia snapped.

Rupert's eyes narrowed, and I could almost see the last of his patience evaporating. "I'll explain later. Now, would you please get off our subject before she infects this entire planet?"

Please or no, the open threat was clear in Rupert's voice, but Natalia *still* didn't remove her knee from my back, and she hadn't put her gun away. "I'm afraid I can't do that, sir," she said. "I have direct orders not to release the subject until she is secured, and, with all due respect, the probability that you have been compromised is too high to ignore." She threw up her arm, pointing the disrupter pistol at Rupert's head. "I'm sorry, sir."

Despite the gun pointed directly between his eyes, Rupert didn't panic or raise his hands. Instead, he sighed and shook his head, the perfect picture of the put-out officer dealing with an idiot subordinate who was messing up his operation. "It's on your head, then," he said. "Make the call."

At that moment, my newfound trust began to waver. Natalia had shifted on top of me, using her free hand to pull her com out of the pocket of her black combat suit, but Rupert still wasn't moving. He didn't even look concerned, just bored and put out, and my heart began to crumble.

Oh god, I thought, I'd done it again. I'd been an idiot *again*. Betrayed again with no one but myself to blame. But just as my faith was teetering, Natalia glanced down at her com, and the moment her attention left him, Rupert moved.

One second he was casually standing a few feet down the pipe, the next he was nearly on top of me, his hand formed in a fist with the first two fingers covered in scales and folded over at the first joint, like he was punching with his knuckles. Natalia stiffened, and I braced for the disrupter pistol's explosion, but it never came. Before she could squeeze the trigger, Rupert slammed his first two knuckles into her forehead, directly between and slightly above the place where her eyebrows met, exactly where I'd shot him on the *Fool*'s bridge so long ago.

The blow sent Natalia flying off me, her gun and handset spinning off wildly into the dark. I'd barely registered the loss of her weight on my back before Rupert snatched me up. "Are you okay?"

"I'm fine," I replied as he set me back on my feet.

Given my record for self-reporting injury, I wasn't insulted when Rupert ran his hands over my ribs and back to check for himself, but other than a little bruising and my wounded pride, I really was fine. When he was satisfied, he let me go and jogged down the pipe toward Natalia's unconscious body. "I'm sorry about how that went," he said, leaning down to grab her. "I wanted to get her gun farther away from you before I attacked, but I ran out of time."

"No worries," I said. "That was good work. You were scary as hell. For a moment there, I thought you were really going to let her turn me in."

The horrified look on Rupert's face destroyed the last of my doubts. Just melted that tiny warning voice away like snow in the sun. In its place, trust sprang up so fast and strong it made my chest hurt.

"I hope you know I'd never do that," he said, turning back to Natalia.

I grabbed his sleeve to stop him, pulling gently until he looked at me again. "I do," I said firmly. "I believe you, Rupert."

It was such a simple thing, a small confession, but the moment the deep, relieved breath left his lips, I knew it had meant as much to Rupert as it had to me. I wished I could have said more. I had the desperate urge to cement the new bond that had settled between us, to build and expand on it until nothing could ever tear it down again, but we were still in enemy territory, and there was work to do.

My thermal shirt and cargo pants were destroyed where Natalia had thrown me down on the pipe, the fabric stained a horrid greasy black all down the front and on the back where her boot had been. I stripped them off and tossed them in the trash around us, leaving myself yet again in only my tank top and underarmor leggings. My filthy socks followed as I got into my armor. Once I was suited up with my guns in place, I shoved my still relatively clean coat and boots into my armor case before locking it tight.

Carrying the Lady's case would be awkward if we had to run and gun, but like hell was I leaving it again. Besides, now that I was back in my Lady Gray with her six-hundred-pound lift limit, I barely felt the weight. What I *did* feel was ready to get some revenge for being dropped on.

When I turned around to find Natalia, I saw that Rupert had

already propped her up against the cluster of vertical pipes I'd used as cover earlier. When she was steady, he hopped down into the trash below us only to return a few seconds later with a long piece of steel rebar. Before I could ask what he needed it for, he bent the heavy metal rod like a rope, lashing the woman to the pipes before twisting the ends together to make sure she stayed that way.

"Will that actually hold her?" I asked as he stepped back.

"Not forever," Rupert admitted. "But it should slow her down. Eyes gain strength with age, and she is much younger than I am. She'll get free eventually, but we'll be long gone by then."

I walked over to join him, tilting my head to look down at Natalia's face. It was relaxed with no sign of trauma, almost like she was just asleep. "What did you do to her? It's like you pressed her off switch."

"I basically did."

At my disbelieving look, he reached up and tapped the part of his forehead just above where his eyebrows met. "The symbiont remakes our bodies when it's implanted, but xith'cal and human physiology can never match up perfectly. One of the reasons the xith'cal's heads are so armored is because the front of their brain is incredibly susceptible to swelling. Since we lack the protective ridges to prevent it when our scales are retracted, a nice, hard blow to the right place on the front of an unarmored symbiont's head will send them into a comalike state for several hours."

"Isn't that dangerous?" I asked, staring down at Natalia's unconscious body. I wasn't a doctor, but brain swelling did not sound good.

Rupert shrugged. "The symbiont's regenerative system repairs the damage eventually, but she will have a massive headache when she wakes. Even so, it's preferable to bleeding her out, which is the only other way to disable a symbiont for long periods of time."

"I don't know," I said, reaching for my gun. "Seems like it would be a lot simpler just to kill her."

"It would," Rupert agreed, bending down to check her pulse one last time. "But I won't. Maria was just following orders, and she's not a bad person. Or, at least, no worse than any of us." He smiled. "She was kind to her daughters whenever she could be. I always liked that about her."

As he fussed over her, I felt a strange pang of emotion I didn't like. It was such an odd, uncomfortable feeling that it took me several moments to recognize it as a twinge of jealousy.

That realization made me like it even less. I'd barely come around to the idea of being in love; jealousy was *way* outside of my comfort zone. But when Rupert stood to walk away, I was the one he looked back for, and low as love had brought me, I was not above giving Natalia a superior look before I turned to follow him.

"We don't have much time," he said, jogging down the pipe, back the way we'd come. "She would have reported her intention before chasing us, and the others will come looking when she doesn't check in."

"How did they find us so quickly, anyway?" I said as I struggled to keep up. "Drones move faster through hyperspace than manned ships, but even if Anthony sent his report the second we took off, it couldn't have gotten to Paradox in less than five hours."

Rupert slowed down until we were running side by side. "Once the message got to Paradox, all they'd have to do was tell a daughter. What one daughter knows, they all know. After that, tracking down a rogue Paradoxian military ship would have been simple. Once they found our destination, all they had to do was scramble the closest teams."

"You keep teams way out here?" I asked.

"The Eyes have a maximum two-hour response time to ninety-seven percent of colonized worlds," Rupert said proudly. "Teams are evenly spread all across the jump gate network to ensure this. Otherwise, we'd show up too late to stop most phantom attacks."

"Even for a pirate camp?"

Rupert's face fell into a scowl. "All people, no matter their status, deserve protection from phantoms."

I was a little surprised by how fiercely he said this, but I really shouldn't have been. Considering what the phantoms had taken from him—his home, his family, his entire culture—I could understand exactly why Rupert would never want that to happen to anyone, pirates or not. Not that it helped us at the moment.

"Well, good on them for being on the ball," I muttered. "But what do we do now?"

"What we were already planning to do," Rupert said. "Get a ship and get off-planet." He glanced at me. "Your armor is going to be a problem."

"Not as big a problem as we're going to have if you try to make me take it off," I snapped.

He sighed, but I didn't care. I was in full-on fight mode now, and there was no way in hell I was taking off my suit. Fortunately, Rupert didn't push the issue.

"They've locked down the starport for sure," he said, pulling out his handset.

"Even here?" I asked.

Rupert nodded. "Kessel might be run by pirates, but the Eyes can swing a lot of power when they want to. Even the head of a criminal haven wouldn't dare deny someone with that kind of clearance, not if he wants to avoid bringing a battleship down on his head. The governor's probably falling all over himself to make sure the Eye team has no reason to call for backup."

"If that's how it is, we'll just have to find another way off-world," I said, looking up at the shanty city above us. "That's the good thing about smuggling holes, though. There's always another way out."

I already had a pretty good idea how we'd do it, too. We'd reached the ladder back up by this point, and Rupert was taking the opportunity to stop and check the system warnings on his handset to see what the Eyes had closed down. While he did that, I pulled up my suit's records on Kessel and started rooting through my old mission notes.

Sure enough, a bit of searching turned up an old briefing about an illegal airfield that had been a possible escape route for a target we'd been hunting. We'd gotten him before he'd made it anywhere near the place, but I still had the location saved in my suit's memory. When I told Rupert my plan, though, he didn't seem enthused.

"I don't know," he said. "You're a high-value target, and the Eyes like to work quietly. Even if we could convince a smuggler to sell us a hyperdrive-capable ship, they'd just sell us out to the Eyes the moment they were offered the right price."

"Better sold out and in the air than waiting around down here," I said. "It'll be fine. We'll just have to be sneaky."

"With your armor standing out like a silver beacon?" Rupert said. "I don't see that happening."

I blew out an angry breath. Rupert made a good point, but again, no armor was not an option. I was trying to think of some way to reconcile the two when I looked down to see that the pipe's thick grime had formed a crust on the bottom of my Lady's lovely silver boots during the run over here. I leaned down to wipe the stuff off, cursing under my breath, but as I struggled futilely with the oily dirt, a brilliant idea came to me.

"Rupert," I said, straightening up. "I think I know how we're going to get out, but you're going to have to help me." Because there was absolutely no way I could do this on my own.

"Always," Rupert said. "What did you have in mind?"

I told him, and Rupert's face broke into a smile. "That just might work," he said, pointing at the ground. "Get down, let's try."

I swallowed. Even though it had been my idea, I suddenly felt like a prisoner on her way to the gallows. Fortunately, Rupert was there to make me go through with it, glaring at me until I fell to my knees. But it wasn't until he leaned over to coat his hand in pipe grime that I realized just how much this was going to *suck*.

And oh god, it did.

"Did you have to be so damn thorough?" I groaned.

"Devi, relax," Rupert said, his voice infinitely patient as he finished cleaning his hands with a cloth bandage from our first-aid kit. "It will come off."

I barely heard him. All I could think about was my suit. Rupert had smeared pipe grime over every inch of my Lady's silver surface. I could already feel the oily dirt working its way into my joints, and even my helmet was caked in it. Rupert had used his claws to scuff my finish as well, leaving my priceless custom suit looking like a banged up, filthy piece of scavenged spacer gear. Which, admittedly, was the entire point, still. "My baby," I whimpered, brushing my hands over what had been a peerless, mist silver paint job. "My beautiful girl."

"Three hours in your case's nano-repair and your Lady will be back to her usual pristine condition," Rupert reminded me. "This is only temporary. Everything will be fine."

"Don't 'fine' me," I snapped, pulling Sasha out to make sure he hadn't gummed up her trigger. "I don't see you rolling around in the dirt."

That was a little harsh considering this whole thing had been my idea, but Rupert laughed it off. "That's because there are, at most, five people on this entire planet who could recognize me, one of whom is currently tied to a pipe." He grinned at me as he slung our bags over his shoulder. "Think of this as the price of fame."

I rolled my eyes and holstered my gun. "Let's just get to the airfield. The sooner we're off this rock, the sooner I can get this gunk off my baby."

Rupert stepped aside, motioning for me to lead the way.

Now that I had my suit, going up through the Pipes took significantly less time than going down. Between the maps I'd logged on my previous visits and my density sensors, I was able to find the quickest, safest path no problem. Unfortunately, this made me feel even worse about covering my Lady in grime. Such a good, wonderful suit did *not* deserve such treatment.

But the disguise seemed to be working. Every time I'd come to Kessel before, people had stared at my shining armor in fear and respect. Now, dirt made me invisible. I would have thought the Lady's custom profile would have been a dead giveaway, dirt or no, but I always forget how little non-Paradoxians know about good armor. Other than a few sideways glances at my plasma shotgun, we made it all the way back up to the underground bazaar without a hitch.

"We should disguise your suit more often," Rupert murmured as we wove our way through the crowded tables. "This is nice, almost like I'm undercover again."

"What's the point of having an amazing suit if no one notices?" I scoffed, checking my map. "Okay, unless they closed down in the last three years, our exit should be through there." I nodded at the doors on the opposite side of the building. "Let's go."

We struck out across the market floor, passing booths full of guns, supplies, Republic Starfleet patrol maps, scan-proof cargo containers, and pirated corporate AIs. But as we walked through the panoply of everything a professional criminal could possibly need, I finally understood how Rupert had been able to get cash for his Warrant. You don't exactly do a lot of sightseeing on a crash mission, so I'd never noticed it before, but most businesses down here were operating on paper money. It felt quaintly old-fashioned, like one of those historic villages they took you to on school trips, only with contraband instead of cheap souvenirs. If the stakes hadn't been so high, it might have been fun to look around now that I wasn't here as a raider. But we had no time, so Rupert and I pushed through the crowd as fast as we dared, making a beeline for the door I'd marked on my map.

I kept my eyes peeled for symbionts the whole way, though even I had to admit they'd be impossible to spot in the crowd. Fortunately, so were we. My plan was actually working better than I'd thought. Since there was cash everywhere, most of the shops employed armored guards, several of which had suits even dirtier than mine.

There were also plenty of buyers with bodyguards walking beside them just like I was walking with Rupert. With so many pairs, we blended in seamlessly, especially now that the sun was going down and the resulting cold was driving everyone underground, filling the market to bursting.

The doors led out into a covered loading zone full of merchant cruisers, small atmospheric cargo ships undoubtedly used to ferry goods from the smuggler hideouts in the mountains down to market. Our airfield was supposed to be straight through the next set of doors that led outside, and the second we were out, I knew it must still be here. There were no signs or markers, of course, but the huge, snow-free stacks of shipping containers were a dead giveaway. Also, the road leading up from the base of the dug-out factory back to ground level was amazingly well maintained for a supposedly abandoned back alley. Grinning triumphantly at Rupert through my grimy visor, I picked up the pace, jogging up the road until I reached the crest of the hill.

The wind hit me like a wall as soon as I left the shelter of the dug-in ramp. My suit adjusted at once, protecting me far better than my coat ever could, but I still couldn't help shivering as the blowing snow engulfed me. According to my map, I should have been right at the edge of the airfield, but now that I was up here, all I saw was trash.

The ramp had led us straight to the town dump. There were plenty of spaceship hulls in the scrap metal heaps that filled the little valley between the mountains, but they were hollowed out skeletons picked clean of all salvageable parts. Definitely not spaceworthy, even by smuggler standards. But when I turned to tell Rupert we had the wrong place, he was already jogging ahead.

"This isn't it," I said when I caught up. "Let's get back inside before my disguise is ruined." Now that night was falling, the snow was starting to come down in earnest. Up here in the open with no protection against the wind, the fat, wet flakes were hitting my suit hard enough to make holes in the heavy layer of oily dirt.

"Actually, I think your information is spot-on," Rupert said, pointing ahead. "Ever see a dump with a jump gate relay tower?"

I looked where he pointed, and my mouth fell open. Now that Rupert had drawn my attention to it, the scrap pile at the center of the junkyard *did* look strangely regular, exactly like a relay tower someone had welded over with scrap metal to hide. It was the right height, too, and my hopes began to pick up again. A few feet later, I was doubly glad Rupert hadn't let me turn back, because as we cleared the top of the first trash rise, the airfield came into view.

I should have known. Like everything else on this planet, the airfield was dug down for protection against the wind. But despite the piled trash that ringed it on all sides, hiding it from view, the airfield itself was orderly and filled with ships, mostly atmospheric craft, but there was a whole line of small starships with clearly visible hyperdrives, and I broke into a grin.

"There's our ride," I said, hopping up onto the edge of the trash pile. "Come on. Let's blow this—"

A boom cut me off. The sound was warped by the wind, bouncing off the trash until I couldn't tell where it was coming from. Because of this, I didn't even recognize it as a disrupter pistol shot until Rupert fell, toppling forward into the now-bloody snow at my feet.

CHAPTER

5

I caught him before he hit the ground.

Moving faster than I ever had in my life, I snatched Rupert up and dashed under the rusted out hull of a freighter, the only cover I could see. This turned out to be a lucky break. The old freighter was about as large as the *Fool* had been, and it was picked clean down to the struts, leaving only a hollow metal shell. Better still, it was half buried at an angle with its nose sticking up, creating a sort of crooked metal tent with the empty hole where the bridge window had been as the only one way in.

I couldn't have asked for a better fort given the circumstances, and I said a prayer to the king as I ran Rupert to the far end, setting him down under the metal cage that had once held the navigation array, the only part of our shelter that wasn't covered in dirty snow. "Where'd they get you?"

"Back," Rupert panted through gritted teeth.

I leaned him forward at once, but I already knew what I'd find. Sure enough, Rupert's back was a burned, bloody mess under the smoking tatters of his coat. It was even worse than when Rashid had shot him in the forest, because this time Rupert hadn't had his scales to protect him. I cursed at the damage and dropped my armor case, which I'd somehow managed not to lose, in the dirt beside me. I was about to open it and get out my coat to tie over the wound when Rupert grabbed my wrist.

"I'll heal," he said, his voice tight. "You're their target. Go on, I'll catch up."

"Hell no," I said, yanking my wrist out of his grip. "I'm not leaving you."

For a second, Rupert looked amazingly touched, but then his face broke into a pained grimace. "You have to get out of here," he said. "I'll—"

A loud bang cut him off as something landed on the old hull above us. Something far too heavy to be only human. Two more bangs sounded a second later, and the rusty ship began to groan.

"Company," I whispered, reaching into Rupert's bag to grab his disrupter pistol. Rupert watched me, scowling as he tried to push himself up. I scowled back and motioned sharply for him to stay put. He must have been really hurting, because he sagged in defeat almost immediately. Smiling, I lowered his gun and crept silently across the icy ground to the edge of our little shelter.

Though there was only one opening big enough to fit a person, the old hull was pitted with rusted out cracks where the wind howled through. I positioned myself right next to one of these and ducked low, disrupter pistol ready in my hand as I listened. The wind was too loud to make out voices, but I could feel the metal vibrating as they moved on top of it. I moved with them, repositioning myself until I was standing by the wall of the hull closest to their perch, and then I stuck out my foot.

My suit had six cameras in total: four on my head to achieve my 360-degree view, one looking straight down, and one that looked up at myself, located on the top of my right boot. The purpose of this last camera was ostensibly to let me see things above and behind me as well as give me a full view of my suit for damage checks, but I'd quickly learned it could also be used to look around corners and up walls, which was what I did now.

Quiet as a mouse, I slid the toe of my boot through one of the rusted out spots where the hull met the ground. As my camera cleared the metal, I got a shot straight up the hull's curved side. An inch later, I spotted the men who were standing on top of it.

There were three of them, standing in a tight cluster on top of what had once been the ship's forward gun. All three of them were wearing plain, black suits like Rupert's under their heavy winter gear, which made me roll my eyes. Considering the Eye's lifestyle, you'd think their dress code would be a little more practical. But even though it looked like I was being hunted by a trio of stuffy businessmen, they were all clearly symbionts, and they were watching the hole we'd used to duck under the hull like wolves eying a rabbit den. Since I was on the opposite side of the hull, this meant that my camera was looking up at their backs, and that gave me a great idea.

I marked each man on my targeting system and then pulled my boot back in. Stepping away from the wall, I slung Mia off my back, holding her one handed with Rupert's disrupter in my other. I took a second to get a feel for the unusual configuration before I hit Mia's charge, sending her whistling to life. The distinctive sound meant I'd have to move fast, a dangerous thing when your enemies were faster, but I was confident. Even if they heard me coming, they wouldn't suspect this.

When Mia hit her highest octave, I leveled my plasma shotgun at the old freighter's rusted wall and jumped forward, pulling the trigger at the same time. My plasma shotgun fired in a blaze of white light, the plasma shot hitting the hull only a fraction of a second before I did. The metal was still melting when I crashed into it, but Mia had done her job well, and I busted through the old starship hull like it was wet cardboard. As I broke through, I dropped Mia on the ground so I could focus everything on the disrupter pistol, watching my rear camera for the moment when my targets appeared.

Under normal circumstances I wouldn't have cut it so close. The disrupter pistol was so old my suit didn't know what to make of it, which meant my targeting computer was lagging dangerously behind. With symbiont speed, though, I didn't have a choice.

I'd been out for less than a second—the echo of Mia's shot was still bouncing across the dump—but the symbionts on top of the hull were already turning. I threw back my arm at the same time, using my suit's rear camera and years of experience to aim the disrupter pistol, but I didn't shoot yet. I couldn't afford to mess this up, not with two shots and no computer, so I waited, holding my breath until my enemy spun completely around. The moment their surprised faces came into view, I pulled the trigger.

The first time I fired a disrupter pistol, the burn had seared my palm. This time, with my suit to protect me, all I felt was a pleasant warmth as the shot went off without a whisper of recoil. Since the energy-based shot moved at the speed of light, I didn't even see it fly. From my point of view, all I did was pull the trigger and the symbiont in the middle of the trio fell backward, downed by a perfect shot to the head.

Considering the angle and how fast I'd had to line that sucker up, the fact that I'd hit a target that small on a quick draw with no computer-assisted targeting while shooting *backward* was nothing short of a career best. I didn't have time to be cocky, though. The boom of the shot had barely sounded before both the remaining Eyes jumped me.

If I'd had any lingering doubts these men were symbionts, that jump would have done them in. They leaped off the hull like the fifteen-foot drop was nothing, angling to come down right on my head. But I must have gotten spoiled from my time with Rupert, because while the two men were faster than any human should be, they still weren't as fast as I expected, and I dove out of the way with time to spare. We all came up at the same time, the symbionts recovering from their landing as I rolled to my feet, my disrupter pistol already up and aimed square at the taller Eye's head.

I was fully prepared to take the shot right then, but the symbiont threw his hands up in surrender. That surprised me enough to make me pause. His partner also looked shocked, his eyes darting to the taller man for a signal, but the other symbiont wasn't looking at him at all. Instead, he lowered his raised arms just enough to pull off his snow goggles and hat, revealing a thick head of dark blond hair and a handsome, young face set with a kind smile.

"Please don't shoot," he said. "You're Devi Morris, right?"

He was speaking King's Tongue like a good old boy from the Summerlands, warm and friendly as could be. A few months ago, that alone would have been enough to make me smile back, but I'd been around far too many Eyes at this point to buy it now.

"Depends on who's asking," I said, sticking to Universal to show him just how much I was not playing along. "Tell your buddy hands up."

Even though they had to know there was no way I could get both of them with the one shot I had left, the other symbiont put up his hands as soon as I asked, and the taller Eye, who looked every inch the big, handsome farm boy his accent suggested, gave me an apologetic look so sincere I wondered how long he'd practiced it. "I'm real sorry about this misunderstanding, ma'am," he said, his drawling voice deep and contrite. "We're not here to hurt you."

"Really?" I said, tightening my finger on the trigger. "Then why don't you just let us go?"

"I'm afraid we can't do that," the Eye said. "The man you're with is very dangerous. Rupert Charkov has been deemed extremely unstable, unfit for civilian interaction. We were sent here for your protection. Please, all we want is to get you somewhere safe."

I opened my mouth to tell him what a load of bull that was, but before I could get a word out, something screamed to our left. Neither the Eyes nor I were amateur enough to turn and look, but I swung a camera over to the hole I'd blasted in the hull, desperate to know if that horrible sound had come from Rupert. The shadows inside were so deep I couldn't make out a thing. A second later, though, it didn't matter, because a man flew out of the hole I'd made and slammed headfirst into the Eye I hadn't been talking to.

The thrown man must have weighed a ton, because he took out the other symbiont like a wrecking ball. I didn't dare take my attention off the smooth-talking Eye I'd been dealing with, so I didn't see where they landed, but my computer reported they'd crashed into a pile of trash some thirty feet away. The fake farm boy had stayed locked on me through the whole exchange as well, which was both good and bad for him. Good, because he'd given me no opportunity to run, bad because with his full attention on me, he didn't see what was coming up behind him until Rupert's arm closed around his throat.

Rupert wrenched the symbiont backward, taking him off his feet. "Devi! Behind you!"

I glanced at my cameras just in time to see the man Rupert had thrown into the trash heap roll off the symbiont he'd bowled over and launch at me. At that point, instinct took over. I didn't even make a conscious decision to attack. I simply turned and fired, pegging the charging symbiont in the head with the disrupter a second before he crashed into me.

I knew as soon as it went off that my shot had killed him, but death didn't stop his momentum. The symbiont crashed into me anyway, knocking me back into the hull. Without Mia's heat to soften the way, we didn't go through the metal this time, but we made a hell of a dent. Even with my stabilizers, the impact hit me so hard my vision went dark, but it didn't matter, because my Lady had me.

I have never loved my suit as much as I did right then. I was still reeling when the Lady Gray rolled me over, kicking the symbiont off me and flipping me back to my feet. I landed perfectly right in front of Rupert, back in the fight after only a few seconds down. Unfortunately, it was a few seconds too many, because my disrupter pistol was now out of shots, and the smooth-talking farm boy knew it.

I heard Rupert hiss as the symbiont tore out of his hold, and then a hand grabbed my left arm, nearly ripping it out of its socket as the symbiont swung me around. By the time I stopped moving, the farm boy had a disrupter pistol of his own out and pointed at Rupert's head. I held my breath at the sight, waiting for a threat or an ultimatum, but the man's sweet-talking front must have been pure fiction, because he didn't say a word. He simply pulled the trigger.

I screamed as the shot went off, but after all the times I'd fired at Rupert and missed, I should have had more faith. By the time the other man finished squeezing the trigger, Rupert was long gone. The disrupter blast slammed into the hull behind him instead, turning the old metal to molten sludge.

The symbiont didn't even seem fazed by the miss. He just followed Rupert with his gun, lining up for the second shot. He might have gotten it, too, because Rupert was watching me and not his enemy, but fortunately for him, I wasn't an idle prisoner. My suit wasn't strong enough to break the symbiont's death grip on my left arm, but Elsie was on my right. I had her out and fired before the echo of the symbiont's first shot had faded, and by the time he pulled the trigger for his second, I was jamming my thermite blade into his unprotected ribs.

The man hissed in pain as his shot went crooked, flying off harmlessly into the air above Rupert's head, but even though I had a thermite knife in his ribs, he didn't let me go. That was fine with me. I leaned in like a lover, using my suit's weight to dig the blade deeper.

Thanks to my fight with Rupert in the forest, I had some experience cutting symbionts. They were surprisingly dense and tough, more like cutting cement than flesh. That made it easy to slip and cut shallow if you went too fast, so I kept it slow, focusing on making every inch count as I worked my blade up the man's chest toward his heart.

I'd almost made it before he kicked me away. The blow sent

me flying, but not far. I was only in the air for a heartbeat before Rupert caught me, setting me down on my feet again as we both turned to face our enemy.

At this point, there were only two symbionts left. One really, since the man who'd tried to sweet-talk me was on his knees clutching his bleeding chest. His friendly farm-boy affect was gone completely now, and he shot me a murderous look as his scales blossomed over his skin, shredding his clothing as they spread up to staunch the wound.

Like hell was I letting that happen. This man had chased us down, lied to me, and tried to blow Rupert's brains out. He was going to die. But as I stepped in and swung Elsie down to cut off his lying head, Rupert grabbed my shoulder.

I jerked to a halt, Elsie's white thermite steaming in the blowing snow just inches away from the man's exposed throat. But before I could yell at Rupert to stop ruining my strike, he grabbed Sasha out of my holster, pressed her against the man's forehead, and pulled the trigger.

I saw the force of my anti-armor pistol's shot ripple across the man's changing skin just before her blast sent him flying. He landed on his back a good fifteen feet away, skipping over the snow-covered trash like a stone over a pond. By the time he stopped, his scales covered him completely, and he lay still, a black shape in the howling snow. I watched him just long enough to be sure he wasn't getting up again before I turned on Rupert.

"What the hell did you do that for?" I shouted, snatching Sasha out of his hand. "That man tried to kill you!"

"Because, like Natalia, he was only following orders," Rupert said with a sigh. He stretched as he spoke, reaching up to rub Sasha's kick out of his shoulder with a hand I only now saw he'd transformed into a claw. "And I have enough blood on my conscience already."

I itched to point out that Rupert had stopped *my* kill, which meant the blood would have been on *my* conscience, and, unlike him, I had absolutely no problem with that. But any recriminations would have to wait, because my thermite was ticking down and there was still one enemy left.

The farm boy's companion, the quiet symbiont Rupert had sent flying when he'd thrown the other man into him, had gotten up from the trash heap while we'd been fighting. Unlike the others, he'd hung back, not helping his team or taking any of the openings I was sure we'd given him. In fact, he didn't seem interested in attacking at all. For all that he was clearly a symbiont, he was quaking in fear, staring at Rupert like the man was death incarnate, which I found pretty insulting since I was the who'd been doing all the killing.

"I've got left," I whispered to Rupert, nodding for him to move right for the pincer before breaking into a run. The shaking man didn't look like a real threat, but I only had thirty seconds left on my thermite. Once Elsie's fire was gone, I was out of symbiont killers, so if I was going to do this, it had to be now. I'd thought Rupert understood this, but despite my hurry, he took his time, walking straight across the trash yard toward the other man like he was just coming over to say hello.

I couldn't yell at him about it either, because whatever Rupert was doing, it was working. The symbiont wasn't even looking at me or my burning blade. His eyes were riveted on Rupert, and he started scrambling back up the trash heap, pressing his back to the flat wall of a burned-out power adapter as Rupert closed the final distance.

I slowed down as well, lowering my blade in confusion. The man was clearly a symbiont, and Rupert was obviously injured. Now that I had the time to look at him, I was actually surprised Rupert was still standing.

He'd transformed his upper body beneath his tattered coat, including his arms and hands, but even that hadn't been enough to stop the bleeding. Blood streaked his cheek and neck where the scales ended, and though no sign of what must be horrible pain showed on his face, his stiff walk gave the whole thing away. If Rupert had been *my* enemy, I would have been on him in an instant, using his wounds for an easy victory. But even though he looked so beaten up I might have been able to take him without my suit, the symbiont on the ground was cowering harder than ever, his face pale and sweaty as Rupert stopped in front of him.

"Mr. Kendris?" Rupert said, his voice colder than the biting wind. "Correct?"

The other man nodded, and Rupert smiled that icy killer smile of his, the one that still made the hairs on the back of my neck prickle. "How many more of you are there?"

"Just me, Natalia, and Ross, who's watching the daughter," Kendris croaked out, sinking deeper into the snowy trash. "Please, Eye Charkov, don't go after them. This daughter has serious stability issues already. If—"

He cut off when Rupert scowled, snapping his mouth shut, but it wasn't until he started nearly hyperventilating that I finally understood what was going on. This man wasn't seeing the real Rupert, who was shot up and barely standing. He saw Eye Charkov, the cold killer, now gone rogue. From that angle, I could totally understand why he was so scared. Standing there with blood dripping from his claws and his loose black hair catching the blowing snow around his cold killer mask, Rupert looked every inch the monster his reputation said he was.

"I'm not interested in the daughter," Rupert said, tilting his head toward me. "I'm guarding Deviana Morris. She's your target, right?"

The man nodded. "They say she can stop the phantoms. Please, I don't know why you took the Paradoxian, but we must have her back. If you turn her in, I'm sure Commander Martin will overlook—"

"Hey, I'm right here, asshole," I said, leaning down to shove the tip of my rapidly dying thermite blade so close to his nose that his skin started to blister. "Don't talk about me like I'm a thing," I growled, giving him a quelling look before glancing up at Rupert. "We're not killing this one either, I guess?"

The man on the ground made a little choking sound, and Rupert sighed. "I would appreciate it if you didn't."

"Fine," I said, sheathing Elsie as the last of her fire flickered out. "Listen up, then, Eye Whatever-Your-Name-Was, here's what you're going to do. You're going to run on back and tell your boss that Charkov didn't take me anywhere. The Paradoxian is running her own show, and if the Eyes want any part of it, they're going to have to meet some requirements. Now, I'm sure you assholes can find us anywhere in the universe, so next time you decide to drop in, come up peaceably and we'll talk this over like civilized people. But try to kidnap me again and you'll regret it, because unlike Eye Charkov, I'm *not* nice, and I have no problem whatsoever chopping up your head and playing dice with your teeth if you mess with me. Understand?"

The man's face went gray as the dirty snow that was quickly piling up around us. I don't know what scared him more—that I was giving him orders to relay to the commander of the Eyes or the idea that I could be worse than Rupert Charkov. Whichever it was, he nodded frantically, and I gave him a nice, bloodthirsty smile through my visor. And then, since Sasha was already in my hand, I snapped her up and took aim at the symbiont's forehead. "Night night, starlight."

The man didn't even seem to realize what was happening before I pulled the trigger, blowing him back into the trash. When he didn't get up again, I slid Sasha back into her holster. "God and king, what's a cupcake like him doing in the Eyes?"

"He's not actually an Eye," Rupert said, his voice strained as he shifted his weight. "Kendris works on the Dark Star as one of Maat's handlers. He's basically a technician who was given a symbiont to protect him from Maat's plasmex rather than to aid in combat. If Commander Martin sent him here, they must be quite short handed."

"Scraping the bottom of the barrel, you mean," I said, walking over to turn the unconscious Kendris over with the toe of my boot. "But then, they *were* coming to take down the great and terrible Eye Charkov. Guess they wanted all the manpower they could get."

Rupert didn't seem to find that funny. "You didn't have to knock him out, you know. He wasn't going to stop us."

"Better safe than sorry," I said with a shrug. "No offense, but I learned the hard way not to trust Eyes."

Rupert sighed. "Fair enough." He glanced around at the scattered bodies. "We'd better clean up."

It took us just under five minutes to move everyone, dead and alive, under the cover of the rusted out ship hull. Considering we were a symbiont and a powered armor user, this shouldn't have been a big deal, but by the time we had everyone safely out of the elements and, more importantly, out of sight, Rupert was looking pale, even for him.

"Are you okay?" I asked, grabbing Mia off the ground where I'd dropped her.

"I will be," Rupert said, wrapping his arms tight around his chest. He'd traded out his ruined coat for mine. The gray snow jacket was a bit small for him, but at least it wasn't full of holes. But even though he was zipped up tight, he hadn't pulled his scales back, and his hands were still claws when he shoved them in his pockets. "I just need a little time. Getting hit with a disrupter blast takes it out of you."

He said this like it was nothing, just an inconvenience, but I knew Rupert pretty well by this point, and I wasn't fooled. I locked Mia on my back and walked over, pulling off my glove as I went. Before Rupert could react, I pressed my bare hand against his cheek, and what I felt wasn't good.

"You're freezing." The words came out more sharply than I'd meant, but I couldn't help it. I was so used to Rupert's warmth that the feel of his cold skin was like a slap in the face. "How bad is it really?"

"Not life threatening," he admitted. "But I did lose a lot of blood."

It wasn't until he said this that I realized he was leaning against the wall of the hull for support. "You're dizzy, aren't you?" I said, glaring at him. "Dammit, Rupert, why didn't you tell me you were this hurt earlier?"

Rupert sighed. "This from the woman who wouldn't admit she was injured if she was missing an arm."

I rolled my eyes. "Okay, fair point, but you're supposed to be the sensible one here. I'm not going to think less of you if you need a minute after getting shot in the back, okay?" I shook my head and walked over to grab my armor case and his bags. "If you're injured, just tell me and we'll deal with it, but don't try to play it off."

Rupert smiled at me. "Can I quote that back at you later?"

"You can try," I said, sliding my shoulder under his.

Rupert chuckled at that, but it still took him all the way to the edge of the hull before he gave in and actually leaned on me. We hobbled together to the ledge where the trash pile gave way to the airfield, but he insisted on making the jump down himself. Once we landed, he let me help him over to the loading deck for one of the big cargo transports. By this point, he was terrifyingly pale, and he didn't even complain when I sat him down and set my armor case on the step beside him so he could lean on it.

"You stay here, try to get warm, and keep a lookout," I said, grabbing the black duffel bag full of money. "I'm going to get us a ride."

For a moment I thought Rupert was going to try and argue, but he just nodded. "Be careful."

"Always am," I said cheerfully.

We both knew that was a lie, but I didn't give Rupert a chance to call me on it before I walked into the snowy night, making my way across the now dark airfield toward the tiny office that was lit up like a lantern on the other side.

———

I've patronized a lot of sketchy establishments in my life, but this had to be some kind of record. The airfield's "office" turned out to be a modified shipping container half buried in the wall of trash. There was a hole cut in the front to make a window, but it was covered by a sheet of bulletproof glass so thick I couldn't see the person inside until I was standing right in front of the damn thing.

The woman working the counter looked to be in her midfifties, though she could have been thirty and it was life that made her look old. She was hugely overweight with bright blond dyed hair, lounging behind the window in a recliner like she'd grown there and sucking on a red speeder, the candy-coated mix of nicotine and amphetamines on a stick that spacers used to stay awake for days. She didn't look up when I approached, too transfixed by the screen in the corner that was playing one of those awful Terran tear-jerker serials, the kind where you know everyone's going to die but they make you wait five years to see how, to notice she had a customer. I banged on the glass, but all that got me was a rude gesture. Seething, I cranked my suit's volume to max and yelled into the iced over microphone welded to the tiny counter. "I want to buy a ship!"

That got her attention. The woman's heavily made up eyes swiveled to me, her exaggerated eyebrows arching up even farther as she popped the speeder out of her mouth and hit the intercom button with one tattooed finger. "You want what?"

"I. Want. To. Buy. A. Ship," I said, pronouncing each word like I was being paid by the consonant. "Now."

"Oh, well, we got those," the woman said, sticking the speeder back in her mouth. "But you'll have to speak clearer if you want me to understand, Doxie."

I almost shot the glass. You *never* called a Paradoxian a Doxie, not if you want to live. Also, my accent was *not* that thick. But I couldn't get mad here. One, I had the virus to think about, and two, I really needed that damn ship. So, in a display of control that would have made my mother weep tears of joy, I pried my hand off my gun and lifted my visor so she could see my lips. "Listen, lady,"

I said, slow and clear. "I need to buy a ship right now. So what have you got?"

Slowly, like she was doing me a huge personal favor and didn't intend to let me forget it, the woman turned her chair around and started tapping on a screen bolted to the top of the welded counter. "Hyperdrive or atmospheric?"

"Hyperdrive," I said, relaxing a bit now that we were getting somewhere.

She punched that in. "How big's your crew?"

"Two."

She gave me a cutting look. "We ain't running a taxi service."

"I know," I snapped. "Look, I'm in a hurry and I have money. I will pay you. I just need a ship."

The moment the words were out of my mouth, I knew I'd stepped in it. The woman's face lit up in a feral grin, making her look like a wolf who'd just spotted a tender lamb. "Well, then, hon, let's see what we can do for you."

She touched her screen again, and a semi-transparent grid appeared on the glass between us, displaying three-dimensional images of three ships. "This is what I've got right now with hyperdrives that can be flown by two people," she said, nodding at the slowly spinning projected vessels. "Just say the word and it's yours."

Now this was more like it. The three ships on display were all planet hoppers, single-cabin vessels similar to the little stealthers Brenton and Rupert had used, but older, crappier, and with far fewer guns. Still, they were much better than I'd been expecting from an airfield that was literally in the middle of a trash heap, and after a minute of looking, I pointed at the revolving image that seemed to have the fewest patches. "How much for this one?"

"Ten mil."

"Are you out of your damn mind?" I shouted. "I could get a space yacht for that much!"

"Don't got no yachts," the woman said, clicking the red speeder against her back teeth. "You asked for the price, I gave it to you.

You don't like it, go somewhere else." She paused, leaning back in her chair. "Of course, no one else is selling this time of night, and the starport's shut down at present. Something about a fugitive hiding out on-planet." Her flat face spread into that cruel hunter's smile again. "Say, do you think that fugitive business could have anything to do with those gunshots I heard a few minutes ago? Word on the network is there's a reward out, so if you're not buying tonight, I think I'll just go ahead and drop them a word."

I gritted my teeth, wishing like hell that I'd let Rupert come along. He was the charming one. He'd probably have had her eating out of his hand after a minute like he did with the nurse. I normally dealt with these kinds of situations by shooting something, but I was pretty sure even Sasha couldn't get through that much safety glass. Even if she could, I wasn't about to descend to robbery. So shooting was out, but I couldn't afford to ignore the woman's threat. All my big words to the symbiont would mean nothing if those Eyes woke up and we were still trapped here.

"Okay, listen," I said, opening Rupert's bag to do a quick count. "I've got three million cash on hand. What can you give me for that?"

The woman gave me a look like I was insulting her, which was just insane. Three million Republic Script was a hell of a lot of money. I could have bought myself a decent racer with a brand-new hyperdrive for less back on Paradox. Surely even with the middle-of-the-night-smuggler-planet-suspected-fugitive markup, three million should be able to buy me *something*.

Finally, the woman rolled her eyes and tapped her long nails against the screen, bringing up a picture of an ugly metal rectangle not much bigger than the shipping crate she was using as an office. If it hadn't had a hyperdrive coil sticking out the back, I wouldn't even have recognized it as a ship.

"What the hell is that?" I asked, reaching up to rotate the projected image. Not that it did any good. The thing looked like crap from every angle.

"It's a Caravaner," the woman said. "Classic piece of Terran engineering for family traders working the colony circuit. This one here was owned by a little old lady who went around selling fancy soap."

I glanced at the multiple patched over cannon blast holes in the hull. "Saw a lot of fire for a soap trader."

"Universe is a dangerous place," the woman said with a shrug. "Look, Doxie, you asked what I had for three mil, that's it. She ain't much to look at, but the engine works and it ain't like you're in a position to say no."

My hand had started creeping back to my gun before I caught it. I'd had it up to here with this woman, but she had me over a barrel. "Can I see it first?"

"Right around the corner," she said, jerking her head to my left.

I left the counter, walking as she directed through the snow, which was now so thick I had to use my density scanner to spot the ships before I walked into them. It took me a while to find the Caravaner, mostly because it was even smaller than I'd thought. I couldn't even go inside because the ship wasn't rated for armor, but I managed to lean in far enough to see the cabin, which was cleaner than I'd expected. It was also furnished, which was just weird.

I'd heard of Terran traders who lived in their ships exclusively for years, but this vessel actually looked like the inside of a house. The walls had been paneled with plastic done up to look like wood grain, and there were lace curtains on the porthole windows. The floor was smothered in thick, salmon pink carpeting, and the tiny bathroom with its waterless chem shower and toilet had been painted a nauseating shade of tangerine. The main cabin was barely big enough for the foldout bench and table attached to the wall, and I didn't see a bed at all. I was making a note to ask the woman about that when I looked up and saw it was stowed on the ceiling.

The soap lady must not have sold her soap alone, I thought with a smirk. The double bunk would fill the cabin once I pulled it down.

Other than that telling detail, though, it really did look like a little old lady's parlor. The only parts of the ship that actually looked like a ship were the flight console up front and the hatch by the door that opened into the tiny cargo hold.

"All the comforts of home," I muttered, leaning back out to go look at the engines.

These at least looked pretty good. I'm no expert on hyperdrives, but it was clean and lacking in obvious patches, which I took as a good sign. The rest of the engine wasn't quite as nice, but it looked like it would fly, and it wasn't like I had another choice.

"Pretty, ain't she?" the woman said when I got back to the window. "Had everything sterilized when she came in. Fluids are topped off and her tank's full, so you should be ready to go." She sighed longingly. "Classic old Caravaners like that are so hard to find these days. They stopped making them twenty years ago. Don't see why."

I did. "And you want three million for that?"

"Empty out the bag and she's all yours," the woman said, nodding to the duffel resting on my shoulder. "I'll even throw in a prepaid jump clearance. No offense, but the jump gate don't take cash, and you don't look like you've got another method of payment at the moment."

I hadn't even thought about how we would pay the gate fee. If I didn't know for a fact that this lady was epically ripping me off, I would have been grateful for her forethought. She transferred over our jump clearance to my suit while I dumped the cash from my bag into the metal drop chute welded to the side of her shipping crate office. Once the full three million was in, the woman transferred me the Caravaner's flight codes.

"She's all yours," the woman said, hitting the chute lever to suck all my money straight into her hands. "And if anyone asks, you didn't buy it from me, and I never saw you. Standard Kessel courtesy."

I shook my head, marveling at how, for once, the pirate's code of silence was actually working in my favor. God and king, how things could change. But done was done, so I hefted the now much lighter bag back onto my shoulder and set off to break the news to Rupert that I'd spent all our money on a flying living room.

He was exactly where I'd left him, sitting on the lip of the loader and leaning against my armor case. He'd pulled his scales back, which was a relief, but his eyes were closed and his legs were drawn up defensively in front of him. The snow had blown up around him while I'd been gone, coating his jacket and sticking in his long hair. This combined with his paleness made him look dead, and my chest tightened like a clamp.

Thankfully, he opened his eyes when I got close. "Well?"

"Success," I said, trying to keep my voice steady as I bent down to help him up. "Let's get you somewhere warmer."

"That sounds lovely," Rupert said, leaning on me as I grabbed my armor case. I tucked the case under one arm and slid the other around Rupert's waist to steady him, taking great care to avoid his wound. When I had everything positioned like I wanted, I turned us around, keeping my arm close on Rupert as we started across the snowy field. We'd barely made it three feet before Rupert said, "What's wrong?"

I looked up at him in surprise, and he gave me a weak smile. "Not that I'm complaining, but you're holding me very tight."

"Nothing's wrong," I said, relaxing my grip. "I just want to get moving."

I don't think Rupert bought that, but I kept us going too fast for him to ask again. It was a cop-out, but helping him hobble over an uneven, snow-covered, dirt landing field on a dark night felt a lot safer than admitting just how badly I'd taken the idea of him being dead. Still, no amount of hustling could stop his reaction when he saw the hunk of junk I'd blown our three million on.

"I know, I know," I grumbled, opening the door of the Cara-vaner. "Options were limited, okay? I did my best."

"You never do anything less," Rupert said, letting go of me to pull himself up the ship's tiny ramp. "Actually, I think it looks quite cozy."

"Cozy" wasn't the word I'd use, but I'd take it.

Since the Caravaner wasn't rated for armor, I had to strip out of my suit before I could fit through the door. I did it in record time, too, shoving my filthy suit into her case as fast as I could in my rush to get out of the freezing wind. Even so, I was covered in snow by the time I slammed my case shut and jumped into the Caravaner, sealing the door against the cold.

Though he'd gone up ahead of me, Rupert hadn't gotten far. He was leaning on the fake wood panel at the top of the little stair, his face tight and pale as he watched me come in. "You have snow in your hair," he said softly.

"I have snow everywhere," I replied, teeth chattering. Since I'd been in my suit, I hadn't actually realized how cold it had gotten when the sun set. Now, shivering in my tank top and bare feet, I was amazed Rupert hadn't gotten hypothermia out there with only a coat for cover and a wound like that. Though looking at his slightly glassy eyes and paper pale skin, I wasn't so sure.

I reached up and hit the lever that lowered the double bunk stowed in the ceiling. Rupert jumped when it swung down behind him, but I got a smile out of him when the thing unfolded to its full size, taking up all the room in the main cabin. "Sit down," I commanded, opening the storage cabinets that lined the back walls. I wasn't sure what I was looking for, but since the whole ship was furnished like an old lady's apartment, I was betting there'd be something useful stowed away. Sure enough, the second cabinet I opened was packed full of blankets and towels. They were threadbare and musty, but I was miles past picky at this point, and I grabbed a handful off the top with glee.

"Here," I said, tossing them at Rupert. I pulled out a second armful for me, not even bothering to unfold the blanket fully before I wrapped it around my shoulder. Even with the power off, the Caravaner was warmer than the air outside thanks to a day of sitting in the sun, and the snow on my clothes was melting rapidly. Unfortunately, while it was warm enough to melt the snow, the ship was still uncomfortably cold, and now that my clothes were soaked, I was getting the shakes bad.

Since Rupert had seen me naked before, I didn't even hesitate before peeling off my wet shirt and bra. I hung them from a knob to dry, wrapping the blanket even tighter around my now bare shoulders. This helped enormously, but when I glanced at Rupert, he was just sitting there, staring at me.

"Oh for the love of the king," I snapped, grabbing a blanket off his pile and throwing it at his head. "Here, wrap up. I'll go get the engines started."

I didn't even wait to see if he did it before I crawled across the bunk to the flight console and flopped myself into the pilot's seat. The ship had come online when I'd used the access code to open it, but the control setup was like nothing I'd ever used before, and it took me a few minutes to figure out how to start the engines so I could turn on the heat. I'd just found the temperature settings when I heard Rupert land in the navigator's chair beside me.

"What are you doing?"

"Helping," Rupert said, his breathing labored as he reached over to hit a button on my console. "We need to get in the air quickly."

"There's quick and there's dead," I said. "You said yourself the Eyes won't be awake for an hour at least, so we can take five minutes to not freeze and have a look at your back."

"Normally, that would be correct," Rupert said. "But you killed an Eye."

I shrugged. "So?"

"So," Rupert went on, hitting something that made the whole ship start to shake. "A daughter can feel when an Eye near her dies, and as I told you earlier, what one daughter knows, they all know." He pushed a knob between us, and the shaking got worse. "Reinforcements are undoubtedly being scrambled as we speak, and I'd like to be gone before they arrive."

I gaped at him. "And you didn't tell me this earlier because…?"

"I didn't want to pressure you," he said. "You were already going as fast as you could. Now we need to pick up the pace."

His hands kept working as he spoke, moving over the console like he'd been flying one of these boxes all his life. A few seconds later, the engine beeped, and Rupert reached over to hit the red button at the center of my flight stick. The moment he touched it, we jumped into the air, and I had to scramble to keep up straight as we rocketed into the snowy clouds.

Fortunately, despite the unfamiliar controls, flying was still flying. Once we were in the air, I caught on fast, steadying our ascent until we blasted through the upper atmosphere to enter orbit. "How did you learn to fly one of these antiques so well?" I asked as Rupert cut the thrusters.

"Because I used them before they were antiques," he said. "Up until two decades ago, this was the standard console assembly for all Terran small crew vessels. I flew a ship with a flight deck just like this for fifteen years." He shot me a mirthless smile. "You forget, I'm old."

I had forgotten, but I didn't like the bitter, self-recriminating tone in his voice when he reminded me. "Well, I'm glad," I said, crossing my arms over my chest. "Your experience has saved our bacon plenty of times now. And anyway, the only time you act like an old man is when you remind me that you are one, so just knock that off and we'll be good."

Rupert blew out a long breath. "It's not something I can just forget," he said as he turned our ship toward the ugly lump of Kessel's jump gate. "You're twenty-seven. I'm almost three times—"

I'd already opened my mouth to tell him to stop bringing up crap that didn't matter, but I didn't get a word out, because at that moment, four Republic battleships came out of hyperspace on top of us.

CHAPTER

6

For several seconds, all I could do was stare. I'd never actually seen a Republic battleship this close in person. The longer I looked, the more I wished I'd kept that record, because what I saw did not make me hopeful.

They weren't nearly as big and menacing as the xith'cal's ships or as beautiful and deadly as the lelgis, but what the Republic's battleships lacked in size and grandeur they made up for in sleek, deadly efficiency. Every line of the long, tapering silver hull—the perfectly placed gun batteries, the arc of the command bridge, the frictionless doors of the fighter bays—fit together like parts in an exactingly crafted machine meant to do only one thing: destroy everything in its path as quickly as possible. But then, the Terrans had been waging wars in space almost constantly since humanity had first left Earth nearly a thousand years ago, so it was no wonder their tools would be so perfected.

"Rupert," I said quietly as the largest ship passed between us and Kessel's distant sun, plunging our tiny Caravaner into deep shadow. "You think they're here for us?"

"Unless the Republic suddenly decided to enforce the law on Kessel, I would say that's a safe assumption."

I looked at him, clutching the blanket tighter around my shoulders. Suddenly, my bragging to the symbiont back in the trash heap sounded incredibly naïve. "What should we do? I mean, we can't outrun that."

Rupert blew out a long breath. "Maybe we won't have to. You said you had a jump clearance already?"

I nodded, hopping out of the chair. I climbed over the bunk and grabbed my armor case. It was in the middle of its cleaning cycle, but I popped it open anyway, reaching through the foamy pink clouds of reparative nanite gel to pluck out my helmet. I wiped it clean on my blanket and put it on my head just long enough to send the ticket info the lady had given me to the ship's computer, which I would have done before if I'd been thinking. As soon as it was sent, I packed my suit back in and started the cleaning cycle over from the top.

"Do you think they'll let us through?" I asked, scrubbing my hair with the corner of my blanket to get any bits of gel I'd missed.

"The Terrans, no," Rupert said, typing furiously on the console. "They've already instigated a blockade. But that clearance was issued before the travel ban was implemented, so I'm hoping the gate office will let us slip by."

"Why would they do that?" I asked, climbing back into my seat. "We have no money left to bribe them, and they're not going to do anything funny with four battleships breathing down their necks."

Rupert gave me a wry smile as he sent the jump request. "Ah, but we're not criminals. We're a young married couple whose long-dreamed-of honeymoon is about to be ruined by the Terran Republic's completely unwarranted travel embargo. Unless, of course, a brave gate officer comes to the rescue and lets us through."

I gaped at him. "Oh, come on. That can't actually work."

"Never underestimate the power of sympathy," Rupert said sagely. "Or how readily colonists who consider themselves independent will jump at the chance to undermine the Republic's authority."

I still couldn't buy it. I mean, I could completely understand the appeal of sticking it to the Terrans, but it *couldn't* be that simple.

But not a minute later, our ship's com beeped. "Caravaner, you are cleared for jump," said a man's voice. "Transmitting calculations now, and congratulations on the wedding."

"Thank you, sir," Rupert said humbly, starting the hyperdrive. "We are deeply in your debt."

"Don't let the bastards get you down," the man replied, and then the com went silent.

I stared at Rupert in amazement as the ship began to shake. He smiled back at me, strapping his harness on over the blanket he'd wrapped around his shoulders as the ship's little hyperdrive spun faster and faster. Once I'd recovered from my shock, I did the same, lashing myself in as our com began to blare an emergency signal.

"Unidentified ship," a stern woman's voice said. "All jumps are prohibited at this time. Power down now or—"

Before she could finish her threat, the jump flash washed over us, lurching the Caravaner sideways. Not surprisingly, our little junker took the bump into hyperspace like a barrel rolling down a mountain. As always, though, it was over in seconds, leaving only deep stillness as the menacing wall of battleships was replaced by the dull, purple-gray nothing of hyperspace.

I flopped back into my chair with a sigh that turned into a relieved laugh. "You sly bastard. I can't believe you pulled that off."

"Experience does have its advantages on occasion," Rupert said, leaning back in his own chair.

I grinned at him, but Rupert didn't see. He was lying still with his eyes shut and his mouth pressed in a thin line, breathing in shallow, quick gasps.

"Okay," I said, undoing my harness. "Enough. We're stuck in hyperspace for how long?"

"Nine hours," Rupert said.

"Plenty of time," I said, hopping up. "Now stop stalling and let's see your back."

"There's not much left to see," Rupert said as I tugged him out of his seat and ushered him to the bed. "The wound is healed."

"Then why are you still acting like you're dying?" I asked, sitting him down on the edge of the mattress.

"Blood loss," Rupert replied. "I didn't get my scales up fast enough, and it takes me a while to regenerate that much blood without food."

I rolled my eyes and reached down, digging through his bag. "If that's all, here," I said, tossing him a large handful of the ration bars he'd taken from Anthony's ship. "Eat."

Rupert glanced down at the ration bars like I'd tossed him a pile of dead bugs. "That's not food."

"You're the one who packed them," I reminded him, grabbing the first-aid kit and crawling around until I was kneeling behind him.

"For emergencies," Rupert protested. "I learned to cook so I wouldn't have to eat stuff like this."

"I thought you learned to cook to impress girls," I teased him, pulling out a can of wound disinfectant spray.

"That only worked once."

"What, you mean you didn't make breakfast in bed for all your Eye ladies?" I asked, ignoring the barb of jealousy as I pulled the blanket off his shoulders.

He went stiff as the blanket came off, sucking in a pained breath. "There were none," he said at last. "You were the first since I got my symbiont."

I froze, blanket dangling from my hand. "You mean that night in your bunk was the first time you'd been laid in forty years?"

Even though he was about faint from blood loss, Rupert's ears began to redden. "I didn't exactly have many opportunities," he said in a voice that was very clearly trying not to sound defensive. "And even when I did, I was too focused on work to notice women. At least, until I met you."

I couldn't help leaning down to plant a kiss on the top of his snow-damp hair for that one. "And was I worth the wait?"

The utterly incredulous look he shot me over his shoulder was all the answer I needed. Honestly, I hadn't needed to ask. I had Rupert's memories of that night, which meant I knew exactly how hard I'd rocked his world. But knowing was nothing compared to having him confirm it in person, and I was still basking in the glow when I pulled off his jacket.

That sobered me up real quick.

"God and king," I muttered, staring in horror at the burned tatters that had been his shirt. "Did they leave any blood in you?"

As he'd said, the wound was gone, but the aftermath was enough to turn my stomach. Dark, clammy blood coated his entire back. All his clothes were cold and sodden with it, the lining of the heavy coat I'd given him so soaked that the blood had actually started crawling down the stuffing in the sleeves. That was bad enough, but when you added in the blood he'd left on the ground, I was amazed Rupert had been able to walk, let alone fight.

"You should have told me it was this bad earlier," I said angrily, dropping the disinfectant spray and grabbing the first-aid scissors instead to cut off his ruined shirt.

"We were in a dangerous situation. I didn't want to distract you," Rupert said as I peeled the bloody fabric away from his shoulders. "It was my fault anyway for not getting my scales up faster."

"What stopped you?" I asked, cutting along the seam to his neck.

"The burn," he said. "Disrupter pistols scorch you from the inside, which makes it much more painful to push the scales through. That slowed me down."

I paused, looking down at the smooth, bloody skin of his back. "Does it hurt when they come out?"

"Yes," Rupert said. "But you get used to it. Burns are the worst by far."

"I'll stick to my suit, thanks," I said, peeling the shirt off him completely. I wrapped the blood-soaked rags and his bloody jacket in a towel and tossed them into the corner. Once they were safely out of my sight, I started looking for something to clean his skin.

Since the blood had already started drying, I needed something wet, but this ship was waterless and like hell was I putting Rupert under the Caravaner's chem shower. Those things were bad enough on modern ships. On an old rig like this, it was probably toxic.

Eventually, I grabbed my snow-soaked tank top. It wasn't exactly sanitary, but Rupert's wound was healed already, so I decided it would do. Though the snow had melted, my shirt was still freezing cold. I held the wet cloth against my stomach to warm it before folding it in half and sliding it across Rupert's back, wiping the blood away in long, soft strokes.

Since Rupert wasn't actually injured anymore, he could have done this himself, but I knew from experience how hard it was to get blood off your back by yourself without a shower. Anyway, it was nice to touch him, especially since I could feel his skin warming under my hands as he ate.

Though he clearly didn't enjoy it, once he got going, Rupert ate all of the ration bars I'd tossed him. By the time I'd finished cleaning the blood off his back and dried him off with one of the Caravaner's threadbare towels, his body was back to its usual near-feverish temperature, and though he'd never be anything but pale, he didn't look like death anymore. But even though the blood was gone and Rupert was practically back to normal, I didn't let him go.

Couldn't let him go would have been more accurate. I'd gotten so used to thinking of Rupert as indestructible, an implacable, superhuman monster. Seeing him hurt had hit me like a slug to the chest, and I was still reeling. I'd had no idea just how seriously he'd been injured until his jacket had come off, and I was furious with myself for not paying more attention. Rupert could have died in that rusted out hull while I was dealing with the other symbionts and I wouldn't even have known until it was too late. A bit more blood, that's all it would have taken, and I could have lost him forever.

"Devi?"

I blinked and looked up to see Rupert staring at me over his shoulder. "What's wrong? You're shaking."

I was, embarrassingly so, but I couldn't seem to stop, or care. Suddenly, life felt very short, and I was so tired. Tired of being angry, tired of fighting this, and as I stared at the smooth wall of Rupert's blessedly healed back in the Caravaner's dim light, all I could think was, *So what?* So what if he made me weak, undermining my resolve and my reason. Whatever he did to me now, it wasn't a fraction as pathetic as I'd be if I lost him.

I curled my fingers against his skin. That I was even thinking this should have been a red flag the size of a battleship. I'd let myself become hopelessly lost for Rupert despite every warning, and if I wanted to have a prayer of keeping myself together, I needed to retreat, right now. But even though the warning was pounding through my head, I didn't move.

I didn't want to fight Rupert anymore. I didn't want to retreat, to keep myself back. It had been a losing battle anyway, a waste of resources right from the start, and if I kept stubbornly trying to press on, I was going to waste this moment now where Rupert was warm and alive under my fingers.

I glanced up at Rupert only to find him still watching me over his shoulder, his blue eyes wary. He must have known I was making some kind of decision, because he'd gone very still, holding his breath as he waited to see what I'd do. And as I watched him watching me like my decision was the most important thing in his world, my choice became obvious.

Slowly, reverently, I lowered my head to Rupert's back, pressing my mouth against the fall of his long hair just below his neck. The soft strands were cool against my lips, still slightly damp from the snow, but the skin beneath was hot and flushed as he took a sharp breath.

Hearing how much my touch affected him only cemented my decision further, but then, everything about him did. His warmth, the wintry smell of his hair, the way his muscles rippled under my hands where I'd rested them on his shoulders, the sound of his breath, every little sensation added to my certainty that this was the right choice. I was utterly lost for him, had been for a long time now, and life suddenly seemed too short to be stubborn. The weakness he'd opened in me was here to stay no matter what, so why not enjoy the fall? Sliding my fingers over Rupert's shoulders to his chest, I had to admit I couldn't imagine a more enjoyable defeat.

I was about to start kissing my way down his back when Rupert suddenly moved away. I looked up in confusion to see he'd turned around to face me, the wariness in his eyes replaced by that same ravenous longing I'd seen back in the rain on Seni Major. "Devi," he said, his voice hoarse. "I—"

I cut him off with a kiss, rising up on my knees to press my lips to his like it was the most natural thing in the world. And it was, because unlike every other kiss we'd shared up to this point, it wasn't a surrender or a bad decision made in the heat of the moment. It wasn't clouded by lies, wasn't angry or desperate or pleading. It was just a kiss, the inevitable end that came when two people as attracted as Rupert and I had always been finally found their common ground.

Rupert froze when our lips met, his body going rigid. Then, slowly, he leaned into me, his hands settling on my hips softly as new fallen snow. His touches were gentle, like he was scared he'd spook me if he moved too fast. Given my record for running, I couldn't blame him, but things were different now. *I* was different, because even though I'd loved him almost since the beginning, I hadn't trusted him. Now I did, and it felt like coming home.

The kiss was long and chaste, but when we broke at last, we were both panting. Rupert got control of his breathing first, leaning in to rest his forehead against mine. "Does this mean we're back on kissing terms?" he whispered, his accent thick.

I don't normally appreciate having my words turned around on me, but this one time, I didn't mind so much. "Yeah," I said, laughing. "Yeah, I guess it—"

Rupert swooped in before I could finish, crushing me to his chest as his lips found mine.

It was just like our first time in the *Fool*'s hallway. Now as then, Rupert was kissing me like he'd never stop, only this time, he didn't. Instead, he slid one hand up to cradle my head while he locked the other around my waist, pulling me so tight against him you couldn't have slipped a knife between us.

I was just as bad, digging my fingers into his shoulders until I was practically crawling up his body in my fight to get as close as possible. When Rupert finally let go of my waist to tear the blanket off my shoulders, I lurched forward, using my weight to send us both toppling back on the bed.

We landed with a bounce on the pile of towels and blankets with me on top, and I pressed my advantage immediately, sliding my hands down his hard chest toward the fly of his pants. But when I hooked my fingers under the button to pull it free, Rupert grabbed my wrists.

"Stop," he panted, breaking our kiss. "We can't do this."

It took about five seconds before my lust-addled brain could process that. "What?" I cried, sitting up. "Why the hell not?"

Rupert lowered his arms to his sides, fisting his hands like he was desperately trying to keep them off me. "I'm sorry," he said. "I didn't expect—" He broke off with a frustrated sound. "I promised myself we wouldn't do this again without protection."

I frowned, uncomprehending. I mean, I knew Rupert was old-fashioned and I certainly had a history, but with the mandatory adaptive vaccinations you had to get to enter Terran space, sexual diseases hadn't been a problem in fifty years. Maybe he was worried about the plasmex virus? But I'd been infected the first time we had sex, and he hadn't gotten it then. Anyway, I was pretty sure I was only contagious when the black stuff was showing, which was definitely not the case now. I was going to just ask him what the problem was, but Rupert was looking spectacularly flustered by this point, a very endearing thing for a man who never lost his cool, so I decided to wait and see where this was going.

"The symbiont changed my body a lot," Rupert said at last, his face determined despite the flush that had spread over his cheeks. "But I'm still capable of getting you pregnant."

That was definitely *not* what I'd expected. "You can't be serious," I said, half laughing, but his look told me he was.

I sat back on his stomach and stared at him in disbelief. It was clear as day that he wanted me feverishly, and yet he wasn't going to do it, wasn't going to take what I freely offered and he desperately wanted, if he couldn't do it right. That thought filled me with tenderness, and I leaned down to press a kiss against his nose. "You are too damn responsible for your own good."

Rupert broke away, grabbing my shoulders to push me up again. "I'm serious, Devi. I was unforgivably reckless before, but I won't take a risk like that with you ever again. So let me up and—"

I couldn't help it. I burst out laughing. It was horribly inappropriate, but I couldn't stop. He just looked so damn earnest. "You can't get me pregnant," I said when I finally got a hold of myself. "I'm Paradoxian, remember?"

The look on Rupert's face at that moment was absolutely priceless. "What does that have to do with it?"

"I never got out from under the ban," I said, wiping my eyes. "Honestly, Rupert, what kind of girl did you think I was?"

If Rupert had looked bewildered before, he looked absolutely dumbfounded now. "Ban?"

My smile faded. "The king's fertility ban." When that got nothing, I spelled it out for him. "All Paradoxians are sterilized at twelve. Breeding rights aren't returned until you've finished your military service."

Rupert's bewildered expression had turned horrified by the time I finished, and I put my hands on my hips. "How do you not know this? The ban's been in place for over a century. It was all over the Terran propaganda during the Border Wars."

"Exactly," Rupert said. "I always thought it was just propaganda." He pushed up on his elbows, looking me straight in the face. "You're seriously saying your government forcibly sterilized you?"

"Not *forcibly*," I said. "My mom took me in to get it done on my birthday. The whole thing was over in ten minutes. And it's not like it's forever. I've been eligible to have it reversed for years. I just never saw the point. I mean, do I look like the sort of person who wants to worry about babies?"

I finished with a grin at the ridiculousness of that idea, but Rupert was still staring at me like I'd grown a second head. "I'm sorry," he said, falling back on the bed as he reached up to rub his temples. "It's just, it sounds a bit barbaric."

"How so?" I asked, lifting my chin. "All Paradoxian children are wards of the king. You can't let just anyone have them. We're not animals, having babies all over the place. Barbaric, indeed. If you ask me, we're the civilized ones. You Terrans let anybody be a parent no matter how young or unprepared or undeserving they are."

As I said this, I was again reminded how blessed I was to have been born under the Sacred King's prudence. I couldn't imagine growing up in the Republic with no living saint to watch over you. But while I was feeling rightly superior, Rupert had started to chuckle.

"What?" I snapped, glaring at him.

"Nothing, nothing," he said, his face breaking into a grin. "It's just...you're *very* Paradoxian."

"You say that like it's a bad thing," I huffed. "If you've got a problem—"

Rupert sat up at once, causing me to slide down his body until I was sitting in his lap. "No, never," he said, wrapping his arms tight around me. "I love you exactly the way you are. You just caught me by surprise, that's all."

The earnestness in his voice washed away my anger, but I wasn't ready to let him off the hook just yet. "So do you still want to stop?"

I asked, arching up to brush my lips against his. "Because if you're going to keep being a Terran prude…"

Rupert's answer to that was to drag me back down to the bed.

After that, we didn't waste any more time talking. I was on top, and I used my superior position to strip him completely naked before shedding the last of my clothes. Even though we both knew Rupert was strong enough to do whatever he wanted, he let me take control, and I did so ruthlessly, teasing him and kissing him until he was shaking in my arms.

Brenton had once accused Rupert of being an iceberg, a cold, calculating man without feelings or heart. I almost wished the old windbag could have seen Rupert now, because there'd be no going back to the cold after this. He was like a live wire beneath me, his blue eyes wide and dazed and beautifully dark as I finally started to ride him. And when he threw his head back in compete abandon, grabbing my hips hard but not nearly as hard as I knew he could, I couldn't help leaning down to kiss him like I'd never let go.

As always, his intensity lit me on fire. The man did nothing halfway. Every kiss was a gallows kiss, his fingers digging into me like I was the only thing holding him down, but best of all was his voice. When he wasn't kissing me, he was whispering, repeating words into my hair and neck. Usually, Rupert never said anything without thinking it over first. Now he was babbling frantically, whispering through clenched teeth that he loved me, that I was beautiful, that he'd thought he'd lost me forever, and that he was never letting me go.

Or, at least, I think that's what he said. Halfway through, he switched from Universal to a beautiful language I didn't know, which was a bit of an ego boost for me. I'd never screwed a man into his native tongue before.

But just as I was enjoying the sight of Rupert in a true frenzy, he flipped the tables, rolling us over and trapping me beneath him. At this point we were so tangled I wasn't sure where I ended and he began, but it didn't matter. Once Rupert started moving, any illusion of control I had left vanished completely. In the space of a few seconds, I was as gone as he was. I writhed against his hold, panting and clinging to his body as everything I'd fought to hold back for so long came crashing down at last, taking us both with it.

When it was over, we collapsed into the blanket-strewn bunk, panting together in a breathless, tangled heap. All around us, the deep stillness of hyperspace pressed in like a fog, and the utter isolation was soothing in a way I couldn't describe. Lying here in the tiny, warm cabin of the Caravaner with Rupert's naked body pressed full against mine, the universe and all its dangers felt far away. All my anxiety and fear and turmoil had vanished like smoke, leaving only a deep sense of contentment and satisfaction. I was still savoring the wonder of it when I caught a flash of movement from the corner of my eye.

I stiffened, then relaxed. It was just the phantoms. There were four this time, floating in the air above the tiny door to the bathroom like little glowing puffballs. Just like the phantoms I'd seen on Anthony's ship, they'd arranged themselves in a line and were waving their hair-thin antennae at me like they were trying to get my attention.

If that was their intent, it worked. Once was strange enough, but seeing this phenomenon twice was definitely creepy. I was wracking my brain to try and figure out what it could mean when Rupert broke the silence.

"You're looking at a phantom, aren't you?"

I glanced up at see him staring down at me. It felt incredibly odd to talk to someone else about the things I'd thought of as hallucinations for so long, but Rupert had already seen me at my worst and he was still here, so I shrugged and told the truth. "Four of them, actually."

"Where are they?"

I pointed at the line of phantoms, and Rupert bent over, looking down my arm like he was taking aim. When he had it, he reached out, flicking his hand at the phantom in a shooing motion. "Go away," he said sternly. "She's mine."

This didn't do a damn thing, of course. The phantoms just kept waving like nothing had happened. But the effort made me smile, and I stretched up to kiss Rupert's cheek. "My hero."

He grinned and wrapped his arms around me, lying back with a purely masculine sound of contentment. Closing my eyes against the phantoms, I relaxed into his grip, taking shelter in his warmth, the peace of the quiet ship, and the luxury of not having to worry about universe-sized problems for at least eight more hours. I was debating whether or not to fall asleep when Rupert rolled over and began kissing a line down my body.

I laughed at his affections, but my laughter died when he settled on top of me.

"What?" I asked, slightly shocked. "Again? So soon?"

Rupert kissed his way back up to my ear. "Being a symbiont does have a few advantages," he whispered. "And I've wanted you for a very long time."

After that, I didn't waste any more time with stupid questions.

———

The next few hours were some of the most delightful of my life. If Rupert's injury slowed him down at all, I couldn't tell. I was actually the one who had to cry uncle first, much to my chagrin. Unlike Rupert, though, I was only human, so it was forgivable.

When he let me go, I flopped back onto the blanket-scattered bunk, sore, exhausted, and utterly content. Rupert stretched out on his side next to me, a wide smile on his face. "Happy with yourself?" I asked.

Rupert leaned down, kissing me soft and slow and so sweetly my mind went blank for a moment. "I'm happy with you," he said when he finally pulled back.

Once I managed to get my scattered thoughts back together, that bothered me. "You sure? Those Eyes were serious about killing you. Are you really happy about being on the run?"

"Absolutely," Rupert said without missing a beat. He propped himself up on his elbow, looking down at me like this was the most important thing he'd ever said. "I love you and I believe in what you're doing. You've given me more purpose and happiness in the last few months than I'd found in sixty years. I thought I'd lost everything when I lost you, and I was prepared to spend the rest of my life making amends, but then you forgave me." His voice sounded incredulous, like he still couldn't believe that was true. "You forgave the unforgivable, welcomed me back into your arms, and you ask if I'm happy?" He broke into a boyish grin. "Do I really have to answer that?"

I grinned back, mortified as a blush spread over my cheeks. "Just making sure."

"You can be *absolutely* sure," Rupert said, leaning down to kiss me again. "I would rather be on the run with you than anywhere else in the universe."

"Even if it gets you shot?"

Rupert's grin turned devilish. "If it gets me the same reaction you showed tonight, I'll get shot as much as possible."

"Don't even joke about that," I snapped, smacking him on the chest. "I'm serious, Rupert."

"I'm serious, too," he said, reaching down to brush my damp hair away from my face. "I'm in this with you to the end, Devi. No matter what happens, no matter who comes after you, so long as you want me at your side, that's where I'll be." He leaned down, pressing his lips against my forehead. "You are the future I want, and I will never surrender you to anyone."

I closed my eyes as he whispered against me, only now it was in shame, not pleasure. I shouldn't be letting Rupert make those promises to me. I might have finally given in to my feelings, but nothing had actually changed. I was still going to die, and since I believed him when he said he wasn't letting me go, I was now certain Rupert would be there when it happened. That actually upset me more than the idea of my own death, because I'd probably end up getting him killed, too.

I wanted to explain this to him, to warn him, but I knew it wouldn't do any good. Rupert was no idiot; he knew this was a doomed endeavor. Hell, he'd already paid the price for sticking by me in blood, and he was still determined to stay. Even if I could make him leave, I didn't want to let him go, and that shamed me more than anything. It was one thing to be weak and give in to love, but it was another altogether to be a selfish bitch who would rather keep her lover in danger with her than go without.

But just as I was getting really upset, Rupert settled into the bed, pulling me into his arms. Even after the last several hours, the intimacy was new and delightful, and I decided my self-recriminations could wait. Soon enough the jump would end and we'd be thrust back into reality. Until then, though, I was determined to savor every second.

I reached out, snaking my arms around Rupert and pulling myself tight. I felt him raise his head in question, but I didn't look up. Instead, I clung to him belligerently, pressing my face into his chest as I forced everything else out of my head until all that remained was the deep contentedness of lying in the dark with someone you loved. And it was in that quiet happiness that I gave in to my exhaustion, falling asleep with my lips pressed over Rupert's heart.

I woke to the hyperspace exit alarm. That in itself was nothing unusual, but the fact that Rupert was still in bed with me was. "Hi," he said softly, leaning down to kiss me.

I kissed him back, marveling. It felt so strange to be openly affectionate like this. Wonderful, but strange and a little reckless, like we were tempting fate, probably because we were. "Which alarm was that?" I asked when he broke away.

"Ten-minute warning," he answered, sliding out of bed and padding over to the flight console to turn off the alarm. I gave myself a long moment to gaze appreciatively at his naked back before I made myself get up as well, wincing when my tired muscles protested. The phantoms were still floating in the corner where I'd left them, though they'd stopped waving now. I rolled my eyes and put my back to them, facing the bathroom as I kneeled down to check my clothing.

It was a short inspection. Between the disrupter blast, Rupert's blood, and the dirty snow, everything I'd worn yesterday was ruined. I sighed, wondering if I was going to have to go meet this doctor in my underwear when I caught sight of my reflection in the bathroom mirror.

I looked exhausted and pale, which was to be expected, but what really got my attention was my hair. It had been down when I'd fallen asleep, the wavy mess too wet and tangled to even put in a ponytail. Now, two neat brown plaits framed my face.

"You braided my hair?" I called, looking over my shoulder. "Why?"

"Because it was beautiful and soft," Rupert answered, giving me a *duh* look.

I looked back at the mirror, turning my head from side to side. As someone who'd struggled her whole life with it, I knew exactly how long it must have taken him to coax my crazy, fluffy hair into those two neat braids. Actually, maybe I didn't, because Rupert had done a better job than I'd ever managed. He'd woven my brown hair back and down in two perfect halves, keeping the braid loose so the tines of my helmet's neuronet wouldn't snag but still tight enough to make sure no curls escaped to get in my eyes. How he'd managed to do it without waking me I would never know, but then, he would have had plenty of time to work it out, considering he couldn't sleep next to me.

"You must have been crazy bored," I said, flipping my new braids over my shoulders.

"Quite the opposite," Rupert said, walking back to the bed. "You were very entertaining. Did you know you talk in your sleep?"

"Really?" I frowned. "No one's ever mentioned that before."

Rupert smiled wide as he leaned over the bed to snatch up his bag. "Maybe I just make you more comfortable than they did."

From anyone else, that would have sounded smug. This was Rupert, though, so it just sounded like the truth. "Maybe," I agreed. "I didn't say anything embarrassing, did I?"

"No," Rupert said. "It was cute."

Not many people called anything I did "cute," but Rupert's judgment was historically impaired when it came to me, so I decided to just accept the compliment. I was about to ask him if we had any ration bars left when he pulled out a folded parcel and tossed it at me. "Here."

I caught it without thinking, but when I looked down, I was astonished to see I was holding a man's underarmor shirt. Rupert tossed me a pair of fatigues next, the same type and size I'd grabbed for myself before we'd fled Anthony's cruiser. When he pulled out another, larger set for himself, I could only shake my head in astonishment. "I can't believe you thought to bring all this."

"Symbionts go through a lot of clothes," Rupert replied, reaching back to pull his long hair into a ponytail. "You learn to overpack."

The clean clothes felt marvelous against my skin. I would have killed for a shower, but I wasn't about to trust the Caravaner's. Anyway, a shower would have required unbraiding my hair, and I was suddenly very disinclined to undo Rupert's painstaking work.

While I put on my boots, Rupert packed up the bunk. Not surprisingly, he folded everything, neatly organizing all the blankets and towels I'd pulled out when we first got on into stacks before stowing them back in their cabinets. He set us in order, too, giving me our last ration bar, a sacrifice I would have been more impressed with if I hadn't known how much he hated the things. He even found the Caravaner's tiny supply of potable water, which I hadn't even realized was there. The water would have been far more useful last night, but I was happy enough to get anything to drink.

As I sat in the navigator's chair, eating my ration and drinking my small cup of water that tasted like it had been sitting in a plastic tank for ten years while Rupert tapped at the flight console beside me, I couldn't help marveling at how easily I'd fallen into the couple routine. I'd expected to wake up to crippling regret, but I didn't regret a thing. I didn't even feel guilty. Quite the opposite, I felt proud sitting next to Rupert, ready to take on the universe. There could be an army waiting for us on the other side of this jump, and I almost wished there would be. I was eager to fight, to challenge anyone who thought they could take this new, wonderful thing I'd found with Rupert away from me. Weaknesses? Screw 'em. If anyone tried to use Rupert against me, I would pound their goddamn face in.

Okay, I knew that wasn't actually a viable long-term solution, but I didn't care. Right now, I felt like I could take down a team of Devastators using only my teeth.

Rupert glanced over at me, lifting his dark eyebrows. "You look happy."

"Just readjusting some priorities," I answered, cracking my knuckles. "So where are we, anyway?"

"I don't actually know if it has a name," Rupert said. "We're outside of Republic borders."

I gave him a skeptical look. "What kind of doctor lives in open space?"

"You'll see in a second," he said as the final alarm sounded.

I grabbed my seat as the jump flash washed over our ship, bringing with it that awful feeling of being sucked back into reality as we left hyperspace and reemerged into the universe. I looked around expectantly as soon as the light faded, but I didn't see anything that could give me a hint of what kind of place we'd arrived at. In fact, I didn't see much of anything at all. We'd emerged into what looked like deep space. I didn't see a planet or a moon or even a sun, just a wall of unfamiliar stars shining like little penlights in the deep,

deep blackness. I was about to ask Rupert if the Kessel gate had jumped us to the wrong place when he caught my eye and pointed down.

I'll be the first to admit that I'm not much of a pilot. Years of working on-planet and on-ship had taught me to keep my eyes straight. Unless my suit tipped me off, I didn't tend to look down when I was searching for things because xith'cal didn't normally spring up from under your feet. But space was another matter. Out here, down was as valid as any other direction, and when I followed Rupert's lead, what I saw made me gasp.

Directly below our little ship was an enormous space station. Or at least, I assumed it was a space station. I'd never actually seen anything like the glittering structure hanging in the blackness like a work of art. From above, it was shaped like a galaxy with long arms radiating out in a spiral from a relatively tiny central hub, but when Rupert flew us closer, I saw that the spiral was actually stretched out. Instead of being a flat disk, the long arms were curved both up and down, so that from the side it looked like a sphere. It was the strangest, most beautiful setup for a space station I'd ever seen, but weirdest of all was the fact that every one of those long, gently curving tubes looked to be made entirely of clear glass.

Inside the clear tubes, people walked on the sloping surfaces at all different directions. Some tubes had gravity on the bottom relative to our position, but in others the people seemed to be walking upside down. Still others looked to have no gravity at all. I was starting to wonder if they were having some kind of malfunction when I realized that all the people inside those clear tubes were wearing the brightest, most ridiculously fluttery outfits I'd ever seen.

"God and king," I muttered, leaning in for a closer look. "It's that space church place, isn't it? Nova's home."

"The Church of the Cosmos," Rupert said with a nod. "They have several stations, actually, but this is their main facility."

"And *this* is where your doctor is hiding?" I hadn't meant that to come out quite so skeptical, but I just couldn't reconcile the idea of a doctor who'd worked with Maat living in the same place that had produced someone like Nova. Then again, the Church of the Cosmos had also produced Nic, who'd been hard enough to run with Brenton, and their dad *was* supposed to be some kind of church leader who knew both Caldswell and Brenton, so I guessed it made sense that—

"Oh no," I moaned, flopping back in my chair. "It's Nova's dad, isn't it?"

Rupert nodded.

"Why didn't you just tell me?" I cried. "I mean, why not just say 'we're going to see Dr. Starchild' instead of 'the doctor' or whoever. It wouldn't have put me off. I like Nova, remember?"

"Old habits die hard," Rupert confessed. "We never talk about him. Dr. Starchild's affiliation with the Eyes is a deeply held secret. I only know about him because I'm old enough to remember his departure. The newer Eyes have no idea the head of the Church of the Cosmos was ever part of our operation."

I looked up at the glittering station in front of us. "Why is it such a big deal? I can understand the Eyes not wanting Dr. Starchild to talk about *them*, but why wouldn't they talk about *him*?"

"Because of what he did," Rupert said. "Dr. Starchild was with the Eyes from the very beginning. He knew enough to bury our entire organization, but he wanted out. When the Eyes refused to let him go, he loaded all that damning knowledge, and proof that it was true, onto satellites, which he then hid throughout the galaxy to use as blackmail. Unless they wanted the story of Maat, her daughters, and the phantoms sent to all the major news organizations, the Eyes had no choice but to let him make a clean break."

I whistled, impressed. A stunt like that took serious guts. It was also surprisingly ruthless, though I could completely understand why the Eyes would never want his name mentioned again after getting shown up so badly. What I didn't understand was: "How the hell is he still alive? This place is so isolated it would be an easy hit, so why haven't the Eyes taken him out?"

Rupert chuckled. "Believe me, there are plenty of Eyes who think we should destroy this place, including our current commander. Fortunately for Dr. Starchild, they can't afford to. He's the only person left in the universe who understands exactly how the plasmex part of Maat's prison works."

A cold shiver ran up my spine. "And why is that?"

"Because he's the one who built it."

My eyes went wide, but before I could ask any more, a beautiful chime sounded over our com.

CHAPTER

7

Most announcement alarms were beeps designed to get your attention. This one sounded like a wind chime, a leisurely string of notes followed by a woman's dreamy voice.

"Welcome, traveler. We are pleased to share space in harmony with you. How do you identify and what is your intent?"

The woman sounded so much like Nova I felt nostalgic, but my calm was ruined when Rupert answered. "My name is Rupert Charkov. I'm here with Deviana Morris to see Dr. Starchild."

"The Solarium Dock is currently available," the woman replied. "Abbot Starchild's envoy will join you shortly. May you be as one with the cosmos."

"Thank you," Rupert said, cutting off the com.

The moment the channel closed, I whirled on him. "Why did you give her our real names? We're on the run, remember?"

"Trust me, it will be much easier this way," Rupert said, glancing over at the station map that had just popped up on my console, along with a blinking marker at the end of one of the long arms that I could only guess was the Solarium Dock. "We're on a timeline and Dr. Starchild is an enlightened holy man with an entire religion clamoring to see him. This is the only way we have a hope of getting on his calendar in any sort of a timely fashion."

"But I thought he didn't want anything to do with the Eyes," I said, confused. "Why would he make an exception for you?"

"Not me," Rupert replied. "The important name was yours."

"Me?" I said, eyes wide. "Why? Because of the virus?"

"If Dr. Starchild already knew about your virus, he really would be psychic," Rupert said with a smile. "No, not that. I'm hoping he'll let you in because Nova adores you, and if Dr. Starchild has a weakness, it's his children."

I hadn't even considered that Nova might have told people about me. Now that I thought about it, though, I recalled she had written about me to Nic, so it made sense that she would have done the same to her father. But even if that was the case, I didn't share Rupert's certainty that the abbot of the Church of the Cosmos would make time to meet someone his daughter had mentioned in a letter. My virus seemed like a much more certain way of getting his attention, but somehow I didn't think he'd respond well to a note informing him that I was carrying a plasmex disease that could wipe out his entire station and oh, by the way, would he mind helping me with that?

At least I wouldn't have to worry about infecting anyone here by accident. After weeks of living with the thing, I had ample evidence that my virus was not contagious unless it was showing. So long as I didn't lose my temper, everything should be fine, and considering where I was headed, I didn't think that was going to be a problem. It would be downright impossible to get mad on a station full of people who talked like Nova.

Our dock was set at the tip of one of the longest spiral arms, and like everything else here, it was weird. There were no doors or metal safeguards to allow them to shut down entry. Instead, the "dock" was just a hole in the glass covered in a shield to keep the atmosphere in and the radiation out. There wasn't even a gun emplacement, which just struck me as dumb. How the hell a place like this survived in open space, I had no idea, but the glass where we landed was clean and unmarked by bullets or energy blasts, so they couldn't have had much trouble with pirates. Maybe they were too poor for criminals to bother with?

As soon as Rupert set the Caravaner down, the station's gravity took hold, making me feel like I'd lost fifty pounds. That wasn't surprising considering what Nova had told me about this place, but I didn't know what to expect as Rupert and I grabbed our stuff and headed out. Something gaudy and weird I was sure, but when we left the plain glass enclosure of the landing dock, walking through a set of clear sliding doors into what looked like a garden, all I found was beauty.

The tube was about twenty feet in diameter, and it was filled with flowering trees. Spindly, alien trees with dark trunks and blue-green leaves rose up from planters set along the tube's edges like sculptures, their roots set not in dirt but in clear balls of hydroponic gel that in turn were bolted onto gyroscopic platforms, which made sense once I remembered what Nova had said about her home's love of flipping gravity around.

They smelled nice, too. Most space stations smelled like chemical sanitizers, which wasn't bad when you considered what that many people living together in a small space would smell like without them. By contrast, the Church of the Cosmos smelled like leaves and sweet flowers, and it *glowed*. At first I thought the trees were bioluminescent, but then I saw the tiny lamps embedded in the trunks, using the tree's own energy to power their soft, bluish light. This eerie brilliance combined with the sweet scent and the majestic sweep of the stars visible above our heads and below our feet through the tube's crystal-clear walls made me feel like I was walking through some sort of heavenly garden, and it was so distractingly lovely I didn't even notice the woman coming until she spoke.

"Salutations, visitors."

I dragged my eyes away from the glowing trees to see a woman in an impossibly bright yellow dress striding toward us through the trees. Unlike Nova, who was pale as flour, this woman was dark skinned with close-cropped curling black hair, but she had the same serene, dreamy expression on her face as she drifted to a stop. "I am Solara," she said, her voice as soft and cool as the light from the trees overhead. "Spiritual guide and priestess of the oneness. It is my great pleasure to share space with any friends of Novascape's. I understand you seek to harmonize with Abbot Nebulon Starchild?"

I had to bite my tongue to keep from laughing. Nova's dad's name was *Nebulon*? I guess that was better than Galaxior, but still... Nebulon Starchild.

Just thinking about it was enough to give me the giggles something fierce. Thankfully, Rupert was there to cover my ass. As soon as he saw me start to lose my composure, he stepped in to save the conversation. "Yes, Priestess," he said, smooth as silk. "We'd like a meeting with him, if possible. Do you know if he has any time today?"

"We do not indulge in the illusion that the infinite flow of time is divisible here," the woman said. "But I would be happy to guide you to the abbot's place of refuge. If events align such that he is not otherwise occupied, I'm sure he would be delighted to share in oneness with you."

Suddenly, I wasn't so sure this place was going to be as safe for my temper as I thought. "Let me get this straight," I said. "You don't use clocks, so you can't make us an appointment, but you're going to take us to the abbot's house and he'll see us if he's not busy?"

"That is the basic summation," the woman said, completely unfazed by my sharpness.

I gaped at her. "How the hell do you run a space station with no clocks?"

Rupert elbowed me, but the woman only smiled wider. "This is a place of healing and freedom, Deviana." She raised her head, looking lovingly up at the stars. "Here we can only surrender to the infinite, for it is only through surrender to that which we cannot change that we free ourselves from the illusion of control and, in doing so, find true peace."

I boggled at her when she looked back down, but rather than explaining what the hell she'd just said, the madwoman gave me a wink. "It always works out in the end. After all, we are always exactly where we are meant to be. Now"—she turned around—"if you would care to follow me, I can lead you to the abbot's. Normally we let pilgrims find their own path, but the station can be confusing if you're not used to it."

"And we're not pilgrims," I reminded her.

"We are all pilgrims on the path of life," the woman said dreamily, walking off down the tube. "This way."

I gave Rupert a long-suffering look as I hoisted my armor case onto my shoulder. Since the gravity was so low here, I was able to carry it easily. Good thing, too, because the curving tube seemed to go on for miles. We passed several more gardens of lit plants, but we also walked through places that looked like classrooms filled with people in plain robes. Sometimes these people were listening to lectures given by men and women dressed like our guide; other times they were just sitting, staring off at the stars.

I also saw people using plasmex. Before Nova had made her cards float for me, I hadn't actually believed it was real, but lots of people apparently had it here. I saw several people levitating objects on their own, and I passed an entire class of children playing a color guessing game that apparently involved *reading each other's minds*. Considering all that, then, it wasn't surprising that I also saw phantoms.

Once I'd gotten used to the strange glow from the trees, I noticed the tiny ones everywhere. There were larger ones, too, phantoms as big as my hand drifting in and out of the tubes like fish swimming through a reef. Though I didn't see any more phantoms in lines, thank god, all of them seemed to notice me when I passed. Some even tried to follow, but I picked up the pace, determinedly ignoring them as we followed the tube in toward the nexus of the station.

The longer we walked, the more I understood the reasoning behind the station's strange construction. By building in spiraling tubes rather than a more normal spherical, ring, or cross-shaped setup, every part of the station had an unobstructed view of the stars. Also, the tubes made you feel like you were walking through space rather than through a structure, which definitely fit the Church of the Cosmos's mission statement. Finally, building in tubes allowed each one to maintain its own gravity environment, a fact I learned the hard way when we reached the place where our tube met the station's center.

As soon as I stepped over the threshold, the gravity vanished like a rug tugged out from under my feet, and I would have gone tumbling if Rupert hadn't grabbed me. The center of the station was a huge, open space that, as I'd just discovered, had no gravity at all. Every tube on the station looked like it fed into this place, which seemed to be an amphitheater of some kind. There was even a floating dais at the center, just the sort where an enlightened religious leader would sit while preaching to his followers, and I realized I'd just entered the church part of the Church of the Cosmos.

I don't have a lot of experience dealing with zero G outside of my suit. While I was struggling to get a leg up, our guide flipped over graceful as a mermaid, pushing off the wall with practiced ease to fly across the space to an unassuming door that was set into the church's roof. "Don't fight the air," she called when she saw me struggling. "Just use your surroundings."

Like hell did I need this bitch to give me flying instructions. Gritting my teeth in frustration, I got myself angled the right way and kicked off, making it more or less on target. Rupert followed with his usual effortless grace, which I normally loved but found highly annoying under current circumstances. Our guide gave him an impressed look as she opened the door and stepped inside. The moment her foot was through the door, she dropped like a stone, falling *up* a long tunnel to land neatly on the carpeted ceiling, which I now realized was the *floor* of a well-appointed waiting room.

At that, my annoyance at being the worst flier was replaced by overwhelming dizziness. "I think I'm going to be sick," I whispered, grabbing Rupert's arm.

"Just close your eyes," he said, brushing a kiss over my hair.

I obeyed, squeezing my eyes tight as Rupert helped me through the door. I didn't open them again until we'd cleared the long tunnel and my feet were firmly planted on what I decided would now and forever be the floor. When I managed to crack them open at last, the first thing I saw was our guide looking at me with sympathy.

"It's all right," she said softly. "You'll learn to let go of your expectations eventually."

I shot her a killing glare. I didn't want to let go. Things like up and down and clocks that she called restrictions I called *useful*, and I'd about had it up to here with her cosmos nonsense talk. But before I could get myself too worked up, Rupert squeezed my hand tight, a pointed reminder to keep it cool. After a deep breath, I decided he was probably right. Virus aside, there was no point in blowing up at someone who didn't get angry and wouldn't fight back.

"This is the entry to the abbot's private refuge," the woman said, holding out her hands. "You may wait here if you desire convergence."

This place was different than the others on the station. It was less like a tube and more like a knob that had been divided into two unequal sections by a long and, surprisingly for this place, opaque wall. We were in the smaller section, a curving room full of glowing trees and sitting pillows with the usual stars visible through the clear walls, which only made the black wall separating us from the abbot more mysterious, like a black hole. The gravity was even lighter in this place than in the tube where we'd entered, and I had to be careful not to throw my armor case as I slung it off my shoulder. "When can we see him?"

The woman frowned. "As I said earlier, we don't restrict our flow to—"

"We'll just wait," I said, cutting her off before I had to listen to all that again.

The woman flashed me what probably passed for a dirty look in this place, but before she could say anything else, Rupert took her hand. "Thank you very much, Solara," he said, giving her a slow smile. "We appreciate your guidance."

And just like that, the woman forgot I existed. "No need for thanks," she said, turning her attention fully to Rupert as she clasped his hand in both of hers. "It is my pleasure to welcome new minds into harmony. If our paths cross again, you are welcome to attend one of my classes on cultivating oneness. I think you'd do very well. You seem to have a very flexible mind."

"Thank you for the offer," Rupert said, his low voice full of promise while I fought to keep from rolling my eyes. "Hopefully, I'll see you soon."

The guide smiled warmly at him and left, hopping up to grab the edge of the door in the ceiling where we'd come in. The moment she had a good grip, she pulled herself up, using the change in gravity to send her body flying back out into the enormous space with such grace I knew she had to be showing off.

"Flexible mind," I muttered as Rupert returned to my side. "That's not all she wanted to flex."

"You catch more flies with honey," Rupert said, putting an arm around my shoulders. "You should try it sometime."

"No thanks," I grumbled. "I don't want any flies, and I've got better things to do than attend classes on how to talk like a space-case." I glanced up through the transparent ceiling at the huge structure above us. "Though I have to say, this place isn't quite what I expected. Where did a group who doesn't even believe in timekeeping get the money to build something like this?"

Rupert shrugged. "Dr. Starchild holds many patents."

That made sense. Patents meant corp money, and lots of it. I was about to ask Rupert what kind of patents when the sound of a door opening made us both turn.

What came next just made me feel awkward. I'd expected another guide, or maybe even the abbot himself. Instead, Copernicus Starchild walked out through the door, his pale face lighting up when he saw me. "Deviana!" he cried, hurrying forward to shake my hand. "I'm delighted to see you're all right!"

I let him take my palm, not at all sure what the proper etiquette was when meeting someone you'd tricked, drugged, and abandoned the last time you were together. But if Nova's brother harbored any ill will about the way I'd ditched him, I couldn't see it. Nic looked every bit as delighted as he claimed, his smile large and genuine. He did not, however, look at Rupert.

"I'm happy to see you as well," I said. And I was, sort of. "I'm glad you made it home."

"It seemed the best choice, all things considered," Nic said, guiding me toward the door. "Montblanc ended up on lockdown, and when we heard you'd died on Reaper's ship, well..." He faded off. "Death might be only an illusion, but personally, I'm very glad you're still with us."

"Me too," I said honestly, glancing at the door. "So does your dad know about—"

"Oh yes," Nic said, suddenly fearful. "I told him the whole story. But you have to understand, we thought you were dead."

"No, no," I said. "That actually makes things easier. Can we see him?"

I'd been trying to reassure him, but if anything, Nic only looked more uncomfortable. "He'll see you," he said, darting his eyes toward Rupert. "But he refuses to see the Eye."

Rupert stiffened beside me, but when I looked up, his face was passive and calm. "Go ahead," he said. "This is your visit, not mine. I'll wait here."

I didn't like the idea of leaving him, and I definitely didn't want to go in to meet the plasmex doctor who'd designed Maat's prison without backup, but there was nothing for it. "I'll be out as soon as I can," I said softly. And then, after a brief hesitation, I rose up on my toes and pressed a quick kiss against his lips.

He caught me, deepening the kiss so swiftly I almost dropped my armor case. When I pulled away at last, Nic was determinedly looking everywhere except at us. "Um, this way," he muttered, walking to the door.

I gave Rupert a final smile and walked to the sleek, solid, black glass sliding door. He watched me the whole way, his eyes on mine until the door closed, leaving me sealed inside the strangest room I'd ever been in.

Other than the wall behind me and the ceiling that connected this room to the zero G amphitheater above, it was completely made of clear glass. There were no lights, no large furniture, just open space. The tunnel we'd fallen up to get here must have been longer than I'd thought, because I was high above the rest of the station's snaking tubes with nothing but open space all around me. Even though I knew logically that there was glass between me and all that space, staring at the sweep of the open universe with no suit to protect me was overwhelming. Looking up, I couldn't help feeling tiny, an insignificant speck, and the only reason I didn't press my back into the wall was because I had an audience.

In the middle of the huge starry room, a man was sitting on a pillow. He was sitting in the dark, but I could see his shape because there were phantoms crawling all over him, lighting him up with their soft, bluish radiance. I was trying to make out his features through the glow of the little phantom sitting on his forehead when he reached out and turned on a light.

The soft, yellow light canceled out the phantom's blue radiance, revealing a man sitting on the same kind of meditation pillows Nova used. The lamp was set on a kneeling table in front of him, as was a chessboard, the pieces already arranged for a game. But

I noticed all of this only on the fringes, because the rest of me was gawking at the man himself.

My first thought was that this couldn't possibly be Dr. Starchild. Maat had been locked up for nigh on sixty years. That meant the person who designed her prison would have to be eighty at the very least, but the man in front of me didn't look any older than Rupert. As soon as I thought it, though, I realized I was being stupid. Of *course* he looked young. He'd worked directly with Maat, which meant he had a symbiont. He could be a hundred years old and not show a day.

He did look uncannily like Nova, though. He had the same pale hair and bleached complexion, like he'd never seen the sun, which didn't seem so far-fetched anymore now that I'd seen where they lived. He had her smile, too, wide and friendly, and I started to smile back out of habit when he held out his hand, gesturing to the pillow opposite him. "Hello, Deviana," he said, his voice calm and dreamy. "It is always a pleasure to share space with any companion of my darling Novascape and Copernicus. I was just about to start a game. Do you play chess?"

My smile vanished. Why did all these former Eye types keep asking me that? "No," I said, "I don't know how."

"Would you like to learn?" he asked. "It is a very enjoyable mental exercise. There are many good moves that might bring victory. The game lies in picking the best one. It makes for a challenging puzzle."

"I don't much like puzzles," I said. "I—"

"You don't?" Dr. Starchild replied, looking dismayed. "How unfortunate, because as I understand it, you're neck-deep in one at present."

I took a deep breath. "With all due respect, Dr. Starchild, I'm not here to play games. I'm sure Nic told you already, so you should know that I have a plasmex virus that's killing me and might just kill everything else if I can't get it under control. Rupert said you might be able to help, and we're short on time because the Eyes are after us, so if we could just cut to the chase, I'd really appreciate it."

Dr. Starchild lifted his wispy eyebrows, and then, to my astonishment, he picked up his game, set it aside, and turned back to me, folding his hands on the now empty table. "Very well, Deviana. I would never wish to upset your harmony. Tell me, then, what do you want me to do?"

I didn't actually know how to answer that. To buy time, I set my armor case down by the door and walked over to kneel on the pillow across from him. Unlike the ones in hyperspace, the phantoms crawling on Dr. Starchild skittered away like normal when I got close. That made me feel a little better before it made me feel worse. Had my life really gotten so crazy that I had standards of normal behavior for invisible bugs?

I shook my head in despair, clearing my throat as I got to the point. "What I want depends on what you can do, I guess," I said. "But let's start with the part where I've got a killer virus."

He nodded. "So you want me to save your life?"

"Yes," I said, and then I sighed. "No, well, it's not that simple. Did Nic tell you what the virus does?"

The doctor's look grew distant. "As much as he knew, though I feel I should point out that it's not really a *virus* by the strictest definition. What the xith'cal created is more like a corruption. It spreads through plasmex in a chain reaction, picking up strength as it grows. The more plasmex a creature has, the bigger it blows. You have very little plasmex, so it was never able to achieve critical mass in you, so to speak, which is probably the only reason you're still alive."

I nodded frantically. That sounded right to me. I was also very happy he'd started talking more like a normal person. "It didn't kill me, but I can use it to see and kill phantoms. So, what I'd ultimately like is to pull the virus out of me safely, but in a way that would still allow the Eyes to use it as a weapon to replace the daughters."

His face grew dour. "You want me to synthesize a weapon from your virus that can replace the current daughter system and wipe out the phantoms?"

"Not wipe them out," I said. "They're not evil monsters. They're more like animals." I stopped, trying to think of how best to put this. "I don't want to kill all wolves. I just want to make a gun that lets farmers protect their fields."

As I spoke, Dr. Starchild started to smile. "It stabilizes my calm to hear you say that," he said. "When you arrived with Charkov, I was worried you'd been misinformed. The Eyes know full well that the phantoms are not malevolent, but it makes their lives easier to demonize them." His smile turned bitter. "Monsters make much better villains than lost animals who are blind and frightened."

"Rupert's not like that," I said quickly. "At least, not anymore. He's helping me against them because he wants to find a better solution. That's why he brought me to you." I held out my hands. "I'll freely submit to any tests you want. I just want this virus to be used the right way."

"And you think the Eyes won't do that?" Dr. Starchild said. His voice was no longer dreamy now, but sharp, like he was testing me. "They have much better facilities than I do, especially when it comes to making weapons. I'm just a humble hermit."

I had to fight not to roll my eyes at that last comment. "Of course I don't trust them. The Eyes are the ones who thought it was acceptable to brainwash little girls into being child soldiers in the first place. They took kids from their families and used them up with no thought for the damage they were doing because, hey, everything's okay if it's in the name of saving the universe, right?"

He chuckled. "And you do not share this belief?"

"Hell no," I said, eying him. "Honestly, I don't know if I can trust you either, but I don't have much of a choice. I have to do something. I have in me the means to end a whole lot of suffering, and I'd be a terrible person if I didn't do my best to see that through. So if you can help me at all, even if it's a long shot, I'd really appreciate it."

Dr. Starchild breathed out a long breath and looked down at his hands, still folded on the smooth wood of the small kneeling table between us. "I am honored by your faith in my abilities," he said after a pause. "Unfortunately, Deviana, I cannot do what you ask."

He raised his head again, looking at me with deep sympathy. "You are dying," he said. "I can see it in your aura. There is no mistake. The corruption has permanently altered you, becoming part of your inherent plasmex, and I cannot cleanse it."

His soft words were like shots landing in my body. I'd thought I'd steeled against this, that I'd accepted my death long ago, but hearing it spelled out like that brought forth an unexpected surge of survival instincts and anger. "Aura?" I snapped. "I can see phantoms, but I don't see any auras. How do you know for sure that I'm dying? Maybe you're just seeing what you want to see?"

I was snarling by the end, but Dr. Starchild didn't seem ruffled in the least. "Aura reading is a complex art that requires years to master," he explained. "It takes a great deal of plasmex to even attempt the technique, so of course you with your tiny spark of plasmex can't 'see' auras because we don't *see* them at all. They are an expression of pure plasmex completely disconnected from our physical senses. You see phantoms, Deviana, because your plasmex is no longer human."

The chill I felt at his words doused my anger like a bucket of snow. "What do you mean?"

"I mean I can't say for certain what you are," Dr. Starchild replied. "Other than a unique anomaly, which isn't actually so unique when you consider the infinite possibility of the universe. For example, Maat is also a unique anomaly. Like you, her plasmex was changed by the xith'cal, though her change was not accidental. She was the sole survivor of Reaper's experiments to turn humans into plasmex-generating vessels when Caldswell found and freed her during one of his slave raids."

Caldswell had mentioned that much before, but the doctor wasn't finished. "This was back when Brian was a simple Starfleet captain and I was the plasmex researcher assigned to him by the

Scientific Council to study xith'cal experimentation," Dr. Starchild went on. "Had the timing been different, Maat might have been rehabilitated, but then we discovered she could *see* the strange deep space phenomena we'd been having problems with, the invisible force that disrupted electricity and ate ships. She was actually the one who first named them 'phantoms' when she was trying to describe what she saw."

He stared up at the stars, lost in the memory. "I thought they were fascinating, Brian thought they were dangerous, but Maat always said they were beautiful. She used to cry when we made her kill them." He frowned, and then shook himself, like he was waking up. "Anyway, what I'm trying to communicate is that you are an oddity, Deviana. By all factors, you should be dead, and yet you live." He shrugged. "The universe is infinite and strange. We cannot predict, only marvel at what it creates."

I closed my eyes with a curse. I hadn't even realized I was still holding out hope until it withered. "So there's no way to make a weapon out of this thing?" I asked, fighting very hard to keep my voice from cracking. "Nothing?"

"I could not speculate," Dr. Starchild said. "I can't do it, but that doesn't mean the Eyes couldn't find a way. However, since the lelgis would never permit such a weapon to be created, the likelihood of any research, however enthusiastically undertaken, reaching an actionable point is very slim."

"But there's a chance," I said, grasping.

"Oh, there's always a chance," Dr. Starchild admitted. "However, unless they find it in the next month, it will be a moot point."

"Next month?" I repeated dumbly. "I'm going to die in a month?"

He gave me a sad look, and his voice grew gentle. "I'm sorry, Deviana. I wish I had better news, but at this point, the corruption is simply too deep. The only beings who could possibly cleanse your plasmex now are Maat and the lelgis queens, and even then, doing so would require them to take the corruption into themselves in the process, essentially trading their life for yours." He shook his head. "The infinite is always possible, but it does not seem likely they would make such a sacrifice."

I disagreed. "But Maat *wants* to die," I said. "That's why she came to me in the first place."

Dr. Starchild scowled. "Maat spoke to you?"

"She wanted me to kill her," I said. "With the virus, actually." I took a sharp breath. "This is *perfect*. She could take the virus from me. She'd die and I'd live. We'd both get what we want!"

"It would also kill all the daughters and forever remove the chance of making more," Dr. Starchild pointed out.

My shoulders slumped. Oh yeah, I'd forgotten about that tidbit in my desperate grasping. Still. "Is there any way around that? If I give the virus to Maat, the Eyes are already set up to study her. We'd be replacing one weapon with another, only this one isn't actively suffering. Could we do that? Infect Maat but spare the daughters?"

He frowned, thinking. "Perhaps, but this is all a moot point. Even if you could snap your fingers and make every phantom vanish, the Eyes would never let you kill Maat. Above all else, they will never let her die."

I glared hard at him. Caldswell had said much the same thing when I'd tried to get him to agree to let Maat go, but he'd refused to explain why. At the time, I'd let it slide. Now, though, I didn't have the time to waste. Dr. Starchild knew the Eyes' secrets, and if I was going to die for this bullshit, I was at least going to know *why*.

"Why can't Maat die?" I demanded. "It's not just because she's the only one who can make the daughters, is it? The lelgis have something going on with her, too, so what is it about her that's so important?"

Dr. Starchild leaned back on his pillow, staring up at the stars like he was trying to make a decision. Whatever it was, he must have decided in my favor, because when he looked at me again, his face was all business. "Maat can never die," he said ominously. "Because Maat is the one who holds the door closed."

"What door?" I asked.

"The phantoms aren't from our universe," he explained. "They came to this place from another, and they did it by slipping through what I can only term a *hole*."

"A hole?" I said. "What, like a mouse hole?"

He made a face. "That is a very simplistic way of putting it, but the general idea is correct. It was the lelgis who found the breach first. They saw the phantoms as intruders, dangerous ones. Being almost entirely made of plasmex, the lelgis fear little, but phantoms are made *entirely* of plasmex. They don't even exist on the physical plane unless they've reached a certain size and made a determined effort to manifest." He paused. "How much do you know about the oneness?"

"Been there," I said, which earned me an impressed look.

"Extraordinary," he replied. "That makes you almost unique. I brush it sometimes in my deeper meditations, but I've never been able to truly ascend."

I smiled. He sounded almost jealous. "It isn't all it's cracked up to be."

He held up his hand. "Please don't spoil the experience for me. Now, as I was saying, phantoms are creatures of plasmex, even more than the lelgis. They live *within* the oneness, the unified flow of plasmex that connects all living things. Plasmex is everything to them—it's what they eat and breathe. It also connects them to each other, allowing communication and, I believe, spontaneous relocation within the physical realm." He stopped, looking suddenly sheepish. "This is all conjecture, of course. I have no proof since the phantom phenomenon is nearly impossible to study."

"It sounds right to me," I said. Eating plasmex would certainly explain why phantoms loved plasmex users so much. Even now, with me sitting so close, the little phantoms were trying to ease their way back toward Dr. Starchild. "But where does Maat come in?"

"Maat was the key," he said excitedly. "So we have this hole in the universe, right? And phantoms are able to move through it freely. However, since we've already established phantoms are made of plasmex, this meant they were also now able to move freely into the *oneness*, which upset the lelgis greatly."

"Why?" I asked. "You said the oneness is touched by every living thing there is. What do a few phantoms matter to all that?"

"Ah, but unlike the rest of us, who merely brush the oneness, the phantoms move through it like fish in the sea," Dr. Starchild explained, his face going grim. "The lelgis consider themselves to be the queens of heaven, custodians of infinite space with the oneness as their private domain. You can see, then, why the phantom's invasion would upset them."

As he said this, my mind flitted back to the craziness right after I'd killed Reaper, to the voices in the dark, the lelgis. They'd described themselves as queens to me then as well, guardians of everything. They seemed to think they were gods.

"To the lelgis overminds, the oneness is their pure land," Dr. Starchild went on. "But when the phantoms began to pour in, they brought their own plasmex with them. The lelgis saw this as corruption and sought to stem the tide, but even they can't manipulate the fabric of space itself. Repairing the hole between our universe and the phantom's was impossible, so they had to settle for plugging it. But even this was risky. While any queen could have easily used her control over plasmex to build a wall, doing so would have exposed her to the phantom's home universe, and not a single one of them would dare risk being corrupted herself to save the others. Being a hive mind, they all knew this, and so they decided to find someone else. An outsider."

"Maat," I said.

He nodded sadly. "Looking back, she tried to warn us what was coming. She used to tell me she could hear their voices in the dark, though I didn't know what that meant at the time. Now I know she was touching the oneness, touching the flow of plasmex itself, and when the lelgis decided they needed a sacrifice, she was the obvious choice."

"But why did you give her to them?" I said. "It was their problem. Why not tell them to suck it up and do it themselves?"

"Because we had no choice," Dr. Starchild said tiredly. "At that point, the phantoms looked to be on the brink of wiping out all of humanity. Maat was the only weapon we had against them, and she was becoming more and more unstable. And then Svenya happened." He sighed. "You have to understand, we were desperate. All the lelgis had to do was hint they had a solution, and we gave them everything. Caldswell handed Maat over to them himself, and when they gave her back, she was changed."

The way he said that made me shudder. "How?"

"I've never been able to figure that out exactly," he confessed. "Maat was always unstable, but that was to be expected from a girl who grew up as both a xith'cal slave and an enormously powerful plasmex user. Actually, I'd often thought she did very well, all things considered. She could be rational, calm, even friendly when we weren't pushing her. When she came back from the lelgis, though, she was mad, truly so, and she's only gotten worse."

I didn't need him to tell me that. I'd seen Maat myself. "So that's why she can't die. She's the plug."

Dr. Starchild nodded. "She is the dam against the phantoms, the wall that stops the tide. Every phantom currently inside our universe came here in the few years the hole was open, before Maat closed the door and blocked the flow. The purpose of the Eyes and the daughters was always cleanup. Their job was to eliminate the remaining phantoms, after which it was thought the program would shut down."

He ran a thin hand through his pale hair. "I haven't been involved with the Eyes for thirty years, so I don't know how that's going for them, but we always did this with an end in sight. If we keep killing them, so the logic goes, eventually we'll kill them out. When that happens, the universe will be phantom free and all the Eyes and daughters can retire. But Maat is different. That's why she can never leave the Dark Star, the Eyes' space station, which is positioned directly over the tear in the universe where all this began. She was the sacrifice, the queen whose position holds the phantoms in checkmate, and until the game ends, that's where she'll stay."

I let out a long breath. As he'd told the story, Dr. Starchild's voice had grown painfully bitter. "So you're like Brenton, then," I said. "You don't think Maat should have to suffer."

He scowled. "John Brenton's objections were purely personal. He didn't care that *a girl* was being sacrificed. He cared that it was *her*. If he could have traded some other poor soul into her fate, he would have done so in a heartbeat. I, on the other hand, was not a lonely, violent man infatuated with a mentally unstable teenager. I objected to the *principle* of the matter."

"But you still went through with it," I said.

"Yes," Dr. Starchild admitted. "And I regret doing so. Like everyone else, I acted out of fear. A planet of billions had just been destroyed and we couldn't even find the monster who'd done it, let alone kill it. We didn't know where it would strike next, or if there were more. It felt like the end of everything, and when the lelgis appeared like avenging angels to kill the unkillable, there was nothing we wouldn't do to keep their protection."

He gave me a bitter smile. "I've often wondered if they planned it that way, letting us get a real taste of the phantom's destructive power to make sure we'd go along without a fight. Now, however, I am no longer under the illusion that we have control over the universe, and I would act very differently if I were given the chance to live those days again."

I didn't agree with what had been done to Maat at all, but the way he said that sat wrong with me. "So what would you have done?" I asked. "The phantoms were pouring through that hole, right?"

He nodded. "Their numbers were increasing exponentially, yes."

"So you would have just let them keep coming?" I snapped. "I'm not saying Maat should have to stay and do this all alone forever—that's way too much on one person—but at the beginning, it might really have been the only way. If the phantoms hadn't been stopped, they would have overwhelmed us before we figured out another solution."

If I'd been in charge back then, I would have bargained for a time limit on Maat's duty and then put every plasmex expert in the galaxy on figuring out how to make a wall that didn't require a person to hold it up. Stopping the initial flow of the enemy was vital, but once we'd gotten ground, there was no reason to let Maat keep fighting all by herself other than laziness and selfishness. That was how I saw it, anyway, but from the look Dr. Starchild was giving me, I don't think that was what he had an issue with.

"The greatest illusion is the illusion of control," he said softly. "We humans are little more than specks of dust in the infinite sea of the cosmos. To protect ourselves from that dreadful truth, we have developed an elaborate fiction that we have control over our lives. But our species is not alone in this. The lelgis are worse, seeking to control and protect something that is infinitely larger than their greatest efforts. Trying to preserve the oneness is like trying to preserve time, or gravity."

He lifted his head to the stars. "This is why the lelgis chose us as their pawns. We both share the delusion that we can control the universe, but we can't. We think we have power, but we don't, and in trying to assert what we do not have, we only hurt ourselves. In the end, all we can really do is accept our powerlessness and be at peace."

I stared at him, disbelieving. "What are you talking about?" I said. "We can't control everything, sure, but there's tons of stuff we have enormous power over. I'm not saying he did the absolute right thing, but if Caldswell hadn't handed Maat over to the lelgis, the phantom situation could have gotten completely out of control. Our entire *race* could have been wiped out."

"It would not have been the first," Dr. Starchild said with a shrug. "The tools of evolution are time and death, Deviana. The second greatest illusion is that of our own importance. Our lives are not sacred; the universe does not care about little specks. We in our hubris care, and when we try to fight the universe, we will always lose, because we are finite, and the finite can never defeat the infinite. Maat may endure in her suffering for another hundred years, but eventually she will fall, and the phantoms will come anyway. We know this, and yet we keep fighting. We suffer and strive and do great evil to each other to preserve lives that will end in the blink of an eye. Even you."

I gave him a curious look, and he explained. "I can't enter the oneness, but even I can feel when an entire xith'cal tribe dies in an instant. Your virus is the only thing that could do that, and yet here you are. Did you do it to save your own life? Kill thirty million thinking, feeling individuals so you could walk away?"

I gritted my teeth. "They were xith'cal."

"Xith'cal have a right to live," he said.

"You don't know shit about me, old man," I yelled. "I did what I felt I had to do at the time, and I don't have to explain my actions to you."

"You're right, you don't," he said. "Because I do not sit in judgment, Deviana. Not of you, nor of Caldswell, nor of anyone."

"You judged Brenton," I snapped.

"I stated fact," he corrected.

I threw up my hands. "So are you saying we should just do nothing? That I should have given up and rotted in Reaper's cell and let him use me as a weapon because, hey, I'm mortal and I'm going to die anyway? Bullshit. If that was how I thought, I'd never get anywhere. Would you sit back and do nothing if Nova was on a planet that was about to be overrun by phantoms?"

"It is possible to love someone without giving in to attachment," Dr. Starchild said. "I love my children dearly, but I accept that I cannot control their fates. Why else do you think I allowed Nova to go with Caldswell?"

I shot him a murderous glare, and the doctor sighed. "I am sorry to have offended you, Deviana. I did not mean to make you upset. But you came to me for aid, and I am doing my best to give it to you. The truth is that we are a constantly evolving picture, and the phantoms are part of that now. If we try to fight that, all we do is cause more suffering for ourselves."

I bared my teeth. "I am not just going to give up."

"Acceptance is not the same as giving up."

I growled deep in my throat. I was past fed up with this guru bullshit. But instead of getting out of my way like someone with a healthy sense of self-preservation, Dr. Starchild leaned over, snatching the smaller of the two crowned figures from the white side of his chessboard.

"In chess," he said, holding the game piece up between his fingers, "the queen is the most powerful piece, but even she is still just a piece on a board. For all her power, she is trapped by her role so long as the game is in play. If she truly wishes to be free, she must change the game."

I rolled my eyes. "What does that mean?"

"You said yourself that the phantoms are not monsters," he replied, placing the little queen on the table. "With that in mind, it might behoove us to cease treating them as such. If we bend and adapt, work with rather than against, we might discover that the wall we perceive at our backs is actually a foundation for something else entirely."

I shook my head. "If you want me to talk to them, I already tried. Doesn't work."

"Maybe not yet," he said with a smile. "But you must agree that it's time to change our approach. For far too long now, we have been sacrificing our pieces in pursuit of a victory we cannot obtain and which may not even exist. If we continue in this fashion, if we keep clinging to our dream of control, then we have no future but failure."

He sat back on his pillow as he finished, looking at me calmly like he expected me to throw myself at his feet and bless him for his wisdom. But I'd had all the lecturing I could stomach, and I stood up instead.

"Thanks for the sermon, Doc," I said. "But you forget, I'm not in this for the long game anymore. I might be a speck in the maelstrom, but this speck means to go out like a supernova. So if you'll pardon me, I'm going to go and see if the Eyes can't do something with this virus. Because while they might have their heads up their asses about it, at least they're *doing* something, not just sitting around in a pretty space station in the middle of nowhere pontificating about acceptance while people are dying."

I lifted my chin, daring him to come back after that, but Dr. Starchild just gave me a warm smile. "Then I wish you nothing but harmony and fulfillment in all your endeavors."

When I gave him a frankly skeptical look, his smile only widened. "We may not agree on all things, Deviana Morris, but you are still clearly a brave woman who is trying very hard to do the right thing. Just because your path is not one I would follow myself does not mean I cannot respect it or wish you well. Though I would appreciate it if you would tell Eye Charkov to stop beating on my door. It's upsetting Copernicus's calm."

I blinked. I hadn't heard any beating. I couldn't hear a damn thing, actually, but when I turned on my heel and marched over to open the door, Rupert nearly fell on top of me.

He caught himself at once, lowering the fist he'd clearly been using to pound a hole in the amazingly soundproof black glass. He looked at Dr. Starchild, then at my scowl, but though he was clearly curious, urgency won out. "We have to go," he said, reaching down to grab my armor case. "Now."

"Why?" I asked. "We got company?"

Rather than answer, he stepped aside so I could see the Terran battleship that was waiting just outside.

"I thought they'd search the planet before chasing down the final jumpers," he said quickly. "I didn't realize they'd be on to us so quickly. I'm sorry."

"Don't be," I told him, taking my armor case back as I led him out into the waiting area where Copernicus was still hovering. "This actually saves time."

Rupert gave me an odd look, but I didn't explain yet. Instead, I gave Nova's brother the "scram" glare, which cleared the room nicely. Copernicus scrambled out without another word, hurrying into his father's room and shutting the door behind him. The moment we were alone, I told Rupert the truth.

"I'm done running," I said, my voice impressively calm and determined as I set my armor case on the floor by my feet. "The doctor can't help. My options are wait for the virus to slowly kill me, die to the lelgis, or let the Eyes have a shot. So I'm going to have a talk with whoever's on that ship and make sure that this thing"—I thumped my chest—"pays its dues for all the trouble it's caused, and I don't want you to go with me."

Rupert jerked like I'd hit him. "What?"

"I want you to run," I said sternly. "I'm going to be dead soon no matter what, but there's no reason you should suffer, too. I'll distract them. I'm the primary target. You take the Caravaner and get out of here."

As I spoke, Rupert went very still, his eyes narrowing. "And where would I run?" he said quietly, reaching up to press his long-fingered hand firmly against my chest. "My heart is here."

I sighed. " Rupert."

"I am a defector," he went on like I hadn't spoken. "I am no longer taking orders." His lips curled into a warm smile. "I am free to follow my heart wherever she goes."

"It'll be a short trip," I grumbled, eyes flicking to the enormous battleship outside. Already, fear was burning up my throat. I could face my own death like a hero, but at the thought of Rupert's, I became a coward. Cowardly enough for the cheap stunt I pulled next.

I snatched my hand down, grabbing Sasha from where I'd lashed her to my armor case. In the low gravity, my anti-armor pistol's normally oppressive weight was nothing, and my hand shot up like a cork to press her muzzle against the skin of Rupert's forehead. I would knock him out, get the Starchilds to hide him as a final favor out of my friendship for Nova, and go up to meet the Eyes alone, explaining away the arm I was about to break as an injury from Kessel.

It was a good plan, clean and simple, but I'd miscalculated. I'd thought surprise and low gravity would give me the edge I needed to beat Rupert's speed, but I wasn't even close. I'd barely touched Sasha to his skin before he grabbed my wrist, pressing hard on the pressure point until my hand opened.

The sound of my gun clattering to the glass floor was painfully loud in the silence, but I couldn't tear my eyes away from Rupert. He was right above me now, his hand still crushing my wrist, though I barely felt the pain. All I felt was a mix of fear and love so strong I didn't know what to do with it. So I kissed him, rising up on my toes like I had before, only this time I was the savage one, grabbing Rupert and yanking him against me as hard as I could.

"You are such a jerk," I said when I pulled away at last. "Why won't you let me save you?"

"Because you wouldn't be," he said, dropping my wrist to cup my face with both hands. "Leaving you behind would be no salvation at all." He leaned into me, smiling softly. "Haven't you listened to anything I've told you?"

I stared up at him for a long moment, and then I lurched forward, burying my face against his chest while my arms wrapped around him so tight I'd have broken something if he'd been human. He held me more gently, but not much, his head pressed against my braided hair as he whispered that he loved me, that I was his brave girl, and didn't I know he would never leave me?

I wanted to tell him I did know and that was why I'd pulled the gun, but I couldn't get any words past the lump in my throat. So I just stood there, clinging to him like I was trying to make up for a lost lifetime until I heard the sound of boots landing at the foot of the vertical tunnel. But it wasn't until a man cleared his throat that I finally found the courage to let go of Rupert and turn to face my fate.

CHAPTER

8

After the force they'd sent against us on Kessel, I was expecting ten symbionts at least, but the Eyes must have been on short notice, because the squad waiting for us when I looked up consisted of only four people who could possibly be symbionts. The rest were soldiers, ten Terrans in classic light-assault gear, the kind Paradoxian armor chewed up like chaff. That almost made me regret not taking a stand, because Rupert and I could have smoked these idiots. But then I noticed that the symbionts had their disrupters out, and, more importantly, all the soldiers were carrying heavy anti-armor shotguns, the big, expensive, multifractal spread kind that could rip my Lady to shreds in seconds, and I knew my decision not to fight had been the right one.

I glanced at Rupert out of the corner of my eye, but he was looking at the person standing at the front of the group. Though his straight posture and physical prowess clearly marked him as a symbiont, the man at the head of the force looked more like a gentle old grandpa than a killer. He wore the same type of plain black suit Rupert used to, but unlike Rupert, he managed to make it look old-fashioned and frumpy rather than dashing. His hair and full beard were snowy white and neatly trimmed, and the soft smile on his lips looked like a permanent fixture on his face. He reminded me of the kindly old mentors you saw in dramas, the ones who always gave the hero that key bit of life advice before dying, so you can imagine my shock when Rupert inclined his head and said, "Commander Martin."

The grandfatherly man nodded back. "Charkov."

My heart began to sink. The old man might look benign, but when he spoke, his voice was dry and crisp without a hint of smugness, despite having cornered us at last. I knew that tone well; it was the voice of an officer who saw you not as a soldier but as a tool. A piece to be moved efficiently to secure advantage, and no amount of heroics would ever make him see you differently. I'd had a few commanders like him in my time, and it had always been a degrading experience, which was why I wasn't surprised at all that the next words out of Commander Martin's mouth were, "Cuff them."

The Eyes started toward us while the normal soldiers hung back to provide cover fire. I squeezed the handle of the Lady Gray's case as they approached, shifting the fingerprint lock to its highest setting. I couldn't stop them from taking my suit, but at least this way anyone who tried to break in would get cooked. It was cold comfort, especially since, at its highest setting, the security shock would slag my suit's electronics as well, but I'd rather destroy my Lady than let these bastards have her.

The symbiont who stepped up to cuff me was a nondescript man who didn't look nearly as impressive as the blond, sweet-talking Eye I'd faced off with on Kessel, especially since he seemed reluctant to touch me. Naturally, then, I couldn't resist leaning into him as he took my case and locked my wrists behind my back with a pair of sticky cuffs from as far away as possible. He was shaking when our skin made contact, so I made sure to bump into him whenever possible. Couldn't let them forget who the plague bearer was around here.

My sticky cuffs were pretty standard stuff, a tough band of semi-liquid plastic that only got tighter when you pulled. The sticky underside adhered to flesh on contact, meaning you'd have to rip off your own skin to get free without the chemical key. Nasty business, but nothing I hadn't encountered, and used, before. The rig they'd brought for Rupert, on the other hand, was like nothing I'd ever seen.

The two Eyes who'd stepped up to restrain him were even more skittish than my guy, visibly shaking as they pulled Rupert's arms behind him and locked them together in an enormous metal cuff that ran from his fists to his elbows. They cuffed his ankles as well, two metal enclosures connected by what looked like a titanium snake just long enough to allow short steps, but he'd take out his own feet if he even tried to kick. Finally, they fixed a shock collar to his neck, which I was pretty sure was actually illegal in Terran space. But the Eyes had never cared much for the law, and they seemed bent on making sure Rupert couldn't so much as twitch without their say-so. Of course, considering his reputation and my own knowledge of what he was capable of, I'd have done no less.

Dr. Starchild had come out of his office while they were securing us, probably to make sure we didn't hurt his station by making a scene. Nic was standing beside his father, looking like he wanted to help, but he didn't make a move. Good thing, too, because Martin didn't seem like a man who took interference well. He watched with cold detachment as the pair of Eyes led Rupert away, pulling him out a side door I hadn't noticed before toward the embarkation shuttle they'd hooked to the abbot's emergency exit. When they got there, Rupert shot me one last look before they shoved a black bag over his head and forced him onto the tiny shuttle for the trip back to the battleship waiting outside.

Even though I couldn't see him anymore, I watched the shuttle until it flew out of view before turning my glare on Martin. "Was that really necessary? He wasn't going to resist."

"It was absolutely necessary," Martin said in that dry voice. "Rupert Charkov has proven himself to be a violent and unpredictable element. I am only taking the necessary precautions to ensure the safety of those under my command."

"If you think *Rupert's* the violent and unpredictable element here, then you haven't been paying attention," I said proudly, striking a pose like my hands were behind my back because it was comfortable and not because they were bound. "So, it's Martin, right? Are you here for our civil discussion?"

"I do not believe you are capable of such a thing, Miss Morris," he said, holding out his hand.

Of all the symbionts, Martin had been the only one not brandishing a disrupter pistol. Now, one of the normal soldiers handed him a gun I hadn't seen before. It was small and lightly constructed, like a civilian-grade concealable pistol. But before I could ask if he meant to tickle me to death with that peashooter, he raised the gun and fired.

A spike of pain exploded in my left arm, and I looked down to see a dart the size of my pinky sticking out of my bicep just before my vision started going fuzzy. "What?" I slurred, forcing my now heavy head up to glare at the commander. "Right to the stick? Not even going to try the carrot?"

"You were the one who forced me to get personally involved, Miss Morris," Commander Martin said, his voice far away. "Now you will learn that when I get involved, we do things one way: mine. And my way does not involve taking chances."

I closed my eyes and took a deep breath, letting my body slump, but it was all for show. My anger was flaring nice and sharp now, scraping the drug haze away. It was the impotent anger of a trapped animal, but after getting cornered, learning I was going to die for certain, and losing Rupert, I was feeling the need to act out.

"If that was your intent, then you haven't done your research," I slurred, pulling myself straight again in slow, exaggerated motions. "Otherwise you'd know shooting me only makes me mad."

A flicker of confusion ghosted over Martin's face at my words. I answered with a crocodile smile before pushing back with all my strength to slam my bound fists into my guard's crotch.

I never could have caught someone like Rupert or Caldswell with a move like that, but this idiot must have been another back-line symbiont, because he doubled over with a yelp, letting me go. His pained cry was music to my ears. Not so armored there, asshole. I was about to rush Martin when I felt three more pricks hit my back.

This time, the dizziness hit me like a tidal wave. I was on the ground in seconds, knocked forward by my own fumbled charge. I was staring down at the stars through the clear floor, trying to decide whether it was worth the effort to raise my finger for a final rude gesture before I passed out when I heard a gruff voice I'd never expected to hear again.

"Never did know when to quit, did you?"

My breath caught, and I looked up, letting shock do what strength couldn't as I raised my head to see Brian Caldswell staring down at me with Commander Martin's tranq gun in his hands. He'd traded out his spacer captain's flight vest and collared shirt for Terran military surplus fatigues, but otherwise, the captain looked exactly as he had the day he'd hired me. This time, though, his glare was far more personal.

"Sorry about this, Morris," he said, not sounding sorry at all. "But it's time to stop being stubborn and go to sleep."

I wanted to tell him I hadn't even gotten to stubborn yet, but my mouth didn't work anymore. I couldn't even feel the pain from the darts now, or Caldswell's hands when he slid them under my shoulders to hoist me up. As he carried me unceremoniously toward the emergency exit, the last thing I saw through my darkening vision were the phantoms. There were a dozen of them now, floating along behind me like little glowing ducklings chasing their mother. My mind was drifting so badly that I actually took a breath to apologize to them since I was probably being dragged off to a lab to become the instrument of their extinction. Before I could form the words, though, I fell into unconsciousness, slumping over Caldswell's shoulder as he hauled me onto the waiting shuttle.

I woke up strapped down to a medical bed with a woman cutting off my clothes.

She squeaked when I jerked, jumping back like she thought I was going to bite something off. Which, to be fair, I would have if I could. "Where am I?" I demanded, wincing when the words came out a slurred mess. My body felt like wet sand and my head was killing me. I lay back with a string of garbled curses. The next time I saw Caldswell, he was a dead man.

The woman, a timid-looking lady of indeterminate middle age, looked at something behind me like she was appealing for help, and then I heard a clicking sound, like a little dog running over a polished floor before a handset appeared above my head.

Don't worry, it read. *A decade of drug abuse has rendered Morris incapable of responding normally to sedatives, hence the restraints.*

I pushed against the straps, rolling over just enough to see the xith'cal standing at my bedside. Considering Caldswell had been the one to put me down, waking up to Hyrek didn't even surprise me, though I couldn't say I was happy about it. "Hey," I said, turning back to the nurse. "There's a crazy lizard in here. Cut me loose and I'll take him out before he can eat you."

Hilarious as ever, I see, Hyrek wrote on his screen. He flashed me a wall of sharp teeth before turning his handset back to the woman. *Please continue.*

The woman looked more frightened of me than of the xith'cal, but she obeyed, reaching out to lift my shirt from my body to resume her cutting. Tied up, I couldn't do a thing to stop her, so I turned back to Hyrek, keeping my words steady in the hopes he wouldn't realize how groggy I still was. "What's going on? Where's Caldswell?"

You are being prepped for surgery, and the captain is with Charkov, Hyrek typed before putting down his handset to shine a light into my eyes.

The word "surgery" went through me like an icy splash, but it was hearing that Rupert was with Caldswell that really worried me. That was not going to be a happy reunion. "What kind of surgery?" I asked, working hard to keep the whimper out of my voice.

We haven't decided yet, Hyrek typed once he was done shining his light into every part of my face. *But Commander Martin ordered you be ready for anything the moment we left hyperspace, and I wanted to get that out of the way while you were still being a good patient, meaning asleep. Alas, it seems even four darts' worth of military-grade tranquilizers can't take down the raging Deviana Morris for more than two hours, so here we are.*

I frowned, struggling to take all that in. The room we were in was a tiny closet with barely enough room for Hyrek and the nurse around my bed. Sleek medical equipment covered every inch of the walls except for the door, arranged with the sort of precise economy of space you'd expect from a Terran battleship. There was no window, so I couldn't see if we were in hyperspace, but I had no reason to think Hyrek was lying. If I'd been in Martin's position, I would have gotten me into hyperspace as quickly as possible, too.

I sighed, sinking into my restraints as the nurse finished cutting off my shirt and started working on my bra. I would have felt more self-conscious about being naked in front of strangers, but Hyrek was an asexual alien and the nurse was a nurse. Mostly I felt exposed and vulnerable. I don't do being tied down in front of people who are trying to help me, but being tied down and naked in front of my enemies, even familiar ones like Hyrek, was putting me on edge something fierce. I tried to remind myself that I'd chosen this, chosen to surrender because it was my last chance at making sure my death meant something, but that knowledge didn't stop the trapped animal anger from sending my whole body rigid, especially when Hyrek started prepping my arm to draw blood.

"So," I said, trying to distract myself from the needle Hyrek was shoving into me. "I guess since you're here, you know everything now?"

Hyrek filled three vials before he removed the needle and typed out an answer. *I've known everything since before you were born*, his handset read. *I've worked with Brian Caldswell for over thirty years. If I was still ignorant of the captain's true nature after so long, I would have had to be either dangerously in denial or dangerously stupid.*

He stopped to label the vials and ready an IV before picking up his handset again. *I am also the Eyes' leading expert on symbionts. I accompany the captain to Dark Star station every year to assist in the implantation process.*

The moment he said it, it made perfect sense. Who could have a better understanding of a xith'cal modification in a human body than a xith'cal doctor who specialized in humans? I also wasn't surprised to hear that Hyrek had been in Caldswell's pocket way before I started poking my nose in. He and Basil had always been the most loyal of the captain's crew.

"What about the rest of the *Fool?*" I asked. "Where's Nova and Basil?" I would have thought for sure the captain would have brought Nova to help with her father. That fact that he hadn't struck me as ominous, a feeling that was only confirmed when Hyrek took his time answering.

We exited hyperspace at Dark Star station seven hours ago, his handset read when he turned it to me at last. *The others are still there. Considering the circumstances, the captain thought it would be safer if they remained under supervision.*

"Under supervision," I said, glaring. "You mean in prison, right?"

Hyrek shrugged, and I lay back with a sigh. Poor Nova. Still, compared to how the Eyes usually dealt with people who'd seen things they shouldn't, prison wasn't half bad. "Are they okay?"

The crew of the Glorious Fool is quite adroit at bearing up under difficulties, Hyrek replied, which actually made me feel better. Prison wasn't the same as safe by any stretch, but I was very happy to hear they were alive. At the moment, I was ready to welcome any good news at all.

"Hyrek," I said quietly as he slid the IV into my hand. The nurse had me down to my underwear at this point, leaving me shivering under the restraints. "Am I going to get a chance to talk to Caldswell before they do…whatever it is they're going to do?"

Hyrek blew out a breath as he taped the tube to my skin. *I don't know,* he typed at last. *If you're wondering about the deal you made with the captain, I don't know anything. Things have changed a great deal while we were in hyperspace. But I will let him know you want to speak with him.*

"Thanks," I said. Now that the IV was in my hand, I could feel the pressure of the high-grade drugs on my mind. Since I hadn't even fully shaken off the last round, these grabbed me quick. I lay still as the room began to spin, wondering if I'd ever be clearheaded again. Considering my future, some would consider that a blessing, but I'd always been the sort who preferred to see death coming, and I fought the drugs as long as I could, staring up at the phantoms hanging below the tiny room's ceiling.

There were a lot, I realized dimly. Thanks to the blindly bright medical lamp, I hadn't noticed before, but now I saw there were dozens of phantoms floating above my bed, watching me with that eerie stillness, their little tendrils waving. I stared a moment longer and then closed my eyes against them, turning my head away as the drugs snuffed out the last of my consciousness.

———

Coming back the second time was a lot harder.

I opened my eyes with a heavy gasp, my lungs thumping and shuddering like an old engine as my head reeled from the sudden, stabbing pain at the back of my skull. Sadly, this was actually the highlight. The rest of me was even worse. *Everything* hurt. I felt like I'd just fought a ranked gladiator match without my armor. My skin was tender as a bruise, my tongue swollen, my joints stiff. I couldn't move my legs or my arms, couldn't even shift my weight to take the pressure off my throbbing back. All I could do was lie there and try to breathe through the pain, staring up at the beautiful lights moving across the ceiling.

There were so many, it took me about thirty seconds to realize they were phantoms. I dimly remembered seeing them on the ceiling before I'd gone under, but this was another level. The room was packed to bursting with the little glowing bugs. They were crawling across the ceiling, up the walls, and bobbing in and out of the light fixtures. Still more were hovering in the air all around me, twitching their little tentacles like they were waving hello across the empty space that always separated me from them. I had the distinct feeling that should creep me out, but I was in too much pain to care. And anyway, they were beautiful, their blue-white glow shining down on me like summer moonlight.

Well, I thought, staring up at the beautiful moving lights, at least I wasn't naked anymore. They must have redressed me while I was out, because I was now wearing a loose set of beige medical scrubs with what felt like a whole lot of tape underneath. Probably sensors, or another IV. There were a ton of tubes running out of me, so I had no idea. For all I knew, I didn't even have blood anymore.

Given my general hatred for all things medical, I probably should have cared more about this, but I kept getting distracted by the hair that kept falling into my face. Even in my pain-induced haze, that stuck me as wrong. Rupert had braided my hair so carefully; nothing should be drifting—

Clarity came back in a rush, and I jerked on the table, shoving painfully against my restraints. I tried to lift just my head next, but it was caught by wires. Someone had glued a whole network of neural leads to my skull, and they'd *unbraided my hair* to do it.

Rage hit me like a spark to dry tinder. I'd never felt anything like it before, but the idea that some random Terran had handled me while I was asleep and vulnerable to take away the last thing I had of Rupert mashed every button I had all at the same time. I was so furious I didn't even care that this would flare the virus. They wanted it? They could *have* it. I would kill every last person on this goddamned boat. And when the lelgis came, I'd kill them, too. I'd—

A wave of pain sent me back to the bed like a punch, knocking my plans for vengeance right out of me. It was like someone had thrown a switch and given me twenty-four hours of the universe's worst migraine all at once. There was no breathing through this pain. I couldn't even think beyond it. All I could do was wait and hope that it would fade and something would be left when it did.

And then, while the shock was still working its way through my system, the pain left as suddenly as it had come. I collapsed back onto the mattress, sputtering and confused. A quick check confirmed all the pains I'd woken up with were still there, though they felt like nothing after what I'd just been through, but the headache from hell was completely gone. I looked up at the swarming phantoms, my mind spinning over in hopeless confusion. What had just happened?

"Well, well," said a gruff voice that put me right back on the edge. "Up twenty minutes before you should be. Why am I not surprised?"

The flash of anger I felt at hearing Caldswell's voice brought another stab of pain so intense my eyes watered. Now that I'd experienced it once, I could actually feel the headache rushing toward me like a freighter, and I forced myself to be calm out of self-defense. Usually, such a thing would take me a bit, but that sort of pain is a hell of a good teacher, and I got myself back down to manageable anger real quick. Like it was rewarding me for my good behavior, the pain retreated, and I let out a relieved breath before I tilted my head to see my guest.

Captain Caldswell was sitting in a tiny plastic folding chair at the end of my bed, his feet propped up on my armor case, which he'd leaned against the opposite wall. That sight nearly made me lose control all over again, but I managed to catch my anger before the pain slapped me by focusing on the fact that my Lady was safe with me rather than locked up in some Terran armory. The relief I felt at that was almost enough to excuse the boot the captain was resting on her control panel. Almost.

"Would you get your damn feet off my baby?" I asked, far more politely than I would have if I wasn't strapped to a bed and having

weird, anger-induced flash headaches. Despite the relative politeness of my request, Caldswell didn't remove his feet. When I looked
at his face to see why, I wished I hadn't.

Unlike Rupert, Caldswell had never been any good at hiding
his emotions, and right now he was radiating anger like a furnace.
Being in the same room with that much raw fury while tied down
on my back was enough to make me sweat, but that still didn't stop
me from demanding, "Where's Rupert?"

Caldswell tilted his head back, resting it against the wall. "You
really don't want to ask me about him right now."

No, I really did. "What did you do to him?" I said, pushing up as
much as the restraints allowed. Talking must be helping, or maybe
the migraine had made everything else seem trivial, because I was
shaking off the stiff pain quickly now. There was still plenty to go
around, but I could work though it, and I wasn't going to stop until
I had some answers. "Where is he?"

"He's already been moved to Dark Star Station," Caldswell said,
pulling his feet off my baby at last as he sat up. "And trust me, that's
a mercy. Martin was going to execute him. It's not often done, but
seeing how he helped you fight, kill, and then escape an Eye team,
the top brass felt an example needed to be made. If I hadn't inter-
ceded, he would already be dead, but I pulled some strings and
managed to convince the Scientific Council that killing such an old
and well-adapted symbiont would be an unforgivable waste. He's
a test subject now, their own private symbiont lab rat. Maybe after
a decade or so, they'll let him out of solitary confinement, but he'll
never be an Eye again."

I took a deep breath. A test subject? Death might have been
kinder. I closed my eyes, trying not to think about Rupert in solitary,
Rupert suffering because of me. Trying not to cry. Fortunately, love
hadn't made me weak enough to bawl in front of Caldswell yet,
though it was a near thing. I kept myself together by remembering the bleak despair in Rupert's voice when he'd talked about how

much he hated being an Eye. He might be a Terran lab rat, but at least he'd never have to shoot another daughter. That was some comfort.

"I'm glad," I said at last. "He hated working for you."

"You don't get it at all, do you?" Caldswell snapped, glaring at me harder than ever. "You don't even understand how much damage you've done."

I opened my mouth to shoot him down, but Caldswell cut me off. "Let me tell you a little story about Rupert Charkov. Do you know where his accent's from?"

"It's Svenyan," I said slowly, buying myself time to spot the trap I knew Caldswell was leading me toward.

"That's right," Caldswell said. "We've recruited several agents from the survivors of Svenya, and all of them lost their accent within a decade of working for the Eyes. All except for Rupert. No matter how long he worked or how many languages we made him learn, his Svenyan accent never faded. Not because he couldn't lose it— Rupert can speak perfect Universal if it suits him—but because he *wouldn't*. That's what Charkov does. He *clings*. He holds on to what's important tooth and nail. No matter what we asked of him, he did it perfectly. He never argued, never abused his power, because all he cared about was clinging to what he'd lost and making sure no one else ever suffered that way again. That was his purpose, his all-powering drive, and it allowed him to do anything. He was the best of all of us, and then he met you."

Caldswell stood up then, looming over me until I was pressing myself into the bed to get away from his fury. "You *ruined* him," he said, his voice shaking with rage. "You did more damage in three months than I've seen him take in sixty years. I would know, too. I've been watching over that boy since he was eleven years old. I was the one who got him out of that prison of a refugee camp, who got him his training. And whenever I got sick of running this circus, whenever the Republic bureaucrats stuck some new idiot like Martin, who'd never even fought a phantom, above me, I'd look at Rupert and remember, aha, *that's* why I put up with this shit. Because that little boy lost everything, and he's still fighting. Forty-three years now he's been fighting with us, and then you came along and broke him." Caldswell bared his teeth. "You snapped him up and refused to let go of your prize for anything, even when his hand was wrapped around your throat."

I swallowed before I could think better of it. Caldswell caught the motion, but if anything, his eyes only grew more disgusted. "Don't worry, Charkov didn't tell me that one. I figured it out for myself when Hyrek reported the black market patch job on your neck." He shot me a bitter sneer. "Your trained love bird wouldn't say shit about you even when I was saving his goddamn life."

I'd had about enough of this. "What did you expect him to do?" I shouted, ignoring the growing pain in my head. "Throw me over and beg your forgiveness?"

Caldswell gave me a warning look that I ignored completely. "You're not his father! And even if you were, Rupert's a grown man. You can blame me all you like, but this isn't my fault and you know it. He made his decisions himself!"

"And I'm happy to blame both of you for being goddamn idiots!" Caldswell shouted. "We had a *deal*, Morris. *Your* deal. I would have thought you'd be more committed to it, seeing how you put a gun to your head, but I leave you alone for four goddamn days and you manage to piss off the Paradoxian Home Guard, beat up your retrieval team, kill two Eyes in the process, and then you run to *Ben*, who no one is supposed to know is even connected to us, and—"

That last one threw me. "Ben?"

Caldswell rolled his eyes. "What, you didn't think he was born Nebulon Starchild, did you? When he worked for me, he was Dr. Ben Strauss, and if you'd only waited for me to get back, I could have told you he was too busy navel-gazing to help anyone and saved you a trip."

"We didn't know if you were coming back!" I shouted, slamming my fists on the bed. My anger was rising to match Caldswell's, and though I couldn't blow up like I really wanted to before the pain took me down, I was determined to go right up to the edge. "You were lost in hyperspace! For all we knew, you could have been in there forever. Did you forget I was on a very limited timeline? No one even thought to tell me about Dr. Starchild until Rupert. I wasn't trying to run out on our deal. I just wanted a second opinion." And for all that I hadn't agreed with a word he'd said at the end, Dr. Starchild had given me some very useful information. "Anyway, I refuse to apologize for exploring *my* options since this is *my* death we're talking about."

"When are you going to get it through your thick Paradoxian skull that this *isn't about you?*" Caldswell roared, making me wince. "The virus in your body could save trillions of lives. *Trillions*, and you nearly wasted it. You could have gotten yourself shot on Kessel by some drunk pirate and we'd have lost everything."

"I didn't get shot," I said, though my voice sounded sulky even to me. "Look, I'm not saying I did the exact perfect right thing attacking the Eyes on Kessel, but they came at me like a crash team trying to bag a fugitive." And I took getting jumped on and shot at very personally. "I didn't know when you'd be back and I didn't trust the Eyes without you there. What was I supposed to do? Roll over and let them lock me in a lab?"

"*Yes!*" Caldswell shouted in my face. "Because this isn't about *your* death and *your* demands and how *you* got shot at. This is about doing what's best for *everyone*, and that means getting into a lab as quickly as possible before you start a disaster."

I looked away with a disgusted sound, but Caldswell wasn't finished. "That wasn't even the worst," he said, his voice thick with rage. "The worst, most selfish thing you did in all of this was taking Rupert off the edge with you. I wasn't surprised to hear you'd gone rogue again—you go crazy every time I turn my back—but Charkov was one of us. When he knocked out Natalia, he doomed his career. You made him a traitor because you were too damn proud and stubborn to surrender to any situation where you weren't in charge and getting everything you wanted. All of his suffering from here on is *your fault*."

I didn't need him to tell me that. I wished like hell I'd been faster on the draw outside back at Dr. Starchild's. Rupert would have been furious with me when he'd woken up, but at least he'd be free. Guilty as I felt over it, though, I wasn't about to let Caldswell twist this entirely around on me.

"They shot him," I said. "His own people shot him in the back on Kessel. They didn't even give him a chance—"

"Eyes don't take chances!" Caldswell roared. "Because unlike you, we don't gamble what we can't afford to lose!"

"You're one to talk!" I screamed at him. "You don't have anything left to lose!"

The headache was bearing down on me now, but I didn't give a shit. My anger had me tight by the throat, and I didn't care if it ripped it out. I was going to speak my piece.

"If you really cared about Rupert, you would be happy that he'd let go of his past and started looking ahead," I snarled. "But you don't care about him at all. You're upset that you lost your cold killer, your damn perfect Eye." I wrenched myself up off the bed as far as I could go, almost spitting in his face. "I didn't break Rupert—*you* did. You knew the kind of pressure he was under his whole life. Are you really so shocked that when he found something that wasn't horrible and bloody, he ran with it? Tried his best to protect it? Damn you, Caldswell, you had a family once. You were in love. Have some compassion!"

The moment I said it, I knew I'd gone too far. If Caldswell's anger had been a furnace before, it was a nuclear explosion now. I could almost feel it burning my skin as he stared down at me, and I braced for a tirade. But when he spoke at last, he didn't shout. Quite the opposite, his words were calm, clear, and deadly, which was much, much worse.

"Compassion," he repeated, looking down at me with such old, bitter anger that I dropped my eyes. "It's because of what I did that—"

He broke off with a ragged breath. "It's because of what I did that I can't have compassion," he continued. "You think I don't understand what was going through Rupert's head? Trust me, I know. I've felt all that and more, because whatever lust-fueled infatuation you and Rupert fell into over the last few months, it can't possibly be greater than the love I had for my wife of seventeen years, than the love I had for my daughter." His voice broke, and he shot me an angry look. "Rupert told you what happened to them."

It wasn't a question, but I nodded all the same, and Caldswell closed his eyes. "I'd heard all the warnings," he said quietly. "At that time, though, they were just military safety write-ups. Drab language, no punch. They were easy to dismiss. I was a full commander then, and I thought I was better than the usual soldier who grappled with the symbiont. I thought my love was so great I'd never do anything like the stories, but I was wrong. Terribly, unforgivably wrong, and they were the ones who paid."

He sat back down in the chair then, collapsing into the plastic seat like his legs had given out as he dropped his head to his hands. "Nothing can bring my girls back, Morris," he whispered. "They're gone forever by my own hand, and you want me to have compassion? Sympathy for Rupert for making the same mistake?" His head shot back up, glaring me down. "Why the hell do you think I told him that story?"

I swallowed. "But—"

"But nothing," Caldswell snapped. "There is no room for error in what we do, no margin for forgiveness. Rupert knew that. I told him, I *warned* him over and over, but still he followed you like a lamb to slaughter, and now that it's all gone to hell, you have the gall to ask me for compassion."

He heaved a huge sigh, and I could almost feel the rage leaving him like steam. The sudden change took my own anger with it, and I shifted awkwardly on the bed. I was starting to realize that I wasn't the only one who'd lost Rupert today, and to my surprise, I felt sympathy for Caldswell. I wanted to say something, to offer some kind of comfort, but I didn't know what. I didn't even know if there was comfort for people like us anymore. I was still trying when Caldswell took a deep breath.

He filled his broad chest with air like he was trying to force himself up with it. When he managed to stand at last, he didn't look angry anymore. Just bone tired, staring at me like I was his death and wasn't sure if he wanted to shoot me dead or welcome me with open arms.

"Dammit, Morris," he whispered, scrubbing his hands through hair that had been graying for longer than I'd been alive. "You never make anything easy, do you? Everything would be so much simpler if I could just hate you, but I can't seem to manage it. I know you mean well, and though I still think it was stupid, I understand why you acted as you did. You don't trust the Eyes, and frankly, I don't blame you. We've never given you much cause to trust, but you can't forget that we're all on the same side here. We all want the same thing."

"Do we?"

Caldswell gave me a funny look, but I kept going, because if we were going to have it out today, then I meant to have it *all* out. "Dr. Starchild told me that you were the one who gave Maat to the lelgis to be the wall that stopped new phantoms from coming into our universe. Is that true?"

Caldswell sighed. "Ben has been airing old laundry, I see."

I scowled. That wasn't an answer. "Is that true?" I repeated.

Now it was Caldswell's turn to scowl. "Yes," he said. "And before you ask, no I'm not proud of it, and yes I'd do it again. I did what needed to be done to save us all."

"I believe you," I said, making Caldswell blink in surprise. He clearly had not been expecting me to agree, but I wasn't finished. "I believe that it had to be done in the beginning, but that was decades ago. Maat and her daughters have been suffering for all of us ever since, and that's not fair."

"You sound like Brenton," Caldswell muttered.

"Well, maybe he's right about this," I said, my voice heating. "You know what I think? I think you're afraid. You're afraid to do the right thing because Maat works and you don't want to mess with it. You'd rather let her be a slave forever than even consider a new solution."

"Afraid?" Caldswell said, staring at me like I was nuts. "Of *course* I'm afraid. Have you not been paying attention? We're talking about the end of human life as we know it. Maat is one person. You can't possibly argue that one crazy girl is more important than the security of all mankind."

"Just because she's crazy doesn't mean you can do this to her," I said. "I don't know about you, but I was raised to fight my own fights. This kind of thinking, that the greater good justifies all evils, is exactly why I tried so hard to find some other way to do this that didn't require working with the Eyes. Because I *don't* buy the company motto. I *don't* believe saving trillions of lives excuses all other sins wholesale forever."

I lifted my chin, uncaring that I was on my back for this. For once, that didn't change a thing. "I am prideful," I said. "And stubborn, but this isn't about being proud or stubborn. It's not even about getting everything I want. It's about having a moral standard."

I didn't often get to take the moral high ground. I was a mercenary, a killer for hire, and I made no apologies or excuses for how I lived my life. But while my hands would never be clean, I had honor. I knew where my line was, and I knew the Eyes were firmly on the other side. And even though I no longer had a choice, what with being lashed to a bed and drugged, I knew what was right. That had to count for something.

Caldswell stared at me for a long time after that, and then, slowly, he spread his hands in defeat. "You're not wrong, Morris," he said.

"But you're not right, either. Morals are for people who can afford them, and that's not us. Not with so much on the line. I thought I'd made that clear to you, but I see now that we'll never agree. I'm sorry, I wish things had turned out differently, but this is the end."

I'd thought it was the end when he'd tranq'ed me back at Dr. Starchild's, but apparently things could keep going downhill, because Caldswell was still talking. "Thanks to your stunt on Kessel and that show you put on back at the church, Martin considers you too volatile for any kind of trust. The only reason you're even awake right now is because you're tied down and that IV you're sporting has enough anti-plasmex drugs in it to knock Maat over."

My eyes flicked to the IV needle in my hand. Anti-plasmex drugs? I didn't even know something like that existed, though it would explain my weird anger-related headaches since I apparently reached for plasmex when I got mad. "I guess this means our deal is off, then?"

"Not at all," Caldswell said. "I'm a man of my word. If your virus can be turned into a weapon, and if the lelgis don't kill us all for trying to use it, I'm going to do my best to free the daughters as promised." He shot me a bitter smile. "That was always the plan in the end, you know. I'll try to get the Eyes, too, though targeted phantom killing will be nigh impossible now. Commander Martin was always a political man, but he's been under a lot more pressure to deliver since we lost Unity."

It took me an embarrassingly long time to remember that Unity was the name of the Aeon Sevalis planet destroyed by the emperor phantom, the one I'd seen floating in the rubble and freaked out about, tipping off Rupert that my hallucinations weren't hallucinatory at all. That realization was followed by a flood of guilt that I'd just forgotten about the deaths of billions of aeons, but in my defense, a lot had happened since then. Also, I'd never actually seen the planet in question, just the rubble and the giant space monster, which was a pretty big distraction. Still, the slipup made me feel just awful, and I had to focus to get my mind back on Caldswell.

"...Paradox, even the free colonies are in his ear about it, demanding results," he was saying. "Martin needed a miracle, and then you came back from the dead. The moment he had confirmation that you were alive, he started selling you as the magic bullet solution to his superiors, and they ate it up. The Scientific Council is outfitting a ship right now for long-term hyperspace travel to serve as a safe quarantine where you, or your remains, can be studied until something comes of it."

That made a lot of sense, I thought morbidly. The lelgis couldn't get me in hyperspace, and if my virus went haywire, the plague couldn't spread to the rest of the universe. But that did remind me of a question I'd wanted to ask earlier. "Where are we now?"

"By the Dark Star Station," Caldswell said. "Don't worry, we're well outside of Maat's range, but still closer than the lelgis will ever come."

Because they feared Maat's contagion, I realized. But that wasn't the part of Caldswell's announcement that bothered me. The longer this went on, the more I saw that he was right. This was the end.

I bit my lip. After facing my death so many times, I'd never thought the truth would be so quiet. So anticlimactic, and yet so terrifying. Could the king's death guides even find you in hyperspace? I wanted to ask Caldswell if he could pull some strings to make sure they didn't kill me for good until we were back in the universe, just in case, but copping to such a fear felt cowardly, and I'd been cowardly enough for one day. I'd ask when they moved me to the other ship, I compromised, staring up at the phantoms on the ceiling. Anything to prevent admitting more weakness in front of Caldswell.

I didn't even know why he was still here, actually. I wished like hell he'd just leave me alone so I could have my breakdown in peace. But as I glared at the phantoms on the ceiling so I wouldn't have to look at him any longer, I noticed they were changing.

When I'd first come to, the phantoms had been packed in like a locust swarm above me. Now that swarm seemed to be merging, the smaller phantoms pulling together like drops of water on a slick surface. At first I thought it was just a trick of the light, or maybe I was having a real hallucination at last, but the longer I watched, the more sure I became that it was real. The crowd of tiny phantoms was merging into a single creature before my eyes, a long, flat glowing mass that took up the whole ceiling, complete with tiny, hairlike appendages that were *still* waving at me.

Just when I was getting good and freaked out by this, the mass changed again, growing longer and thicker until one end passed through the wall at my feet. My first thought was that the swarm of phantoms was changing shape again, but when I saw their surface shimmer, I realized they were actually merging into something I couldn't see on the other side of the wall. A second later, the phantom mass changed again, and I saw I was right. The phantoms that had swarmed together on my ceiling had hooked into another group, forming what now looked like a glowing pipe so long only a tiny fraction could fit into my room. It wasn't even doing anything, but the sight alone was enough to make my blood run cold. Just how many phantoms were on this ship?

A hand closed on my shoulder, making me jump, and I tore my eyes off the phantoms to see Caldswell standing over me. "What's wrong?" he asked sharply.

I didn't know how to begin to answer that. The mass of phantoms above my head was now a single phantom far larger than the one I'd killed on the asteroid. I couldn't even see how big it was thanks to the walls, but the bit I could see was undulating, almost like it was part of something even larger than I'd envisioned. *Much* larger. I was wondering just how big it could actually be when the ship's power cut out, leaving only the glow of the phantom as the scream punched into my mind.

CHAPTER

9

The scream went off like a siren, a sharp spike piercing right through the center of my skull. It would have sent me curling into a ball with my hands over my ears if I hadn't been strapped down, not that that would have helped. Just like back in the clearing on Mycant and the emperor at Unity and the poor dead phantom on the asteroid and every single one of these bastards I'd ever encountered, this phantom's scream wasn't a sound. It was a force, as huge and immutable as gravity, and all I could do was grit my teeth and wait for it to end.

But as I lay there trying to keep myself together, a distant part of my mind noted that this scream sounded different from the others. Maybe I was grasping at straws, or maybe I was finally cracking for real, but where most phantom cries sounded angry or pained, this one struck me as excited, like the shout you give when you find something you've been looking for. That didn't stop it from hurting like hell, of course, but there's only so long a body can be shocked into stillness, and a few seconds later, mine had recovered enough to open my eyes…

Just in time to see the glowing tentacle slam down right by my head.

I rolled sideways on instinct, straining as far as the straps would allow, but that didn't save me when the equipment bank beside me exploded into shrapnel. The phantom's aura had killed the ship's power, which meant I didn't get showered in sparks when the breaker came off the wall, but I still ended up with a lattice-work of thin cuts down my right arm and toxic-smelling plastic dust everywhere.

I was still coughing to clear my lungs when I saw the glowing mass rise up again for another blow. Tied down as I was, though, I couldn't do anything to get away. Fortunately, Caldswell was already on it.

Whatever our differences, the captain and I had always been on the same wavelength when it came to trouble. He couldn't see the phantom like I could, but he'd been at my side when it had crashed down. By the time it lifted up again, he had his claws out and was slicing through my restraints. The second he was done, he shoved his arms under me, yanking me off the bed a split second before the phantom flattened it.

The crash of breaking metal was deafening in the tiny room, but the phantom didn't lift up for another blow. Instead, the glow-ing appendage that had been hundreds of tiny phantoms less than a minute ago froze, almost like it was taking stock of the situation. But then, just as I leaned against Caldswell's hold for a better look, the glowing flesh dimmed and sank through the floor like a ghost, plunging the room into darkness. I was blinking to adjust my eyes when I realized Caldswell was calling my name.

"Morris!"

"What?" I asked, looking up.

"You tell me," he said, his voice growling with annoyance as he tugged the now useless IV tube out of my hand. "What the hell was that?"

"A phantom," I said, reaching up to dig the sensors out of my hair.

"I guessed that much," Caldswell snapped. "How big? How many?"

I bit my lip. How to answer that? "One," I decided finally. "And really big."

It was too dark to see the captain's face, but I could feel his scowl. "Define 'really.'"

The room was about eight feet long, but the thing the little phantoms had formed had been much bigger. I'd taken to thinking of it as a tentacle because that's what it looked like. Now, though, I was starting to wonder if that wasn't more accurate than I realized. Phantoms came in all different shapes, but the ones with tentacles tended to have long ones. A piece of this one was big enough to fill an eight-foot-long room, which meant the creature it belonged to would have to be ship sized, if not bigger.

"I think it's an emperor," I said honestly. "Or whatever the next step down is. Big enough to take on the ship."

Caldswell cursed loudly, shifting me in his arms to reach for his com, but it was dark just like everything else. He cursed again and shoved it back in his pocket. "Come on."

Before I could ask where, he'd tossed me over his shoulder and turned to the door, which, with the power out, was locked tight. Not that that stopped Caldswell. I'd barely gotten my balance on his shoulder before he kicked it down, his foot going through the metal like it was paper.

The hall outside was just as dark as the room we'd left. Whatever the phantom did, it worked on the self-powered emergency lights as well as it did on the other systems. By some miracle, the gravity was still working, but everything else was dead, leaving only darkness and chaos. I couldn't see a thing, but I could hear the soldiers shouting. That didn't stop Caldswell, though. Even though I knew he was as blind as I was, he cleared the busted door and started running into the dark without missing a beat.

"Where the hell are we going?" I asked, clinging to him for dear life as I tried in vain to find the patch of darkness behind us that was the door to my room. "My suit's back there!"

"Forget it. It wouldn't work anyway," Caldswell said, hopping over something I couldn't see. "Our only hope is to get to the bridge." I felt his chest tense as he bellowed, "Officer coming through!"

I couldn't see the soldiers, but I heard them clear the hall, giving

Caldswell a wide berth as he raced forward. "Mabel has a daughter on board," he went on, like nothing had happened. "Her aura can restore enough power for us to get to a fighter and jump. The drugs should keep the virus down long enough to—"

He broke off with a gasp as a huge clang reverberated through the ship, and everything pitched sideways. For one terrifying second, the enormous battleship rocked like a skiff on a stormy sea, and then the gravity sputtered out at last, flinging us into the ceiling.

Thanks to Caldswell's bellow, the soldiers had moved out of our way, so we didn't crash into anyone. Caldswell let me go when we hit, and even my rubbery limbs were enough to catch myself without gravity to weigh me down. The ship stopped spinning after a few seconds, and for a crazy moment, I thought they'd actually gotten the thrusters back online. But then I heard it, the same horrible creaking noise I'd heard on the *Fool*, and even though there was no gravity, my whole body started to sink.

"It's wrapped around the ship," I said, my blind eyes darting in the dark.

"I'm well aware," Caldswell muttered beside me, and then I felt his hand on my arm before he yanked me forward. "Stick to the plan," he said, dragging me around until I was pointed the right direction. "We go up this hall until we hit the central elevator shaft. From there, we..."

He was still talking, giving directions in that clipped captain's voice of his, but I'd stopped listening, because I'd just realized I could see. Some part of the ship must still have power, because there was a light up ahead, and it was getting brighter. I grinned and turned to Caldswell to make sure he saw it, too, but the captain wasn't even looking at the light.

And that was when my sinking feeling doubled, because that was when I realized the captain didn't see the light at all. Neither did the soldiers I could now clearly see clinging to the walls around us. No one did but me, because it wasn't a light. It was the phantom.

I'd been unconscious when they'd loaded me onto the battleship, so I'd never actually seen the dark hall we were climbing through. Now I didn't know if I'd ever forget the sight of that plain, straight, efficient, military ship's hall lit up with the bluish moonlight glow of the enormous phantom tentacle sliding through the closed off elevator shaft at the far end like a ghost. I couldn't say if this was the same tentacle that had nearly smashed me earlier, but I didn't think it was. First, this one was reaching in from the opposite direction, and second, it looked even bigger. That one had been as wide as my bed once it had finished forming. This one was big enough to nearly fill the five-foot-wide hall.

It looked more transparent than the one before, too, but when it had reached in far enough to cross the first of the doors that lined the hall, its rounded tip grew suddenly brighter, and the door exploded inward like it had been hit with mortar shell. Considering it could go through walls, knocking down a door seemed pretty pointless, but when the tentacle turned to slide into the room it had blown open, passing through the screaming soldiers who floated out to root around inside, I suddenly realized what was going on. The phantom was looking for something, something it couldn't drag through a wall, and I had a pretty good idea what.

"Caldswell," I said, cutting off his instructions. "The phantom's inside. We have to go another way."

He stopped at once. "Where?"

I pointed before I remembered he couldn't see. "Did you hear the bang up ahead?" I said instead. "That was it blowing out a door. It's about to hit another one."

As though my words were the signal, the tip of the phantom's tentacle brightened again, and the second door flew off its track, slamming into the wall on the far side of the room. Caldswell hissed as the sound echoed down the hall. "What the hell is it doing?"

"Looking for something," I said. *Looking for me*, I added to myself as I tugged on Caldswell's sleeve. "We need to get out of here."

"That's what we're trying to do," the captain snapped.

"No, I mean we have to get out of this hall," I said, letting him go and pushing off the ceiling with my feet. "Right now."

Caldswell grabbed blindly, catching my foot by pure luck. "You're not going anywhere."

A stab of annoyance hit me, followed by a flash of pain as the remainders of the anti-plasmex drug did their job. Now that I was off the IV, my system was clearing out and the pain wasn't nearly so bad, but it was still sharp enough to make me gasp, and the light at the end of the hall brightened as the phantom's tentacle froze. And then, like a hunting snake, it yanked out of the room it had been rummaging through and snapped back into the hall, coming up with its tip pointed directly at me.

The blood drained from my face. "I need to go now," I said, yanking against Caldswell's hold, but his fingers only tightened on my foot.

"I am not—"

I kicked. Hard. Slamming his hand into the ceiling. If he'd been human, I would have broken his fingers, but since Caldswell was a tried and true monster, I was just aiming to weaken his grip. And for a second, it worked. His hand opened enough for me to snatch my foot away, but before I could pull more than an inch, he grabbed me again, his fingers locking around the arch of my bare foot in a vise.

"Morris!" he snarled, but I barely heard him, because that was when the phantom's tentacle lunged at me.

"No!" I screamed, writhing out of the way. "Let go!"

The tentacle was fast but not agile. It must have been hard for such a huge creature to move such a tiny part of itself, because even though Caldswell had ruined my dodge, it missed me by a mile, landing with a flat thump on the ceiling beside us. Part of it actually phased through the metal before it brightened again, ripping a fair-sized chunk out of a support beam when it pulled back for another try.

It was such an odd sight I actually paused for a moment. The phantom must have to concentrate to interact with the physical world, I realized. That was what the brighter glow meant. Maybe if I aimed for the dimmer parts, I could pass through the phantom just like it passed through everything else and get away?

It was a crap plan to be sure, but I ran with it. There was nothing else to do. The phantom's tentacle was already racing toward me again, knocking floating debris out of the way as it flew at my stomach like a spear.

Funny enough, it was the lack of gravity that saved me. In a move I never could have pulled off otherwise, I braced my leg against Caldswell's grip and swung sideways, using his hand on my foot as a pivot for my entire body. The tentacle missed me again, but this time, instead of slamming into the ceiling, it slammed into a soldier I hadn't noticed coming up behind us. It was glowing at the time, and it hit the poor woman like a missile, throwing her all the way back down the hall to slam against the far wall so hard I heard her bones crack.

"What the hell is going on?" Caldswell shouted at me.

"The phantom!" I shouted back, reaching out to grab the wall so I'd have something to push off. "It's after me. You have to let me go!"

Caldswell's grip tightened on my foot, and I bit down against the stream of swear words I wanted to lay into him. Satisfying as chewing him out would be, I didn't have the time. He had ample reason to think I'd run. I'd run from him every time before. What I needed was to make him understand, so with a will I'd never known I possessed until this moment, I forced my voice to be calm and reached up to grab his shoulder.

"Listen," I said, squeezing hard. "I swear to the king this isn't an escape ploy. But there's a phantom tentacle in the hall with us right now that's already grabbed for me twice, and unless you let me go, I don't think I can dodge it again. So would you *please* release my foot and help me get out of here?"

Though I knew he couldn't see me, Caldswell turned toward my voice in the dark, his face set in such a scowl I didn't think he was going to listen. But then he nodded, unlocking his death grip on my foot. "Which way?"

Since he couldn't see, I grinned in triumph. "Back," I said, scrambling over him.

At this point, my fight-or-flight instinct was pinned firmly on flight, and the corresponding adrenaline rush was rapidly cleaning the remaining drugs from my system. Instead of hurting, my body felt wired and ready as I wedged my hand against a support beam and shoved myself backward, flying down the hall away from the phantom like a shot.

Other than my short jaunt in the Church of the Cosmos, I hadn't been weightless outside my suit in years, but the need to get away filled the void left by experience. Caldswell followed right behind me, kicking off the walls with practiced ease. We'd nearly made it back to my busted door and the rest of what I could now see was the medical area when the tentacle attacked again.

This time, I was ready. I flattened myself against the wall to let it pass, already plotting my next push to get around the corner into the next long, drab hall. I didn't even know where I was going, other than away, but as I prepared to jump, the tentacle snapped back and up unexpectedly, brushing against my leg in the process.

The first thing I felt was cold. Even through the fabric of my scrubs and the tape beneath, the phantom's slick surface seemed to leach the heat right out of me, making me gasp. The touch must have surprised the phantom as well, because the tentacle froze against me.

Looking back, that should have been my chance. I should have kicked off, dropped down, anything. But I was too shocked by the chill to move, and that was my undoing.

Quick as a whip, the tentacle wrapped around my leg and plucked me off the wall. I saw Caldswell's hand shoot out for me when I yelped, but he was miles too late. The tentacle was already dragging me up the hall toward the elevator, its slimy, freezing coils sliding up my body until they'd wrapped me to the neck.

I fought them the whole way, but it was like trying to wrestle an icy current. The phantom's flesh was slick as oiled gelatin under my fingers and even colder than the one I'd touched in the xith'cal's asteroid. My whole body was numb in seconds, but even though I couldn't feel my hands, I kept punching anyway. There was nothing else I could do.

"Let me go!" I screamed, my voice shrill with fear and frustration. "Goddamn you, idiot monster! I'm going to kill you if you *don't let go!*"

And I was, too, because the drugs were gone now. Numbed by the phantom's cold, I couldn't feel the pins and needles, but I didn't need to. I could see the black stain spreading up my arms in the monster's light, and my heart began to hammer so hard I thought I'd pass out.

"No!" I screamed, writhing against its grip harder than ever. I absolutely refused to die this way, but I didn't see how else this was going to end. Already the phantom had yanked me around the corner and away from the elevator Caldswell had been going for, dragging me through a pair of blown out doors into a huge open space, but it wasn't until we passed the first row of neatly arranged single-pilot ships that I realized it had taken me into the battleship's fighter bay.

My heart began to pound even harder. The lights were out here, too, but I could see the bay's enormous doors clearly in the phantom's glow, the stars glittering like pinpricks in the dark through the huge exterior windows, and I knew what it was doing at last. The phantom was going to drag me outside, kill me with the vacuum before the virus could touch it.

That thought made me go absolutely insane. I hadn't gone through all this shit, hadn't lost Rupert, hadn't swallowed my pride and gone back to the Eyes, to die like *this*. It insulted every sense

I had, and I fought wildly, snarling like a trapped animal. I was getting ready to bite the damn thing when the phantom stopped moving.

I stopped as well, blinking as I looked around. We were at the very edge of the battleship's fighter bay, right beneath the huge doors that opened when they scrambled the fleet, the ones I'd expected the phantom to smash open. But though the tentacle passed through the jointed metal in front of me, it remained semi-transparent, incorporeal as a projection. In fact, the only part of the phantom that was still shining bright enough to be physical was the bit wrapped around me. Apparently, we weren't going outside, at least not yet. I was wondering why it had brought me here, then, when the phantom jerked me up.

The move came without warning, snapping my neck painfully. By the time I recovered, I was twenty feet in the air, flying up past the doors toward the huge observation windows above them. As the phantom lifted me past the window's bottom edge, harsh white light broke like a sunrise, and my panting breath vanished completely.

Through the huge window I could see the full sweep of the ship's port side, as well as a second battleship floating in formation with ours. The other ship was unexpected, but they could have had the entire Republic Starfleet out there and I wouldn't have given them more than a passing glance. My eyes were only for the phantom.

As I'd told Caldswell, it was indeed wrapped around the ship, though not like I'd expected. I'd imagined a giant squid clutching the battleship in its tendrils, but the emperor looked more like a nest of beautiful, glowing snakes that had simply cozied up to us. There were so many overlapping parts, I couldn't actually tell where the phantom began until the shimmering mass in front of me shifted, and its head came into view.

Normally, I had a hard time determining which part of a phantom was which. They seemed to follow no rules, at least none I was familiar with. But while I'd seen phantoms with thousands of jointed legs and phantoms that were little more than blobs, I'd never seen one with eyes until right now.

Its head was clearly delineated, a huge and majestic sweep of glowing flesh leading up to four perfectly round spheres. They were bulging and beady, like the eyes of a shrimp, but they glowed the most beautiful, deep blue I'd ever seen. And though, since they had no pupils, there was no way I should have been able to know they were looking at me, I felt that fathomless gaze locked on my face, all four eyes glittering with intelligence as they looked me over.

As we stared at each other, a bolt of pure cold slid into my chest, making my heart stutter. Even with that, I had to struggle to tear my eyes away from the phantom's in order to see what had stabbed me. But when I looked down, my chest was uninjured. What I'd felt was the tip of the phantom's now transparent tentacle passing through my ribs into my body.

It was astonishingly cold, but it didn't actually hurt. At least, it didn't hurt me. The phantom, on the other hand, gave a deep moan that set my teeth on edge, but it didn't let go. Instead, it slid the tentacle in farther until I could feel the icy edge of it inside my lungs. And then, right before my eyes, the tentacle in my chest began to turn black.

For a second, all I could do was stare as the black ink swirl of the virus began to seep up the beautiful glow of the phantom's body. I was still staring at it when the world fell away, plunging me into the dark.

————

Just like all the times before, my journey into the oneness happened in an instant. This time around, though, I at least knew what to expect. The second the universe vanished, I braced, ready to face the others, the crowd of lelgis I knew were waiting in the dark. And that's where things took a turn for the unusual, because when I opened my eyes—something, by the way, I'd never realized I could do here—it was no longer dark.

I was floating weightless in the nothing, and hanging in front of me like a silver moon was the emperor phantom. It looked just as it had when I'd seen it from the window with its clear blue eyes and beautiful snaking tendrils, only there was no window anymore. There was no battleship either, no stars, nothing. Just the phantom and myself floating in the infinite dark.

No, that wasn't quite right. As my mind adjusted to the beautiful monster filling my vision, I realized I could still feel the unseen watchers out in the dark beyond. I looked around, craning my neck, but the phantom's glow ruined my vision, or what passed for vision in this place. All I could see beyond the glimmer of its moon-white light was blackness as thick as tar, and so I gave up, turning back to face the monster I could see.

"Okay," I said, folding my arms over my chest, which I could now see was covered in the same medical scrubs I'd been wearing back in reality. "You brought me here. Now, what do you want?"

I can't tell you how stupid I felt shouting across what had to be miles of emptiness. Now that I'd lost all points of reference, it was hard to actually tell how big the phantom was, or how far away, other than *very*. But the lelgis had been able to talk to me here no problem, and I figured the phantom, being plasmex as well, would be the same. So I waited, clearing my mind for an encore of the strange mix of impressions and words the lelgis queens had put me through when Reaper died.

What I got was a roar.

The phantom shifted, lifting its mass of snakelike tentacles as it made a deep, musical sound. "Hurrrrrrrrrrrrrm."

The call was so loud I could feel it to my core, churning my guts until I thought I was going to be sick, but what really got me was the fact that it was a *sound*. Not a psychic message or a scream-that-wasn't-a-scream, but a real, make-your-ears-ache noise that went on for almost a minute before finally trailing off. Then, after a few seconds of blessed silence, the phantom roared again, even louder this time.

"HURRRRRRRRRRM," it roared. *"HURRRRRRRRRRM!"*

I clapped my hands over my ears, but my palms were a poor guard against the vibrations rolling through me like an earthquake. I had no idea what this was about or why I was here or what the hell this phantom thought it was going to gain by yelling at me, but the whole mess was giving me a splitting headache. Worse, the phantom seemed just as frustrated as I was. The whole time it sat there *hurrm*ing, it was staring at me with those huge eyes, waving its huge tentacles in increasingly sharp motions, like it was trying to tell me something and it was angry that I wasn't getting it.

"What?" I shouted in the gaps. "What are you trying to tell me? What do you want me to do?"

The phantom waved its tentacles more frantically than ever, and then it stopped, tapping the ends of its appendages together in a way that gave me the distinct impression it was thinking. After almost a minute of this, it reached its two longest tentacles out toward me, tightening the coils in its snake nest body to get enough slack. I worried it was going to make a grab for me, but the phantom's tentacles stopped a few dozen feet away. For a second, I was stuck again by how huge it was, and how beautiful. Its body glowed like water lit from within, sparkling in the dark as the longer of the two tentacles bent to form a rectangle.

It was a nice rectangle, too. The phantom's squishy flesh squeezed itself neatly into four perfect corners. Of course, I still didn't know what the hell "rectangle" was supposed to mean, but it was nice to see something recognizable. Just when I was starting to feel like maybe we could work with this, though, the phantom took its second tentacle and placed it in front of the rectangle, blocking it from view. Then, slow and deliberately, it pulled the covering tentacle away.

"Hurrrrrrrrrrrm," it sang when the rectangle was fully revealed again. "Hurrrrrm."

I folded my arms over my chest, wracking my brain as I tried to guess what that could mean. I sucked at puzzles in general, and this was way out of my league. I bit my lip, wishing with all my might that Rupert were here. He was clever at this sort of thing, and he knew a ton about languages. He could probably figure this out. But he wasn't here, and I didn't have the first clue what the phantom wanted, or how to tell it I was stumped.

"Hurrrrrrrrrrrm," the phantom called again, moving its tentacle back and forth in front of the rectangle like it was playing peekaboo. "HURRRRRRRRRRRM!"

"I hear you!" I shouted. "I'm trying, okay?"

"Horrrrrrrrum," it said, varying the intonation until it sounded like whale song from the largest, angriest whale imaginable. "Hoooooorum. Hoooooooooooorum."

I felt like ripping my hair out. God and king, why of all the people in the universe did this stupid alien pick me to play charades with? What the hell was a horum? I couldn't even think with the phantom roaring like that, so I tuned it out as best I could, combing my brain as I tried to remember if I'd heard that word before in any context. I even tried to search Rupert's memories, which was incredibly hard with nothing to help trigger them, but he didn't have anything either so far as I could tell. I was pretty sure "horum" wasn't even a word, but when I looked up to tell the phantom I had nothing and this was a waste of time, I realized its roar had changed again.

"Hooooooome," it sang, looking at me as its tentacle went back and forth, the motion no longer just revealing and hiding the rectangle, but pivoting against it, like a door opening and shutting. "Hoooooooome."

And just like that, the puzzle fell into place. "Home," I repeated, my face breaking into a grin. "You want to go home."

The phantom dropped its tentacles, and though I might well have been imagining things, I would have sworn its blue eyes looked happy. "Hoooooome," it roared, making my ears ring. "Hoooooooome!"

"You want to go back," I said, getting excited as well. I could almost hear Dr. Starchild's voice in my head telling me that Maat was the wall that held back the flood of phantoms. But walls worked both ways. In cutting off the place where their universe broke through into ours, we'd kept new phantoms from entering, but we'd also prevented the ones who were already here from *leaving*. By plugging the hole, we'd cut off their way home. But even as the thrill of solving the riddle raced through me, I realized it didn't make sense. "Wait," I said. "Why are you telling me about this?"

The phantom dropped the rectangle and reached out its tentacle again, stretching until the tip was barely touching me. I paused, waiting, but the creature didn't move. It just hung there, motionless, pointing at me with a glowing tentacle that seemed to be getting shorter.

I took a hissing breath. The tentacle wasn't getting shorter; it was getting dimmer. Its light was going out, eaten from the tip by a creeping black stain.

I jerked away with a curse. My virus was crawling up the emperor phantom's tentacle like ink seeping up paper. At my horrified sound, the phantom pushed its dying tentacle at me in a motion that seemed to say *See what you've done?* But I didn't see. I didn't know—

Stay away.

The words exploded into my head so suddenly I would have jumped twice my height if my feet had had anything to press down on. They didn't, though, so I just kicked, craning my neck out of a frantic, instinctive need to see where the threat was. Frantic and futile, because I couldn't see anything except the phantom. It didn't matter, though; I knew that voice. Or, rather, voices. But just when I was sure I was wasting my time, I spotted something moving out in the dark beyond the phantom's light.

I'd felt the lelgis when I'd first arrived, before the phantom had distracted me. I'd known they were out there, watching. Now, though, I could feel their hate and fear like bugs crawling over my skin. *We warned you, death bringer,* they whispered in the dark. *We told you, never return.*

The words hit me like slaps, but I barely noticed. I was too focused on the great, black, mountain of a shape rearing up out at the light's edge. I'd seen the lelgis queens before, in the vision they'd showed me of Caldswell bringing them Maat, but that had been just a glimpse, an impression of something enormous and alien. I still couldn't see them clearly because they stayed in the shadows, keeping away from the phantom's glow, but I could make out the glassy reflections of millions of eyes set in bodies even larger than the phantom before me coupled with slick flashes of long, sharp barbs the size of battleships creeping in the dark, waiting for their chance to strike.

You will not undo our work, they hissed, their voices like cutting claws in my mind. *Be gone.*

Like before, the word was accompanied by a blow meant to knock me out of the oneness. This time, though, I didn't go anywhere. Right before the hit had landed, the phantom had wrapped its dying tentacle around my waist, holding me in place as it turned on the monsters in the dark and roared. Not the plaintive whale song it had sung for me, but a true bellow of fury. And as the sound filled the emptiness, the lelgis screamed in reply, their voices shrill and terrified as they skittered back into the shadows.

Once the lelgis had retreated, the phantom turned back to me, dropping the tentacle it had used to catch me, which was now completely black. I expected it to cradle its dying limb, or at least show some sign of pain. Instead, the phantom used the second of the two tentacles it had reached toward me, the one that was still moon bright and uninjured, to form the rectangle again. Once the shape was made, it placed the tentacle I'd infected, the one that was now crumbling into black dust, in front of the pantomime door.

"Home," it said again, its whale song voice filled with longing. "Home."

As the last of the phantom's plea rumbled through me, I couldn't help thinking that I should have guessed the truth a long time ago. Maat had told me herself that the phantoms were prisoners and she was their jailer. She'd told me, too, that the phantoms were the ones who told her to find me. Small voices, she'd said.

I smiled at the enormous emperor. Apparently, I got the big one. But then, I needed it. They'd been trying to get my attention ever since I'd left Reaper's ship, but I hadn't spared them a thought other than annoyance. Now, though, I heard them at last, and I understood. Maat was the door, the force that kept them in, and as she'd always told me, my virus was the only thing that could kill her. The only way I could set the phantoms free. Before I did, though, there were a few things I had to be sure of.

"Will you *all* go home?" I asked, gazing up at the phantom shining like the moon above me, tilting my head back to stare into the bluest of its eyes like I could make it understand my question through sheer will. "If I open that door, will you and all your kind leave us in peace?"

The phantom made a deep keening sound, and then, slowly, it reached with its remaining clean tentacle, the one my virus hadn't destroyed, and pressed the tip gently into my chest.

I hadn't felt its other touches in the oneness, not when it had taken my virus the first time or when it had steadied me against the lelgis, but I felt this one loud and clear. Just like when it had gone into my chest in the real world, its flesh was unbearably cold. Cold enough to knock my breath out, like I'd jumped naked into an icy lake, and in the moment when my body seized up, the vision filled me.

It wasn't like the lelgis' many layered images or Rupert's memories with their intense feelings. It wasn't even like the daughter's hand in my mind. I'd been on a ship with aliens and visited the farthest reaches of known space. I'd fought lelgis and felt an entire xith'cal tribe die one by one, but I'd never felt anything as alien as the phantom's touch in my mind. I didn't even think I had all the senses I needed to process the confusing torrent of experiences it was pouring into me, but below all the stuff I was sure I could never understand was a basic need that I got completely: hunger. Horrible, crippling, overwhelming hunger.

For one terrible moment, I saw our universe as the phantoms must: a great, barren waste without food or shelter. They'd come as explorers, but when Maat had closed the door, they'd gotten trapped in a land of death and hunger and darkness, and they couldn't go home.

The vision vanished in a flash as air exploded back into my body. I floated panting in the nothing as my brain tried to recover, but I wasn't sure there *was* a recovery from this. Even now that I was alone in my head again, I could feel the alien echo of the phantom in my brain, and when I looked down at my own body, at the faint glimmer of plasmex I could now see shining under my skin below the black film of the virus, part of me saw it as food. Thin, terrible, insufficient food.

"You eat plasmex," I said dumbly, more to myself than to the phantom. Dr. Starchild had said as much, but I'd never really understood. Never known. "You're starving," I said, my head shooting up. "That's why you want to go—"

The word died on my lips. When the phantom's cold had left my body, I'd assumed it was because it had removed its tentacle. Now I saw I was wrong. The tentacle was still pressed against my chest, but it was black as the void around us. *All* of it.

When the phantom had taken the virus into itself before to make a point, the darkness had crept slowly, eating the phantom's light in little bites. But if that had been a drop, then whatever the phantom had done to pour the knowledge of its home into my head must have been a mainline, because in the few seconds I'd been out, my sickness had overwhelmed the emperor phantom completely.

The beautiful snake's nest of tentacles was now a blackened knot, and where the virus hadn't yet reached, it was spreading in waves. I could actually see the light vanishing before my eyes, but I didn't understand why. It had formed itself out of smaller phantoms, hadn't it? Why didn't it break apart again? Cut off the sickness and go back to how it was?

But the phantom did no such thing. It just hung there, its blue eyes watching me even as they succumbed to the dark, and I couldn't do a damn thing but watch back as the phantom died.

"Home." Its booming voice was thin and brittle now, but the word was clearer than ever as its last glowing tentacle, the last light of its entire body, reached up to point at my face.

I met it on instinct, grabbing the offered tentacle with both my hands. I didn't even have a name for the emotion tearing through me. No word seemed big enough. I hadn't understood before, but I knew now on a deep, primal level that this phantom had given up its life so that I would believe. It had sought me, found me, *grabbed* me knowing that I was death so that it could show me the truth. Even now, I could feel its longing, the phantom's—maybe *all* phantoms'—desperate need to go back, and as the last of its light faded, I swore.

"I'll take you home," I whispered. "On my honor, by my king, I swear it. I will open the door. I will end this. All of it."

I don't know if the phantom heard me. I don't know if it understood. But as the final light snuffed out, the tip of the enormous, snakelike tentacle curled very slightly around my hand, brushing my fingers like a promise, and it was enough. And as the darkness fell again and I felt the lelgis returning, I was not afraid. I didn't fight or answer or acknowledge the wordless rush of rage and fear that threatened to stomp my mind to nothing. I just closed my eyes and let go, falling out of the dark and back into my freezing body.

———

When I opened my eyes again, the lights were back on and Caldswell was in my face.

"Morris!" he yelled, his voice hoarse, like he'd been yelling for a while. I also caught a hint of panic, though that part might have been my imagination. *"Morris!"*

I rolled away from him with a groan, curling into a ball on my side. God and king I was cold. Cold and achy, like I'd just woken up from death itself. But when I reached up to rub my eyes, my hand felt funny, almost like it was asleep.

My eyes popped fully open and I sat up with a gasp, holding my hands in front of me. Sure enough, they were black as the void outside, but the mark was already fading, slipping away down my arms. Usually that would have made me feel better, but now all I felt was tired. Tired and empty and flat, like I should lie down and never move again. But I couldn't, because as the pins and needles faded, I could still feel the slick residue of the dead phantom on my fingers, reminding me of what I had to do.

I took a deep breath and looked around to check where I was. Still in the fighter bay was the answer, though it took me a moment to recognize the place with the lights on. They must not have moved me at all, because I was lying right below the window where the phantom had lifted me up. I could hear alarms blaring from other decks of the battleship, but other than Caldswell, I was alone in the huge hangar. That struck me as odd for a second before I saw the blast doors over the exits were in lockdown position. Of course. Caldswell had quarantined the area.

"Morris," he said again, leaning closer. "You okay?"

"Yeah," I said with a sigh, wiping my now virus-free hands on my baggy scrubs only to realize that my pants were also covered in the phantom's slick slime. "I think so."

"Good," Caldswell snapped, reaching down to grab my arm and haul me to my feet. "Because I need you to tell me what just happened. The emperor's field isn't jamming us anymore and it released you. Why? Did it go back into hyperspace?"

I blinked, caught off guard. I opened my mouth to tell him the emperor hadn't come out of hyperspace at all, that it had formed itself out of the millions of tiny phantoms, but one look at his face told me I should skip the particulars and get right to the point. "It's not gone," I said, finding it surprisingly difficult to get the words out. "It's dead. I killed it."

Caldswell's eyes widened, and then his face fell into a relieved smile, but before he could congratulate me, I held up my hand. "That's not a good thing," I said. "Listen, I'm not sure how to explain this, so I'm just going to lay it out. That phantom didn't come randomly. It came to talk to me."

The captain's eyebrows shot up, and I took another deep breath. Oh boy, where to begin?

"They want me to set them free," I said at last. "The door Maat holds closed isn't just keeping new phantoms out. It's also keeping the old ones *in*. They don't want to be here. They want to go home but they can't because Maat's in the way. The phantom came to explain that to me."

Caldswell's face, which had been growing more and more skeptical as I spoke, was now set in a firm scowl. "It told you, did it?" he said. "The phantom just popped in to talk to you?"

"Yes," I snapped. "Sort of. That's not the point." I leaned closer, dropping my voice even though there was no one to hear. "Look, Caldswell, I think this is the solution we've been looking for. The phantoms don't want to fight. They never did. They eat plasmex. That's why they're drawn to inhabited planets. The fact that they destroy things in the process is pure accident. They're not our enemies. They don't want to kill us or wipe us out. They just want to go home where there's food, but Maat's in their way. All we have to do is take down the barrier she puts up and, bam, we fix the phantom problem."

Like saying the words out loud made them real, my whole body started to shake with excitement. "Don't you see?" I asked, grinning. "We don't have to use the daughters or the virus to kill them. We don't have to kill them at all. All we have to do is clear the way and they'll leave on their own!"

By the time I'd finished, hope had filled me to bursting. After days of fighting, even resigning myself to death on the mere hope for a compromise, I felt like I'd just been given another chance at everything. Thanks to the phantom, I'd solved the unsolvable problem, and now everyone could live, maybe even *me*. Just the idea made me want to jump around and sing for joy, and in my happiness, I didn't see the deadly frown stealing over Caldswell's face until it was too late.

"The phantom told you this?"

"Yes," I said, my smile fading. "But—"

"And you believed it?"

"Yes," I said again, staring at him. "Caldswell, it *died* to tell me. Of course I believe it."

"There's no 'of course' about it," he said, his voice rising. "I thought you were smarter than this, Morris. If you close off the path of attack for an invasion force, do you go open it again because the surrounded soldiers caught on the inside tell you to?"

"It's not like that!" I cried. "They're not soldiers and this isn't an invasion. They just want—"

"You don't know that," Caldswell said, crossing his arms. "Intent doesn't change the crime. Even if they meant no harm, phantoms destroy everything. They disrupt the flow of space and time just by their presence. What's to say if we open that door we won't just be trading out new phantoms for the old?"

"That won't happen," I said. "They know there's no food for them here now. Compared to what they're used to, our universe is a desert. If you'd just open the door for a moment you'd see."

Caldswell's face went from angry to incredulous. "You honestly expect me to open the floodgates for the phantoms and possibly undo seven decades of work because you saw something in a dream? Are you completely out of your skull?"

I glowered, grinding my teeth in frustration. It was hard to be really mad at Caldswell, though. Had our positions been reversed, I would have been a lot less kind. But I *knew* I was right. I just didn't know how to make him believe. I was still trying to think of something when Caldswell held up his hand.

"I can see your wheels turning," he said. "But you're wasting your time. Even if I did buy your story as told, I can't open the door. The setup the lelgis created with Maat is a combination of machinery and plasmex mumbo jumbo even I don't understand, but I know it's not something you can just turn on and off. Whatever the lelgis did to her that lets Maat hold the universe closed, it's forever. It doesn't matter if she's completely nuts or drugged catatonic, her barrier never goes down. The only way to open the door is if Maat dies, and that's completely off the table."

"But Maat wants to die," I said, pleading. "You *know* how much she wants to die, Caldswell. This is our chance to break this endless cycle, to set us all free. Dr. Starchild said Maat could possibly remove my virus, and that if she did, she would die with it. But that could also mean the virus dies *with her.* Maat would finally be able to rest, and if the threat of the virus was gone, the lelgis would leave us alone. Don't you see? We all *win.* Maat, the phantoms, all the daughters, the Eyes, even me, we'd *all* be free."

I poured my confidence into the words as I spoke them, trying to make Caldswell understand, even if he wasn't really listening. I'd never pleaded so hard for something in my life, but I'd only get one shot at this; I had to make it count. And for a moment, I thought it did. When I finished, I could almost see my hope reflected in Caldswell's eyes, but then the captain sighed, dropping his head to rub his temples with his fingers, and for the first time ever, I saw how old and tired Caldswell really was.

"I want to believe you, Devi," he said quietly. "It's like I said before, your heart's in the right place, but you're asking the impossible. Only fools gamble what they can't afford to lose, and I was done being a fool a long time ago." He lifted his head, and the flash of weakness was gone, replaced by the captain I knew too well. "Your request is denied. The plan does not change. Hyrek's already preparing your new quarantine chamber. As soon as it's ready, you'll be going back under sedation until the ship arrives to take you into hyperspace for study. I'm really sorry, but this is for the best. For everyone."

My fists clenched so tight my hands ached. "Don't do this, Caldswell," I said. "Don't—"

The piercing shriek of an alarm cut me off, making me jump. Caldswell jumped, too, though not in surprise. He'd jumped to his feet to go to the bay's window, yanking out his com as he did. But there was no need to call to ask what this new emergency was. Even from my spot on the floor, I could see the bright flashes outside as ships came out of hyperspace. And came. And came.

I swore and pulled myself to my feet, crawling up the heavy bay door until I was finally standing beside Caldswell. Something funny was going on, I told myself. There couldn't possibly be as many ships out there as the flashes suggested. But I was wrong. There were more.

"King protect us," I whispered, eyes going wide.

Out past the battleship flying in formation with ours, in space where the emperor phantom had been, lelgis cruisers were popping in one after another. Already, they filled the sky as far as I could see through the small window, more ships than I could ever count, and still they were coming, surrounding us in a wall of beautiful, deadly force.

I swallowed, turning to Caldswell because, for once, he was less frightening. "How long was I out?"

"Not five minutes."

"How did they get here so fast?"

"Lelgis move through hyperspace instantly when they know where they're going," the captain explained, leaning into the little window like he was trying to get a count. "The queens are much better at navigating than our jump gates."

"I thought you said they wouldn't come so close to Maat."

"Guess they decided you were worth the risk," he said, squinting. "What the hell is that…" He faded off, his face going pale. I pressed my nose against the glass, searching frantically for whatever was awful enough to make Caldswell speechless. In hindsight, I should have taken the warning and backed off, because what I saw only made everything worse.

Something enormous was lurking behind the wall of ships. Not enormous like a battleship; our Republic cruiser was barely big enough to match the lelgis ships. No, this thing was big like the emperor phantom had been, a great looming shadow so huge it blotted out the stars behind it. Unlike the lelgis ships, though, it didn't glow with its own soft, iridescent light. It was black, visible only in the light thrown up by the ships that surrounded it and the shape of the stars it blocked. And though it wasn't nearly as large as a xith'cal's tribe ship, it scared me more, because this wasn't a ship. It was *alive.*

Caldswell shoved off the wall with a stream of profanity that blistered even my ears. "Goddamn queen," he finished, half shouting. "They brought a goddamn *queen* into this." He punched his handset as he jogged for the door, yelling into the com. "Bridge! This is Commander Caldswell. I'm ordering a full weapons lockdown. Do not engage the lelgis. I repeat, do not—"

The blinding flash of cannon fire outside cut off the end of his orders.

"*Who the hell fired that?*" Caldswell bellowed, whirling back to the window.

"I don't think that was us," I whispered, my voice trembling.

On our port, the second Republic battleship was now listing, a huge column of debris shooting out of its far side. I'd been watching Caldswell, so I hadn't seen the first shot, but I saw the second clear as day when the closest lelgis ship fired again, lighting up the sky with blue-white fire. The same fire that had consumed Stoneclaw's ghost ship was now eating ours, burning the battleship from the inside out. In the light, I could actually see the tiny shadows of the soldiers as they burned, and bile rose in my throat, scalding my mouth as I realized what this meant.

"They're going to destroy us all," I whispered. "Just like they did the xith'cal."

"No, they're not," Caldswell snapped, marching toward the farthest of the bay's sealed doors. "They *need* us. They're just trying to scare us into handing you over, but I can bluff back. I just have to get the queen to talk before she burns half my fleet. Mabel!"

I almost yelped when Mabel stepped out from where she'd been leaning against one of the fighters. I would have sworn there was no one in the bay but Caldswell and myself, and yet there she was. Looking back, I don't know why that surprised me. Even when she'd been playing engineer, Mabel Cobb was Caldswell's shadow, but I hated that I hadn't spotted her, especially since she hadn't even been hiding. She'd been standing practically in plain sight, just very still. So still I'd looked right over her, and that made me angry. I despised feeling like an idiot.

But there was no time for that. Mabel was already walking toward me, a wry smile on her face, like she'd been just waiting for her chance to push me around. Caldswell was already at the door, barking orders into his com while he punched in the code to unlock the bay. I pressed my back against the wall, trying to think of some way out of this, but deep down, I knew there was no hope. I couldn't escape Mabel, not without my suit, which was still back in the room where I'd woken up. And even if I'd had my Lady, there was nowhere to run.

Still, I couldn't bring myself to surrender just yet, so while Mabel stalked toward me, I stalked backward, letting her push me toward the corner. It was pure pigheadedness. I didn't have a plan and baiting her was only going to make it hurt more when she finally took me down. Even so, I didn't mean to stop moving until I had to, and I would have made it all the way to the back of the bay if a small hand hadn't landed on my shoulder.

I did yelp this time, jumping almost a foot in the air before whirling around, fists ready to punch whoever had the gall to be behind me, only to come up nose to nose with Maat.

No matter how many times she did it, I would never get used to seeing her appear like magic. *You have to leave.*

I almost rolled my eyes. "Tell me something I don't know!"

We will not let them have you, Maat hissed in my head. Phantoms were swarming all around her now, their glow drowning out even the harsh white lights of the fighter bay. *They will **never** have you. You are ours.* She thrust out her hand at me. *Come. Help is on the way. Maat will guide you.*

"Who are you talking to, Morris?" Mabel called behind me. "We already know you're nuts. Proving it won't change a thing."

I decided to ignore that. "Guide me *where?*" I snapped, batting at the phantoms swarming above Maat's head. "Would you please just speak like a normal person for two minutes and tell me—"

I never got to finish. I couldn't even remember what I'd been about to say, because at that moment, a roar tore through my mind like shrapnel. I gasped in shock, looking out the window just in time to see the emperor phantom appear above the wall of lelgis ships.

For a beautiful second, I thought maybe I hadn't killed that phantom, but then I saw this one was smaller than the emperor who'd spoken to me. Of course, this one was still forming, pulling itself together from the ambient glow all around us that I now realized was the phantoms. Millions and millions of tiny phantoms no bigger than the ones I always saw were coming together in a single, soundless cry of fury. They formed before my eyes, growing bigger and bigger into a huge, glowing mass that opened like a mouth. I had a fleeting impression of shining teeth and snaking tongues before the trap snapped down, consuming the lelgis cruiser that had been burning the other battleship in one fearsome gulp.

The first giant phantom had barely finished its attack before a new cry shot through me, and I lifted my eyes just in time to see a second emperor coalesce out of the still expanding sea of tiny phantoms right in front of the lelgis queen. As it formed, its light bloomed over the thing I'd only glimpsed in the dark, showing the queen in all her terrible glory until I thought I would be sick at the sight. But before the new-formed phantom could attack, the queen skittered back into the dark as the lelgis ships guarding her opened fire.

The white flame scorched over the phantom, lighting up its transparent body like a star going supernova. But even though it almost blinded me, I couldn't turn away. I would have stood there watching the battle forever, or at least until Mabel grabbed me, but Maat had already gripped my head, snatching my jaw between her palms as she shoved a command into my head.

Run.

I blinked at her, feeling almost drunk from everything that had happened. "Run where?"

Maat smiled a beautiful, mad smile. *With me.*

As she spoke, one of the emperor phantoms roared again, causing the battleship's lights to flicker, and then go out altogether. I heard Mabel gasp and stumble behind me, but though the bay was now lightless, I could see just fine. Without the harsh lights to hide them, I could make out the haze of tiny phantoms floating all around us. Their collective glow filled the air like summer moonlight, making Maat's hand shine like a beacon when she held it out.

It's time to keep your promise, she whispered in my mind, nodding to the emperor phantoms outside. *They tell Maat, 'We save her so she may save us.' They are doing their part, so now it's your turn.* The cloud of phantoms edged closer, waving their tiny feelers at me like a plea as Maat shoved her hand at my face. *Come and end this.*

I sucked in a long, deep breath and reached out, slapping my hand in hers. I hadn't expected to actually feel anything, but Maat's glowing skin was warm as Rupert's when I touched it, and her grip was tight as a clamp when she grabbed me back. *This way,* she said, pulling me toward the door.

With our hands locked together, I didn't have a choice. I ran, legs pumping as we left Mabel groping blindly in our dust and made for the door the emperor had used to drag me in here the first time. Behind us, the little phantoms gave chase, lighting our footsteps with their soft, ghostly glow.

CHAPTER

10

I didn't even think about the problems this latest power outage presented until we reached the blast door. The gravity was still working, so I knew there had to be power somewhere on the ship, just not here, which really sucked when you were facing down a solid steel automatic door with no juice to run the automatic part and no suit to kick it down. I hit the button anyway, just to be sure. When nothing happened, I turned to Maat. "Now what?"

I was hoping she'd blast the thing open like she'd done to Caldswell's window the first time she'd sprung me. Whatever she did, it had better be quick. Mabel had found her pace now, and though she couldn't see us, I could see her closing the distance fast. But while I was working myself into fight or flight, Maat was looking at the locked door like a kid genius who's just been presented with an interesting puzzle. Finally, when Mabel was only ten feet away, Maat reached out and plunged her fingers straight into the door's control panel.

From where I stood, it looked like she'd just broken her hand, but real as she looked and felt to me, Maat wasn't actually here. She passed through the electronics like air, and everywhere she touched, the lights came back on. For a moment, I thought she'd done real, honest to god magic, but then I remembered that one of the big reasons the daughters were used was because they negated the phantom's disruptive field. And if her daughters could do it, of *course* Maat could. That made me grin wide, because if Maat could light up a door, maybe she could do the same for my suit, and if that was the case, then we were playing a whole new game.

I didn't have much time to enjoy the idea, though. The glowing console had alerted Mabel to our location. By the time the little wheels spun up to lift the blast door's weight, she was tearing toward us, her hands already reaching out to grab me.

I didn't give her a chance. The second the blast door left the floor, I dropped, squeezing through the crack like a dog wiggling under a fence. As soon as I was through, Maat removed her hand, and the door dropped like a stone, slamming back to the floor just in time for me to hear Mabel collide with the other side.

"Don't run, Morris!" she shouted, slamming her fist down so hard the door warped. "You're only making things worse for yourself!"

I didn't see how that was possible, and I didn't hang around to find out. By the time Mabel pounded the door again, I was already running full tilt down the hallway, dodging the mess left from the recent loss of gravity and the emperor phantom's search for me. There were soldiers here, too, whole crews that were far too busy clearing the out passage and moving the wounded to pay any attention to me. But when we reached the elevator and turned to head for the medical area, Maat grabbed my shoulder.

Not this way.

"Yes, this way," I snapped, shrugging out of her hold. "I'm not going anywhere without my suit."

The hallway where the emperor phantom had grabbed me looked even worse than it had when I'd left. The phantom hadn't exactly been gentle in its ransacking, and the resulting chaos had left the military hallway looking like a war zone. The floor was strewn with broken furniture, glass, blood, and other things I couldn't identify. But for all that, the emergency lights were back on, and soldiers were already working to clear the way for the wounded that were being brought into the medical bay from other parts of the ship.

Everyone was too busy to look at me, so I picked up the pace, vaulting over a toppled desk to get to the busted out door of the room I'd woken up in, which I could already see at the end of the hall. Unfortunately, I'd put my body through a lot recently, and what was supposed to be a graceful jump ended up more like a half tumble, half roll. I landed badly, too, grunting as I caught myself on the wall. I was about to haul up and keep going when someone touched my shoulder.

"Hey, are you okay?"

I didn't recognize the voice, and I raised my head to see a Terran soldier standing over me. He looked like a kid, not more than twenty and wearing the simple uniform and short haircut of a first-year crewman. He also clearly had absolutely no idea who he was talking to.

"Thanks," I said, concentrating very, very hard to keep my accent as neutral as possible as I let him help me to my feet. "And sorry."

I had just enough time to catch the look of confusion that flashed over his face before my fist landed in his gut. The kid doubled over with a grunt, and I reached down, snatching his gun out of its holster. A few of the other workers looked up at the sound, but the emergency lights were far too poor for them to see what I'd done.

"Sorry, kiddo," I said again, taking careful aim before I slammed the edge of my hand down on the back of his neck. He didn't make a sound when I hit him this time, just fell to the ground like a dead weight. I tucked him up against the wall so he wouldn't get trampled and started back down the hall, pistol ready.

In all the chaos earlier, I hadn't realized that my little room was located on the main hall leading into the battleship's medbay. Considering the medical bunk and all the equipment I'd woken up to, I probably should have guessed as much way before this. I hadn't, though, and I was now at a disadvantage.

Medical bays on big ships were always hives of activity after emergencies, even relatively minor ones like a sudden loss of gravity, and my suit was right in the middle. Worse, I was losing my cover. The emperor phantoms must have moved farther away, because the ship lights were starting to flicker back on. It was only a matter of time before Caldswell put the word out about my escape, which meant I needed to move now. So, putting on my best I'm-working-don't-bother-me scowl, I tucked my stolen gun into the waistband of my scrubs and marched into the fray, glaring at any medic who dared to get in my way as I made a beeline for the busted door of the quarantine room.

There's a lot to be said for putting on a good front. Despite the fact that I clearly didn't belong here, no one moved to stop me. They were all busy with their own work, and those who did glance at me glanced away just as fast, their faces afraid. That just made me smug. Terrans never did know how to handle a little old-fashioned animal aggression.

By the time I reached the quarantine room, I was starting to really believe we could make it. Maat was still tugging at me, glancing over her shoulder like Caldswell was going to appear and kill us both at any moment, but I refused to let her throw me off. I was committed to getting my damn suit, and I ducked through the door Caldswell had kicked open, bold as you please, only to come up face to snout with Hyrek.

He'd been squatting beside the destroyed lab equipment in dismay, trying to salvage some machine or other. Crouched down like that, his head was only slightly lower than mine, which meant when he looked up to see who'd just come in, we were eye to eye. We stayed that way for several seconds, both of us frozen, staring at each other, and then Hyrek dove for his handset.

Hyrek might be a xith'cal, but he was a noncombat one. I beat him by miles, grabbing his handset with my free hand while I shoved my stolen gun into the scales of his stomach with the other. He went perfectly still when the barrel touched him, his snake eyes darting from the gun to the people walking outside, just behind me. The way I'd come in meant my body hid the gun, but with the door torn down, anyone could see what was going on if they took the time to look. If I didn't move quick, this was going to get very ugly very fast.

"Hyrek," I said softly. "I've always liked you, so I'm not going to shoot unless you make me."

Hyrek rolled his eyes, and I could practically see the lecture on xith'cal anatomy he was writing in his head on how a shot from a standard sidearm wouldn't even make it through his armored belly. "I know it won't kill you," I said with a smile. "But you see, I've got Maat with me right now, and she will. So if you want to keep that brain you're so proud of in working order, you'll keep your trap shut."

That threat got through. Hyrek went very still, his yellow eyes boring into mine. I stared back, letting my certainty shine through until, at last, Hyrek held up his hands.

"Good," I said softly, reaching for my armor case, which was still safely tucked in the corner, right where Caldswell had left it. "Now don't move and don't draw attention or I'll have Maat scramble your neurons."

Maat can't do that from so far away.

With Hyrek standing right there, I couldn't very well tell her he didn't know that, so I just gave her a "shut up" glare and moved into the corner. Crammed in a tiny room between Hyrek, the smashed medical equipment, and the ruined door was hardly the ideal condition for putting on a powered suit. My clothes sucked, too. The medical scrubs were too baggy to fit neatly under my armor, and the thought of all that dirt and slime touching the interior of my suit was almost more than I could bear. That said, I'd been dying to get back into my Lady since this shit began, and even with all these handicaps weighing me down, I had my whole suit on in just under twenty seconds.

I was locking Mia onto my back when a woman in an emergency med-vac uniform came charging through the broken door and smacked right into me. I barely felt the impact through my suit, but the woman went sprawling, and in the second I was distracted, Hyrek reached out and hit the panic button.

A siren kicked on right by my head, screeching so loud I almost went deaf before my computer canceled the noise. By the time my head cleared, the woman I'd knocked down was back on her feet and running the other direction, shouting for security. I glared after her for a second and then turned on Hyrek, shoving Sasha in his face. "You goddamn lizard."

Caldswell's doctor barely blinked an eye at the anti-armor pistol aimed right for the soft spot between his eyes. Instead, he gave me a triumphant look and placed his hand over the center of his chest in a gesture I remembered from my lizard-killing days. Among the xith'cal, it meant loyalty to the tribe, and though Hyrek had no tribe, I didn't have to think too hard to guess who he was swearing to.

"Morris!"

I cringed. That was Caldswell, and he was close. Much closer than I liked.

Deviana, Maat pleaded in my head. I couldn't see her with my cameras on, but I could feel her hands reaching through my armor, tugging on my arm. *Deviana, we have to* **go**.

I glared at Hyrek one last time as I holstered my gun. There was no point in threatening him anymore. Even if killing Hyrek could have stopped the alarm, we both knew I didn't have the heart. "I'll get you for that," I promised, running out the door. Behind me, I heard a sound like cans being crushed in a grinder as Hyrek called his reply. I didn't know what that meant since I didn't speak lizard, but I chose to think it was *Good luck*.

The medbay was on high alert when I came out. All the doctors had pressed themselves against the walls to stay out of the armored Paradoxian's way, proving they were the smart ones. Unfortunately, I had no idea where to go next.

Hurry, Maat whispered, flooding my brain with urgency. *Hurry!*

I didn't need her to tell me that. With a thought, I flipped my suit into combat mode, letting my computer take over as I picked a direction and started running, trusting my Lady to jump and bend and slide me around any obstacles. I spotted Caldswell the second I got into the hall, but what really concerned me was that I didn't see Mabel, which meant she was probably a lot closer than I wanted her. So, since I couldn't be sure, I turned and ran in the other direction.

Symbionts could outrun me no sweat on open ground, but in the chaos of the damaged battleship, I had the advantage. While the captain and Mabel had only their eyes, the combination of my 360-degree view and my density scanner fed my Lady all the information she needed to keep moving. And move we did. With Maat right beside me, the phantom's disruptive aura didn't so much as flicker my display. I raced around the corner, my suit moving so smoothly it felt like I was flying as I cleared the back of the medbay and charged into what looked like a central troop staging area.

This way, Maat said, and then, before I had a chance to remind her I couldn't see where she was pointing, a map shoved its way into my head, showing me the path across the battleship to the docking tube on the other side.

I had no idea where the end of that docking tube connected, but off the ship was good enough for me. I changed direction midstep, thinking through Maat's map in a way my suit could understand. After that, the route appeared on my computer, and I didn't even have to make choices. I just followed my suit, running faster and faster past confused soldiers and technicians until, at last, I reached a huge open staging bay with bold arrows painted on the floor, pointing the way toward a wide, plastic tunnel at the far end.

Battleships like this one were too big to dock at most stations, so they made do with collapsible plastic tubes that could be extended to lock into a docking bay, forming an enclosed path from ship to station. Unsurprisingly, the docking tube for this ship was big enough to drive a tank down. There actually were a few tanks lashed down in the bay around me, ready for deployment, but I didn't have time to give them more than a passing glance before I launched myself at the exit.

The tunnel was guarded by a wide, heavy exterior door, but they must have been pretty secure in their connection, because it had been locked open when the ship's power shut down. There was also clearly supposed to be a shield in place, but it was down at the moment, and I was able to enter the tunnel no problem. As soon as I was inside, the door's exterior locking panel flickered to life, and I flipped up my visor to see Maat working on it, her fingers flexing inside the machinery just as the door slammed closed. Maat pulled her hand back and made a fist, then slammed it down again, destroying the lock in a shower of sparks.

There, she said, snarling at the closed door. *Rot in your prison.*

The cold hate in her voice made me shiver, but I didn't have time to be squeamish. Even though we'd made it out and broken the door so he couldn't follow, I didn't let myself believe for a second that we were safe from Caldswell. He'd be beating his way to us any second, which meant we needed to get a move on. First, though, I intended to find out where we were moving *to*.

We were now on the opposite side of the battleship from the fighter bay where the phantom had spoken to me, but I could still see the fight. Counting the ship we'd just left and the one behind it that the lelgis had opened fire on before the emperor phantom's counterattack, there were four Republic battleships in total. Four battleships were normally considered a hell of a lot of firepower, enough to squash any rebelling colony, but next to the lelgis it wasn't even a blip.

The docking tube was clear all the way around, made of self-formed collapsible plastic with battery lights. There were no wires, no ribs, nothing at all to block my view of the lelgis fleet that had closed in around us like a fist. The emperor phantoms were there as well, three of them now, but even they looked small and helpless in the face of so many ships. Thousands of ships, and behind them, the huge shadow of the queen was still lurking, visible only in the flashes of blue fire and the stars she blotted out.

Deviana?

I took a deep breath and turned to Maat only to find she'd moved ahead of me in the tunnel, her ghostly bare feet moving over the hardened flat plastic floor without even a whisper. The cloud of phantoms around her had only gotten thicker, but the tiny bugs weren't looking at her. They were looking at me, their tentacles waving, and for a moment, I almost thought I could hear their small voices in my mind, begging me to hurry.

"Where am I going?" I asked.

Maat raised her dark eyebrows and pointed down the tunnel.

With Armageddon going on outside, I supposed I could be forgiven for missing the space station. Honestly, though, even if the lelgis fleet hadn't been bearing down on me, I would have had a hard time spotting it, because the station at the end of the docking tunnel was painted matte black. There were no identifiers on its surface, no numbers, not even guide lights to mark its edges, though that could have been due to power loss. Still, I would have bet my suit that the station wouldn't have been lit up, phantoms or no. Everything about it spoke of hiding and secrecy, even its old-fashioned diamond construction with four pointed arms radiating from a central generator core like rays on a star, which made it look like an evil Terran base straight out of a classic Paradoxian war movie. Cinematics aside, the cross star shape was actually very fitting when I realized at last what I was looking at.

"Dark Star Station," I muttered, glaring down the tunnel. The fortress they'd built to hold Maat, the heart of everything that had gone so wrong. It was smaller than I'd expected, and very plain, which was really a shame since nine to ten odds said it was going to be my grave. I'd hoped to smash up something really impressive, but I guessed this made more sense. Whoever heard of a beautiful secret government base?

"Come on," I said, starting down the tunnel. "Let's get this over with."

Why?

Her question made me skip a step, forcing my suit to catch me as I whipped around to face her. "Excuse me?"

Maat folded her arms over her medical gown. *I got you out of the ship to get away from Brian. But we're safe now, so why wait? I'm here. You're here.* She held out her hand, her fingers glimmering as the phantoms scurried over her palm to get away from me. *Give me what you promised,* she demanded. *Give me my death.*

"I can't yet," I said, glaring at her. "If I kill you here, every daughter dies."

Maat doesn't care, Maat said, her eyes glittering dangerously. *Maat never asked for daughters.*

"They didn't ask for you, either," I snapped. "But they're yours now, and I won't kill them if I don't have to."

I'd actually been thinking about this in the back of my head ever since my talk with Dr. Starchild. Caldswell's story about doing my testing on a Republic deep hyperspace ship had given me an idea, and facing Maat now gave me the final push I needed to put it all together. I just had to pray she was sane enough to understand.

"I have a plan," I said calmly. "In order to let the phantoms go home and keep my promise to you, I need to kill you. But if I infect you with the virus now, it will spread to all your daughters."

So? Maat said, shrugging. *They're part of me now. If I want to die, that's what they want, too.* She glared at me. *Do it.*

"No," I said firmly. Seeing Ren die as she wept over her father's body was what had started me down this path in the first place. As wrong as I knew Maat had been done, I'd be damned if I let her kill the poor girls who'd been just as abused simply because she was impatient. But Maat clearly didn't see it that way.

No, her voice ripped through my mind, sending the phantoms fleeing as her body began to tremble with rage. *You can't do this to me. Not now. Not when I'm so close.* She stepped forward. *I will kill you if you betray me!*

Her presence plunged into my mind as she spoke, reaching for the virus. But Maat had always said my plasmex was tiny, impossible to find. This was clearly true, or she would have grabbed it already. So, though the invasion of her hands in my head galled me, I kept my temper, refusing to give her so much as a taste of what she sought.

"I'm not going to betray you," I said calmly. "I swear to the Sacred King that I will set you free, you and the phantoms, just not here."

Then where? Maat's eyes gleamed madly as she threw her arm up, pointing at the beautiful glowing shapes of the emperor phantoms as they faced off against the lelgis. *They are fighting and dying for you, and you would make them wait longer? They cannot hold the lelgis forever. When they fall, it is over. The queens will tear you apart and all will be lost.*

I took a deep breath. She had a point, but I'd made up my mind and I would not back down. I'd never been anything if not ambitious, and with only one shot to get it right, I was going to ace it, all of it, or die trying. "If that's the case, then you'd better quiet down and listen," I told her, putting my hands on my hips. "This is my virus, which means my rules. I'm going to get you everything you want, so do you want to shut up and find out how, or do you want to keep fighting over it?"

Maybe it doesn't matter, Maat snarled, glaring daggers at me. *You claim to be in charge, but Deviana's temper is worse than Brian's. It's only a matter of time before you slip up.*

"Don't count on that," I snapped. "I'm not the same woman I was. I learn and I survive, and if you think I'm going to forget myself and just hand you this virus, you're in for a rude surprise. Now are you ready to hear the plan or not?"

Maat narrowed her eyes, and for one tense moment I could actually see her fighting it out with herself, her lips moving in a silent argument. Whichever side was arguing for me must have won, because a second later she motioned for me to go ahead.

"Good," I said. "But first, let's get something straight. Is it true you can't talk to your daughters in hyperspace?"

Maat nodded. *Even Maat can't go outside the universe.*

I grinned. Bingo. "Here's the plan, then," I said. "I'm going to break you out of that station, steal a ship, and jump into hyperspace, separating you from your daughters. Once we're out there, you clean the virus out of me. I'll get to live, and you'll get your death just like you want, *without* taking the daughters with you. With you gone, the door will be open and the phantoms can go home. It's win-win all around."

My words came faster and faster as I spoke, my heartbeat speeding up in time. Out loud, my plan sounded even better. I was so close, so *close* to pulling it all off, to getting everything I wanted and living to tell about it. But Maat didn't look convinced.

No, she said softly. *It won't work.*

I stopped short. "Why not?"

You can't get to Maat, she said with a helpless shrug. *The Dark Star might be old, but it's been built up over decades to do only one thing: keep Maat in. The entire place is a labyrinth designed to confuse and trap anyone who enters without clearance. Even Brenton was never suicidal enough to assault the Dark Star directly, and he's much stronger than you. It's simply impossible for you to reach Maat. All you'd do is get yourself killed and ruin everything.*

"What do you mean ruin everything?" I said. "You said if I die, the virus goes free."

That was back on Reaper's ship, Maat replied, indignant. *There, Maat was set up to catch you, and only if it was the virus itself doing the killing. If you die to a bullet with your virus still dormant, you'll just be dead.*

"Then I'll make sure to get mad before I go," I said. Shouldn't be hard; failing now would certainly make me angry enough for a final black-hands hurrah. "That way even if I fail, all you'd have to do is be ready to catch."

Maat refuses, Maat said, shoving the words into my mind like needles. *You will not risk my freedom or theirs*—she nodded at the phantoms crawling over her shoulders—*on a stupid gamble.*

I sighed. Deep down, part of me agreed with her. It *would* be much safer to just stop here, give her the virus, and be done with it. That's what a smart merc would do, take the sure bet, keep her nose clean, get the job done. Trouble was, I'd stopped being a merc at some point over the last week. I wasn't sure what I was anymore exactly, but on one thing I was absolutely certain: I was not going to throw anyone to the wolves on this. Not Maat, not the phantoms, and certainly not the daughters, whose plight was the kicked kitten that had made me take up this stupid crusade in the first place. I didn't care if it was nigh impossible. Risk brought reward, and I was too close, had fought too hard, to give up mine now.

"This is not a negotiation," I told Maat, crossing my arms over my chest. "I know the Eyes have hyperdrive-capable ships in there." I could actually see the station's docks now that I was looking for them, four in fact. One of them had to have something we could use. "And if they don't, I'll have you. Caldswell would jump a battleship to save your life, and then you take the virus and make a fool out of him."

I'd thought that image would cheer Maat up, but all she did was bury her face in her hands. *You'll die*, she moaned. *It's not fair. You get to die and Maat doesn't. Maat wants to—*

"You should be hoping I die," I snapped. "Because if I go down at any point during all of this, I swear to the Sacred King that I will give up my virus freely. I'll cover myself in all the black you could ever want, and you can grab it and die at your leisure, no wait, no fuss. But *until that point*, I'm going to try, and if you care about anything other than your own suffering, you'll help me."

Maat dropped her hands as I spoke, her stricken look turning thoughtful as I explained. By the time I was finished, she was staring at me like she was trying to take my measure, worrying her bottom lip between her teeth, and for a fleeting moment I caught a glimpse of the clever, thoughtful girl she must have been once, back before everything went so wrong.

All right, she said at last. *Maat will help. Maat thinks you're crazy, but Maat will help.*

I rolled my eyes. The craziest lady in the universe thought I was nuts, but if she really was ready to help, I wasn't going to argue. We'd lost enough time already.

I turned and started jogging down the plastic tunnel, doing my best to keep my mind off the terrifying battle going on outside and on my own mission. "Can you tell me what's going on inside the station?"

A little, Maat said, frowning. *Maat has been angry lately, so they've been drugging me a lot. They woke me up when the first emperor phantom came, but I held back my aura and let the phantom shut down the station.* Her voice was smug as she said that last part, and I knew she was reveling in their fear. *It's still out, but Maat can hear them in the other room talking about drugging me again. If they do that, Maat will sleep. When that happens, the power will come back and all the station security with it.*

I made a face. That didn't sound fun. "How much longer have we got?"

Not long, Maat replied. She was shaking now, her thoughts bleeding into mine. She hated being drugged. *Hated* it. Now that I'd experienced the anti-plasmex cocktail myself, I couldn't say I blamed her.

"I need you to fight them and keep the power off as long as you can," I said. "I also need you to stick with me and keep my suit functioning." Having the only working piece of hardware in a shut-down station was a vital advantage if I was going to have a prayer of pulling this off. But while I'd thought this was obvious, Maat's brush against my mind only felt confused.

You don't need Maat for that.

"What are you talking about?" I said. "You're the only reason I'm still online."

She shook her head so hard her hair flew. *Maat hasn't touched your suit.*

I looked at her, then back at the dark ship behind us, and then down at my suit, which was functioning just like it always did. "How is that possible?"

Because you're like me, her voice whispered in my mind, bringing with it a feeling of connection not unlike what the lelgis had shown me when they were trying to demonstrate the oneness. *Your range is very small, of course, because your plasmex is like a tiny grain of sand. Still, it is enough.*

She said this like she was telling me I'd never walk again, but I wasn't listening. I was too busy studying my suit. All my systems were perfectly normal, my power humming along to all segments without so much as a sputter, even when I stretched my hand out as far as I could. But when I took the test further, slinging Mia out of her holster and placing her on the floor, her charge light flickered out before I'd backed off three feet.

"Well, I'll be," I said softly, leaning down to scoop up my plasma shotgun again. "So, what? Am I like a daughter now?"

Maat shrugged helplessly. *Who knows? Maat's never seen anything like you. But then, no one had seen anything like Maat before, either.*

I sighed. Great, sisters in freakdom. But unlike everything else the virus had done to me, canceling out the phantom's aura was a welcome development. One I meant to use to my utmost tactical advantage.

By this point, we'd nearly reached the place where the plastic tube hooked into the station. Just past the boarding tube's edge, I could see the heavy casing of what was clearly meant to be a plasma shielded door. Now, with no power, there was no shield, and though I spotted no fewer than four cameras pointed at the entry gate, every one of them was dark and motionless.

The boarding tunnel let out into an entry room that had clearly once been part of a much larger docking area but had since been renovated into something smaller and easier to defend. The initial entry point was wide enough to fit the large tunnel I'd just come out of, but after that the room quickly shrank, funneling into a long hallway lined with inconspicuous turret drops. I froze when I saw them, remembering Maat's warning that this place was a fortress, but without power, the security measures had no teeth, and I relaxed a little, starting down the hall as I opened up my density scanner to get a glimpse of what I was walking into.

A lot of metal seemed to be the answer. I was about to ask Maat if she could give me another map when I realized I didn't need one. Now that I was actually in the hall, it felt deeply familiar. This whole place did, like I'd been here a hundred times before. For a second, I worried Maat was bleeding into my mind again, but the truth turned out to be much simpler. I knew this place because Rupert knew it. Even with the lights out, the entry hall triggered his memories, filling my head with his calm, orderly assessment of the station that had been his headquarters for four decades. He'd hated this place with a cold, dark menace, but he knew it like the back of his hand, and that gave me an idea.

When I reached the end of the hall, I paused, sorting through Rupert's well-ordered memories of the station for the one I wanted. When I found it, I turned and starting following one of the hallways that ringed the station's center toward the turn that would take me out one of the station's arms, the rays of the star. This also meant I was going the exact wrong direction to reach the area Rupert thought of as "Maat's containment." Maat clearly saw this as well, and she appeared in front of me, her face set in a snarl.

Where are you going?

"You can't expect me to pull off a job like this without help, can you?" I asked, jogging faster as my suit's sensors filled in the gaps in Rupert's recollections, drawing me a detailed map in the process.

Who here is going to help you? Maat snarled. *Eyes never help.*

"He's not an Eye anymore," I said simply. "He's mine."

I could feel Maat's bafflement like a fog in my head, but I just grinned and kept going, kicking open the door to the dead elevator so I could jump down the shaft.

———

I'd noted before that Dark Star Station was set up like a pointed cross with four rays extending from a central mass. From the outside, the shape had looked simplistic, but by the time I'd climbed all the way down to the cramped hallway that ran up the spine of the ray farthest from Maat's prison, I was thanking the king for every single one of the memories Rupert had left in my head. Without his intimate knowledge of this place bubbling up like carbonation anytime I saw anything remotely familiar, I would have been lost for days.

The station's interior was every bit the labyrinth Maat had described, a warren of identical metal hallways whose sole purpose seemed to be finding new ways to dead end. The only good part was that the station was big enough for solid-state gravity generation. I might feel like a rat in a maze, but so long as the air pressure stayed normal, at least I wouldn't have to do it flying around.

I had more than enough to process already, especially since even with Rupert's mental map at my fingertips, it was still easy to get turned around when every corner looked exactly the same. There were no directional signs, no emergency exits; there weren't even numbers on the doors, nothing to help me get my bearings. There were, however, a lot of traps.

I lost count of how many automatic turrets I passed. Even the elevator shaft had had them at regular intervals, along with shield generators, gas vents, electrified fields, others I didn't even recognize. If I hadn't been trying to break in, I would have been impressed. Whoever had designed this place was a master of redundant fail-safes. Every trap had overlapping fields of fire and multiple power sources to make sure they kept firing even if you managed to cut the line. Too bad all that didn't do shit against a phantom's field, but then, considering who the Dark Star was built to hold, I bet they'd never thought they'd be in this situation.

"Keep it up, Maat," I said as I stepped over the discolored stripe on the floor marking where a shield normally stood. "Keep it up."

Maat didn't respond. She'd been getting quieter over the last few minutes, floating along silently behind me like a ghost in truth, her eyes flat and overly dilated. Considering what she'd said about their plans to drug her, I was pretty sure that was exactly what was going on, but though the station lights flickered occasionally, they didn't come back on. Drugged or not, she was still holding back her aura and keeping her end of the bargain. For now, anyway.

My destination was the door at the very end of the hall, the tip of the star's ray. The Dark Star's brig was just as guarded as everything else, the entry flanked by auto-fire turrets and overlapping shields. But even with all of those down, I still had to deal with the actual prison door.

My density scanner couldn't even penetrate the solid steel mass, which meant shooting or burning my way through was out. I considered asking Maat for a repeat of the trick she'd used to open the blast door on the battleship, but she was nearly catatonic now, her head lolling, so I decided to try another approach. I flipped my visor back down and turned to the wall beside the door, peering through the much thinner metal to see if I could spot a weak point, and got a flash of good luck.

The prison door was made of two interlocked heavy metal halves on a track, but the pressure that kept them pressed together and locked the interior latches down came from a hydraulic pump, which was buried in the wall. Naturally, the door had locked in place when the main power went out, which meant the pump was still extended, using the pressure from the liquid inside to keep the doors pressed tight together, and that gave me an idea.

I flexed my wrist, popping Elsie from her sheath. Another thought had my thermite blade flaring to life, filling the dark hall with blinding light. Fortunately, I only needed it for a second. I wrenched back, letting my targeting system line up my punch before I slammed my blade through the wall and into the pump inside. My Elsie might not have been able to cut through the prison door, but she cut through this just fine. Once I was sure I was where I needed to be, I braced my legs and pushed her up, slicing the pump, the hydraulics, and reservoir hose clean through. Liquid starting pouring out into the wall immediately, and the prison doors sagged with a clunk as the pressure forcing them closed vanished.

I extinguished my thermite to save the rest of my blade and pulled Elsie back before pressing my shoulder against the door. Normally, there was no way my speed combat suit could lift something this heavy, but without the pressure locking it shut, the enormous door was just a big weight on tracks. I didn't have to lift it; I just had to slide it. Even so, I almost burned out my suit's motor shoving the halves the two feet apart I needed to slip through.

With my visor down, I couldn't see the phantom's light, and the inside of the prison was surprisingly dark. Even darker than the hallways, where a few battery-operated emergency lights still barely glowed, giving my night vision something to work with. In here, though, I didn't have squat, but since I didn't want to raise my visor if I could avoid it and I'd already made enough noise to wake the dead cutting my way in, I took the easy solution and turned on my suit's floodlights, filling the room with light.

There wasn't much to fill. Unlike the rest of the station, Rupert hadn't been to the brig before, so I didn't actually have a clear picture of the area until I saw it for myself. The door opened into a narrow hall lined with glass-fronted cells, though only two looked to be currently occupied. When I saw who by, I nearly cracked up.

"Well, well," I said, putting my hands on my hips. "Fancy running into you folks."

In the cell next to me, the girl who'd been shielding her eyes against the sudden light dropped her hands with a jerk, and my grin widened as Nova's pale face came into view. "Deviana?"

Her startled voice roused the other prisoner, who'd looked like he'd been trying to pull himself into a ball of feathers before he raised his head. "You have got to be *kidding* me."

"Hello, Nova," I said, trying not to laugh. "Hello, Basil."

"What are you doing here?" Nova said, pale eyes wide. "Is the captain here, too?"

"What's going on outside?" Basil spoke over her, hopping to the front of his cell with a flap to tap his beak against the thick glass. "What were those explosions? Are we under attack?"

We were, but I didn't think it would be helpful to let them know the details right now. "The captain's not here," I said, walking up to Nova's cell. The glass was bulletproof and shatterproof, but it didn't look nearly as bad as the box the xith'cal had put me in. Elsie should be able to slice it with a little leverage. "But it's a long story and I'm short on time. Stand back and I'll get you out."

Nova and Basil exchanged a look. "I don't want to project ingratitude for your generous offer, Deviana," Nova said. "But I don't think a prison break is a good idea right now."

I gave her a funny look. Prison breaks were always a good idea in my book, but Basil was nodding furiously. "You're in huge trouble, monkey," he said, eying me up and down. "I don't know what's going on exactly, but you're bad news."

"Worse than being locked up?"

Seeing Basil fluff his feathers in a huff was as nostalgic as it was annoying. "The captain said we were here for our protection, and I believe him," he snipped. "If we go with you, we'll be accomplices to your criminal activities."

I rolled my eyes and turned back to Nova, who gave me a plaintive look. "We appreciate your efforts," she said. "But while Basil and I would like to assist you along your trajectory, unless you need a jump calculated or light plasmex services, we would probably be more of a hindrance than a help. So thank you for the offer, but we'll remain in this space for the current present, if that's all right."

Personally, I would have taken the out anyway, but then, I wasn't Nova. She was a civilian with no combat experience or armor. That prison wall probably looked more like a shield than a blockade to her.

"Suit yourself," I said with a shrug. "But maybe you can help me anyway. Did you see Rupert come through here?"

Nova nodded rapidly. "Oh yes, they brought him in a while ago. He's at the end of the hall." She pointed down the line of glass-fronted cells toward the back of the prison my lights hadn't reached yet.

I took a deep breath to keep my hopes in check. "How did he look? Did you see what they're using to hold him?"

It didn't seem possible, but Nova's paper-white skin went even paler under the glare of my floodlights. "I couldn't say for sure," she whispered, her voice almost too low for me to hear through the thick glass. "I've never seen anything like that, but it looked very bad." She bit her lip. "What did he do?"

Sided with me, I thought with a scowl. "Nothing," I told her. "One last question. Do you know what deck the hyperdrive-capable ships are being stored on?" Because Rupert remembered this place having functional two docks, but only one was kept operational at a time for security reasons, and I didn't want to waste precious minutes going to the wrong one. "Like, did you see any when Caldswell brought you in?"

"The dock we put in at had several hyperdrive-capable ships," Basil chirped, his big yellow bird eyes shining like lamps in my light. "But they were all on lockdown. You'll never get in."

"Thanks for the vote of confidence," I said, starting down the hall. "Was it the top dock or the bottom?"

"There is no up or down in space," Nova reminded me. "But it was the one closest to the observation deck."

Top, then. "Thanks," I said, pushing up my visor so she could see my smile. "You're the best, Nova."

She blushed scarlet in the floodlight before I turned it away.

"Deviana!"

I looked back at my name to see Nova pressed against the glass. "Be careful," she said softly.

I smiled wide. "Careful as I'm able," I promised.

Basil made a sound that was part squawk, part snort, and completely disbelieving. I didn't feel the need to dignify it with a response as I picked up the pace, following the hallway toward the back of the brig.

I'd noted before that the brig wasn't large, and it wasn't. The cells were shallow and the hallway was narrow, barely wide enough for my armor to fit comfortably. But while the prison wasn't wide or spacious, it *was* surprisingly long. By the time I'd left the lower security area with glass-fronted cells and reached the much more serious rooms at the back, I couldn't even see Nova or Basil anymore.

The cells here were smaller and completely closed in, no glass fronts, though I could see from the vents on the walls that the doors were meant to be covered in shields, all of which were down thanks to the power outage Maat was still holding strong for me. With my visor up and my lights on, though, I could see just fine. The phantoms were thick as tar here, opening up only to let me through. Maat, however, was nowhere to be seen. I was pretty sure that meant they'd finally drugged her into oblivion, which meant I needed to get a move on before the power came back on and I ended up being the prisoner who'd broken herself into jail.

Unfortunately, every cell I checked was empty. By the tenth one, I was starting to get really worried. What if Caldswell was wrong? What if they'd just killed Rupert once they got him back here? What if I was too late? But before I could get too worked up, the hallway came to an abrupt end, and I found myself face-to-face with a final pair of cells.

They were both squeezed in at the end of the hall, which didn't make much sense to me. Considering the already claustrophobic width, there was no way either cell could be bigger than a closet. Both doorways had the usual discolorations that showed there was supposed to be a shield over them, but unlike the ones I'd passed on my way back, these cells didn't have actual doors. Instead, they were blocked off from the hallway by thin metal mesh not much thicker than a bug net with yellow caution tape and rubber rollers on the sides.

My eyebrows shot up. Apparently, this netting was supposed to be electrified. *Very* electrified if the grounding wires were anything to go by. With the power off, though, the fancy electric mesh was nothing but a very expensive metal curtain, and I shoved it aside without a second thought to see if I'd found Rupert at last.

When I shone my light in, however, I still wasn't sure, mostly because I couldn't make sense of what I saw. I'd been right about the size of the cell; it *was* little bigger than a closet, barely wide enough for my armor and maybe two feet deep. And in this tiny space was a man, though he was so bound up I wasn't actually sure about that last bit. His body had been wrapped like a corpse in heavy plastic weave straps, the crazy tough kind they used to secure exterior starship cargo, and his feet were anchored to the floor with an inert plasma weight so large I didn't think I could lift it with my suit. But worse than all of this by miles was the mask that engulfed his head.

Aside from the incident in the mines, I'd never thought of myself as claustrophobic, but seeing that horrible, faceless, smooth metal prison wrapped all the way around the prisoner's skull almost gave me a panic attack. It also looked horribly familiar, like I'd seen it before in memories I didn't want to remember. Or maybe Rupert didn't want to remember them? It was getting hard to tell. Wherever I'd seen this mask before, though, it hadn't been good, and I didn't like the look of it now either. There was something unspeakably wrong about the way it covered his entire head with no openings at all, not even air vents, just metal clamped down so hard it cut into the skin of his neck.

And that was where I got my clue. Though the heavy straps covered him everywhere else, a strip of the man's neck right below the helmet was bare, showing enough skin for me to make out the pale color I knew so well. It was Rupert, I'd found him, and I had to get him out of that thing right this second.

"Rupert," I called, ducking under the supposed-to-be-electrified mesh to stand as far inside the cell as I could get. "Rupert!"

He didn't stir at the noise of my entrance or his name, and I cursed. They must have drugged him. I hadn't planned on that. But symbionts recovered quickly from everything. Maybe I just had to get him out?

I reached out to do just that, hooking my hand under the closest of his straps so I could slice him free, but the moment I touched him, Rupert lurched forward, swinging on his tiny bit of slack to slam me into the wall.

"Oof," I grunted, stepping back. He'd hit me hard enough to

knock my wind out even in my suit—no small feat considering his limited range of movement. But rather than being mad at him for body slamming me, pride filled my chest. He might be soft spoken, but my love was a fighter, and apparently not drugged at all. He'd pulled back quick as a switchblade when the blow was done, pressing himself flat against the back wall, no doubt waiting for me to make another move.

"It's me, Rupert," I called, but though my voice was offensively loud in the small cell, Rupert didn't even flinch...and that was when I realized he couldn't hear me. The mask must be a sensory-deprivation device. He probably couldn't make out a thing. I grimaced, a prison indeed, and I was more determined than ever to free him. If the mask was that horrid to look at, I couldn't imagine what it must be like to *wear*.

I reached for him again, gently this time, my fingers landing lightly on his chest, letting him feel it was me since I had no other way of telling him. He tensed when I touched him, but he didn't try to slam me into the wall again. I smiled and squeezed my fingers against his chest in a way I hoped he'd recognize as friendly. Then, after a quick look around to make sure I wasn't about to be unspeakably stupid, I snatched my hands back and pulled off my helmet.

Face bare, I leaned in and pressed my lips softly against his chest. He went stone still at the touch, but it wasn't until I'd moved up to press a soft kiss against the thin strip of skin at his neck that Rupert slumped into me.

"I've got you," I said into his skin. "I'm going to get that helmet off."

I have no idea if he understood me, but when I pulled away he started to twist, ducking his head toward me while turning it sideways like he was trying to show me the back of his neck. On the second turn, I saw it. There was a latch at his nape that held the helmet together. I memorized the target and put my own helmet back on. Next, I wedged in beside him and grabbed his shoulders, gently pushing him as far down as the straps allowed. When I had him where I wanted him, I gave him a firm squeeze followed by an even firmer push, which I hoped he would interpret as *don't move.*

He must have, because when I released him, he didn't move a muscle. When I was sure he'd stay that way, I ejected Elsie, firing her thermite above his head. Then, when the initial flare was over and the blade was burning evenly, I lined up my targeting and slid her into the helmet's latch, carefully slicing the thing in two.

I did it as fast as I could, but the burning hot thermite was still near Rupert's skin for an uncomfortably long time. Even so, he didn't flinch, his body still as bedrock even after I lifted the blade away. I snuffed the thermite and pulled Elsie back, finishing the break with my hands.

Even with Elsie's crack, it was tough work. The mask was crazy hard, and I didn't want to hurt Rupert by accident, so it took me nearly a minute of careful prying before the thing finally split. When it went, though, it went all at once, falling off Rupert's head in two neat halves, leaving him gasping.

I gasped, too, reaching down in dismay. "They cut your hair!"

Okay, so that wasn't the best reaction I could have had, but I was just so shocked. Rupert's lovely, long black hair was gone, shorn off in a tight buzz cut, probably so they could fit the mask. The short black stubble made him look younger and thinner, vulnerable, and even though I knew nothing could hurt Rupert for long, that didn't stop me from throwing my arms around him and squeezing him tight as I could.

He grunted when I grabbed him, but he didn't fight me. Not that he could, bound up like he was, which reminded me. "Let's get you out," I said, letting him go to grab the closest strap.

Rupert shook his head, glaring at me through the brightness of my suit's floodlights. "Get out of here. You shouldn't have come."

"No," I said fiercely, glaring back. "I'm not leaving you here."

"They'll catch you," he pleaded.

I ignored him, popping Elsie again to slice through his restraints, though I didn't bother with the thermite this time. The woven plastic was hell to rip, but it sliced just fine. Elsie's cold edge was more than enough.

When I didn't answer, Rupert's expression turned frantic. "Devi, *please*. Please go. I don't—"

"You were the one who said you wanted to help."

Rupert went still, and I grinned at him before turning back to my cutting. "You said you were on my team, right? Well, you should know I never leave my teammates behind. Anyway, if you think I busted all the way back here just to turn around, you're out of your mind. Now"—I sliced the last strap, freeing his arms—"do you want to help or not?"

The plastic weave was barely off him before Rupert grabbed me, throwing his arms around my shoulders and hugging me so tight I could feel the pressure through my suit. It wasn't the first time we'd been in this situation, but this time I didn't wait for him to ask. I popped the locks on my helmet and swept it off of my own accord, rising up on my toes to meet his kiss halfway.

Just like back on Reaper's ship, he kissed me savagely, his whole body tense like he was trying to wring out all the fear and anguish and worry. I kissed him back just as hard, sliding the hand that wasn't holding my helmet up to run my fingers over his shaved head. Even through my suit, I could feel the soft brush of his stubble under the Lady's sensitive fingers, and that only made me kiss him harder.

Rupert smiled against my mouth when he felt my hand on his head. "It'll grow back," he whispered against my lips.

"I don't care," I whispered back. "I hate that they did this to you, and I'm never going to let them harm a hair on your head ever again. *Literally*. Now let me go so I can finish breaking you out."

He let me go reluctantly and I put my helmet back on, leaning down to examine our final obstacle, the plasma weight holding his feet. Fortunately, while it was heavy, it wasn't terribly hard, and I was able to slice the thick, jellylike substance down enough that Rupert was able to wiggle his feet out no problem.

They'd really given him the full prison treatment. In addition to his shaved head, he was wearing a neon-yellow prison uniform and alarmed shackles on his feet and wrists, though they were dark thanks to the phantoms. I sliced them off next, slipping Elsie carefully between the metal and Rupert's skin. When I was finished, he shredded the jumpsuit on his own, ripping his scales through it from neck to toes.

"Sure that's smart?" I asked as I helped him brush away the shreds of yellow polycotton. "Black scales and claws aren't that much less eye-catching than yellow pants."

"I don't think stealth is going to be an option if anyone sees us," Rupert replied, stepping out of the tiny cell. "What's the plan?"

"Steal Maat and get her onto a hyperdrive-capable ship."

To his credit, Rupert took all of that with only a slight tightening of his jaw. "Anything else?"

"Isn't that enough?" I asked, popping my visor again. Like before, the phantoms were thick as soup, but I still didn't see Maat. That couldn't be good. I didn't know how much longer she'd be able to keep the power out, but my bet was not long enough, which meant we needed to move. I was about to put my visor back down and do just that when I realized the phantoms behind me were acting strangely.

Considering the events of the last few hours, this was enough to make me spin around and reach for my gun on instinct. Rupert gave me a funny look, but I just held up my hand, watching the cloud of tiny phantoms dance back and forth through the non-electrified mesh of the second high-security cell, the one I hadn't checked. Every time they reappeared, they waved at me, almost like they were inviting me inside.

"What are you doing?" Rupert asked as I holstered my gun and stepped forward.

"The phantoms say there's something in here," I replied, giving him a helpless grin as I pulled the mesh aside. "I've learned to roll with it."

Rupert clearly thought this was every bit as crazy as it sounded, but I couldn't explain it any better, so I just kept going, shining my floodlight into the tiny cell. I wasn't sure what I'd expected to find, a trapped phantom, maybe, or something to help me free Maat. Unsurprisingly, considering where we were, what I found instead was a prisoner, bound up just as Rupert had been. Unlike Rupert, though, this prisoner didn't have one of those awful helmets, though I kind of wished he had. Even the blank metal face would have been better than the alien mask of discolored, brittle scales.

Whoever this symbiont was, he'd clearly seen better days. His scales were longer than any I'd ever seen, and the color was wrong, the normally glossy black turned dull brown in my floodlight. I opened my mouth to ask Rupert if this was one of the symbionts they were doing experiments on, the kind Caldswell had said they planned to do on Rupert, but then I saw the tip of a plastic tube jutting out from the side of the symbiont's neck, its end ragged, like it had been shot off.

"Holy shit," I whispered, taking a small step back. "Hello, Brenton."

In the cell, the symbiont raised its head, its scales rattling like old paper blown by the wind.

CHAPTER

11

"Devi," Rupert said softly, placing a clawed hand on my shoulder. "Back away. His symbiont's still enraged."

I frowned, staring at Brenton's buglike eyes. Their glossy surface was cloudy in my light, but I could see something behind them. I glanced at the phantoms, but they'd dispersed as soon as I pulled back the mesh, fading back into the swarm. Apparently, I was on my own.

"Let's get him out," I said.

Rupert's grip tightened on my shoulder, stopping me. "That's not a good idea."

I almost laughed at that. "We ran out of good ideas a loooong time ago."

I could tell he didn't want to let me go, but he didn't fight me when I shrugged out of his hold to start cutting Brenton loose. The old man was bound in much tighter than Rupert had been, which should have been a warning, but the more I cut, the more sure I felt that this was the right choice. After all, if anyone could be counted on to help me free and kill Maat, it would be Brenton.

Despite Rupert's warnings, Brenton didn't move a muscle the entire time I was cutting him down. I thought this was because he understood what was going on, but then I spotted the machine at his feet. Instead of a plasma weight to keep him down, Brenton was hooked up to an automated tank with an IV that ran under the scales by his ankle. When I pulled the tube out, I caught a whiff of the same awful, metallic smell I'd picked up when Caldswell had cut my own IV, which made me pause. Why the hell did they have Brenton on plasmex-suppressing drugs?

Once the IV was gone, Brenton was completely free, but he didn't move until I stepped out of the way. Only then did he slump down from his spot against the wall, stepping out slowly, like an old, old man.

"Brenton," I said softly. "Can you understand me? Do you know where you are?"

For a moment, he just stared at me, and then he nodded, his head bobbing drunkenly.

"Good," I said. "We're going to—"

Rupert grabbed my shoulder hard, yanking me out of the way. A second later, blinding light hit me in the face as the power came back on and the mesh I'd been holding re-electrified, falling back into place with a blast that echoed down the hall.

I jumped back into Rupert, swearing up a storm. The black mesh was now humming with electricity, and Brenton was trapped on the other side. I glowered for a second, then pulled my gun, flipping my visor back into place. "Cover your head," I warned Rupert as my suit traced the wires to line up Sasha's shot.

He obeyed, pulling the scales over his face. When he was protected, I pulled the trigger, plugging a three-shot burst into the three wires that held the mesh up. When the first bullet hit, the sparks flew like a firework. The second one actually started a small fire, but the third one cut the power to the grid completely, and the prison lights flashed wildly as the electricity surged. But the job was done. The mesh fell to the floor, harmless again, and I reached across it to grab Brenton.

"Come on, old man," I said, trying not to wince when his brittle scales crunched a little under my hand. "Time to go."

Brenton let me pull him down the hall as the three of us made for the exit, but though the lights were mostly back, none of the shields over the cells had come back on yet. That made sense; shields took a *lot* of power. The generator must still be warming up. Luckily, the power hadn't unbusted the door I'd cracked to get in, though I could hear the broken pneumatics grinding inside the wall before the alarms started to blare. I cursed and ran faster, racing for the exit. I barely had the chance to see Nova give me a thumbs-up before we were gone, gunning it into the station proper as fast as we could.

As soon as we were in the relatively open hall, Rupert put on a burst of speed to get out in front. "This way," he said, darting confidently around the closest corner.

I followed him gladly, relieved that I didn't have to rely on his memories to tell me the way anymore, especially since I could hear the security around us coming back online as more and more power was restored. "How long until they get the guns back on?" I yelled at Rupert as he turned a blind corner and started up a ladder I'd only vaguely known would be there.

"Ten minutes from cold shutdown," he answered, reaching up to punch the locked hatch in the ceiling. It folded like paper under his strength, and up we went, scrambling onto the floor above. "The cameras will be back on in five. We need to be somewhere safe by then."

I nodded, motioning for him to lead the way while I helped Brenton. It was hard to believe that the sad creature behind me was the same powerful symbiont who'd slammed Rupert around back on Falcon 34, or even the crazed monster I'd fought in Reaper's arena. Even after I got him up the ladder, he moved in jerks, his scales clattering like spent bullet casings with every step. In the glare of the station's restored lights, he looked more brown than ever, sickly and brittle, his breath wheezing. I had to reach back and help pull him along several times before Rupert finally found the door he was looking for.

"What's this?" I asked, looking the door up and down. Damn thing looked like a bank vault.

Instead of answering, Rupert opened a panel beside it and pulled a red lever. Another alarm went off when he did, but there were so many howling already I didn't even jump, especially since the door was already opening, revealing a small storage room packed to the rafters with ammunition.

Rupert waved at me, and I didn't wait to be asked twice before running for cover. Brenton followed more slowly, giving Rupert a wide berth. When he was through, Rupert pulled the lever on the inside wall, shutting the door. He hit a button above it next, turning off the alarm he'd added to the mix. "That should buy us some time," he said, sliding the huge manual bolt into place.

"How much?" I asked, helping Brenton to the back of the room.

"Enough for you to tell me what we're really doing."

I glanced at Brenton, but he was already leaning back against the shelves, his head listing sideways, seemingly oblivious. I had no idea why the phantoms had wanted me to grab him, but it wasn't like I could ask them, and Maat was nowhere to be seen when I shoved up my visor. Apparently, I was on my own, but since we were safe for a moment, I motioned for Rupert to join me in the far corner. Once our backs were to a wall and we were out of earshot of the door, I dropped my voice to a whisper and brought him up to speed.

I'd only meant to give him the basics, but once the story got going, I ended up telling him everything, including my interlude with the emperor phantom in the oneness and what it had shown me about their home. Rupert was far too tactful to let his skepticism show on his face, but I knew he had to be feeling it. How could he not? I mean, even *I* thought what I was saying sounded crazy. To hear me tell it, we were risking our lives to kidnap and kill the most valuable and irreplaceable plasmex user in the universe because a monster had told me to do it in a dream.

If our positions had been reversed, I would have told him he was nuts flat out, but Rupert just looked thoughtful. "And you're sure killing Maat in hyperspace will free the phantoms while sparing the daughters?"

"That's my hope," I said with a shrug. "I realize it's not a lot to go on, but—"

Rupert reached through my open visor, silencing me with a gentle stroke of his claw against my cheek. "You don't have to explain," he said softly. "I believe you."

"You do?"

The words came out far more skeptical than I'd meant, but Rupert just smiled. "Of course," he said, sliding the tip of his claw up to brush a stray curl behind my ear. "You can be frustratingly reckless, but there is always good reason behind what you do. If you're convinced this is the right path, that's proof enough for me."

"And it beats prison."

"That it does," he said, laughing, and then his face turned serious again. "Thank you for that, by the way."

"Save it until we're safe," I warned him. "This might still turn out to be a suicide mission."

He shook his head. "Doesn't change a thing."

I glared at him. "Don't talk like—"

"It's not talk," Rupert said, dropping his hands to mine. "If helping you costs me my life, I count it well spent." He leaned down, giving me that warm, loving look that always melted me into a puddle. "It's because of you I have a life to risk in the first place."

I dropped my eyes, unsure what to say. I wasn't even sure there *was* an answer to a statement like that. I didn't know how to handle being so important to someone or the fact that as Rupert spoke, I realized I'd do the same.

That might not sound like much coming from me. After all, I'd risked my neck for a whole host of reasons: kingdom, honor, pride, ambition. My whole life, these had been drilled into me as good reasons to die, honors worthy of my sacrifice, but as I stared down at our joined hands, his black claws wrapped around the Lady's beautiful silver, I knew love was now on that list, too.

The thought made me shake in my boots. When had Rupert gotten so much power over me? And when had I stopped caring? I squeezed his hands tighter. When had this hole gotten so deep? I was still scrambling for an answer when a terrible sound made us jump apart.

The grating hiss was so awful, so inhuman, it took me a second to believe it was coming from Brenton. He was still leaning against the shelves, but his head was up now, his cloudy eyes watching us as he made that ghastly noise, but it wasn't until I saw his chest shaking that I realized Brenton was *laughing*.

"So you weren't lying before." The words came out as a hiss, almost, but sadly not quite, unintelligible. "You really did melt the iceberg, didn't you?" He started laughing again, setting my teeth on edge. "How the mighty have fallen."

I bristled and turned to tell him to shut his mouth before I shut it for him, but Rupert beat me to the punch.

"Enough," he said, his voice shockingly cold. He'd been so warm to me for so long, I'd half forgotten he could sound like that. "How long have you been aware?"

"Since shortly before Caldswell handed me over," Brenton replied.

"Then why didn't you speak up earlier?" Rupert snapped.

"Easy, killer," Brenton said, tilting his head. "We're both traitors now. You don't get to play high-and-mighty with me anymore."

I looked back and forth between the men. There was a dynamic here I didn't follow. I knew they didn't like each other, but I'd thought the animosity was strictly professional. Apparently, I was wrong, because Rupert's glare was very personal as he turned to Brenton and crossed his arms over his chest. He looked like he was trying to decide just how slowly to gut the older man, and I was starting to worry I'd made the wrong choice listening to the phantoms.

"What do you want?" Rupert said. "And make it quick. We don't have time to play your games."

"I never play games," Brenton replied. "And what I want depends on Morris over there. She's the one who sprung me."

Brenton turned to me then, and I had to focus to keep from cringing at the sight of his symbiont's battered face. "Thank you for that, by the way," he said. "And for the record, despite what Charkov here might be implying, I wasn't trying to give you the silent treatment. I couldn't speak up until just a few minutes ago. The drugs make it . . . difficult to think clearly."

"Why did they have you on anti-plasmex drugs?" I asked. "Are you—"

"Plasmex sensitive?" Brenton finished, shaking his head. "No more than most Eyes." I arched an eyebrow at that, and Brenton explained. "You need a decent amount of natural plasmex to keep the symbiont running, but nothing out of the ordinary curve, and certainly nothing they'd need to drug. The drugs weren't for *my* abilities. They were to dampen my plasmex aura so Maat couldn't talk to me."

"Why would Maat want to talk to you?" I asked.

I couldn't see Brenton's face through the mask, but it didn't matter. I knew he was smiling. "Because she loves me."

"She doesn't love you," Rupert said scornfully. "She was using you to kill herself. Maat is insane. She doesn't love."

"Just because she hates the rest of you doesn't mean hate is all she has," Brenton replied.

Rupert opened his mouth, but I raised my hand. "Actually, I think Brenton's right."

"He's delusional," Rupert said, dropping his voice. "You didn't see what he did when he went rogue, Devi. He used to be one of our top-ranked Eyes. He was Caldswell's own partner for years before Maat's whispers started to get to him. Commander Martin had just taken over then. He ordered Brenton contained, but Caldswell convinced him to give him a second chance, and do you know what he did with it?"

I could guess, but Rupert was going to tell me anyway, so I let him finish.

"He killed his new partner plus five other Eyes," Rupert said, glaring at the symbiont on the other side of the room. "He murdered his entire team in cold blood, stole their three daughters, and ran."

"That's one way to put it," Brenton said with a shrug. "But so long as we're talking about the past, why not tell her how you came after me like Caldswell's attack dog and then killed the daughters we liberated when you couldn't get to me?" He turned his alien mask in my direction. "Three little girls, Devi, can you imagine? Charkov here broke their necks like a farmer killing chickens." He raised his hands and mimed a twisting motion, making Rupert go tense. "Crack, crack, crack."

"I had to kill them because *you* let them degrade," Rupert said, his voice so icy I was surprised I couldn't see his breath. "You let Maat's madness devour them."

"I set them free," Brenton said, his hoarse voice shaking with conviction. "Better they be mad and themselves than your mindless dolls. At least when the daughters were with us, we treated them like people."

Rupert's eyes narrowed to slits. "You used them just as much as we did."

"Ah, but there isn't any 'we' anymore, is there, Charkov?" Brenton replied with a cruel laugh. "You're just as fallen as I am, and for not nearly as good a reason. I left to do what was right, to be a knight in shining armor for a girl who had no one to be her champion. *You* turned traitor because you got hooked on a sweet piece of Paradoxian—"

I had Sasha out before he could finish, my gun trained right at the sweet spot between his cloudy bug eyes. "That will be quite enough of that," I said, making my voice as cold as Rupert's. "In case you've forgotten, Brenton, we're in enemy territory and we're running out of time. Now, how do we get to Maat?"

"I could have told you that," Rupert muttered behind me, but I motioned for him to shut up. The phantoms had told me to save

Brenton, probably at Maat's behest, and I was betting this was why. I certainly hadn't done it for the pleasure of his company.

Brenton sighed and took a seat on an ammo crate. "Finding Maat isn't the problem. It's surviving the trip."

He reached down, using his claw to trace a crude map of the Dark Star Station in the layer of dust that covered the metal ammo crate's surface. "We're here," he said, tapping a spot halfway down the bottom ray. "And Maat is here." He lifted his claw to tap the very tip of the ray on the station's opposite side. "To reach her, we need to go all the way across, cutting through the center of the station below the command deck and around the primary generator."

I whistled, calculating how much ground we'd have to cover. "That's a lot of traps."

"Actually, the first part isn't bad. The real challenge comes when we enter Maat's part of the station." He spread his first two fingers to indicate the entirety of Maat's ray of the star. "This entire wing is known as the kill box."

"I thought this whole place was a kill box."

"Not like this," Brenton said. "The lab and Maat's cell only take up a small portion at the very tip. The rest is a snaking corridor of blast-rated doors and walls broken up into fifteen compartmentalized checkpoints. You don't have the credentials, they lock you in and blast you—with gas if they're feeling generous, bullets if they're not. There are also three break points."

I frowned. "Break points?"

"Explosive rigged airlocks," Rupert said, leaning down to draw three thin lines on Brenton's map, dividing Maat's ray neatly in thirds. "The checkpoints protect against a boarding, but if the Dark Star was ever attacked from the outside and was in danger of falling, command could blow any one of these points, detaching Maat's prison so it could be picked up and ferried away to safety by the battleship on guard."

"Like a lizard shedding its tail," I muttered, only here, the tail was the important part. "What else?"

"I should think that's enough," Rupert said, crossing his arms. "There's a reason no one has ever made it to Maat. We've gotten this far thanks to the power outage, but now that things are back online, I don't know if we can even make it to the kill box, much less through. Once the guns are operational, it will be like shooting fish in a trap. We won't have a chance."

I ground my teeth in frustration. It did look impossible, but I couldn't believe I'd made it all this way just to fail here because of a damn security system. I was about to ask Rupert if there was any chance of cutting the power again when Brenton suddenly spoke up.

"We absolutely have a chance."

Rupert and I both glanced up to see Brenton leaning back, his chin raised proudly. "Unlike your doomsayer boyfriend, I'm actually older than this station, old enough to remember the Dark Star didn't start out as a maze. This place used to be a normal four-corners starbase. Caldswell and I built it up over the years as Maat grew more dangerous and our needs changed, but the problem with building over old equipment is that there are some things, crucial parts of the infrastructure, that you just can't alter no matter how much you spend."

He paused dramatically, and I gave him a killing glare for his trouble. "Where are you going with this?"

"Exactly where you need to be," he replied smugly. "Sometimes it's the old dogs who know the best tricks, and I know one that might get us through the kill box if we move fast. But if we're going to make it, we have to leave right now, no arguments and no backtalk."

His scales made following his eyes impossible, but the tilt of his head told me he was looking straight at Rupert. Rupert returned the favor, scowling at Brenton like he meant to toss him into the hall for the other symbionts to slice into little tiny bits. As someone who's stared down a lot of macho bullshit over her career, I didn't begrudge him the hard feelings in the least, but I didn't have time for them right now either.

"Let's go, then," I said.

"*Devi!*" Rupert hissed, but I just shrugged.

"It's not like we'll be any deader if he screws us over," I reminded him. "I'll take a crazy chance over no chance any day of the week." I turned back to Brenton. "Ready?"

"Whenever you are," he said, pushing himself to his feet.

I headed for the door, looking both ways before darting into the hall. Rupert came out right on my heels and took point at once, and though he was too polite to grumble, I knew he didn't like this one bit. I sighed and promised myself I'd make it up to him later, if there was a later. For now, I ran like my life depended on it. Which, of course, it did.

———

According to the timers I'd set when Rupert had told me our time limits, we left the armory with two minutes, fifty seconds until the station's security measures came back online. That wasn't much time by anyone's standards, especially with Brenton in such bad shape, but we were still two symbionts and a damn fine suit of powered armor. If we didn't make it, no one could.

We went at a full run, choosing speed over stealth. I thought for sure we were going to get jumped any second, but we never even saw another person. Apparently, whoever was running the station was waiting for security to reboot, too, so they could kill us at a distance. A smart choice considering my record versus symbionts and how the tight hallway would eliminate their superior numbers advantage. I should have been disappointed we wouldn't get a chance to thin their numbers with a few easy fights, but all I felt was smug. It was nice to finally get some damn respect.

We had fifty-eight seconds left when Brenton skidded to a halt in the middle of an otherwise unremarkable hallway. "Here we are."

Rupert and I stopped as well, looking around. "Here where?"

Fast as we were going, I hadn't bothered trying to follow Rupert's memories, which meant I was completely lost. Since the hallways here looked more military industrial than military aggressive, I assumed we were in the middle of the station where they kept the power core, shield generators, and other key machinery. But rather than answer my question, Brenton grabbed an important-looking panel covered with warning stickers on the ceiling and yanked it down, breaking the latch to reveal an empty metal pipe just big enough for a person to crawl through.

"What's that?" I asked, craning my head. "Air shaft?"

"Please," Brenton said. "This isn't amateur hour. None of the vents here are anywhere near big enough to crawl through." He nodded up at the open pipe. "This is the shield feeder."

I made a choking sound before I could stop myself. I didn't know much about space station construction, but even I knew about shield feeders. The shields needed to protect something as huge as a space station required enormous amounts of power. Since you didn't want generators that big on the outside of your battle station where they could get hit by stray fire, this often meant the heavy shielding plasma was generated wherever the power core was and then piped out to the station edges for projection. The stuff was crazy hot and crazy dangerous. Most places big enough to need feeder pipes kept them buried deep in the support girders for public safety, and now Brenton wanted us to climb *inside* one?

"Brenton," I said with what I thought was impressive calm, all things considered. "The whole point of this is *not* to die."

"Then we'll have to move quickly," Brenton said. "We are sitting on an unparalleled opportunity here. This pipe runs to the shield generator at the end of Maat's wing, which means it runs directly over the kill box, skipping right over every checkpoint and trap. It's a straight shot."

"A straight shot to the head," I snapped, glaring up at the dark hole above us. Sure the pipe was empty *now*, but: "If we're in there when the shields come back online, we're going to get flooded with superheated heavy shielding plasma. We'll be cooked through before we can even scream."

"Actually, I think Brenton has a point." Rupert's voice told me he *really* hated to admit that, but he was a professional, and he explained his logic quickly and efficiently despite his obvious loathing. "The Dark Star's systems were never meant to be turned off completely, so they're slow to come back online. The shields take the most power, which means they'll come on last. Twenty minutes from power-up, assuming no damage."

We'd lost ten already, so that gave us roughly ten minutes of clean pipe before we got baked. Not great odds, but then, we were talking about a straight shot, which was definitely preferable to a kill box. "I don't know," I said, putting my hands on my hips. "You sure this will take us all the way? I mean, a pipe running straight over a death maze sounds like a pretty obvious vulnerability."

Brenton shrugged. "We couldn't impede the flow if we wanted shields on that side of the station, and anyway, the pipe is normally full of superheated, pressurized plasma. Not exactly a viable path of invasion."

He had a point, and we were running out of time, so, with a long sigh and a prayer to my king, I hopped up and grabbed the edge of the panel Brenton had just yanked down.

Unsurprisingly, considering the power had gone out less than thirty minutes ago, the pipe was burning hot. So much so that I could feel it radiating up even through my suit's thermal shielding. I paused just long enough to make sure I wasn't going to get burned before I swung myself into the pipe, which now felt much smaller than it had looked from the floor. There was room for my suit lying down, but just barely, and though I could pull myself forward on my forearms, I couldn't turn around.

The combination was close enough to the mines that my heart started pounding. Fortunately, my panic was staved off by the fact that I wasn't underwater and, more importantly, I could *see* this time. That might not sound like much since there wasn't anything to look at other than the pipe going off into the distance, but seeing all that open space in front of me helped me get over the heat and the terrible closeness of the walls, and I was able to pull myself forward after only a few seconds of hesitation.

Rupert came up next, then Brenton, who closed up the pipe behind him, blocking off the light and hopefully any chance of us being followed. I set my timer and focused on moving as quickly and quietly as possible, but even with my suit's coolers, the residual heat from the metal quickly grew intolerable. I was sweating buckets before we cleared the first hundred feet, and I had no idea how Brenton and Rupert kept going, though I was sure the promise of impending death was a motivating factor.

All things considered, we made excellent time. Eight minutes and fifty-seven seconds later, my floodlights hit the coil-covered wall of the shield projector. We'd made it to the end of the line; now we just had to get out.

As we'd been crawling, I'd seen several more emergency hatches like the one Brenton had pulled down, spaced at regular intervals. Sure enough, there was one at the tunnel's end. I broke the latch as quietly as I could and lifted the panel, and then let out a relieved breath when I saw it let out into a crawl space and not, say, a gun emplacement. Even so, the power was almost completely restored now, which meant I could see the people gathered through the cracks in the drop ceiling.

I motioned for Rupert and Brenton to be silent and crawled out, using my suit's stabilizer to make sure I made no sound as I let myself down onto the metal grate that shielded the pipes and wires from view. Rupert came down next, followed by Brenton, who quickly replaced the panel. Not a second too soon, either. I could already feel the pipe vibrating as the shield prepared to come back online. Without that panel, we would have gotten covered in molten shield sludge. With it, though, we were safe for the moment, giving me time to examine our enemies.

Symbionts don't show up on density sensors, and the hot pipe beside us blinded my thermo, so I couldn't count how many people were in the room below. Going by the muffled voices that drifted up through the drop ceiling, however, I was guessing quite a few. My density scanner picked up the rest of the room just fine, drawing me a picture of a single room twice as long as it was wide with a door at either end. Thick walls, too, nice and defensible. Unless, of course, your enemy came from above.

I grinned and turned my attention to my suit, arming all of my grenades and setting the variable payloads. When everything was ready, I shot Rupert and Brenton a pointed look and raised three fingers. Two fingers. One finger.

When I had nothing left but a fist, I slammed it down on the metal ceiling panel beside me. The drop ceiling crumpled like cardboard under the blow, and I leaned forward, letting my ordnance payload fall. The *ting ting* of grenades hitting the metal floor was almost musical, and I was treated to a collective gasp as everyone in the room below simultaneously realized what that sound meant. By that point, though, it was too late.

Before they could run, before I could even pull my arms back to cover my head, the whole room exploded in a flash of light that whited out my cameras. As soon as it faded, I shoved myself forward, rolling headfirst through the hole I'd made in the ceiling.

Because I mostly worked ships and compounds, my ordnance was ship-safe. Even when I dumped my full payload like I just had, the combined explosions wouldn't do more than throw a symbiont around. They did, however, make a hell of a lot of smoke, and smoke was what I was after.

I plummeted silently through the billowing clouds that filled the room, my suit flipping me automatically to land neatly on my feet with Sasha ready in my hand. Rupert dropped down next, almost landing on top of me. He fell into a crouch at once, peering around blindly into the smoke before he pulled his scales over his head.

I had no such problems. *I* had thermal scanners, and now that we were away from that damn pipe, they painted a crystal-clear picture of the room, the cool furniture, and the bright shapes of the warm symbionts around us. My computer marked them as I watched, painting a target at the center of each glowing figure's head, and I couldn't help a smug smile. "Bet you wish you had armor right now."

"What?" Rupert said almost in my ear.

My answer was a gunshot followed by the solid *thunk* as the first symbiont hit the far wall, thrown across the room by Sasha's perfectly aimed blast to its head.

I didn't wait to see if he'd get up. I was already on to the next target, my suit moving my pistol into place with millimeter precision. I'd marked Rupert and Brenton as friendlies so my Lady wouldn't let me shoot them, but every other glowing heat shadow on my sensors was fair game as I hopped up on a metal lab table and got to work.

With the thick smoke, surprise, and my thermographics, the fight didn't even deserve the name. This was a slaughter. I normally prefer to do my shooting myself, but this was the sort of situation my Lady was made for, and I didn't dare stand in her way. Letting my suit guide me, we moved together like a turret, firing perfect shot after perfect shot as my firing system unfailingly guided my gun right to the target painted on each symbiont's head. Even though Sasha's bullets couldn't puncture their scales, she was still accurate as hell and hit like a truck, and now that Rupert had revealed the symbiont's weak spot, I was merciless. Every shot I fired sent a scaled body careening into the wall before collapsing in a heap, just like the one I'd shot back on Kessel. It was brutal, unfair, and deeply satisfying. It was also not enough.

I hadn't actually realized until my suit counted them up for me just how full the room had been. At least now I knew why we hadn't run into anyone out in the halls. There must have been thirty symbionts waiting here for us. I'd shot a good fifteen of them by the time someone thought to turn on the lab's ventilation system and suck out the smoke, but as soon as the air began to clear, the tide began to turn.

I'd just finished taking out my sixteenth symbiont when I saw a glowing blur pop up behind me on my thermals. That was all the warning I got before a claw caught my arm, wrenching me back hard enough to overpower my stabilizer. Since not falling was no longer an option, I kicked off the table instead, slamming my body back into my attacker. But symbionts are tough bastards, and heavy as I was, I didn't manage to knock him down. He did stumble, though, and I seized my opening, shoving Sasha back and under the arm he'd grab to plug a shot into his chest. The anti-armor round wasn't enough to really hurt him, but it did blast him back, and when his hand opened on instinct, letting me go to catch himself, I kicked off, jumping clear of his reach to the other side of the table I'd been standing on.

I landed less gracefully than I would have liked, but my suit righted me soon enough, slamming me back against the lab table's built-in cabinet. My smoke was almost completely gone now, and though several symbionts were down, plenty were still up. Worse, when I'd broken line of sight on Rupert, my suit had lost his friendly fire tag, which meant I was no longer sure which of the black-scaled figures was him.

There were four in front of me right now, actually, closing in fast. None of them were tall enough to be Rupert, so I cleared my suit to fire, shooting the first one square in the head before I could blink. Two of the remaining three jumped back at the shot, but the fourth didn't even flinch, and I knew at once that this was my real enemy. The other two were civilians, likely scientists or engineers given symbionts to survive living near Maat, but this man was a soldier like me, and my gunshot had barely finished echoing before he lunged for my throat.

I threw my arm up, ejecting Elsie as I did, but this was a real symbiont, a trained Eye, and I was too slow. His claws shot through my guard to dig into my chest, slicing deep gouges in the Lady's mist-silver plating above my ribs before I could roll away. I came up furious, swiping my now-burning plasma blade across his calves as I rose.

The man fell with a yelp as I cut his legs out from under him. Even if he hadn't, my next punch to his jaw would have knocked him flat. I was burning with anger over the damage to my suit, so much that I felt the first tingles of the virus on my fingers. That snuffed my rage like a candle in a vacuum, but not before I'd sliced the symbiont's neck open.

I kicked his body for good measure and turned, blade ready, only to find I had no more opponents. My anger-fueled execution must have looked even worse than I'd thought, because the remaining two symbionts backed off at once, their hands up in surrender. I switched Sasha to my left hand and kept her trained on them just in case while my cameras scanned the room, looking for the next real threat.

I found it on the other side. Whereas I'd pulled the coward symbionts, Rupert was facing off against four opponents who looked like they knew exactly what they were doing. Brenton was over there, too, holding his own in the back corner against two more, though not nearly as well as he should have been considering how I'd seen him fight before. I hopped up on the table to go help, but as I jumped over the symbiont with the slashed neck, his hand shot out and grabbed my ankle to yank me back down.

I gasped and fell, landing flat on the table before my suit pushed me back up, but I couldn't break the bleeding symbiont's hold as he jumped on top of me. I had no idea where he was getting his strength from; he should have been half bled out by now, not to mention unable to breathe thanks to a filleted windpipe. But I must not have hit him as well as I'd thought, because he was gasping in my ear as he held me down, throwing up his hand to catch something one of the other symbionts tossed. I was still trying to shove him off me, which meant I didn't see what he'd caught until it was too late.

The bolt of lightning crashed into my suit like a spear, and then everything went dark as my Lady overloaded. I went limp a second later, landing hard on the table's edge as my suit's weight crushed me. I didn't even try to catch myself. First, I'd only break my arms without my suit's motors to help with the weight, and second, I was too busy frantically trying to get my Lady back online.

After what felt like an eternity of darkness, my cameras flickered back to life, giving me a clear view of the bastard who'd shot me. He was still leaning into me where I was doubled over the table, resting his weight on my back to avoid putting it on his injured legs. His chest was soaked with blood from what I'd done to his neck and he seemed to be barely holding on. Despite all that, though, he was still up, pressing a clunky anti-armor charge thrower pistol into the back of my neck, the same goddamn gun Brenton's team had used on me on Ample.

"Target secure," he panted. "Call the commander. Tell him we've got—"

I had Sasha down and pressed against his knee before he could finish. I fired three shots in rapid succession, and while the first two only slammed him around, I felt the third one crack bone. The symbiont lurched back a second later, clutching his knee with a pained cry. The second his weight was off me, I whirled and shot him in the head, blasting him into the door that led back to the kill box.

He hit the blast door like a cannon shot, knocking it half off its track. I kept my gun on his limp body, but it wasn't necessary. This time, he wasn't getting up again.

The symbiont had dropped the charge thrower when I'd shot his knee. I stomped on it with all my weight, cracking the plastic casing to tiny bits. Threat eliminated, I turned back to my cowering enemies, Elsie shining like a star on my right and Sasha ready on my left. My targeting system was already lining up the shots for their miserable heads when I heard the unmistakable blast of a disrupter pistol behind me.

Before I could think better of it, I glanced at my rear cameras. I was too late to see who'd fired, but they must not have hit, because a second later, the knot of symbionts surrounding Rupert blew open as he grabbed one of his attackers around the throat and hurled him as hard as he could. I ducked as the man flew over my head to slam into the door I'd just broken with his buddy, taking it clean off its railings this time.

The first man hadn't even landed before Rupert kicked the next one, slamming him into a metal specimen refrigerator hard enough to dent the wall behind it. He slammed the third symbiont into the ground with his heel, stomping the man's chest so hard I heard his ribs crack under his scales.

The snapping sound made me want to cheer. Every other time we'd fought symbionts, with the exception of Brenton's first invasion of the *Fool*, I'd felt that Rupert was holding back. In a way, I couldn't blame him. These were his former teammates; for him, fighting them would be like me attacking Blackbirds. I didn't know what had finally pushed Rupert over the edge—getting locked up maybe, or perhaps it was getting shot. Now that he'd thinned the herd a bit, I could see that his side was burned where the earlier disrupter blast had grazed him. The wound looked painful, but Rupert didn't even seem to feel it as he reached out and crushed the disrupter pistol in the final symbiont's hand.

I wasn't the only one watching, either. Back on my side of the room, the symbionts I'd been preparing to fight were breaking. They turned as I watched, abandoning their fallen comrades as they fled back through the kill box into the station proper, and they weren't alone. The room that had been packed full of symbionts was now nearly empty as the remaining combatants turned and ran for the door.

I didn't bother trying to stop them. My goal was to reach Maat, not slaughter the station, however appealing that might sound while the battle rage was singing through me. But I had a job to do, and anyway, the panic only confirmed my suspicions that most of these people weren't real symbionts but technicians forced into fighting, and bloodthirsty as I can be, I'd never liked hurting civilians.

Elsie had burned out by this point anyway. I broke off her blackened edge and pulled her back into her sheath on my wrist, walking toward Rupert as I did. He was still standing with his foot on the downed symbiont's chest. There was blood on his claws and splattered across his upper body, making his blank, scale-masked face look truly monstrous in the bright white lab lights. This should have been a reminder of what Rupert really was, but as I looked him over, all I felt was a primal, possessive pride. That was *my* man standing victorious over his defeated enemies, and I couldn't have been happier if I'd beaten them all myself.

Rupert must not have been able to see through my visor, though, because when he saw me staring, he dropped his head. "I'm sorry," he said, scraping the blood off his cheek with a scaly claw. "That was...I didn't want you to see—"

I hopped over the table, landing neatly beside him. The second my feet were on the ground, I hugged him. It was very brief, just a squeeze, but when I stepped back, I could practically feel the confusion radiating off his body.

"Very Paradoxian, remember?" I said with a smirk, running my hand over the smooth scales on his back before I let him go. "You were marvelous." I kicked one of the downed symbionts with the toe of my boot. "That'll teach 'em to mess with us."

When Rupert didn't answer, I knew he was staring dumbfounded at me. Normally I would have reveled in my ability to throw him so completely off balance, but I had no time to enjoy it right now. I was already jogging over to help Brenton.

Despite his physical problems, Brenton had defeated the symbionts who'd been trying to corner him, but the fight had taken its toll. He was leaning against the wall, his brittle, brown-black scales rattling with every wheezing breath. He accepted my arm without comment, letting me haul him up. "Where now, Mr. Guide?" I asked when I got him back on his feet.

"Through there," he whispered, nodding at the heavily reinforced door at the opposite end of the room.

I frowned. That door was going to be a problem, especially if there were more symbionts on the other side, which I was sure there must be. Martin would never leave Maat without a final guard.

"That door is the only way into Maat's prison," Rupert said, stepping up beside us. "Devi, if you go down, it's all for nothing, so Brenton and I—"

"No way," I snapped, glaring. "They were going after you with disrupters, but I got charge throwers. The Eyes must still want me alive or that symbiont would have ripped off my head instead of just shocking me. The fact that they want me alive is a weapon we can use, so if anyone does anything, it's going to be me."

I heard Rupert take a breath to argue, but before he could, a loud, mechanical hum filled the air. When I glanced up reflexively to find the source, I was nearly blinded as a pair of huge targeting floodlights flashed on from the far wall. My suit adjusted to the brightness automatically, though not fast enough to save my eyes. I was still blinking away spots when the room filled with a harsh, jangling rattle, like something metal was spinning up very fast. It was a sound I recognized, but it was so out of place here that I couldn't put a name to it until Rupert grabbed my arm.

The next thing I knew, I was on the ground, pinned under Rupert's weight as the heavy door at the end of the lab slid open to reveal two enormous, automated, anti-armor chain guns. They'd already spun up, the noise I'd heard earlier, and the second the door was out of their way, they opened fire, shredding everything in their path.

I gasped in surprise, covering my head, not that it would do any good. The bullets that thing was firing were the size of my hand.

They'd punch right through my arm into my head if they hit. I was scrambling to think of something they wouldn't punch through when Rupert grabbed my arm.

"Door!" he yelled, yanking me up.

I jumped to my feet and bolted for the door the symbionts had fled through, the one our carnage had knocked off its track, turning the corner into a short hallway that dead-ended at another heavy door, the final compartment of the kill box we'd avoided by taking the pipe. Brenton was already here, crouched down behind the final kill box wall, which, since it had been built to keep even symbionts in, was sufficient for keeping bullets *out*, even huge ones. Thankfully, the turrets here had already been yanked down, probably by the fleeing symbionts, so we were able to hole up without fear.

Shaking my head at the irony of using a kill box for cover, I crouched down between my two symbionts, glaring at the rain of bullets pecking a hole in the wall on the opposite side of the sundered blast door not three feet in front of me. "Who the hell uses guns like that inside? Does Martin *want* to slag his station?"

"At this point, I don't think he cares," Brenton said, panting. "Those guns were put in as a last-stand defense."

"More like suicide," I grumbled, nodding at the rapidly disintegrating metal wall. "He's going to puncture the hull and kill us all."

"I don't think he'd mind that," Rupert said quietly. "And I don't think he's worrying about keeping you alive anymore, either."

Couldn't argue with that. The guns in the other room were chewing up everything, including the symbionts we'd knocked out. The two men we'd thrown at the door were such a bloody mess I had to look away, which is saying something when you've seen as much blood as I have. "He's killing everyone," I whispered. "His own people."

"Of course," Brenton said. "He's an Eye."

I snorted. Brenton was one to talk about sacrificing his men. But that was an old argument, and now was not the time. The tiny hall we'd holed up in had no vents or openings, no escape other than the doors at either end, which weren't escapes at all. If we busted the door behind us and retreated, we'd still be trapped inside the kill box, maybe even in a bit where the *kill* part still worked. But if we tried to go forward, we'd get shot. Either way, we'd be dead.

"He can't keep this up forever," I said, taking the chance to reload Sasha. "Those guns have to run out some—"

I was cut off by sudden, deafening silence as the hail of bullets stopped. I held my breath, listening, but I didn't hear the click of a new belt being fed in. They weren't reloading. The guns hadn't spun down on their own, though, which meant something had stopped them. I was about to peek out and see what when I heard the distinct sound of symbiont claws crunching over spent shells.

"You can stop delaying the inevitable, Miss Morris."

I threw my head back with a silent curse. I'd only heard it once before, but that little exchange had been memorable enough for me to forever recognize Commander Martin's dry, genteel voice. It seemed the old bastard had come out to finish the job himself.

"There's no point in being stubborn," he called. "You're dead no matter what. But if you remove your armor and weapons and surrender now with no more fuss, I won't kill Charkov."

I heard Rupert suck in an angry breath, but I put up my hand. "Aren't you supposed to tempt me with my life, too?" I yelled.

"Unfortunately, your death is a foregone conclusion," Martin said. "After your actions today, your risk-to-reward ratio has proven far too dangerous for my blood. But I am a fair man, Miss Morris, and so I'm giving you a choice: come out now, save your lover, and die a hero, or I kill all of you. You have thirty seconds to decide."

I took a step back, bumping into the blast-rated wall. As my back hit the reinforced plates, the awful feeling of being trapped, *really* trapped, curdled in my gut. Fear followed right behind, but not because I was going to die. I'd long accustomed myself to that. No, I was afraid because, with Maat knocked out, I wasn't sure I could give her the virus like I'd promised. Even if I gave in to my anger at Martin and blacked my whole body right now, she wasn't aware enough to grab it, which meant I wasn't just going to *die*, I was going to *fail*. I'd put everyone in danger, Rupert in danger, for *nothing*.

But while these awful thoughts were busy spinning through my head, Brenton and Rupert were moving. They weren't even looking at the guns in the hallway. Instead, they were huddled beside the blown off door with their heads together, talking in rapid whispers. This was odd, because not five minutes ago I would have sworn they hated each other. They must have put their differences aside, though, because when Brenton gave what looked to me like an order, Rupert just nodded and returned to my side.

"Stick close to us," he whispered. "Go for the gun on the left. I'll get the right. Brenton will take Martin."

I blinked. He couldn't be serious. Even if we could miraculously make it to the other side of the room under fire, Martin was a full symbiont who hadn't lifted a claw yet. Brenton was a nasty customer, but he was in a bad way. If it came to a fight, he wouldn't have a chance.

"Ten seconds, Miss Morris," Martin called from the other room.

I clenched my teeth as I looked at Rupert, and then I made a field decision. The second I nodded, Rupert walked to the mangled door and heaved it up, setting it in front of him. Before I could figure out why, Rupert rushed into the room, using the battered door as a shield. I followed a few steps behind with Brenton, throwing myself entirely into whatever we were doing, even though I still wasn't quite sure what it was.

Once we were through the door, I understood what Rupert and Brenton had been planning. At the other end of the bullet-riddled lab, a fully changed symbiont was standing between the two deployed chain guns. If I hadn't heard him speaking earlier, I wouldn't have guessed the muscular man was Martin. But though his scaled mask covered his graying beard and false, grandfatherly face, nothing could hide the surprise and fear in his body as he stumbled backward, hitting the switch in his hands.

The huge, belt-fed chain guns spun up at Martin's command, but their motors were no match for symbiont speed. The door in Rupert's hands ate the first shot, the bullet nearly breaking through. The second would have made it for sure, but it never got the chance. By the time the second shot fired, Rupert was already on top of the guns.

He brought the door down like a hammer, slamming it into the motor of the right turret. I heard the thing squeal as its metal casing broke, but I was too busy with my own gun to pay attention. As we'd agreed, I took the gun on the left, jumping on top of it before its targeting system could get a lock on me. I popped Elsie as I flew, and though my thermite blade was dark, she was still sharp enough to punch through the turret's control board. The hard circuitry cracked like a plate, and the gun sputtered to a stop, the chain spinning off its gears.

I grinned, yanking my blade out as I turned to see if Rupert needed help, but I should have known better. While I'd been stabbing circuit boards, he'd ripped his gun completely out of the floor. He hurled it as I watched, launching it into the far wall. It landed with a crash I felt through my stabilizers, and I sagged with relief. All this back-and-forth between hope and despair was starting to take its toll. But while we'd eliminated the guns, the battle wasn't done yet.

Brenton and Martin were on the floor in front of Maat's door, brawling like schoolboys. As I'd feared, Martin's healthy symbiont had a definite edge on Brenton's sickly one, but what I'd failed to take into account was the difference in skill. Forever ago, when I'd watched Brenton fight Rupert in the *Fool*'s lounge, the difference had been a razor's edge. Here it was more like miles.

Despite his superior strength and claws, Martin was on the bottom on his back, and he couldn't seem to get up. Any time he managed to get something free to take a shot, Brenton would just readjust and attack from another direction, methodically pounding the commander into the floor. Martin must have gotten some hits in at some point because Brenton was bleeding freely from his stomach, his brittle scales chipped in several places, but he didn't seem to feel it. If anything, he seemed to be getting stronger, driving his fists into the commander over and over until the floor began to dent beneath them.

The Brenton I knew was normally a calm, rational fighter, but right now he was drowning in blind fury, tearing into Martin like an animal even though he'd clearly already won. And while it was disturbing to watch, I didn't dare try to stop him. I'd been fighting the Eyes for just a few months, but Brenton had been waging a personal war on them for years in his quest to save Maat, and Martin was now feeling the result of all that pent-up anger. I wouldn't have risked getting in the way of that to save someone I liked. Like hell was I risking it for Martin.

Finally, after what felt like an eternity, Brenton stopped swinging. Martin had stopped moving a while ago, but it took Brenton a few tries to actually ease off the man. For a long moment, there was no sound except his labored breathing, and then the tension cracked as Brenton began to chuckle.

"Bastard always was a damn paper pusher," he said, slinging the blood off his claws. "A bureaucrat who took the symbiont because it was part of the job. Never learned to use it, never bothered to learn anything about the real work of being an Eye. I'll hate the man to my dying day, but Caldswell was twice the commander Martin was."

I wasn't sure Caldswell would take that as a compliment. "Let's go," I said softly, offering Brenton my hand. "We've got a princess to save."

"Maat never was a princess," Brenton grunted, nearly pulling me over when he grabbed my hand and hauled himself up. "She was just a little girl."

"They all were," Rupert said bitterly, tapping the panel by the reinforced door Martin's body was still blocking. A second later, the lock turned green, and the door opened with a hiss, revealing a pure white room.

With a deep breath, I stepped forward. "Let's end this."

Brenton and Rupert followed without a word, their claws and my boots leaving bloody tracks on the pure white plastic as we entered Maat's prison.

CHAPTER

12

The room was long and featureless, a white plastic box. The only relief from the unrelenting nothingness was a panel about twice the size of my armor case that had been folded down from the wall. It was quaintly old-fashioned with dusty buttons and old-style screens where you had to actually push your finger down instead of just brushing. Other than this, there was nothing. Not even another door.

"Is this the right place?" I asked, swirling my cameras.

"It's the right place," Brenton wheezed. He was using the wall for support, his shoulder leaving a blood smear as he pulled himself forward. "Maat is kept in seclusion beyond that wall."

He nodded at the back of the room as he said this, but I didn't see anything. Stranger still, this place didn't trigger any of Rupert's memories. When I tried to remember it, all I got was a terrible feeling of unease. One that Rupert apparently still felt if his hunched shoulders were any sign.

"This is the threshold of Maat's quarantine," he said quietly. "There used to be a lab past here, but these days everything beyond this first door is automated. Eyes never set foot in here unless Maat is drugged unconscious."

"Why not?" I asked.

"Because when she's awake, even being a symbiont won't save you at this range," Brenton said bitterly. "This is where they throw the daughters to be changed. No one else would dare come in. This close Maat could pop all our heads like rotten tomatoes if she wanted to." He looked back at the bloody mess he'd left on the floor. "I'm surprised Martin had the guts to hide in here, drugs or no."

"He didn't have a choice," Rupert said, walking up to the dusty console. "Republic command ordered the subcommand station be moved in here two years ago. This room was to be considered the very last line of defense. Martin was following protocol. If things went bad outside, he could detonate the separation charges from this console." He pointed at a large red button placed prominently at the top of the console's slanted control board. "Once he'd blasted this arm free from the rest of the station, we'd have been sucked into space while he and Maat would float off to safety and wait for a pickup."

"So why didn't he?" I asked.

"Maybe he wasn't ready to give you up yet," Rupert said with a shrug. "Maybe he thought the guns would be enough."

"Or maybe he was too chicken to float off into space alone with Maat," Brenton said, pulling himself along the wall until there was a bloody trail leading all the way to the end of the room. "How do we get in?"

I gaped at him. "You don't know?"

Brenton shook his head. "They changed everything. I might not have formally defected until five years ago, but Caldswell mistrusted me long before that. I haven't been here in twenty years. Back then, this was a hallway that led to Maat's room. She had a bed then, even a window, though they never let her out of her restraints long enough to walk over and look out of it. I guess they finally did away with even the pretense." He reached up, running his bloody claws over the white wall at the far end of the room. "Open it, Charkov."

Rupert bristled at the order, but he began fiddling with a console. When nothing happened for several seconds, I walked over to see what was wrong. "They have her on lockdown," he explained before I'd even said a word. "And I used to do this from the other side of the wall. This console is different."

"I wasn't criticizing," I replied, glancing through my cameras at the rapidly spreading pool of red at Brenton's feet before dropping my voice to a whisper. "Do you think he'll make it?"

Rupert dropped his voice to match mine. "If his symbiont hasn't stopped the bleeding by now, it's not going to."

I'd thought as much, but hearing it confirmed hurt more than I'd expected. I didn't like Brenton, but I'd come to grudgingly respect him. It was hard not to respect a man who went after something with everything he had.

Finally, Rupert tapped a sequence into the console, and I heard machinery grind to life somewhere above me. That was all the warning I got before the wall at the end of the white room rolled away and another wall was lifted up on a pneumatic wrench to replace it. And pinned to this wall by a massive web of white straps like a spider's victim was a figure I'd seen before, though not in Rupert's memories. From the way he was staring, I didn't know if he'd actually seen Maat before this moment, but I had. The white wrapped figure with her head trapped in that horrible, faceless mask was exactly the one the lelgis had shown me in their warning. Even now, seeing her, a complex knot of feelings was rolling over and over inside me until I could almost hear the alien whisper.

Mad queen.

But while I was trying to master the flood of dread and revulsion the lelgis had left in my mind, Brenton stumbled forward, falling to his knees at Maat's feet. For a long moment, he knelt there like a pilgrim before the Sainted King, and then he jolted up again without a sound and began shredding the white straps that bound her to the wall.

I stepped forward to help, but then thought better of it. Brenton's claws might have been brittle, but they were more than sharp enough to cut Maat's restraints. Even if they hadn't been, he would have made it work. Brenton was tearing her down like a madman, shredding everything in reach: the IV tubes, the cloth straps, even the metal chains that bound her wrists and ankles. Those last ones he broke by slipping his claws into the links and wrenching them sideways like a lever, snapping off two of his claws in the process. But Brenton seemed to be beyond pain's reach as he pulled Maat free at last, clutching her skeletal body in his arms.

"I've got you," he said, the words crumbling into a sob. "I told you I'd come, Enna. I kept my promise. I told you I'd come." He leaned over, pressing his scaled face against her narrow shoulders, and then his head shot back up. "Help me get her mask off."

That command was clearly meant for me, and though it was on the tip of my tongue to snap that I didn't take orders from him, I swallowed the words. Now wasn't the time. "Let me repack my blade," I muttered, reaching up to grab my block of thermite gel out of Phoebe's old nook.

It took me just under thirty seconds to replenish my thermite blade. Brenton waited impatiently, snapping his fingers like I was taking forever. I ignored him, waving my blade to set the gel before walking over to examine the problem.

Maat's blank faced helmet was just like Rupert's, a metal shell completely encasing her head that locked at the nape of the neck. I motioned for Brenton to ease her head forward and flared my thermite, using what I'd learned from cutting Rupert's to slice the lock with a single clean stroke. The second I was done, Brenton grabbed the still smoldering edge of the crack I'd made and snapped the helmet in two.

I'd seen Maat's face many times, so I thought I knew what to expect. But as the helmet broke away, I realized I was utterly wrong. The girl I knew had olive skin, dark almond eyes, and straight black hair, cut flat above her shoulders. But that projected image must have been how Maat remembered herself from before all this began, because the thing beneath the mask didn't even look human.

She was bald and bone thin, her paper-thin eyelids closed in fitful sleep. Her skin was as gray as my armor and speckled with pale blue patches. Scales, I realized belatedly, from her symbiont, but they were the wrong color. Even Brenton's unhealthy brownish black scales at least looked vaguely xith'cal, but the strange blue-white things poking out of Maat's skin didn't look like any lizard I'd ever seen. Her gaunt face was relatively clear, but once you got past her shoulders, her body was completely covered in the things, poking up in uneven waves beneath her white medical gown like rumpled, razor-sharp feathers.

"Defense mechanism," Brenton said, his voice uneven. "She can't control them like other symbionts. They're only out because her body tried to defend her when they drugged her unconscious. Here"—he reached back toward the wall—"help me."

I didn't realize what Brenton was asking me to do until I saw what his hand was clutching. When I did, I almost threw up. Under the helmet, Maat's head was *open*. A window had been cut in the top of her skull to make way for a nest of wires that seemed to be plugged directly into her brain. Brenton had gathered the lot of them with his broken claws and was now squeezing the multicolored rope in his fist.

"This is how they control her, make her create the daughters," he said, his voice shaking with rage. "She used to say she could feel them, worms in her brain, making her do things." He held the wires up to me. "Cut them."

I swallowed. "Are you sure? They look kind of vital."

"If Maat could be killed this easily, she wouldn't need you," Brenton said bitterly. "Cut her free. Now."

My thermite was still burning, so I did as he asked, slicing through the wrist-thick rope of plastic-coated wires like it was gossamer. Maat's entire body convulsed when I severed the cord, her small, clawed fingers digging into Brenton's arm so hard his scales cracked. It must have hurt, but the only sound he made was a relieved sigh. That twitch was the first sign of life Maat had given.

"Come on," I said softly, touching Brenton's shoulder. "We have to go."

He nodded and held Maat out, but it took me a second to realize he wanted me to take her, and yet another to realize this was because he couldn't stand. The white floor where Brenton had been sitting was now entirely red.

"God and king, Brenton," I whispered, taking Maat from him. "You're leaking everywhere. We've got to get you—"

A loud thump echoed through the walls, cutting me off. I went silent, craning my neck even though there was nothing to see in the blank room. I could hear it, though. The hull around us was groaning softly, and I felt the floor beneath my boots vibrating like a string about to snap. The vibrating got stronger and stronger until, all of a sudden, it stopped with a sharp crack, like something had broken.

"Rupert," I hissed in the sudden silence, clutching Maat tighter. "What was that?"

I'd thought he was still at the console, but when I looked for him, Rupert was right beside me, almost making me jump. "Something hit the hull," he whispered, looking up at the white ceiling. "Maybe the battleships decided to fire after Maat's cell alarm went off?"

I'd been on ships that were getting shot plenty of times, and that hadn't sounded like any missile strike I'd ever heard. From the sound of his voice, I could tell Rupert didn't believe that story either. Whatever it was, though, we needed to move. Now.

"You take Maat," I said, holding her thin body out to Rupert. "I'll find something to patch up Brenton and—"

I cut off, eyes going wide. Behind Rupert, a dark shadow was moving erratically. It left a trail of blood behind it, but it wasn't until the thing threw out its arm to grab the console that I realized what—or rather, *who*—I was looking at.

"No!" I shouted. "*Martin!*"

Rupert had turned before the name left my mouth, but it was too late. Wobbling like a drunk, Commander Martin reached up and slammed his fist down on the red button Rupert had pointed to earlier, the one that blew the charges that would separate Maat's ray from the rest of Dark Star Station. Rupert sent him flying a second later, but the damage was already done, and I braced for the thunder of the explosions...

Which never came.

"What?" I said, looking around bewildered. "Did something go wrong?"

"No," Rupert breathed, stepping back to let me see his hand pressed flat on the console, holding down the button.

"It doesn't fire until the pressure is released," he said, nodding at Martin. "Deal with him, please?"

The please wasn't necessary. I didn't even have to put Maat down. I just shifted her to my left arm and pulled out Sasha as I walked over to where Martin was lying, his chest heaving as he tried to get back the breath Rupert had just slammed out of him.

"You can't do this," he coughed when he saw me standing over him. "You're dooming us all. I won't let—"

I shot him in the head with Sasha, knocking him out just like Rupert had taught me. When I was sure he was down for good this time, I holstered my gun and turned back to Rupert. "So all we've got to do is keep that button pressed and no explosion, right?"

Rupert nodded, but then his head jerked up. I heard it, too, more rumbling out on the hull. Lots more, and closer, like something was crawling over the station. For a moment, I thought it might be phantoms, but phantoms didn't make noise.

"We should probably get moving," Rupert whispered.

That sounded like a good plan to me, and I started looking around for something heavy to hold down the button so we could do just that. Unfortunately, the console was steeply slanted, and the button had to be held at its lowest point below the metal surface. To keep it punched, we'd need something pointed as well as rope to make sure it stayed. There was nothing in the room since Brenton had slashed

Maat's prison into unusably small bits. I was about to go search the shot-up lab when I saw Brenton pushing himself to his feet.

"Sit down," I snapped. "Do you *want* to bleed out?"

"I think that's inevitable."

I froze. Brenton's voice was thin and strained, but his words were unmistakably resolute. I'd heard that same tone in countless soldiers' voices, including my own. It was the sound of someone who had accepted death.

Using the wall for balance, Brenton pulled himself to the console. When he got there, he pressed his thumb against the button Rupert was holding down. "My symbiont is dying," he said softly. "Reaper's lizards poisoned it when they made me go mad. I will never never regenerate the damage, but that doesn't mean I can't do my duty to her."

"No, Brenton," I said fiercely. "I won't tell you not to die, but I'm not going to let you throw yourself away doing the job of a goddamn paperweight. Just give me five minutes to rig something and—"

"We don't have five minutes," Brenton said calmly. "Listen."

As though to prove his point, the rattling on the hull chose that moment to get exponentially louder, the metal grinding like someone was ripping it apart.

"I've done a lot of bad things in my time," Brenton said. "So many sins I can't possibly atone for. But this one thing I'm determined to do right."

Rupert went stiff at his words, and Brenton took his chance to shove the younger symbiont away. Despite his injuries, the blow was still enough to knock Rupert off the button. The moment he was out of the way, Brenton stepped up to block the console with his body, holding the trigger like a last stand as he turned his ruined symbiont face to us.

"I'm dead," he announced. "You're not. Seems to me, then, that the way ahead is simple. I'll hold this button as long as I can, you go and do what I should have done seventy years ago." He nodded at

Maat's body in my arms. "Go and save her so we can both rest in peace at last."

I looked at Rupert, but he was still staring at Brenton. Finally, he nodded. "Let's go."

I nodded back, gripping Maat to my chest as I turned to Brenton. "Don't let go, whatever you do," I warned, and then I shifted to King's Tongue. "King's rest be on you, John Brenton."

"Of course it will," he replied, and though I couldn't see, I could hear the smile in his words. "I told you I was one of the good guys."

If things had been less dire, I would have called bullshit on that. Brenton's ends might have been well intentioned, but no one with any sort of conscience could ever call his methods "good." If the situation were anything other than what it was, I would have told him exactly that. Now I could only turn and run for the door with Rupert at my heels.

The last sight I had of John Brenton, he was framed against the blood-smeared whiteness of Maat's prison. His feet were braced against the plastic floor as he pinned his weight against the console, like he could somehow push the button down farther to buy us more time. But though the pool of blood at his feet was growing before my eyes, he did not falter and he did not move, not even when the entire station began to shake.

Even with no one left to run it, getting through the kill box was dangerous and annoying. The doors were all symbiont rated, which meant they were huge, stubborn slabs of metal, and several of the turrets were automated, including one really nasty disrupter cannon. If we'd tried to come in this way, we would have been shot full of holes before we reached the end of the second hall. Now, though, we had two circumstances in our favor: first, the entire station seemed to have abandoned their posts, leaving all the systems running on auto, and second, we were going through the kill box maze backward, out of Maat's prison toward the lower security zones, which meant everything was facing the wrong way.

Rupert went first, opening each locked door from the inside and pulling down all the traps before they could turn to fire on us. But even with his speed, it was tricky work. Without a live person arming the guns, their movements were predictable, but they were still fast as hell. If they hadn't had to turn completely around to fire backward every time, there was no way we could have managed it. As it was, Rupert was able to handle them all right, which was good, because I couldn't seem to keep my mind on the task at hand.

The clanging against the hull was getting louder as we neared the center of the station. I could feel the vibrations through my boots as I ran, but while that was nerve-racking, it wasn't actually the cause of the lump in my stomach. I wasn't sure what was, but whenever Maat twitched in my arms, the feeling of doom grew stronger. The third time it happened, I gave in and flicked up my visor to have a look.

The moment my eyeballs took over for my camera feeds, the tiny dark kill box corridor filled with light. The flood of phantoms was a surprisingly welcome sight, but though I took comfort in the glow of the little aliens I'd started thinking of as allies somewhere along the line, my feeling of dread didn't go away. Though we were running toward the station's center, the phantoms were all going the other way, flowing past us like a swift river back toward Maat's chamber.

That wouldn't have been so odd except that the only time I ever saw phantoms move at anything other than a leisurely crawl was when they were trying to run away from me. I was trying to think what I could have done to scare so many of them when I realized the truth. These phantoms *were* running; they just weren't running from *me*.

"Rupert."

Rupert looked over his shoulder from where he was pulling down a drop turret.

"We have to go back."

"Why?" Rupert asked, trashing the turret with a swipe of his claws. "What's wrong?"

My eyes flicked over the mass exodus going on around us. "The phantoms are running the other way," I said, knowing full well how dumb that sounded. "I don't think we should keep going."

"There is no other way out," Rupert said, his calm strained. "We have to go this way."

As he spoke, the loudest bang yet sounded directly above us. It was like something had crashed into the hull right above our heads. Maat jerked in my arms at the sound, her thin mouth falling open in a silent cry. Cursing, I moved her onto my shoulder so I could pull my gun. I didn't know what I was going to shoot yet, but I felt better with Sasha in my hand. The whole time, my gut was telling me it was no good and we should run, but Rupert was right. Everything we'd done so far had been for one purpose: to get Maat onto a ship and into hyperspace. If this was the only way out to the station's docks, then we had no choice.

"Let's go fast, then," I whispered, jogging up to the door he'd just cleared. "How much farther?"

"We're almost there," Rupert said, joining me. "Just a few mo—"

A deafening bang ate the rest of his words as the door we were standing at dented inward like it had been hit with a battering ram. A second blow came right on the heels of the first, and this time the heavy door broke, bashed off its hinges by a black hooked, armored tentacle as big as the hallway.

My first thought was that it was another emperor phantom coming for me like back on the battleship, but when Rupert shouted in surprise and jumped back, I knew I was wrong, because he could see it, too. Still, it wasn't until the tentacle withdrew and a huge, bulbous head started wedging itself through the door that I realized at last what was going on.

"Lelgis!"

I should have known, I thought bitterly as we retreated down the tiny hall. Should have guessed. The clanging on the hull around us was louder than ever, but now I recognized it. It was the sound of squids tearing the station apart, ripping open the metal to get to me. And if the lelgis were *here*, that meant the emperor phantoms who'd been keeping them back must have been defeated, which would also explain why the power was still on even though we'd removed Maat from her prison. I didn't think we'd be getting reinforcements, either. My visor was still up, but I couldn't even see the phantom's glow anymore. The hallway was now completely empty of even the tiniest phantoms. It was down to us and the lelgis.

Well, that was fine with me, I thought, dropping my visor with a growl. I owed the damn squids for my leg. From the bits I'd seen, this looked to be the same armored lelgis Brenton and I had fought on the asteroid, the one that had bounced Sasha's shot. I wasn't about to eat another of my own bullets, so I slammed Sasha into her holster and reached for Mia instead, dialing up her charge as I yelled at Rupert, "Go!"

He obeyed, slashing at the lelgis with his claws, forcing it to retreat back through the door. At the same time, I fired a narrow slug of white fire straight at the base where the thing's barbed tentacles connected to its body. The squid might ignore gravity, but with no room to dodge in the small tunnel and Rupert occupying its attention, it didn't even get a shield up in time before my plasma shotgun's blast slammed into its body.

The burning slug hit its tender flesh like a rock splashing into a pond, and for a moment, I could actually see the white fire spreading through it. But just like every other one of these bastards I'd fought, this lelgis didn't seem to feel pain. Even while it was burning, it kept coming, shooting its barbed tentacle up to grab Rupert's chest.

He sliced it out of the air, stabbing his claws into the appendage that had been grabbing for him and yanking it forward instead. The lelgis fought back with a vengeance, writhing against Rupert's grip, but even the squid's strength was no match for Rupert's as he pulled it forward and stabbed his free hand deep into the burning hole I'd made.

"Go!" he shouted as he ripped the tentacle free at the base. "Run for the dock!"

He didn't have to tell me twice. I darted forward, vaulting over the wounded lelgis' wildly thrashing body with Rupert right behind me. I had Maat slung over my left shoulder and Mia in my hand, ready to fire again, but the next hallway was much bigger than the one we'd just left. We'd cleared the kill box at last, I realized, my hopes soaring. We were back in the station proper, but while that was enough to make me want to cheer, I didn't know which way to go.

Fortunately, Rupert did. "This way," he said, sprinting past me. "Follow this to the end, then down the stairs and—"

He cut off with a grunt as something slammed into him. It hit me a second later, and the impact was enough to knock my breath clean out. As I struggled to get it back, my suit informed me that I'd hit a tentacle, a huge one that had shot out of one of the side corridors to bar our path. That was news to me, because from the way my stomach felt, I'd have guessed we ran into a metal bar. As it was, the blow was so hard and unexpected that my stabilizers couldn't keep me up. All I could do I as fell backward was curl over to make sure I didn't crush Maat when I hit.

As always, Rupert recovered before I did. He was up and at my side before I'd finished landing, yanking me back to my feet. But even after I was up, we didn't move. We couldn't. In the time it had taken us to recover, every way we could have escaped had been blocked.

The hallway we were in was much larger than the squirrelly little corridors of the kill box maze. This was the sort of wide, efficient passage you could drive a fully stocked supply loader down with room to spare, and every inch of it, from the flat industrial lights overhead to the scuffed metal floor, was packed full of lelgis.

There were tall, dainty lelgis perched on spindly legs like the one I'd jumped over back on the asteroid and heavy ones with barbed tentacles like the creature Rupert and I had left writhing in the doorway. There were squat lelgis with armored heads and long lelgis that looked more like snakes, and others so alien my brain had trouble making sense of them. There were lelgis no larger than dogs and lelgis so huge they had to double over to fit beneath the hall's twelve-foot ceiling. Still more lelgis were packed in behind the ones we could see, their bodies forming a mottled wall of purples and blues and blacks under the station's harsh white lights. But even though the aliens had us completely surrounded, they didn't move in for the kill.

"Why aren't they attacking?" I whispered, putting my back to Rupert's.

"I think they're afraid of you," he whispered back.

That didn't make sense. We'd just been smacked with a tentacle, and the lelgis we'd cut up in the hall hadn't had a problem attacking us. But as I thought about it, I realized the lelgis we'd cut down hadn't been after *us*; it had been after *Rupert*. Other than the one I'd just run headfirst into, not a single tentacle had touched me or Maat despite ample opportunity to do so, and that gave me courage.

I bared my teeth and took a threatening step forward, and then broke into a grin when the wall of lelgis inched back. I was about to tell Rupert to follow me, that I was busting us out of here, but when I glanced at him through my rear camera, my heart almost stopped.

One lelgis had entered the clear circle the others had left around us. It was huge, filling the hallway, its head brushing the ceiling as it floated forward on a cloud of tentacles that looked soft as a cloud, but it wasn't the size that got me. Actually, compared to the last time I'd seen it, the lelgis was practically a miniature. What got me was that I *had* seen it before. The lelgis in front of me was black as pitch, its shape the same as the dark shadows I'd seen skittering at the edge of the emperor phantom's light both in the oneness and behind the wall of ships outside. It was the queen, I realized as my throat went dry. And it was coming for me.

Peace, death bringer.

The words floated through my mind like a warm summer wind, bringing with them a feeling of calm and confidence, a crisis managed. All around us, the writhing lelgis fell still, and I had the sudden uncanny feeling that the crowd of aliens that had boxed us in wasn't a crowd at all, but pieces of a whole commanded entirely by the entity in front of me. I set my jaw. Queen indeed.

"Back off," I said, my voice sneering with false bravado. "You don't order me around."

I felt Rupert tense beside me, and his head turned quizzically. I thought this was because he couldn't hear the lelgis talking in my head, but then I realized he was looking around like he didn't see the giant black thing in front of us at all.

He doesn't.

I winced at the pity that came with the lelgis' words, and then, before I could shout a warning, the black queen reached out and flicked a tentacle at Rupert's chest.

The unexpected impact sent him flying, and he crashed headlong into the wall of lelgis behind us. The queen's amusement suffused my mind when he hit, but I was too busy to care. I was already running to help him. Before I'd taken two steps, though, the queen's black tentacles flew up in front of me, blocking my path, and as she encircled me, all light vanished.

I stumbled in the sudden darkness, cursing as the familiar, weightless feeling of the oneness clamped down on me like a trap.

"*No!*" I screamed, flailing wildly. I didn't even know what I was doing, other than fighting, shoving against the darkness like I could bust through it and get to where Rupert was. He was no pushover, but even he couldn't possibly fight so many on his own. I had to reach him, I thought frantically. I had to save him.

You can't.

"Shut up!" I screamed, fighting harder. This was all in my head. I just had to break free. Had to—

The queen landed on me like a hammer, its black tendrils wrapping around me, squeezing the breath from my lungs.

It is done, it said, layering the words with the same inevitability as gravity as the feathery tentacles tightened, cutting off my air. *I am your death, death bringer.*

"Like hell you are," I croaked, grabbing at my neck. I had not come this far to die here. I absolutely refused, and so I fought, writhing like a caught fish as I willed my virus to rise up and turn this overgrown octopus to ash. But though my rage was running red hot, sending the pins and needles sweeping over my body, the lelgis did not let go.

I do not fear you, it snarled in my mind. *I am the youngest of us all, the last to enter the oneness and the first to leave. I was sacrificed for this, cut off so that your poison could not spread. Your destruction is my purpose now.* The tentacles tightened as the queen rose before me, eyes glinting in the endless dark. *I do not fear you, death.*

By this point, my panic over my vanishing air was making it difficult to think, but even my frantic thrashing couldn't completely drown out the oddness of the lelgis' statement, and that oddness made me realize others. For example, I'd never had a problem with air in the oneness before, because I hadn't had a body. There was nothing theoretical about the pain in my limbs now, though, and I was still clearly wearing my suit, but strangest of all was the fact that I could *see* the monster in front of me.

Save for the time with the emperor phantom, I'd never been able to see in the darkness. There was no light in the oneness, only endless nothing and the feeling of the others watching. Now there were no others, just me and the queen and the light shining over its black, alien eyes. The light that was coming from right under my nose.

Like a mirage, the real world flickered back into view. I could see the wall of lelgis writhing like shadows cast by a fire. I could also hear the blast of Mia's plasma echoing from very far away, and all at once, I realized this wasn't the oneness at all. The darkness was too small, too thin, too finite. And there was light here, a soft glow radiating from the girl in my arms, the girl I was still holding despite the fact that I was sure I'd just been using both hands to snatch tentacles away from my neck.

I must not have actually moved my arms at all, because Maat was still clutched to my chest, only now she was glowing. In the strange, thin dark the lelgis queen had pulled me into, Maat shone like the moon. The light radiating from her was the same soft blue-white radiance that rose from the phantoms themselves, and it was getting brighter.

No!

Fast as they'd grabbed me, the queen's black tendrils let me go, and I fell choking on the floor. The blackness wobbled when I hit, and for a moment I was back in the hallway with Rupert standing over me, Mia in his hands as he blasted the lelgis back. Before I could do anything, I was sucked back in the dark, but this time, Maat was standing beside me.

That wasn't quite true. Maat's body was still in my arms, fragile and limp as ever, but the scale-covered skeleton was just her shell, her mortal shadow. The girl standing beside me in the dark looked like the Maat I knew, the dark-haired, bright-eyed girl in the hospital gown who'd freed me from Caldswell, and her skin glowed like phosphorus as she reached down to help me stand.

"You came," she said, her voice amazed.

"Of course I came," I said, grabbing her hand. "I promised you I would."

She yanked me to my feet with a grip that was every bit as strong as it had been back on Io5, and I felt new confidence wash over me as we turned together to face the lelgis, who was now cowering at the edge of Maat's light.

Corrupt madness, the alien whispered, the words carrying a stab of hate and fear so intense it made me dizzy. *Death will not be yours, mad one. You were given your purpose for the good of all. Go back to your duties now before you spread your corruption any—*

"I will never go back," Maat snarled, gripping my hand so hard I thought she'd break it right off. "I will never be your slave again! Maat will be free!"

You have no choice, the lelgis hissed. *You are the wall that must not fall, the barrier against the flood.*

"Never," Maat spat. "Never, never, never, never."

The repeated words began bumping into each other, but now that I wasn't being choked to death, I was starting to realize this whole situation was off. "Hold on just a second," I said. "Why does Maat have to keep being a wall? She was put here to plug the hole the phantoms came through, right? But they just want to go home. I can understand why you'd want to kill me, but why does Maat have to stay? If she opens the door, the phantoms go home and this whole goddamn mess solves itself."

I cannot begin to describe how weird it felt trying to reason with a black monster I could only see in flashes, but my tolerance for weird shit had gotten pretty high of late, and I'd be damned if I kept my mouth shut when my life was one of the topics being discussed. Besides, I was genuinely confused. From what I knew of the lelgis, they considered themselves the immortal caretakers of the oneness. Heaven's queens, Dr. Starchild had called them. That in mind, it just made no sense to keep the invading phantoms locked into a universe they only wanted to leave.

When I finished my question, a wave of pity and condescension washed over me. *Poor dying mind,* the queen whispered. *You understand so little. You think we do not hear the aliens' cries? Their pleading to go home? It has plagued us from the moment we shut the door, but what is that to us?*

A lot, it seemed to me, but the lelgis wasn't finished.

Our concern lies with this universe, it said, filling my mind with a sense of infinity. *We are…*The thing that came into my head next had no word to go with it, probably because there wasn't a word in any language to represent the mix of motherhood and stewardship that rolled into my mind.

We were the first to touch the infinite, the lelgis continued. *Therefore, it falls to us to protect it, to preserve the purity we were given. The creatures*—a picture of an emperor phantom formed in my mind before falling away—*are but annoyances, distractions best left to the lesser races. We care not if they come or go or live or die. Our priority is and will forever be to halt the corruption they brought with them.*

As the lelgis finished, a story shoved its way into my mind. It was like watching a soundless movie. In it, I saw the oneness as the lelgis had shown it to me before: the infinite expanse of all things hanging in perfect darkness. Then, without warning, a tiny light broke through, carrying pollution into perfection. Everything the light touched was lessened, corrupted, in some cases completely broken down, and so the decision was made that it must be blocked. A queen was the only one who could manage such a feat, but queens were so vital and so few. To sacrifice one would lessen all, but who else could do such a task?

And then, like a gift, the answer appeared. A bumbling insect from one of the lower races who could brush the oneness. She would do. With her to block the light, the perfect darkness could be protected, and none of the great, powerful, irreplaceable queens of heaven would have to die. The perfect solution.

Now do you see, death? the lelgis said, shaping the tale back into words once more. *It is not the phantoms that matter. We care nothing for your destroyed planets or the lives of your death-bound kind. Being mortal, your death is inevitable, but we are better. Even your limited mind can understand sacrifice, can it not? And so I ask you, what is one mad, death-doomed creature's life to that of an eternal queen? What is her suffering next to the preservation of the perfect oneness? Her cries of slavery are mere selfish madness, but you are different.* The lelgis' presence curled to the very back of my head, its presence filling every nook and cranny until nothing was hidden. *After all, are you not the one who does what must be done?*

I swallowed against the dryness in my throat and glanced down at Maat's glowing hand, still gripping my own. With the queen's overwhelming presence in my mind, I couldn't help seeing things from her perspective. Under her influence, Maat's light was no longer beautiful, but a corruption, an alien influence from another dimension that disrupted the purity the lelgis had guarded since time untold. Seeing that, Maat's sacrifice to keep it back felt noble and right. The queens were immortal, superior to humans in every way. It was only fair that we should die for them, suffer for them. Even Maat's pain was nothing compared to what she guarded, and anyway, I wouldn't be around to worry about it much longer, since I would be dead. I should go ahead and kill myself, actually, so this beautiful, noble queen who was better than me in every way wouldn't have to be bothered with something as unclean as death.

That's right, the lelgis whispered. *Listen to reason, little death bringer, and let go of the mad one's hand. You are the brave hero, and you have fought very hard, but the end has come. Let me end your suffering and save the universe, and when all of humanity is dead and gone, we will remember you. Is that not glory enough?*

The words made me shiver. All I had to do was obey and I would have everything I'd ever wanted: glory, honor, a noble death known by all, my name handed down forever. But if that was the case, why was I still so angry?

As I mulled this over, I realized Maat was tugging on my arm. She was tugging on everything, actually, yanking the queen's black tentacles off me with her plasmex while her mouth moved silently. She looked like she was screaming at me, her face wet with tears, but I didn't hear anything. That was wrong, I thought, frowning. I should be able to hear.

I tried to pull my hand out of the mad queen's so I could rub my ears, but she wouldn't let go, because I'd promised her. There were other hands on me as well, a man's rough, urgent grip on my shoulders, begging me to wake up. The feeling was so distant it could have been in another world, but it was very precious to me. *He* was precious to me, and if I gave in and died here, I'd hurt him.

Forget him, the queen whispered.

My whole body went rigid. "No," I growled. I'd forgotten Rupert once and it had been terrible. Like hell was I doing it again. And why was I thinking about killing myself for some alien? Why was I listening to any of this crap?

Like a shot out a window, the queen's illusion crashed to pieces around me. Sound came back in a rush, bringing fury with it. All at once, I could feel the alien's hold like a sticky film on my mind, and rage like nothing I'd ever felt was rising to meet it. The virus followed on its heels, howling up from the depths like a hellhound to devour the invader whole. The queen must have felt it coming, because the last thing that touched my mind was horrible fear before the black haze fled and I exploded back into the real world.

I was kneeling on the floor with Maat's body clutched against my chest. Rupert was crouched over me with one hand on my shoulder and the other angling my head to his. Mia was on the ground beside him, her charge spent, and Sasha was right next to her, her ammo counter blinking zero. But though I was back and the darkness was over, the lelgis queen was still floating in front of me. I braced at once, clutching my tingling fingers, ready to use the virus if it twitched so much as a tentacle toward me. But even though I could feel the alien's anger like pressure in my ears, it didn't touch my mind again.

"They are afraid of you."

I looked up in alarm to see Maat's projection standing next to me. She was transparent now, her body glowing like a phantom's, and she was staring at the queen with such hate it made my blood run cold. Which was fine with me, I realized. If anyone deserved her anger, it was the lelgis.

"You can kill them," she said, speaking the words out loud instead of in my head, which was probably for the best. What the lelgis had shown me was still in my head, fanning my rage even hotter, and I knew from the tingling the virus was nearly to my throat.

That wouldn't do. I couldn't lose control here, so I closed my eyes and focused my anger by concentrating on what I had to do. What I *really* had to do, because for the first time, I felt like I was seeing the entire picture.

All this time, I'd thought of Maat as the sacrifice. Now, thanks to the lelgis, I knew Maat was just the focus, the crux of the suffering. The truth was we were *all* the lelgis' sacrifice. They could fight the phantoms no problem. They could have hunted down and killed every single glowing bug if they'd wanted to, but they hadn't. Instead, they'd used us, the disposable lesser races, to hunt down and kill what they were too afraid of risking their precious purity to touch. The only reason they'd risked themselves today was because of me. Because I could kill them, which made me more dangerous than even the phantoms.

I gritted my teeth. Caldswell might have given Maat over, but it was the lelgis who'd come to him. It was the lelgis who'd let us suffer so they could go on unharmed, only bothering to intervene when the emperors got too big for us to handle. They were cowards, I realized. Immortality had done nothing but make them afraid. They clung to their perfection and let others do their dying while they hid away, not even watching.

That made them even worse than the Eyes. Even Caldswell had fought alongside the daughters, but the lelgis had just left us to our fate. They'd let the entire aeon colony of Unity be destroyed because they couldn't be bothered to take a moment from stomping out the xith'cal's virus to bother saving the place. Billions dead because the lelgis chose their own safety over everything else.

Even the phantoms were victims, I realized. The lelgis heard their voices, they knew the truth, but they'd kept the poor things locked up and starving because they couldn't bear to crack the door to let them go home. It was all more of the same bullshit I'd been fighting since I started to learn the truth, everyone sacrificing everyone else and claiming the greater good made it worth it. But there was a line, I decided. The answer to all of this was sitting in my lap, and so long as I had a say, the universe was going to change. I looked down at Maat. I was going to end this.

At that thought, my anger crystallized into action, and the virus faded, falling under my control. It was just like back in Reaper's cell, only now I understood exactly how I'd done it, and I knew I could do it again. The virus was now mine to control, mine completely, and I knew what I had to do.

I stood up in a rush, making Rupert jump. Maat's body was still clutched in my arms, but I held out my hand anyway. My clean, uninfected hand. She took it a second later, and I smiled as the warmth of Maat's illusionary touch pass through my suit to grip my skin. United, we turned back to face the lelgis queen, who backed up several feet.

You don't know what you do! it cried. *We are the mothers! Guardians of that which touches everything! If you persist, if you tear down the wall, we will diminish and all will suffer.*

"That's what you say," I replied, lifting my chin. "But let me tell you what I see. *I* see a bunch of cowards hiding behind us and saying their lives and happiness are worth more than ours because they've been alive a long time. That our deaths are justified because your lives are more important. But they're not. You might live in the oneness, but it doesn't belong to you."

Foolish child, the lelgis hissed. *You would destroy the infinite to save those who are already doomed to die?*

"That's the thing about infinity," I said. "You can't destroy it, and you can't control it." Even as the words left my mouth, I couldn't believe I was quoting Dr. Starchild, but truth was the truth, no matter where it came from. "Death and change are part of life," I went on. "You can plug that hole and hold back the phantoms for a long time, but eventually they'll get through, and there's nothing you can do to stop it. Because the infinite *isn't* pure. It *isn't* static. Like it or not, the universe goes on with or without your help, and we're done dying so you can maintain your illusion of control."

So you would have us stand by and do nothing while the oneness is corrupted? The lelgis roared, weighing the words down with so much doom I almost couldn't breathe. I found the air somehow, and though I'd asked nearly the same question myself not twenty-four hours ago, I wasn't surprised to find the answer waiting on the tip of my tongue.

"What you do is your business," I said. "But just because you're too cowardly to fight for yourselves doesn't give you the right to sacrifice us or the phantoms or anyone else." I held up Maat's hand. "We're done suffering for your comfort. This ends right now. I'm freeing Maat. I'm freeing the phantoms. I'm freeing the daughters and the Eyes and all of humanity from your bullshit war to keep your pond clean. I'm going to fling that door wide open and set us all free. If you don't like it, you can go cower at the other end of the universe, but this cycle of forcing us to suffer and die so you can maintain the status quo is over, and if you don't back off, you will be, too."

I pulled away from Maat as I finished, unlocking my glove to reveal my bare hand. When my fingers were free, I focused until the tips turned black and reached out, holding my dirty hand out toward the lelgis' soft, midnight flesh.

Before I could even extend my arm completely, the alien turned and fled. They all did. The huge crowd of lelgis, all the different types, turned and ran as one, vanishing from the halls as quickly as they'd appeared until Maat, Rupert, and I were alone.

I dropped my black hand, pulling my controlled anger back. The virus vanished as well, and I felt a surge of pride as I bent down to retrieve my glove. When I looked up again, Maat was standing right in front of me.

"The queen ran," she whispered.

"Cowards always run," I replied, grinning as I slipped my glove back on. "I have to admit, though, I'm surprised you held back. I was all blacked out for a while there, but you didn't even touch me."

Maat set her jaw stubbornly. "You kept your promise. You're the only one who's ever kept a promise to Maat, so I will hold faith, too. Maat will not touch you until we're safe in hyperspace and the daughters will not die."

"Brenton kept his promise, too," I said softly. "We couldn't have gotten you out without him."

Maat went very still as I said this, and then tears began to roll down her cheeks. She blinked in surprise, reaching up to touch them. "I can't remember," she whispered. "John was always important, but there are so many memories, Maat can't tell which are hers anymore."

She started to cry in earnest then, and I reached out to lay a hand on her shoulder. "Come on," I said softly. "Let's finish this."

Maat nodded and faded away, her glowing image vanishing like a projection after the power's cut. I stared at the space where she'd been for a long second before turning back to Rupert.

He was still where he'd been when I'd woken up, standing right behind me to guard my back. Now that the lelgis were gone, he'd pulled the scales back from his face and was looking at me with blatant confusion. "Do I want to know what just happened?"

"Sure," I said, shifting Maat's unconscious body so that it was resting comfortably against my chest again. "The lelgis are cowards who tried to brainwash me into shooting myself, but I broke free with Maat's help, told them straight up that we were done with their bullshit, and then I sent them packing. So that's over and now we're back on the 'get Maat into hyperspace' plan. Which way was it to the dock again?"

Rupert stared at me for almost half a minute after that, opening his mouth and then closing it again like he'd thought better of whatever he'd been about to say. Finally, he didn't say anything at all, just shook his head and bent down to retrieve my guns.

"Thanks for watching my back," I said as he fixed Mia to my back for me since my hands were full with Maat.

"Always," he replied, slipping Sasha back into her holster as well. "I'm afraid I used up all your ammo."

"I've got another clip," I said, but Rupert was already shaking his head.

"You *had* another clip," he corrected, giving me a sheepish look. "There were a lot of them."

That was the understatement of the decade. There'd been so many lelgis that you couldn't even see down the hall, but Rupert had held them all back so he could watch over me, and if that wasn't worth every bullet I owned, nothing was. "Thank you," I said again, leaning into him.

He froze for a moment, and then his arm slipped around my waist. "I'll always fight for you," he said softly. "Always, until I die."

I believed him. At this point, I'd have to be an idiot not to. I stayed like that a moment longer, resting on his strength, and then I pushed away. "Let's go."

Rupert nodded and we started down the hall toward the stairs he'd mentioned earlier, but though we were still in enemy territory, he didn't let go of my waist, and though I knew this was a damn stupid way to proceed that would likely get us shot, I didn't make him.

CHAPTER

13

The rest of the station must have abandoned ship when the lelgis started tearing the place apart, because we didn't see a soul. The traps were still there, but with the hull breach alarm going off like crazy, all of them seemed to have gone on emergency lockdown, and with no one to take them off, they gave us no more trouble. The dock, however, was another story.

Thanks to the swath the lelgis had cut getting to me, the station had subdivided, locking the remaining atmosphere into sealed compartments. A computer voice was announcing the compromised sections by code, and though I couldn't make heads or tails of the alphanumeric strings, Rupert recognized one of them as our dock, which meant we were now stuck.

"Please tell me there's another one," I groaned, because seriously, how much worse could this shit get? The only good news was that Maat's arm of the station hadn't blown yet, which meant Brenton was either still alive or the charges had malfunctioned. I preferred to believe the former, because horrid as the old man was, I wanted Brenton to at least live long enough to know his sacrifice hadn't been in vain. Assuming, of course, we could get off this hunk of junk.

"They haven't said anything about the second wing," Rupert said. "The old fighter deck might still be functional. Let's try that."

Anything known as "old" in this antique didn't sound too promising to me, but I followed Rupert as he shifted course, doubling back to the station's center before setting off into what was clearly a less used area. The lights were off here, probably an automatic shutdown in deference to what were usually the more vital areas of the station. The orange glow of the emergency lights was still enough to see by, though, and when the big bay doors for the dock came into view, safety lights on and clearly functional, I started to let myself believe we were actually going to make it.

Rupert opened the doors and went in first, motioning for me to stay back. He returned a few seconds later, his face excited. "It looks clear. There's a bomber at the end of the bay that's unhooked and ready to go. All we'll need to do is get in, hit the engines, and we're gone."

It sounded too good to be true, but I followed him anyway, hugging Maat to my chest as we ducked through the door. Just as Rupert had said, the dock was clearly out of use. The fighters and the larger bombers clamped to the high walls were all a decade or more out of date, and the bay floor, rather than being kept open for crews to assemble like Republic regulation demanded, was stacked with dusty boxes. Even so, there was plenty of room to see the line of ships prepped at the edge of the bay for immediate deployment, including the bomber Rupert had mentioned, which was sitting like a forgotten trophy at the far end of the deck with its dusty ready light still shining a bright, cheery green.

"I just hope it flies," I said as we started to run through the stacks of storage crates.

"It should," Rupert said, jogging beside me. "These ships were all rated for fifty-year storage. All I have to do is get the bay doors open and we'll be good to—"

I couldn't hear what he said next, because at that moment, my suit alarm started blaring in my ear as a huge message flashed over my entire view space.

Weapon lock detected.

My heart jumped into my throat, and for a terrifying second,

I was frozen in panic. Then, like a kick to the gut, nine years of combat experience snapped into place, and I threw up my sensors. But though it took my suit less than a second to pin down the source of the lock, dodging wasn't an option. I barely had time to glimpse Mabel sitting behind one of the stacked crates we'd just passed before she raised the Terran anti-armor shotgun to her shoulder and unloaded the huge twin barrels straight into my back.

Anti-armor shotguns are short-range weapons, meant for taking down armored targets in close quarters, but this was just ridiculous. Mabel had shot me from less than three feet away, close enough that she hadn't even needed the stupid lock. But I guess she wasn't taking any chances, because the shot my Lady took across the back was full bore, and every alarm I had started going off as the barbed shrapnel ripped through my beautiful baby like she was made of paper.

If I'd been wearing a cheaper suit, that would have been the end. But my Lady is quality through and through. Still, even custom Verdemont armor can't stop everything. Pain exploded down my left leg as one of the metal barbs punched through, digging into my thigh. I actually felt the damn metal sliver hit bone before my breach foam kicked in to stop the bleeding. Unfortunately, nothing could stop me from falling.

"Devi!"

Rupert's frantic shout came from far away as I crashed to the floor, rolling just in time to keep from crushing Maat. For a second, I couldn't even believe Mabel had shot me considering just who I was carrying, but then sense kicked back in. For all that she looked delicate, Maat was still a symbiont. If something like this could kill her, we wouldn't have had to go through all this nonsense in the first place.

It could kill *me*, however. The breach foam made it hard to tell where else I was injured, but my suit's vitals only showed my leg wound, and though the shard of metal hurt like hell, the bone wasn't broken, which was why my suit hadn't injected the cock-

326

tail automatically. It was still giving me the option, but I pushed it away. I couldn't afford to be drugged now, not with my Lady in this condition.

My suit was far worse off than I was. Nearly every gauge I had was in the red or unresponsive. I wasn't even sure if I could sit up. I was about to try when I felt Rupert grab me. Before he'd even gotten me off the ground, though, another shot echoed through the dusty bay, the familiar boom of a disrupter pistol.

This time, I did panic. Rupert's hold on my armor vanished as he crashed to the floor beside me, gripping his chest, which was now a bloody mess. I reached out to help him automatically, but my arm wouldn't move. I couldn't do anything except lie there and stare as Rupert began to bleed out, and then I felt the soft vibration of footsteps near my head.

The man standing over me when I looked up was a black, bulky shadow against the bright dock lights. The pearl-handled disrupter pistol in his hand looked just like every other Eye gun I'd ever seen, but that didn't matter. I knew who it was.

"End of the line, Morris."

I bared my teeth as Brian Caldswell leaned over to pull Maat's body out of my limp hold. Gentle as a new father, he gathered her in his arms. The moment he had her clear, he said, "Shuck her."

I didn't take his meaning until Mabel appeared above me with that damned anti-armor shotgun still propped on her shoulder. She set her gun down to grab me, using her claws to peel away my damaged armor, shucking me like a shellfish, just as Caldswell had ordered. I fought her for every inch, but unarmored and bloody against symbiont strength, I might as well have been trying to box a mountain. She yanked me around like an unruly toddler, kicking my damaged suit, my beautiful custom Verdemont armor aside like so much trash. The sight made me so mad I would have infected us all right then, but two things held me back: my newfound control and my fear for Rupert.

From the way he was gasping, I knew Caldswell had hit a lung with that shot. He was pale, too, even paler than he'd been back on Kessel, and my fear that Rupert was dying before my eyes was even greater than my rage over the damage to my suit, which I would never have thought possible a few days ago.

My feelings must have been clear on my face, because Caldswell sighed and shifted Maat under his arm. "Relax," he said, nudging Rupert with his clawed foot. "Charkov was always one of our best regenerators. He won't die from this. You, however, are another matter."

I tossed my head at his threat, struggling uselessly against Mabel's hold to get in his face so I could yell at him properly. "Do you even know what you're doing?" I cried. "We're on the *same side*, you moron! The lelgis have been using us! Goddamn you, *let me go!*"

Caldswell answered my hysterics with a pitying look. "You think I don't know that?"

His calm voice shocked me out of my fury. "What?"

"We knew the lelgis were using us from the beginning," he explained, his voice frustratingly calm, like he was talking to a child. "But it didn't matter, because we were using them, too. That's what negotiation is, Morris. Using and being used in return. We had to stop the phantoms, they had a way, and up until recently, they kept their part of the bargain to the letter." His eyes narrowed. "You were the one who messed things up."

"Me?" I roared, twisting in Mabel's grip. She kneed my injured leg in response, and the wave of pain that followed was almost enough to black me out. I didn't go under, though. I wasn't going to give these bastards an inch if it killed me.

"I was the only damn person with the guts to try anything new!" I shouted at Caldswell. "You said you hated the system of using up the daughters more than anyone, and you have the gall to stand there and blame me for trying to take it down?"

"Did you know how much I wanted to believe you?" Caldswell shouted back. He was losing his temper, too, his lips pulling back in a snarl. "Your virus was the first real hope I've had for a change in seven decades. That's why I fought so hard to try and meet you halfway. You want change? I was ready to bend over backwards to make this bullshit work. The *only* thing I couldn't give you was her." He tightened his arm around Maat's body. "But that wasn't good enough. You had to run off half cocked after god knows what, and now you've left me no choice."

"That's not how it is!" I cried, my anger giving way to the furious, desperate need to make him understand. "We *can* have everything. We can end this suffering. All of it, for everyone. Just *let us go.*"

"No," Caldswell said. "Shut up for once and listen, Morris. This isn't something we can afford to mess up. It may well be that you're right. That if I let you do as you like and kill Maat in hyperspace, all our problems will vanish and the whole universe lives happily ever after. But as much as I'd like that to be true, I can't risk it, because Maat is the *one thing* we can't afford to lose. We've tried everything we know to reproduce the circumstances that created her, but the daughters are the best we could ever manage, and even they're just shadows."

He looked down at Maat in despair. "She's irreplaceable," he said softly. "If you kill her, and the phantoms don't leave, or worse, if more come in, it's over. Without her, we can't close the door again and we can't make more daughters. The ones we have now will go mad like they always do, only we'll no longer be able to replace them."

He turned back to me. "Don't you get it? Without Maat, we have *nothing.* I don't care what you promised. I cannot allow you to gamble away our only defense against the phantoms and our only bargaining chip with the lelgis. There are simply no odds good enough or payoff large enough to justify that risk, and I will not play dice with the lives of all mankind just to satisfy your damned Paradoxian honor!"

I looked away. When he put it like that, my mission did sound unforgivably reckless. But though I knew he had good reason to doubt, I couldn't, because every time the thought tried to cross my mind, all I could see was the emperor phantom lighting up the dark, dying as it begged me to open the door and let them go home.

"I know I'm right," I said at last, pouring every ounce of my conviction into the words as I lifted my eyes to his. "This isn't a gamble, Captain. It's a leap of faith. You can't change anything without risk. If you cling to safety, if you refuse to jump, all you'll ever have is the hell you've got. So please, sir, I'm begging you, take a chance."

I have never begged for anything in my life, but I did it now. If Mabel hadn't had me pinned against her, I would have been on my knees, because this was more important than my pride, more important than anything. And for a second, I saw the doubt in Caldswell's eyes. He looked down at Maat, then back at me, then back to Maat like he was arguing with himself, and I held my breath. *Please*, I begged the Sainted King. *Please please please.*

In the end, though, my prayers came to nothing. "I can't," Caldswell said softly, looking at me with pity. "For what it's worth, Morris, I believe you, but it's not enough. I can't risk everything on a story you got from a phantom."

"Then take me back into custody." The surrender was like ash in my mouth, but I figured if I could just draw things out a little bit more, maybe I could make him see. But Caldswell was already shaking his head.

"I'm afraid that bridge is burned," he said, raising the arm he wasn't using to hold Maat to point the disrupter's barrel straight at my head.

"I'm sorry about this, Morris," he said as Mabel forced me to my knees. "For all the hell you raised, you were the best merc I ever had. I'd even thought about inviting you to be an Eye if you could ever learn to follow orders. But after two escapes, there's no way I can risk taking you as a prisoner again, virus or no. You're just too much of a liability. I'm sure you understand."

I did, but that didn't mean I was going to make it easy for them. I fought the whole way, ignoring the pain and the blood running down my leg, forcing Mable to push for every inch. In the end, she hit me so hard I saw stars and moved while I was stunned, scooting around so that she was standing off to the side, holding me in place with one iron-strong hand on my shoulder as Caldswell pressed the barrel of the disrupter pistol against my forehead.

Funny enough, when the metal cylinder bit into my skin, its hard edge still uncomfortably warm from the shot that had downed Rupert, all I could think was that this was the same pose I'd seen back in the snowy bunker on Io5. This time, though, there was no illusion, and unlike Rupert, I knew Caldswell wouldn't hesitate before pulling the trigger.

"For what it's worth, you have my word your body will be returned to Paradox for a proper burial once the scientists are done," he said, shifting to King's Tongue for the final blessing. "King's rest be on you, Devi Morris."

I kept my eyes open, staring my death in the face, determined to make him watch as he shot me. It was petty revenge to be sure, but I was ready to take what I could get. But as Caldswell's finger moved on the trigger, bright light broke over the fighter bay like a sunrise.

It was so sudden and blinding, I thought the shot had gone off prematurely, but when my vision cleared, I saw that the light was a *hand*. Maat's bony, glowing hand was gripping the barrel of Caldswell's disrupter pistol so hard the metal dented. Maat's physical body was still tucked under Caldswell's arm, but Maat, the real Maat, was standing practically on top of me with light pouring off her like a star going supernova. And though I was the only one who could see her like this, everyone winced when her voice boomed through the dusty bay.

"She is mine."

The words went off like a cannon blast, a throbbing mix of sound and metal pressure. I wasn't sure how she did it, whether it was her physical proximity or the drugs wearing off or something else entirely. Whatever it was, though, Maat's voice cut through the air like a phantom's scream, and as it echoed through the enormous dock, every light in the place went out.

Silence fell like a stone as the station's engines died. For one long second, I don't think anyone so much as breathed, and then Maat reached out, placing her glowing hand flat on Caldswell's chest. "She is Maat's freedom," Maat said, her voice ringing. "And Maat is not alone!"

As she spoke, a wave of force so strong it made my ears pop rose up around her. I could actually see the plasmex moving as it coiled like a fist, and then that fist slammed into Caldswell, punching him into a wall of crates twenty feet away. The whole station rocked as he landed, and a new sound took over, a deep, shaking roar that made my mind go blank. That was all the warning we got before the emperor phantoms descended.

I never did know for sure how many there were. All I knew was that they were enormous, bigger than the phantom who'd spoken to me, bigger than the one I'd seen floating among the broken rocks that had been the aeon colony of Unity, bigger than anything I'd ever seen. They were so huge I didn't actually know how I was seeing all of them, but I did.

It was like I was looking with two sets of eyes. With one, I saw the dark fighter bay and Caldswell rolling to his feet, shouting at Mabel to keep hold of me. With the other, I saw the phantoms writhing together like a serpent pit the size of a planet, their combined light so bright I thought I'd burn. But Maat was brightest of all. She was crouching over her own body where Caldswell had dropped it when she'd sent him flying, staring at me with eyes so wide I could see the tears she hadn't yet shed.

"*Please,*" she cried, the word stabbing into my head even as the sound rattled my ears. "Please, Devi!"

She didn't need to ask. I was already straining to get to her, but I couldn't. Despite all the chaos, Mabel was following orders and holding me down, and though the emperor phantoms were everywhere now, they couldn't get close enough to knock her off without entering the three-foot dead zone phantoms always maintained around me.

"No!" I screamed, clawing at her arms. I couldn't be stopped now, not after all this, not by something so stupid. I fought tooth and nail, clawing and biting and screaming. But the more I struggled, the tighter Mabel held me, her claws digging into my shoulders so hard she broke the skin through my shirt.

I knew it hurt, but I didn't feel it. I was beyond pain. All I cared about was getting to Maat and finishing what I'd started, which was why I didn't see Rupert until he was on top of me.

He must have moved all at once, because when I'd seen him a second ago, he'd been on his back. Now he was in Mabel's face, his claws buried in the side she'd left open trying to keep me in line. I felt her body tense as the blow went through her, and then Rupert's arms slipped around my waist and tore me free.

That hurt enough that the pain got through, but it was quickly overwhelmed by a glorious rush of love and victory as Rupert turned and started for Maat. Behind me, I heard Mabel cry out as the phantoms grabbed her at last, but I didn't have time to look. I was too busy trying not to touch Rupert's barely mended chest as he reached down through the spectral Maat he couldn't see to scoop up the unconscious body he could. Once he grabbed her, he didn't even slow down to get a good grip. He just kept running, shooting like a bullet toward the bomber at the bay's far end.

Now that we were closer, I could see the ship's rear bomb bay door was already open and waiting, an oversight of some forgotten officer a decade ago. There wasn't a ramp, but the ship wasn't that much bigger than Rupert's little stealther. Even injured and burdened with Maat and myself, Rupert could make the five-foot jump into the back of the ship no problem. We just had to get there.

I was egging him on when a furious roar caught my attention. I looked back just in time to see Caldswell slice his way free, his claws cutting through the bright tendrils the phantom had been forced to physically manifest in order to hold him. His body was bright with the phantom's slick, freezing blood, painting him like a glowing target as he turned to charge after us, bellowing at the top of his lungs.

"Charkov!"

In a fair race, Rupert could have beat Caldswell. He was younger, and his legs were longer. But this wasn't a fair race, and with his injuries and the two of us weighing him down, Caldswell was catching up fast, sprinting through the phantoms' glowing bodies before they could make themselves physical enough to trip him. But though the captain was gaining, our head start gave us the edge, and we reached the bomber well ahead of him.

Rupert tossed Maat up first, sliding her onto the rusted metal floor of the bomber's empty bay. The Maat only I could see was already inside. The old engine creaked to life as soon as she came in touching range, her power canceling the phantom's nullification field as she hurried toward the front of the ship, sliding through the cockpit chairs like a ghost.

I was still watching her when Rupert shoved me inside, tossing me unceremoniously just inside the door. I scrambled onto my knees at once, turning to help pull Rupert into the ship. But as I came around to face him, I saw Caldswell's arm fly up, leveling the disrupter pistol directly at my head.

Time slowed to a crawl. Caldswell had been running the whole time Rupert had been loading us in. He was now less than five feet from the bomber, almost in arm's reach. He was so close that I could see the decision in his eyes and the strain in his hand as he squeezed the trigger, and my heart stuttered to a stop.

At this distance, there was no way Caldswell could miss. Crouching on the bomber's bay floor, I was at eye level with Rupert, and I could see the trajectory of the shot clearly. It would blast through Rupert's head and into mine, killing us both. But though I could see the danger, understand it, practically feel the heat of the shot cutting through my head, I couldn't move fast enough. All I could do was meet Rupert's eyes for a final good-bye, a thank you, everything. He was already staring at me when I looked over, his blue eyes warm and determined as they bored into mine.

"Love you," he said, his hand shooting up for what I thought would be our final touch. But instead of falling gently on my cheek, his clawed hand curled into a fist as he brought it down on the red button on the ship's hull.

The bomber's emergency blast door slammed down, blocking the room and nearly taking off my hand in the process. I didn't care. I was already beating on the wall of metal, screaming, *"Rupert!"*

My answer was the muffled blast of a disrupter shot outside, followed by a sliding, hollow thud I knew I'd hear every moment for the rest of my life. The sound cut me off like a switch. I sat there dumbstruck, my hands pressed against the metal door that was quickly becoming too hot to touch. But even when my hands started to burn from the shot's dissipating heat, I didn't move.

Behind me, I could hear the sound of someone throwing switches, and then the bomber's engine roared to life. In my peripheral vision, I saw Maat's glowing projection standing over the flight console as the dusty touch screens worked themselves, and then the whole ship started to shake as the hyperdrive coil spun to life.

Outside, something slammed into the emergency door. Caldswell, I thought numbly. Trying to get in.

I knew I should do something about that, but I couldn't move. For the first time in my life, I was shocked completely still, my mind spinning like a wheel cut loose even as the jump flash washed over the ship, pulling us out of reality. Pulling me away from the world where Rupert no longer was.

And with that, something inside me broke.

I crumpled, collapsing on the floor with a sob so sharp it ached. I didn't care that Maat was watching, didn't care that I was weak. I curled up on the bomber's dusty metal floor and bawled, crying in great heaves until I could barely breathe. But even my lack of air seemed trivial next to the fact that Rupert would never smile at me again, never kiss me again. He was dead, and I'd never even told him I loved him.

That sent me to pieces all over again. Why the hell hadn't I told him I loved him? How could I have been so stupid? The answer came to me as soon as I asked the question, and the truth was scalding. Even though I'd admitted it to myself, I'd never told him I loved him because that would have given him power over me. So long as he was the only one who'd admitted his feelings, I was safe, in command, my pride protected.

I choked on a sob. What a joke. What a stupid, prideful, childish way to think, and now I'd never get to set it right. Rupert was gone, and even if I said I loved him a thousand times, he'd never hear it.

I slammed my burned fists against the door one last time and rolled onto my side, crying in great heaves until the strain on my abs from the gasps began to make me nauseous. As I tried to get back some control before I made myself sick, it occurred to me that this was exactly why I'd never let anyone in, but I couldn't even work up the strength to be angry. Grief had filled me to bursting, and there was simply no room for anything else.

I couldn't say how long I cried like that, curled over in my own blood on the dusty, rusted floor. It could have been minutes or hours. It felt like forever, but when I'd finally managed to cry enough out that a bit of the world could creep back in, the first sensation I registered was a hand stroking my back.

I looked up with a hiccuping breath to see Maat kneeling beside me. The real Maat, not the physical shell we'd stolen. That was still lying motionless on the floor beside me, tiny and pathetic and broken. By contrast, the glowing, semitransparent girl petting my back looked almost normal, her brown eyes brimming with tears as she stared down at me.

"I'm so sorry," she whispered.

Her words triggered an anger so sharp and deep I barely recognized it. "Why are you sorry?" I snarled, pulling away. "You hated him."

"I did," Maat admitted. "But you loved him, and you saved me, so for your sake, I'm sorry."

Her voice was worlds calmer than mine. Calmer than I'd ever

heard it, actually. Now that my brain was capable of thinking such things again, I realized she sounded almost sane.

"What happened?" I whispered, pushing myself up. I wasn't done crying yet. I wasn't sure if I ever would be, actually, but I never could stand to be in a prone position when other people were over me.

Maat courteously waited until I was sitting with my injured leg propped in front of me before she answered. "The voices are gone."

"Does that mean you're sane?" I asked.

She tilted her head and smiled at me. Not a mad smile either, a relieved one, like someone experiencing freedom from pain after years of suffering. "I don't know," she admitted. "But I'm alone in my head for the first time since I can remember. That has to count for something."

Her answer irritated me. "Where did you go?" I demanded. If she'd been with us the whole time instead of disappearing after the queen ran, Rupert might still be alive. I wasn't sure how she could have changed things, but I jumped on the possibility with a viciousness that shocked me. I was desperate for someone to blame, someone to hate, and Maat was convenient. But as much as I wanted to make her the outlet of all my loss and rage, I couldn't, because as soon as I spoke, she started to cry.

"I went to Brenton," she admitted. "I wanted to help him, but he was already dead. He died standing up, holding the button. Died for me."

She started crying in earnest after that. Not sure what else to do, I put my hand awkwardly over hers and waited. "I think I loved him once," she said at last, her voice thick even though she had no body, no throat to contract. "There were so many voices, so many memories, I could never tell which were actually mine and which were stolen. I could never be sure of anything except how I hated them." She covered her face. "I hated so much."

"It's okay," I said softly, patting her arm. "It's over now."

Until the words left my mouth, I hadn't actually thought about what our situation actually meant. While I'd been falling to pieces over Rupert, Maat had jumped us. We were now in hyperspace, which meant we'd done it. We'd won. I tried to conjure up some pride at that. Happiness, accomplishment, something, but all I felt was tired and lacking, like I'd left something vital behind when we'd jumped, and I was never getting it back.

Despite everything that had happened, though, some things never changed. I'd always used work as a form of comfort and coping, and now that Maat had reminded me of the job left unfinished, my reeling mind grabbed on to it as hard as it had latched on to my vicious anger earlier.

Moving slowly so as not to jostle my throbbing leg, I reached over and grabbed Maat's body, pulling it into my lap. Maat and I must have been more alike than I'd given her credit for, because she also stopped crying when she saw what I was doing. Her face grew even more determined when I pressed my fingers down against the skin of her cheek where the scales didn't block me.

"You know," I said quietly, "you don't have to die. You seem a lot better out here, and you're free now. You could take this ship and run, go somewhere and live the life they took from you."

Maat shook her head. "If I don't take the virus out of you, you'll die."

I sighed and leaned back, wincing when it triggered the throbbing ache in my leg and shoulder, though those were nothing compared to the much greater hurt in my chest. "I'm kind of ready to get off the ride."

I was, too. I had no illusions about what was waiting for me when this jump ended. If he lived through the phantom's attack, Caldswell would have me declared enemy number one, Maat's murderer. He'd probably have a firing squad waiting the second I popped back into the universe. Paradox thought I was dead, so there'd be no running home, and this was assuming there'd still be a Paradox to run home to.

I could see the hyperdrive screen from where we were sitting in the back. Maat hadn't entered a destination; she'd just hit the button, jumping us blind from a dusty old bay. With so much interference, no gate, and no destination, we were cut free of time completely, and who knew when we'd slip back in. Millions of years could be passing and we wouldn't even know. We'd be lucky if humanity still existed. But even if we popped back in a minute after we'd left, Rupert wouldn't be there, and I saw no reason to go back and get executed if I couldn't even give him a good-bye kiss.

"I can't tell you what to do with your life from here," Maat said, reaching down to stroke her own sleeping face. "But I'm not leaving this jump alive."

I opened my mouth, but Maat cut me off. "I'm tired," she said. "Every time I made a daughter, I ate her life. Even if the girl didn't survive the process, I drank her memories. Through them, I've seen my parents murdered in front of me hundreds of times, but I can't remember anymore which of those faces were my real parents. And even after they became my daughters, I was still in them. I felt everything that happened to them, every minute of every day of every year."

Her eyes drifted shut. "All their humiliations," she whispered. "I was there. And at the end…" She took a shuddering breath. "I can't even count how many times I've died, but I never got to rest. It was always another life, another's suffering to eat."

She raised her head sharply, staring at me until I flinched. "It doesn't matter that I'm free of their voices here," she said. "I can never get rid of the memories. Even if you could get my body to function normally again without the machines, the second we go back into reality, all the voices will come back and I'll go mad again."

Her lips curled into a snarl. "You can't make me go through that again. I'll take the virus from you by force if I have to, but after that I'm leaving, and if you try to stop me, I'll kill you, too."

I smiled at her threat. "Then do it, Maat."

"Enna," she said, her face lighting up, like she'd just remembered. "That's my name." Her smile got wider. "My real name."

"Enna," I repeated, holding out my hand.

She took it, grabbing the hand of her poor abused body at the same time. When she motioned, I reached down and took her body's other hand so that the three of us were a triangle. Then, when we were ready, Maat closed her eyes, and a hand grabbed hold of my spine.

Since the virus entered my life, I'd discovered a lot more than I ever wanted to know about plasmex. I'd been ripped out of my body and thrown into terrifying situations that would probably have broken a more sensitive person. But I've always been pigheaded, and I'd muddled through every time. I fully expected to get through this the same way, so even though the ghostly feeling of fingers touching my vertebrae was every bit as unnerving as I remembered, I didn't worry about it too much until Maat's hand slid up my neck to grab my brain.

That was exactly what it felt like, too. Like she'd run her hand up my spinal column and was now squeezing my gray matter like it was clay. The only things that kept me from reaching up to yank her arm out of my head were the fact that I knew it wasn't real and the part where I couldn't move.

Maat's touch had paralyzed me. I could feel my body, but I couldn't so much as twitch my fingers or shut my eyes so long as she was groping around inside my skull. After the lelgis and the oneness, I'd thought the process would be more elegant, but it was almost comically macabre. Across from me, Maat was sitting with her eyes squeezed shut, the tip of her tongue sticking out like she was thinking very hard. But though it felt weird and extremely unpleasant, Maat's digging wasn't painful. I was starting to wonder how long this was going to take when Maat's fumbling hit something I never knew was there, and my mind exploded like a grenade.

But as I was bursting open, Maat was pouring in. Even though she'd told me about the chaos not minutes before, nothing could have prepared me for the onslaught of foreign memories, feelings, pains, entire lives shoved into me like so much flotsam. It was like when Ren had returned my memories multiplied by several powers of ten, only this time there was no Rupert to put things back in order. I didn't even know if this mess *could* be put in order. I'd decided to focus on just trying to get through alive when the black stain blossomed on my fingers.

Pain came right behind. Before, the stain had felt like the tingling after your limb falls asleep. Now, it was like an entire bed of nails was being shoved under my skin, and it was *everywhere.*

The virus spread like wildfire, consuming my entire body in seconds. The pain alone was enough to shock the air out of my lungs. If I could have moved, I would have been thrashing and howling, but I couldn't. All I could do was hold on, wait it out, and hope there was some sanity left at the end.

I was still holding when Maat's grip tightened, and then, without warning, she began to *pull.* And as she pulled, the body between us began to convulse.

From the moment we'd pulled her out of the machine, Maat's sad, scale-covered body hadn't done more than twitch. Now, her blind eyes shot open and her clawed hands reached up to claw at her face like she wanted to tear it off. It was like when I'd killed Brenton's girl back on the *Fool*, only so much worse, because this time I wasn't just watching. With Maat's hand pulling in my head, I was plugged into her directly, and I felt her death like it was my own.

But even as I lived her agonizing pain as the virus dissolved her body, I could feel it leaving mine. As the blackness devoured Maat's hands, mine became clean. As the stain spread up her arms and over her chest, my own skin cleared, and this time, I knew it was forever.

Somewhere in the maelstrom of pain and memories that was raging in my head, I could actually feel the enormous weight of Maat's plasmex cradling my own tiny spark like a giant holding a grain of sand. I'd been told plenty of times by plenty of people who should know that my plasmex was small, but actually feeling the proof was something else entirely. I felt like a leaf adrift in the ocean of Maat's power, but even so, she didn't lose me. Her hand stayed lodged in my mind, patiently teasing out the sickness. And then, when every speck of black had been pulled away, Maat's presence vanished.

I didn't even know what the infection had felt like until it was gone. I felt like I'd been washed clean, purified. It wasn't all pleasant, though. My mind also felt raw, like overscrubbed skin, and everything was too bright and hollow. It took me several seconds to work up the courage to open my eyes. When I did, I was sitting in the pilot's chair.

I looked around in confusion. The last I'd known, I'd been in the back with Maat. Now I was in the dusty cockpit, looking out at the flat, purple-gray nothing of hyperspace through the bomber's front window. But when I turned to ask Maat why she'd moved me to the front of the ship, the question died on my lips.

Behind me, the fire door to the bomber's bay had been lowered, sealing off the tiny cockpit from the rest of the ship. Like everything else, the door was old and heavy, its once-shiny surface turned dull by age, and on that dull metal was a message.

The release lever for the bomb doors is on the far left, it read. *You'll want to hit it as soon as possible to avoid reinfection.*

It took me two tries to understand what the message meant and another try to get over the fact that it had been written in blood, most likely *my* blood since I'd been the one doing all the bleeding. Once I got over that little detail, though, all I felt was gratitude. Maat had taken my infection and moved me away so I wouldn't catch it again when she died. The doors were down because her body was lying on the other side, along with the final remains of Stoneclaw's terrible, stupid weapon.

But when I reached over to follow the note's instructions, I felt something wet and sticky on my skin, and I looked down in alarm to see another message written across the back of my hand. A much shorter one.

Thank you.

The letters on my hand were far shakier than those on the wall, but that only made them feel more real. The bloody words should have been creepy, but after all I'd been through, I was incapable of seeing them as anything other than what they were. Thanks, the most heartfelt and gladly given I had ever, or would ever, receive.

"You're welcome," I said, reaching out to pull the lever.

The whole ship shuddered as the bomb bay doors opened, dumping Maat's body into hyperspace. There was a warning blip on the monitor as the thin shell protecting us from the unknown rippled, and then the corpse with the last of the virus was eaten by the unknown beyond. Another time, that would have upset me. I was a stickler for proper burial. This time, though, I felt nothing, because the girl I knew was gone already. Enna was free, just like I'd promised, and now I was alone.

I sat back in the dusty pilot's chair, casually wiping my bloody hand on my shirt's last remaining clean spot. I wasn't sure how long I'd been out, how long any of this had taken really, but I seemed to have stopped bleeding. My leg still hurt like a bitch, of course. Thanks to the metal barb, my thigh was throbbing so hard I could feel it in every part of my body. My shoulder was a little better, but not much, and I had no energy to deal with any of it. I had no energy for anything.

Now that the job was done, I was tired in a way I'd never been before. I felt hollow and powerless, though I didn't know if that was from what Maat had done to me or from the crying before. Whatever it was, the exhaustion was a blessing, numbing the ache of Rupert's loss and my own fear. Some small part of me that still retained its logic knew this was probably because I was going into shock, but I couldn't remember why that was a bad thing. It was nice to feel muted, to not hurt.

I sat there in the lull for several minutes, idly contemplating whether I should go back or not. I was injured enough that I could easily die here if I did nothing, but whenever I thought about it, the idea seemed insulting. She might have done it for her own reasons, but the fact remained that Maat had given me my life back. Also, if I was going to die, I at least wanted to do it somewhere I knew the king's death guides could find me. Plus, however low I'd sunk, I'd never been a quitter, and the idea of a quiet, ignominious death in hyperspace was simply too maudlin for me to bear.

It took everything I had, but in the end, I forced myself to sit up and hit the button that controlled the hyperspace coil. I fell backward as soon as I did, landing in a cloud of dust as the coil began to spin down. Closing my eyes against the burst of pain my movements had caused, I crossed my fingers and recited a prayer to my king as the stillness of hyperspace vanished and I was yanked back into the universe.

———

When I opened my eyes again, the first thing I saw were the phantoms.

That threw me for several minutes. First, I'd assumed my ability to see the space bugs would have vanished with the virus, and second, there weren't supposed to *be* any more phantoms. They were all supposed to have gone back home, not floating around in our universe, especially not in such vast numbers.

But even while these worries rattled around in my head, I had to admit they were beautiful. The space around my ship was so bright with them I felt like I was flying through a glowing snowstorm. Soon enough, they were in my ship, too, passing through the walls like spirits to land on me.

Having lived at the center of a three-foot no-phantom zone for so long, I couldn't help a little jump when the first one lighted on my arm. A few seconds later, I was covered in them. The little glowing bugs were crawling over my skin and hair and under my clothes, which would have been disturbing except I couldn't feel them at all. After that, I couldn't help a wide grin, because of all the phantoms sitting on me, not a one was turning black.

My moment of happiness was short-lived. Just as I reached up to pet a particularly fluffy-looking little shrimplike phantom that had landed on my stomach, the bomber's alarm started to blare. I jumped, scattering the phantoms, and looked over just in time to see three Terran fighters fly up in tight formation beside me. The next second, my little ship rocked as a harpoon struck the hyperdrive, and a man speaking brisk, no-nonsense Universal hailed my com.

"Unidentified vessel," he said. "You have entered restricted space. You are being taken into custody under special action order number—"

"Save it," I said, leaning back in the bomber's dusty chair. "This is Deviana Morris, here for her funeral. What's today's date?"

The swift response actually gave me a stab of hope. If they were still guarding the Dark Star this actively, I couldn't have lost too much time. The fighters didn't look too different at least, so I couldn't have been gone more than ten years. I waited for the pilot's response, but he didn't speak to me again. Instead, a jammer field landed on my ship, sending my com into a squeal of static. I cut it off with a groan and settled down for the ride as the fighters rearranged their formation to tow me in.

I didn't have to wait long. The fighters ended up pulling me to a Republic battleship that was only about five minutes away. I tried to read the ship's fleet number, but the phantoms were so thick I couldn't even make it out. Still, battleships don't hang around for the fun of it, and by the time the fighters had dragged me into the landing bay, I was starting to get seriously nervous. After all, if there were this many phantoms, then maybe Caldswell had been right. Maybe by killing Maat, I'd opened the floodgates and doomed us all.

But the phantoms were all so tiny and peaceful as they floated by like little jellyfish in a tide that I had trouble believing that. In any case, there was no way to know until someone talked to me. So when the bay doors closed behind us and gravity caught my ship,

I left the landing to the autopilot and popped the front hatch. The ladder was tough on my leg. Going out through the back would have been easier, but even with Maat dead, a little more pain seemed like a small price to pay to avoid going into the bomber's rear bay ever again.

My quick exit must have confused the pilots, because they were still scrambling themselves when I poked my head out the hatch. They had their guns ready by the time I climbed down, and I immediately raised my hands in surrender. Clearly, I hadn't jumped too far in the future, which meant I was probably still in a lot of trouble, and if I was going to be executed, I wanted it done proper, not because I startled some trigger-happy Terran idiot.

"Easy," I said, trying my best to look nonthreatening, which was a lot easier than normal with one leg shot through and my face pale from blood loss. When the soldiers didn't start barking orders at me, though, I got confused. Were they waiting for something or—

"Well, well, look what the cat dragged in."

My whole body froze at the deep voice echoing from the other side of the bay. No. It couldn't possibly...

But it was. When I looked up, Brian Caldswell was strolling across the deck. He looked exactly like he always did—graying reddish hair, late middle age, confident stride—none of which told me anything since he'd looked like this for seventy years that I knew of. What really threw me was the fact that he was *smiling*. That was just unnerving. Maybe the trauma of losing Maat had left him soft in the head?

"I thought they were pulling my leg," Caldswell said as he stepped up to join the pilots, looking me up and down like he was trying to spot a fake. "Damn, Morris, never thought I'd see you again."

"Feeling's mutual," I snarled, glaring at him and fighting the urge to bat at the tiny phantoms flying around my face. "Let's cut to the chase. What year is it? How long was I gone?"

Caldswell's smile got wider, making me cringe, but his answer was what hit me like a sucker punch.

"Six days, twelve hours, thirty-eight minutes, eighteen seconds," he said. "Give or take a second."

I must have stood there for a solid minute, opening and closing my mouth like a fish. "But," I spat out when my brain finally started working again, "*how?*"

"Wild jumps can just as easily be short as long," Caldswell replied with a shrug. "And large phantoms thin space by their very presence. With so many emperors around ripping up the universe and distorting time, your jump was much easier than it should have been. Clearly, you have the devil's own luck."

His words made sense, but I'd been braced so hard for the worst I couldn't wrap my mind around them. I also couldn't understand why he was talking about phantoms in front of men who were clearly common soldiers. All this confusion must have been a pathetic sight, because Caldswell sighed and walked over, putting a hand on my back to steer me forward.

That snapped me out of my shock just fine.

"Don't touch me," I snarled, whipping back. This man had killed Rupert. If I'd thought I had a chance of actually ripping it out, I would have gone for his throat. "If you're going to kill me, then do it. I'm not afraid, and I'd rather die taking you out than go through some sham of a trial."

"Relax, Morris," Caldswell said, putting up his hands. "You have every reason to want to kill me right now, but before you try, I have something I'd like to show you."

I should have punched him. I should have gone for one of the soldiers' guns and plugged him right in his smug face. Unfortunately, appealing as both of those actions sounded, they would have ended up hurting me far more than Caldswell. Also, part of me was curious, and since curious was a lot better than the angry, grieving hurt I'd been swallowing for the past hour, I stalked after him.

I fully expected to be marched into a prison cell. Instead, Caldswell led me down to the ship's medical bay. I blew out a breath, expecting to be told to hop up on one of the triage tables, but though my bloody clothes and marked limp were drawing nurses like vultures to a carcass, Caldswell waved them away and kept going, leading me down a short hallway lined with private patient rooms very much like the one I'd woken up in the last time I was on a Terran battleship.

That memory put a bad taste in my mouth, but I was in this now, so I stomped through the door Caldswell was gentlemanly enough to hold open for me only to come up face to snout with a xith'cal in a lab coat. I stumbled back in shock, though I really shouldn't have been surprised considering my escort. For his part, Hyrek didn't even blink. He just tapped at his handset and turned it to face me.

Oh, it's you.

I blinked at the message, and then fixed him with a glare. "That's it? That's all I get?"

He pulled his handset back and started typing. When he turned the screen to me again, the letters were bright pink and bobbing up and down. *Welcome back from the great beyond! Miracle of miracles!*

I stared at the message so long I think I scared Hyrek, because he quickly typed, *That was a joke.*

"No, I get it," I snapped, suddenly furious. I was in zero mood to be played with. "Why am I here? What's going on?"

Hyrek looked at Caldswell. When the captain nodded, the lizard reached out and pulled back the curtain that shielded the bed from view.

The man lying in it was hooked up to a dozen machines, his body covered in patches and monitoring cuffs everywhere they would fit. His head was wrapped in a bandage that wisps of black hair were already starting to escape, and though there was an oxygen mask over his mouth and a bandage covering his eyes, it didn't matter a jot. I'd know him anywhere.

"Rupert," I whispered, the name coming out in a choked gasp

as I stumbled forward, almost falling in my hurry to grab his warm hand in mine. He didn't move when I touched him, but his chest was rising and falling, his heartbeat measured by the steady beep of the machine on the wall, audible proof that he was alive. He was *alive*.

That was as far as I got before I started to cry.

I should have been ashamed of myself, bawling like that. Caldswell and Hyrek were right next to me, no doubt judging me every second, but it didn't matter. If the king himself had been before me, I couldn't have stopped the tears. My relief was so intense it hurt almost as much as the grief had, and after everything that had happened, I didn't have the strength left to fight it.

It took me a few minutes to get myself together enough to turn back around. When I did, I saw that Caldswell and Hyrek had retreated to the door to give me some privacy. I felt a twinge of annoyance that they'd had to do that, but mostly I was exhausted. I'd pushed past my limits on everything, mentally, physically, emotionally, and overjoyed as I was to find out Rupert wasn't dead, it had been the final blow.

I didn't even have the energy left to be mad at Caldswell. Instead, I leaned on Rupert's bed and caught the captain's eye, waving them over without ceremony as I asked, "What's going on?"

How is he alive? was what I really wanted to know, but I couldn't get that one out just yet, so I settled for something broader.

Caldswell blew out a long breath and jerked his head toward the door. Hyrek took his cue and left at once, locking the room behind him. When the captain and I were alone, he sat down in the chair in the corner with a sigh. "Luck," he said tiredly. "When that phantom or Maat or whatever grabbed my gun to save you, it bent the barrel. So, when I went to shoot to prevent your escape, my aim was off."

"So why is he like this?" I said, nodding down at Rupert's still body.

Caldswell arched a thick eyebrow. "I said my aim was 'off,' not 'gone.' I still hit him in the head, just not as cleanly as I'd meant. He sustained a massive brain injury, which is why Hyrek's keeping him in a coma. We're waiting to see if he'll regenerate."

Panic sent my heart racing as a cold sweat broke out all over my body. "Will he regenerate?"

"We're not sure," Caldswell said. "Hyrek says he's never seen a symbiont this badly damaged who wasn't dead. But he's doing well so far, and if anyone could pull this off, it's Charkov. He never was one to give up."

I let out a shaky breath. He'd make it, I decided. He had to. I wouldn't let him die again.

Even though I had no actual way of enforcing that decision, just thinking it made me feel much better, and I settled a little more comfortably onto Rupert's bed, trying not to get too much blood on things as I cradled his warm hand in my lap.

"I'm sure you hate me right now."

Caldswell's voice caught me by surprise, and I looked up to see him staring like he expected me to disabuse him of this. When I didn't, he continued. "It seems I owe you an apology, Morris."

"You owe me a lot more than that," I said with a snort, lifting my eyes to the phantoms that were still flowing by. "I was right, wasn't I? We opened the door and now the phantoms are leaving, just like I said."

"So they tell me," Caldswell replied. "For the record, I am not apologizing for what I did on the Dark Star. Just because your gamble paid off doesn't mean you had any right to make it. You bet the future of all humanity on the word of a space monster who couldn't even speak, and I was completely in the right for trying to stop you."

"Except for the part where you were wrong," I reminded him. "So what are you apologizing for, then?"

Caldswell lowered his gaze, and for a moment, I would have sworn he looked ashamed. "I'm sorry I tried to keep you and Charkov apart," he said at last. "A great deal of suffering could have been avoided if we'd told you the truth right from the beginning

350

and set out to work with both of your feelings rather than against them. It's been a long time since I was in love and I'd forgotten what an idiot it makes you."

That was hardly an apology, but seeing as this was Caldswell, it was probably as good as I was ever going to get. "What about Maat's daughters?" I asked. "What's being done for them? Are they still..."

"Alive?" Caldswell finished. "Oh yes, very. When you took Maat into hyperspace, her control over them vanished. Some, mostly the older ones, became unstable, but the majority were able to recover once Maat's madness was removed from their shared consciousness." He shot me a curious look. "They've been asking about you."

I couldn't help a smug grin at that one. "Still think I was greedy and prideful for trying to have it all?"

"Incredibly," he said. "If I wasn't so happy about how it all worked out, I would be furious."

"So what happens to me now?" I asked. "Am I going to prison or what?"

"Honestly, I have no idea," Caldswell confessed. "We haven't actually drawn up a list of all the laws you broke during your time on the lam or your escape from and subsequent near destruction of one of the most expensive military installations in the Republic, but when we do, it'll be as long as my arm. That said, you also saved us from the phantoms, ended the abusive daughter system, and gave us a shield against a lelgis retaliation."

I frowned. "Shield?"

"I don't actually understand that part myself," Caldswell said. "But it seems they don't like the door you opened up, and if I understood Dr. Starchild's rather oblique report correctly, they have fled to the farthest reaches of the universe to avoid it."

Served them right, I thought bitterly. The lelgis were cowards; of course they'd run. I just hoped they stayed away.

"Needless to say," Caldswell went on, "these mitigating factors confuse the issue of your future. Technically, since you were signed over to the Eyes, I get to decide, at least until they appoint someone to replace Martin, but I've excused myself on the grounds of personal bias and referred your case up the chain of command."

I shot him a level glare. "Bias for or against?"

Caldswell just smiled. "A little of both. But since no one expected you to come back so soon, or at all, we don't have a decision for you yet. I'll get on the horn about that, but in the meantime, why don't you get some rest and let Hyrek look at your leg? Because you look like hell."

He had a lot of nerve saying as much to me considering most of that hell was his fault, but I didn't disagree. "I'll see him in here," I said. "And if you try to move me, I'll just come right back, so you might as well agree."

"I was planning to," Caldswell said, standing up. He turned to leave, then paused, running his hands through his hair. "I'm really glad you're back, Morris," he said at last, turning back to look at me. "And I'm really glad you didn't let me stop you."

"Me too," I said, smiling at him through the glowing haze of the little drifting phantoms. "Me too."

CHAPTER

14

As usual, Hyrek had me patched up and good to go in less than thirty minutes. The lecture part of the treatment took substantially longer, but seeing as how it had been Mabel who put the shard in my leg, I didn't see how he had any cause to gripe. Unfortunately, since I refused to leave Rupert's room, I couldn't exactly get away, but putting up with Hyrek's typing was a small price to pay for not having to leave the place where Rupert was.

I spent the next two days filling out forms and watching Rupert sleep. I was a little nervous about that last one given his symbiont's dislike of me, but once Hyrek showed me the titanium restraints under his medical gown, I was able to relax and enjoy a life where my lover wasn't dead and I wasn't constantly getting shot at or chased by monsters.

My only true sadness was the loss of my suit. The emperor phantoms had ended up ripping the dock to pieces after we jumped, so even though the majority of the station had been salvaged, my armor and weapons were lost to the void of space. I held a funeral for my Lady and my guns the night Caldswell broke the news, and I'm not ashamed to say I cried again. It was only fitting. She'd been the first suit I'd bought for myself, earned in blood and tested by fire. She was my most cherished possession, more like a friend than an object, and even if I got a new Verdemont suit every year for the rest of my life, I knew none of them would ever hold a candle to my beautiful, beloved Lady Gray.

The combination of the loss of my equipment, the lack of concrete information about my future, and the fact that I was stuck on a Terran battleship with nothing to do should have been enough to sink me into a real depression. The only reason it didn't was that Rupert was improving enormously, his body healing so fast that I had to wonder what the hell he'd looked like in the six days before I'd gotten back. He still hadn't woken up, but Hyrek seemed pleased by his progress, and since Hyrek was hard to please, I took that as a very good sign.

I'd made a sort of nest in the chair by his bed, leaving it only when the guards or Hyrek made me. I was sitting there procrastinating filling out yet another incident report when the door guard informed me I had visitors. That struck me as odd since this was Rupert's room, not mine, but it all made sense when Nova burst through the door, swallowing me in a hug before I could even say hello.

"Oh, Deviana," she gasped, squeezing me so tight I could barely breathe. "I'm so so so happy we're able to share space again!"

"Me too," I choked out, hugging her back. "Guess you didn't need that jailbreak after all, huh?"

Nova shook her head, eyes brimming with tears. "Captain Caldswell and Mabel came to rescue us after the hull breach sealed. The captain broke open my door himself." She smiled at me. "I knew he'd never allow harm to befall us, though I did think you'd beat him to it."

I bit my lip guiltily. Honestly, I hadn't even thought about Nova or Basil during our frantic escape, and even though I knew there were mitigating circumstances, that didn't stop me from feeling like the worst friend ever. Thankfully, Nova didn't seem mad I hadn't come back, not that I could actually imagine Nova angry. "I'm really happy you're okay," I said, hugging her hard. "Basil, too," I added belatedly. "Where is the birdie?"

"On vacation," Nova said. "He says he'll retire if Caldswell doesn't get another ship. He'll only fly for the captain."

"Because Caldswell's the only one who'll put up with him," I grumbled, glancing over her shoulder at the other person, who was still hovering in the hall. "Who's your friend?"

Nova's face lit up. "This is Marielle," she said, reaching back to pull the girl in. "She says she already knows you."

I'd never met anyone named Marielle, but as soon as she came through the door, I understood. The girl holding Nova's hand looked just like Maat. Her hair was shorter and stylishly cut and she wore the same loud colors as Nova did, but clearly this was, or had been, a daughter. But the little, shy smile she gave me had never crossed one of Maat's brainwashed faces. I took her hand gingerly when she held it out, bracing for something—a pull, a touch, her voice in my mind—but all I got was another shy smile as she dropped my hand and moved a little closer to Nova.

"Marielle is coming to help Father at the Church," Nova told me, her pale eyes sparkling. "Can you imagine what their meditations will be like?"

"Awesome, I'm sure," I agreed, and I was actually pretty certain they would be. "Do you want to see Rupert? He's doing a lot better."

Of course Nova did, and while she took my seat at Rupert's bedside, I walked to the corner of the room where Marielle was waiting, looking at me expectantly.

"Hello, Deviana," she said.

I nodded in return, lowering my voice to a whisper. "Are you really Marielle? Like, can you actually remember who you were before?"

The girl shrugged. "We were all mixed in Maat's mind. None of us is really sure who is who, so we divided the pasts up between ourselves. I liked Marielle's, so I became her. Sometimes, though, I switch with the others."

I couldn't stop my horrified look. "You mean, switch minds?"

"Bodies really," she said, nodding like it was nothing. "They're all the same, and we still share most of our minds anyway, so it's not a big thing to switch consciousnesses."

That sounded absolutely awful to me. I felt like I should say something, apologize, even though her situation wasn't my fault. But Marielle didn't look angry. She looked nervous, actually, looking down at her hands as she fiddled with her fingers. "The others wanted me to thank you," she said. "We, um, have all your memories."

I blinked. "*My* memories?"

Marielle nodded. "Up to the moment you took Maat into hyperspace. Maat searched your mind constantly, trying to determine if you were lying to her, but you weren't." She looked up at me, her dark eyes clear and free of Maat's madness, making her look like a totally different person in truth. "We know how hard you fought for us, and we are very grateful," she said earnestly. "Even Maat didn't care what happened to us, but you did, and we will never forget that."

Now it was my turn to look down at my hands. For being such a glory hog, I was surprisingly bad at knowing what to do when people thanked me. Cheering crowds I could handle no problem. Sincere personal gratitude? Clammed right up.

"You're welcome," I said at last. "I'm, um, sorry it took so long."

"There's another thing as well."

I glanced up in alarm. "What other thing?"

Marielle smiled and reached out, brushing a phantom off my shoulder. I'd gotten so used to the things crawling on me, I hadn't even noticed it was there. But when she shooed it away, I understood. "You see them, too."

"We all do," she admitted. "Us and you, but no one else. We're not sure why, but we wanted to tell you in case you ever needed help."

"Thanks," I said, unaccountably touched. "But it won't matter after too long since they're leaving."

"They are," Marielle agreed. "But you aren't." She gave me a secretive smile. "Just because there's nothing to see doesn't mean you're blind, Deviana Morris. What happened changed you, made you like us. That makes you our sister as well as our savior, and we've agreed that we will always stand with you. Remember that the next time Brian tries to bully you. You are not alone."

My eyes widened. *That's* what she was getting at. The most powerful human plasmex users in the entire universe considered me family. I smothered a smug grin. That was going to be some fun leverage if I ever got to use it.

Nova came back at that point, and we talked for a few more minutes about her plans to go home and help her father do outreach. "Unless, of course, the captain needs me for his new ship," she put in. "Then I would have to go back and work for him since he looked after us so well."

"Of course," I said, though I secretly hoped it would never happen. Nova was far too kind to waste on someone like Caldswell.

After giving me half a million ways to stay in touch, Nova and Marielle left. I spent the rest of the afternoon thinking up uses for my newfound power and listening to Rupert breathe. I realize that sounds as dull as watching grass grow, but after everything that had happened, a little dullness was fine with me. I was contemplating getting up to go find some food when Hyrek came in and casually turned my new boring world on its ear by announcing that he was about to wake Rupert up.

———

"So how long is this going to take again?" I asked, hovering over Rupert's bed.

For the last time, I don't know. Hyrek's claws clicked testily across the screen of his com. *All I'm doing is cutting off the drug that's been keeping him unconscious and leaving him to wake up on his own time.*

"Okay," I said, settling back in my chair. "I'll wait."

Hyrek's snout twitched as he removed the last of the gauze from

Rupert's face, followed by the oxygen mask. *You do realize this is not guaranteed? He could wake up in five minutes or five days or not at all.*

"He'll wake up," I said firmly. "And I'll be here. And if you try to kick me out, I will kick your ass."

Hyrek snapped his teeth at me, but he didn't try to make me go. No one did. Caldswell must have given an order, because the petty officers who usually hounded me to do stupid things like sleep or eat or fill out forms vanished altogether, leaving me alone with Rupert and my growing worry.

The first night was hell. I didn't sleep a wink, and I had a new-found appreciation for all the times Rupert had waited at my bedside. The next day was better, but by late afternoon the quiet and exhaustion were taking their toll, and I started drifting off. I caught myself several times, but eventually I slept, my head resting on the mattress right next to Rupert's arm. I couldn't have been out for more than an hour when I felt something move beside me.

I shot up, wide awake in an instant. The lights were dimmed for the battleship's night cycle, but it was still bright enough for me to make out Rupert's sluggish movements under the sheets. I moved away quickly, giving him plenty of room just in case he wasn't really himself yet. But when his eyes opened, they weren't the dilated, crazed eyes of his symbiont. They were hazy and charmingly dazed as he looked around the darkened room in confusion.

I probably should have said something then, but I couldn't make a sound. Relief and happiness and a thousand other emotions I wasn't used to dealing with had stopped my throat tight. So I just sat there and waited until, at last, his eyes fell on me.

He stopped cold, his breath catching like he'd seen a ghost. I gave him a weak smile in return, the best I could manage without break-ing down again like a ninny. "Hi," I whispered. And then, because I'd already lost the chance to tell him once and wasn't about to risk it again, I said, "I love you."

The words fell so easily from my mouth I was ashamed all over again that I hadn't said them earlier. From the expression on

Rupert's face, though, you would have thought I'd just announced my intention to slit his throat. He stared at me in horror, his eyes going so wide I could see the whites all the way around. And then, in a tiny, gravelly, beautifully accented voice, he whispered, "Am I dead?"

I should have told him calmly that he was not. I should have explained things to him like a sensible person, because he'd just woken up from a nine-day coma and was clearly confused. I *should* have done any number of things, but what I *did* was throw myself into his bed and kiss him like I'd been dying to since I'd first realized he was alive.

Rupert must have caught on that he wasn't dead pretty quick, because after a few seconds he was kissing me back just as hard, his arms wrapped around my waist as far as the restraints would allow. When we finally came up for air, he still looked confused, though much, much happier.

"Where are we? What happened?"

"On a Republic battleship," I told him, reaching down to unlock his restraints. "And you got shot in the head, though not by me this time. Caldswell did it, but he missed and you ended up in a coma. You just woke up."

As I released the last hook holding him to the table, Rupert reached up to rub his temple. "The last thing I remember is getting you to the bomber. Did we fail?"

"Nope," I replied, grinning wide. "Other than you getting hurt and both of us possibly going to jail forever, we succeeded spectacularly. Maat's dead, the lelgis turned tail and ran, the phantoms are going home to greener pastures, and the daughters are saved. More importantly," I added, sitting down on the edge of the bed, "you're alive."

I reached out to run my hand down his cheek, but I never made it, because Rupert grabbed me first. He sat up in a rush, crushing me against him as he buried his face in my neck. He didn't say anything, didn't make a sound, but his shoulders were shaking. I hugged him back, squeezing until my arms ached, and though I didn't cry this time, it was a very near thing.

"I'm so happy you're alive," he whispered at last. "You have no idea."

"I think I do," I said, kissing his shoulder before pulling back to look him in the eyes. "Because if you *ever* scare me like that again, I will kill you myself."

Rupert stared at me for a long second, and then he folded me back against his chest, pulling me up on the bed until I was sitting in his lap. "I'll never leave you again," he solemnly. "I swear it."

I leaned into him, perfectly happy, because I knew he meant it. Whatever happened from here out, however screwed we were, we were together. Right now, that felt like the most important thing in the universe, and if thinking so made me a sentimental weakling, I'd just have to learn to deal with it.

We didn't break apart again until Hyrek came in thirty minutes later. After that, I was ordered back to my chair while Rupert was put through the expected battery of tests. He bore the poking and prodding with far more grace than I would have in his situation, but then, it probably helped that he was completely healthy. I asked jokingly if symbionts could regenerate lost limbs as well as brains, which earned me a lengthy lecture on symbiont physiology from our resident lizard.

"You know, a simple yes would have sufficed," I grumbled.

Ah, Hyrek typed. *But then you wouldn't have learned anything.*

Two hours after he entered, Hyrek grudgingly pronounced Rupert cured. I think I was happier about that than Rupert was. I was so damn sick of this room and I wanted nothing more than to take Rupert back to the surprisingly nice cabin Caldswell had assigned me and fall asleep next to him for a week. Unfortunately, Caldswell picked that moment to come in.

He wasn't alone, either. Mabel was there, along with an older man I'd never seen before, who was wearing a very important-looking Terran Starfleet uniform. Admiral was my guess, maybe higher. He also had a daughter with him who wasn't Marielle. This girl's hair was cut very short, and she looked every bit as cold and deadly as Maat at her worst.

I felt Rupert tense on the bed beside me as they entered, but his face was perfectly calm when I looked over. I moved a bit closer anyway, glaring at Caldswell to do something about it. Which meant, of course, that he did.

"Out, Morris," he ordered.

I was opening my mouth to tell him exactly where and how hard he could shove his orders when Rupert squeezed my hand. "It's all right, Devi," he said quietly. "I'll find you later. Go rest."

I gave him a skeptical look, but as scary serious as this group looked, there was a daughter here. Between her and Rupert, that gave me two voices I trusted to be on my side. Besides, I reasoned, if they were going to lock Rupert up, they would have done it while he was unconscious, and they definitely wouldn't have let me stay with him given my record for successful escapes.

That made me feel a bit better, and though I was loathe to leave Rupert so soon after getting him back, I wasn't about to embarrass myself by making some kind of melodramatic scene. But I wasn't above giving him a long, pointed kiss, just to make my intentions clear. He was grinning when I finished, and I grinned back, hopping off the bed and heading for my cabin, shooting Caldswell the mother of all death glares on my way out. I've made hardened mercs in full armor step back with that sort of look. Naturally, then, it rolled off Caldswell like water off a greased duck.

I don't know who he'd kicked out to get it, but Caldswell had given me a very nice diplomatic suite on the ship's port side. It was still cramped, we were on a battleship after all, but I had a full-sized bed, my own bathroom, and a window with a great view of the wrecked Dark Star Station. If I hadn't known for sure what it was, I never would have recognized the place with the work lights all over the cavernous new hole it was sporting on one side.

Caldswell told me that almost all of the Eyes who'd run during our attack had survived. He'd informed me of this gravely, like I should care, but I really didn't. It was his job to worry about symbionts. I didn't give a damn whether they were dead or heading off to form their own symbiont colony so long as I never had to see any of them ever again.

I'd meant to wait up for Rupert to hear what Caldswell was planning, but I'd been awake for almost thirty hours at this point with only an hour's nap in between, and my body was in revolt. By the time I'd showered and changed, I was dead on my feet. I passed out the moment I sat down on the bed, just fell right over. I don't think I moved a muscle until I heard Rupert call my name.

When I opened my eyes, it was like I'd gone back in time. Rupert was sitting on the edge of my bed dressed in a somber black suit identical to the ones he'd worn on the *Fool*. The only difference was his hair, which was still short and slightly damp from the shower he must have taken, and the haze of glowing phantoms that was still flowing through the ship like a river. Otherwise, we could have been in Nova's and my bunk back on the ship, except now Rupert was smiling openly at me, his hand reaching down to brush my hair out of my face with a possessive familiarity I liked a lot more than I'd thought I would.

"Well?" I asked, leaning into the touch. "What's the verdict?"

Rupert frowned. "I'm still not quite sure, actually. Right now, it looks like the Eyes are being disbanded. There was talk of doing bodyguard work for the daughters, but they aren't exactly keen to work with us."

I could see how working with your former jailers wouldn't be ideal. "What are the daughters doing?"

"A little of everything," Rupert said, moving so that he was sitting on the bed with his back to the wall and my feet across his lap.

It was the same position we'd been in when we'd played cards back in my room forever ago, only now he freely rested his hands on me, petting my legs as he talked like he couldn't stop touching me.

"The daughters have all agreed to work willingly with the Republic and other governments in exchange for certain freedoms. Naturally, they can't ever fully reintegrate knowing what they know and being who they are, but they're powerful enough and valuable enough to make sure their confinement is on their own terms." He grinned at me. "They also demanded amnesty for you."

"Well, that's nice," I said with a yawn. "But I'm not up for being confined even if I am the one setting the terms."

"Commander Caldswell said as much," Rupert said with a shrug. "They didn't make a decision about you, though."

"But they did about you," I said, reading between the lines. "What's going to happen?"

Rupert sighed. "I disobeyed orders," he said plainly. "So I'm being discharged."

"Honorably or dishonorably?"

He chuckled. "Would you believe a little of both? There was a move toward court-martial, but Caldswell worked out a deal with the Republic. I've been stripped of my clearances and demoted to special envoy for the Scientific Council."

I frowned. "What kind of job is that?"

"It isn't one, really," he admitted. "The title is just to keep me under all my secrecy clauses and on the books, but I'm currently on indefinite unpaid leave."

"What are you going to do?" I asked. What the hell was Caldswell thinking? Rupert might be a symbiont, but he still had to eat. I understood the need to keep a supersoldier who knew decades of secrets under control, but under this setup, he couldn't even get another job. "What are you going to live on?"

Rupert flashed me a wry smile. "Well, I did work a very high-paying government job for forty-three years without having to worry about living expenses, so I think I'll be all right on that account. Honestly, some time off sounds very appealing, especially if I get to take it with you."

That statement sparked a confused tangle of emotions in my gut. On the one hand, a vacation with Rupert sounded divine. On the other, I didn't have a huge nest egg waiting for me, and like hell was I going to live off Rupert's money. Even though I knew he'd offer it freely, I'd always made my own way, and anyway, I *liked* working. Assuming they ever let me out of here, I'd planned to get a job and start saving up for my next suit, maybe even reapply to the Blackbirds if Anthony hadn't trashed my reputation too badly. I was still thinking about how best to explain this to Rupert when a light flashed outside my window.

I recognized it right off as a jump flash. A *big* one. My first thought was that another battleship had arrived, but when I glanced out the window to be sure, I almost fell off the bed.

A Paradoxian Royal-class battle cruiser was sitting just off our bow. Not just any Royal-class cruiser, either. This was a huge, shiny, golden palace of a battleship with the king's own seal displayed proudly above the elevated bridge, and my heart leaped into my throat. "Rupert," I choked out. "That's the royal ship."

"So it is," he said, leaning over for a better view. "I wonder what they want."

I looked at him like he'd lost his mind. "*The* royal ship," I clarified. "The *king's* ship."

Even as I said it, I knew that couldn't be true. Just because the royal ship was here didn't mean King Stephen was on it. The king never left Paradoxian space. Ever. He was a living saint, the divine king. He didn't even leave the planet unless there was a dire emergency that required his condescension to visit the Marches. He would never come out to a place like this, both Terran space and a recent war zone. The very idea was stupid.

I was still talking myself down when the com Caldswell had given me beeped with a message demanding my immediate presence in the starboard docking bay. Rupert was not mentioned, but

I don't think I could have made him stay if I'd wanted to, which I didn't. I did make him wait while I changed into the nicest set of drab Terran deck clothes they'd given me, and then we set off together, my heart beating louder by the second as we took the elevator down.

Caldswell was waiting for us at the bottom. He gave Rupert a sharp look, but he didn't say a word. He just walked us over to the docking tunnel the royal ship had already extended.

When I opened my mouth to ask what was going on, Caldswell shook his head. "It'll all be explained in a second," he said. "Move quick. We have very little time."

And with that cryptic statement, he shoved Rupert and me into the docking tunnel and activated the entrance shield, sealing us in. I stood bewildered for a second, then whirled around and half marched, half ran toward the golden door at the other end of the long plastic tunnel.

The boarding tunnel wasn't so different from the Terran ones the battleships used, but once we reached the cruiser, it was like stepping into another world. The gold-plated airlock opened when we approached, and two Devastators in full King-class armor came out to meet us. If Caldswell hadn't made it clear we were in some kind of crisis, I would have spent a good five minutes drooling over their suits, but I did not want to be late for whatever was waiting for us, and I definitely did not want to miss my first look at true royal splendor.

The ship did not disappoint. Unlike Terran battleships with their stark military sensibilities and efficient design, the Royal Cruiser was built to impress on every level. It was scaled for armor, which meant everything was enormous, but still luxurious to the point of absurdity. The walls were lined with wood instead of plastic or metal, the floors either lushly carpeted or tiled in slick, polished, gold-flecked stone. I couldn't even begin to calculate how much something like this cost, but then, if the king couldn't have the best, who could?

This was certainly the king's own ship, too. Everything from the door handles to the soft lighting positively smacked of royalty and privilege. Even the deck layout was more like a palace than a warship, with soaring ceilings and sweeping hallways and verandas overlooking ornamental gardens filled with fountains and fishponds. But for all the opulence, the most telling detail of just how noble a presence we were dealing with was the fact that *everyone* was armored, even the servants. Not even dukes bothered with that level of security, Terran space or not, but royals were another matter altogether.

By the time our silent Devastator guides had led us up to the ship's highest level, I was certain we were being taken to a member of the king's own family. The prince maybe, or his sister. Whoever it was, I was so nervous I didn't know if I'd be able to speak a word of sense when the time came. Rupert, of course, looked perfectly together, thought not nearly as impressed by all of this as he should have been. In his defense, though, he was Terran. Terrans never could appreciate true grandeur.

Our trip ended at a beautiful observation room at the very top of the ship. The ceiling was open glass, revealing what should have been the full swath of the stars overhead, but I could barely see them through the ever-present haze of phantoms. The room was as large as the *Fool*'s cargo bay and softly lit with natural light–giving crystals, the sort that glowed all different colors. I'd always thought they were lovely, but I'd never been able to afford even a small one, especially considering they only glowed for a week before they went out. The cost of keeping an entire room like this lit with the things boggled my mind. I was wondering how many suits of armor I could buy with that much money when I heard the hiss of a door opening.

I looked up nervously, expecting to see a royal secretary, or maybe another pair of exalted tour guides to replace the Devastators who'd stayed behind at the door. What I got was a knot of soldiers wearing the most high-end, expertly designed custom armor

I'd ever seen, all golden, and all bearing the insignia of the king's private guard. And standing between them, wearing a suit that made him seven feet tall, was a man whose face I knew so well I didn't actually recognize it now that I was seeing him in the flesh. When I did, I threw myself to the ground, pressing my forehead against the slick stone floor, because that was my king standing in front of me, and I wasn't sure if I was dead or blessed beyond reason.

"Rupert!" I hissed, glancing at his feet, which I shouldn't have been able to see if he'd known the first thing about meeting a living saint. "*Kneel!*"

"Why?" Rupert said. "He's not my king."

I rolled my eyes to the heavens, bracing for the bolt of punishing fire I knew was coming. Before I could beseech my king for mercy, however, a deep, rumbling laugh echoed through the room.

"It is all right, Deviana Morris," said the voice. "We no longer waste our time being offended by Terran arrogance."

The sound of King Stephen's sacred voice, the one I'd heard since childhood, saying *my* name nearly made me faint. But before I could decide if I'd be fainting from fear or religious awe, the king spoke again. "Rise, child, and let us see you."

I shot up like an arrow, desperate to obey. I'd never dreamed that I would be this close to the king, and I'd never wanted to be, either. The Sainted King was as terrible as he was just, the divine will of God made flesh. He was not the sort of power you wanted taking an interest in you if you were smart. He was looking at me now, though, so I stayed perfectly still, praying frantically that he see whatever he wanted even as I realized the futility of praying to a saint who was ten feet in front of you.

This close, I couldn't help noticing how much older the king looked in person. I'd never thought of King Stephen as handsome— one did not have such thoughts about a living saint—but this close I couldn't miss how age had sunken his cheeks, making his high cheekbones and pointed chin even sharper by comparison. He looked gaunt, a blasphemous part of me realized, almost sickly. But then, King Stephen was approaching sixty-five, and no Paradoxian king had ever lived past seventy. His eyes, however, were crystal clear and every bit as electric blue in real life as they appeared on camera.

That scared me the most, actually. I'm as faithful a Paradoxian as you'll find, but I'd always secretly wondered if the eerie glow was added in postproduction, a trick to help the faithful believe. Now I saw for myself that it was no trick. The king's eyes glowed like electric blue fireflies behind the open mask of his suit, and though I forced myself to hold my ground, inside I was shrinking with holy terror.

"You are younger than we thought you'd be," the king said at last, like this disappointed him. "But Caldswell praises you very highly. He wrote to us of what you did here, the services you rendered to our crown, before giving you back into our care."

I swallowed. When Caldswell said he had referred my case up the chain, I hadn't realized he'd gone to the very top.

"What do you want with her?"

I jumped at Rupert's voice, giving him a frantic look. You did *not* speak to any noble unless specifically invited, especially the king. He was going to get both of us hanged if King Stephen took offense. But if the Sainted King was offended by Rupert's lack of deference, he didn't show it. Instead, he answered.

"That depends on young Morris, former Eye Charkov," the king said. "We heard such tales of her that we thought we'd better come see for ourselves, and to bear witness to a unique natural phenomenon."

He turned as he said this, gazing up and out of the observation room's glass bubble at the universe beyond. I looked, too, trying to figure out what he could mean, but all I saw were the phantoms. They'd gotten thicker since we'd arrived, sweeping through the observation room like windblown seeds. But though they blew through Rupert and the king's guard like ghosts, they stopped when they hit King Stephen.

That made me pause. I'd gotten so used to the phantoms going through everyone except me and the daughters, I hadn't paid them any attention, especially since my king was in the room. Now that I'd seen it, though, I wondered how I could have missed them. They were crawling over the king like they loved him, gathering around his body until he was ringed in light. It was a holy sight, and quite fitting, but I didn't understand why. I was still wondering when the king turned back to me.

Having those glowing eyes staring straight through you is a harrowing experience, and when the king raised his hand, I was certain he was about to smite me where I stood. But he didn't. Instead, he turned his hand over, palm up, and like he'd called to them, the phantoms descended, flocking to his fingers like birds to a feeder, their little feelers running over his skin just like they did over mine.

When he saw me looking, the king dropped his hand, scattering the phantoms as his gaunt face broke into a smile. "You have done Paradox a great service," he said, his deep voice rumbling. "By opening the door and freeing those it trapped, not only did you make our sacred kingdom safer, but you also removed our need to support and tolerate the Eyes' interference."

He grinned, like this was a grand joke, and held out his hand again, though not for the phantoms. Instead, one of his knights handed him the hilt of an ornate, and very sharp, sword. The king gripped the hilt with practiced ease, swinging the razor-sharp point up until it was level with my nose.

"Your deeds have made you worthy in our sight," he said, his voice taking on the rhythm of ceremony. "To reward you for your service to our crown, we in our magnanimity have decided to grant you a boon of your choice. Speak, and it shall be."

I swayed on my feet, thunderstruck. A boon from the king. That could be *anything*. Wealth, power, even nobility. The king was offering me anything I could dream of, but when I opened my mind to the possibilities, there was only one wish waiting for me.

"Your Majesty," I said, focusing on each word to keep my voice from shaking. "I ask you to make me a Devastator."

The king frowned. "Are you sure, young Morris? Our Devastators are brave, but they are commoners. We are willing to grant you a barony in the Marches if you desire."

A barony would make me real nobility, something that was almost never offered to peasants like me. I wasn't actually sure which part of what I'd done had set me so high with the king, but even so, I wasn't tempted. For all its importance, nobility was too much like a desk job for my liking, and anyway, I'd only ever had one goal in my life. Now that it was in my reach again, nothing was going to put me off course. "With all due respect and gratitude, Your Highness, I want to be a Devastator."

I was certain I'd messed up the address in that one, but the king merely shrugged. "So be it," he said. "The easiest way to do this is to knight you, which would please us greatly. If that is your wish, then step forward, young Morris, and be sworn to us forever."

I sucked in a breath. Knighthood was a silly childhood dream. Things like that never really happened to mercs. But I didn't wake up when I stepped forward, or when I fell to my knees at the king's feet. I didn't imagine the feel of the king's sharp sword pressing down on my shoulder as he spoke the ancient blessing of knighthood, and though I barely heard myself giving the answers, I was reasonably certain I actually spoke them. Everything was a blur by this point, but I must not have messed up too badly, because when I stood, the king placed his hand, his own sacred hand, upon my shoulder.

"Sir Morris now," he said, smiling. "Go back to Caldswell and tell him you are no longer his. We shall see you back in Kingston, Sir Knight, and all of civilization shall know of your deeds."

I think I might have died of happiness at that moment, or maybe I was just in shock. I was vaguely aware of bowing to the king and stumbling out. I probably would have fallen on my face if Rupert hadn't been there to keep me upright.

I did remember to look back one last time when we reached the door, because it wasn't every day you met a living saint. When I looked back, though, King Stephen wasn't watching me. He was standing at the huge window, staring up at the sea of phantoms as they drifted past on their way out of our universe, his eerie eyes casting a brighter blue tint to their snowy light.

This ghostly sight was the last I saw of my king before the doors cut me off.

———————

The reality of what had just happened didn't really sink in until we reached the docking tube. After that, it took everything I had not to bounce up and down squealing like a pig. After all, I was a knight now, and knights had to be dignified. But though I managed not to act like a *complete* idiot, I couldn't help grabbing Rupert's arm and tugging on it while I told him I was a knight over and over in a breathless voice until the words ran together into mush.

"Yes, you are," he said indulgently, kissing my head. "You made it. I'm proud of you."

But even though his words were warm, I couldn't help noticing Rupert wasn't quite as happy as I was. To be fair, I don't think anyone could have been as happy as I was at that moment, but I'd expected a little more excitement.

To my great surprise, Caldswell seemed over the moon at the news. He congratulated me earnestly, slapping me on the back like we hadn't been trying to kill each other a week ago. Actually, life without Maat seemed to be doing him very well. He looked ten years younger, so when he announced he was retiring, I couldn't quite believe it.

"There's no more need for us," he said, grinning. "The daughters are being integrated into other programs and want nothing to do with us anyway. Maat's gone, no more phantoms, there's nothing for me to do."

"There must be something," I said.

Caldswell just shrugged. "Nothing I care about. I've done my time and then some, and I think I deserve a break from the endless grind of duty. I'm thinking of getting a new ship, actually, try my hand at real trading."

I made a face. "Well, so long as you don't have to make real money doing it, you should be fine."

It was a sign of his good mood that Caldswell burst out laughing at that. He waved farewell to us and walked off down the hall, whistling as he went. Mabel fell into step behind him a few doors down, though I didn't see where she'd come from. That should have unnerved me, but it's hard to be afraid of a woman who was turning around to give me two big thumbs up. After that, I could only shake my head. Vicious, bloodthirsty killers one second, best friends the next. Damn crazy Eyes were as bad as mercs.

"What are you going to do?" I asked, glancing at Rupert as we walked back to my room. "You're free, too."

"I don't know," he said. "I've never been anything except an Eye."

I shrugged. "Why don't you come with me, then?"

He stopped midstep, head snapping up to stare at me. "But you just got made a knight."

"So?" I said. "That just means I'll be in Kingston all the time. The Devastators are part of the Home Guard. Commitment-wise, it's actually easier than being a mercenary since you get to go home at night instead of spending your off hours stranded on some rock."

Rupert cleared his throat, and though his expression was perfectly casual, I knew him too well now to be fooled into thinking the next words out of his mouth didn't mean the world to him. "Are you sure you'd want me around? This is what you've always dreamed of. I wouldn't want to be in the way."

I slugged him in the arm, hard. "Of course I want you," I said, scowling to hide my blush. "Didn't you hear me before? I love you. Besides, you're the one always talking about wanting a future. This is mine, and I want you along. It wouldn't be any fun at all without you."

Rupert stared at me for a long time after that, and then his casual expression vanished as he swooped in to hug me so hard I gasped. "Sorry," he whispered, stepping back. "It's just..." He trailed off with a boyish grin that he couldn't seem to stop. "I'm just very happy."

"Good," I said. "You should be. Always."

He slipped his arm around my waist. "So long as you'll have me, I will be."

"Like I'd ever let you escape," I said, slipping my arm around his waist as well as we walked down the dull, efficient Terran hall toward the rest of our glorious and, with luck, exceedingly happy future.

ACKNOWLEDGMENTS

As always, none of this would be possible without the tireless work of the good people behind the scenes at Orbit Books. Thank you for all your hard work.

extras

meet the author

RACHEL BACH grew up wanting to be an author and a super-villain. Unfortunately, supervillainy proved surprisingly difficult to break into, so she stuck to writing and everything worked out great. She currently lives in Athens, Georgia, with her perpetually energetic toddler, extremely understanding husband, overflowing library, and obese wiener dog. You can find out more about Rachel and all her books at rachelbach.net.

Rachel also writes fantasy under the name Rachel Aaron. Learn more about her first series, The Legend of Eli Monpress, and read sample chapters for yourself at rachelaaron.net!

introducing

If you enjoyed
HEAVEN'S QUEEN,
look out for

ANCILLARY JUSTICE

by Ann Leckie

*On a remote, icy planet, the soldier known as Breq is
drawing closer to completing her quest.*

*Breq is both more than she seems and less than she
was. Years ago, she was the Justice of Toren—a colossal
starship with an artificial intelligence linking thousands
of corpse soldiers in the service of the Radch, the
empire that conquered the galaxy.*

*An act of treachery has ripped it all away,
leaving her with only one fragile human body.
And only one purpose—to revenge herself on
Anaander Mianaai, many-bodied, near-immortal
Lord of the Radch.*

CHAPTER

1

The body lay naked and facedown, a deathly gray, spatters of blood staining the snow around it. It was minus fifteen degrees Celsius and a storm had passed just hours before. The snow stretched smooth in the wan sunrise, only a few tracks leading into a nearby ice-block building. A tavern. Or what passed for a tavern in this town.

There was something itchingly familiar about that outthrown arm, the line from shoulder down to hip. But it was hardly possible I knew this person. I didn't know anyone here. This was the icy back end of a cold and isolated planet, as far from Radchaai ideas of civilization as it was possible to be. I was only here, on this planet, in this town, because I had urgent business of my own. Bodies in the street were none of my concern.

Sometimes I don't know why I do the things I do. Even after all this time it's still a new thing for me not to know, not to have orders to follow from one moment to the next. So I can't explain to you why I stopped and with one foot lifted the naked shoulder so I could see the person's face.

Frozen, bruised, and bloody as she was, I knew her. Her name was Seivarden Vendaai, and a long time ago she had been one of my officers, a young lieutenant, eventually promoted to

382

her own command, another ship. I had thought her a thousand years dead, but she was, undeniably, here. I crouched down and felt for a pulse, for the faintest stir of breath.

Still alive.

Seivarden Vendaai was no concern of mine anymore, wasn't my responsibility. And she had never been one of my favorite officers. I had obeyed her orders, of course, and she had never abused any ancillaries, never harmed any of my segments (as the occasional officer did). I had no reason to think badly of her. On the contrary, her manners were those of an educated, well-bred person of good family. Not toward me, of course—I wasn't a person, I was a piece of equipment, a part of the ship. But I had never particularly cared for her.

I rose and went into the tavern. The place was dark, the white of the ice walls long since covered over with grime or worse. The air smelled of alcohol and vomit. A barkeep stood behind a high bench. She was a native—short and fat, pale and wide-eyed. Three patrons sprawled in seats at a dirty table. Despite the cold they wore only trousers and quilted shirts—it was spring in this hemisphere of Nilt and they were enjoying the warm spell. They pretended not to see me, though they had certainly noticed me in the street and knew what motivated my entrance. Likely one or more of them had been involved; Seivarden hadn't been out there long, or she'd have been dead.

"I'll rent a sledge," I said, "and buy a hypothermia kit."

Behind me one of the patrons chuckled and said, voice mocking, "Aren't you a tough little girl."

I turned to look at her, to study her face. She was taller than most Nilters, but fat and pale as any of them. She out-bulked me, but I was taller, and I was also considerably stronger than I looked. She didn't realize what she was playing with. She was probably male, to judge from the angular mazelike patterns quilting her shirt. I wasn't entirely certain. It wouldn't have mattered, if I had been in Radch space. Radchaai don't care much about gender, and the language they speak—my own first language—doesn't mark gender in any way. This language we were speaking now did, and I could make trouble for myself if I used the wrong forms. It didn't help that cues meant to distinguish gender changed from place to place, sometimes radically, and rarely made much sense to me.

I decided to say nothing. After a couple of seconds she suddenly found something interesting in the tabletop. I could have killed her, right there, without much effort. I found the idea attractive. But right now Seivarden was my first priority. I turned back to the barkeep.

Slouching negligently she said, as though there had been no interruption, "What kind of place you think this is?"

"The kind of place," I said, still safely in linguistic territory that needed no gender marking, "that will rent me a sledge and sell me a hypothermia kit. How much?"

"Two hundred shen." At least twice the going rate, I was sure. "For the sledge. Out back. You'll have to get it yourself. Another hundred for the kit."

"Complete," I said. "Not used."

She pulled one out from under the bench, and the seal looked undamaged. "Your buddy out there had a tab."

Maybe a lie. Maybe not. Either way the number would be pure fiction. "How much?"

"Three hundred fifty."

I could find a way to keep avoiding referring to the barkeep's gender. Or I could guess. It was, at worst, a fifty-fifty chance. "You're very trusting," I said, guessing male, "to let such an indigent"—I knew Seivarden was male, that one was easy—"run up such a debt." The barkeep said nothing. "Six hundred and fifty covers all of it?"

"Yeah," said the barkeep. "Pretty much."

"No, all of it. We will agree now. And if anyone comes after me later demanding more, or tries to rob me, they die."

Silence. Then the sound behind me of someone spitting. "Radchaai scum."

"I'm not Radchaai." Which was true. You have to be human to be Radchaai.

"He is," said the barkeep, with the smallest shrug toward the door. "You don't have the accent but you stink like Radchaai."

"That's the swill you serve your customers." Hoots from the patrons behind me. I reached into a pocket, pulled out a handful of chits, and tossed them on the bench. "Keep the change." I turned to leave.

"Your money better be good."

"Your sledge had better be out back where you said." And I left.

The hypothermia kit first. I rolled Seivarden over. Then I tore the seal on the kit, snapped an internal off the card and pushed it into her bloody, half-frozen mouth. Once the indicator on the card showed green I unfolded the thin wrap, made sure of the charge, wound it around her, and switched it on. Then I went around back for the sledge.

No one was waiting for me, which was fortunate. I didn't want to leave bodies behind just yet, I hadn't come here to cause trouble. I towed the sledge around front, loaded Seivarden onto it, and considered taking my outer coat off and laying it on her, but in the end I decided it wouldn't be that much of an improvement over the hypothermia wrap alone. I powered up the sledge and was off.

I rented a room at the edge of town, one of a dozen two-meter cubes of grimy, gray-green prefab plastic. No bedding, and blankets cost extra, as did heat. I paid—I had already wasted a ridiculous amount of money bringing Seivarden out of the snow.

I cleaned the blood off her as best I could, checked her pulse (still there) and temperature (rising). Once I would have known her core temperature without even thinking, her heart rate, blood oxygen, hormone levels. I would have seen any and every injury merely by wishing it. Now I was blind. Clearly she'd been beaten—her face was swollen, her torso bruised.

The hypothermia kit came with a very basic corrective, but only one, and only suitable for first aid. Seivarden might have internal injuries or severe head trauma, and I was only capable of fixing cuts or sprains. With any luck, the cold and the bruises were all I had to deal with. But I didn't have much medical knowledge, not anymore. Any diagnosis I could make would be of the most basic sort.

I pushed another internal down her throat. Another check—her skin was no more chill than one would expect, considering, and she didn't seem clammy. Her color, given the bruises, was returning to a more normal brown. I brought in a container of snow to melt, set it in a corner where I hoped she wouldn't kick it over if she woke, and then went out, locking the door behind me.

The sun had risen higher in the sky, but the light was hardly any stronger. By now more tracks marred the even snow of last night's storm, and one or two Nilters were about. I hauled the sledge back to the tavern, parked it behind. No one accosted me, no sounds came from the dark doorway. I headed for the center of town.

People were abroad, doing business. Fat, pale children in trousers and quilted shirts kicked snow at each other, and then stopped and stared with large surprised-looking eyes when they saw me. The adults pretended I didn't exist, but their eyes turned toward me as they passed. I went into a shop, going from what passed for daylight here to dimness, into a chill just barely five degrees warmer than outside.

A dozen people stood around talking, but instant silence descended as soon as I entered. I realized that I had no expression on my face, and set my facial muscles to something pleasant and noncommittal.

"What do you want?" growled the shopkeeper.

"Surely these others are before me." Hoping as I spoke that it was a mixed-gender group, as my sentence indicated. I received only silence in response. "I would like four loaves of bread and a slab of fat. Also two hypothermia kits and two general-purpose correctives, if such a thing is available."

"I've got tens, twenties, and thirties."

"Thirties, please."

She stacked my purchases on the counter. "Three hundred seventy-five." There was a cough from someone behind me—I was being overcharged again.

I paid and left. The children were still huddled, laughing, in the street. The adults still passed me as though I weren't there. I made one more stop—Seivarden would need clothes. Then I returned to the room.

Seivarden was still unconscious, and there were still no signs of shock as far as I could see. The snow in the container had mostly melted, and I put half of one brick-hard loaf of bread in it to soak.

A head injury and internal organ damage were the most dangerous possibilities. I broke open the two correctives I'd just bought and lifted the blanket to lay one across Seivarden's abdomen, watched it puddle and stretch and then harden into a clear shell. The other I held to the side of her face that seemed the most bruised. When that one had hardened, I took off my outer coat and lay down and slept.

Slightly more than seven and a half hours later, Seivarden stirred and I woke. "Are you awake?" I asked. The corrective I'd applied held one eye closed, and one half of her mouth, but the bruising and the swelling all over her face was much reduced. I considered for a moment what would be the right facial expression, and made it. "I found you in the snow, in front of a tavern. You looked like you needed help." She gave a faint rasp of breath but didn't turn her head toward me. "Are you hungry?" No answer, just a vacant stare. "Did you hit your head?"

"No," she said, quiet, her face relaxed and slack.

"Are you hungry?"

"No."

"When did you eat last?"

"I don't know." Her voice was calm, without inflection.

I pulled her upright and propped her against the gray-green wall, gingerly, not wanting to cause more injury, wary of her slumping over. She stayed sitting, so I slowly spooned some bread-and-water mush into her mouth, working cautiously around the corrective. "Swallow," I said, and she did. I gave her half of what was in the bowl that way and then I ate the rest myself, and brought in another pan of snow.

She watched me put another half-loaf of hard bread in the pan, but said nothing, her face still placid. "What's your name?" I asked. No answer.

She'd taken kef, I guessed. Most people will tell you that kef suppresses emotion, which it does, but that's not all it does. There was a time when I could have explained exactly what kef does, and how, but I'm not what I once was.

As far as I knew, people took kef so they could stop feeling something. Or because they believed that, emotions out of the

way, supreme rationality would result, utter logic, true enlight-
enment. But it doesn't work that way.

Pulling Seivarden out of the snow had cost me time and
money that I could ill afford, and for what? Left to her own
devices she would find herself another hit or three of kef, and
she would find her way into another place like that grimy tavern and get herself well and truly killed. If that was what she
wanted I had no right to prevent her. But if she had wanted
to die, why hadn't she done the thing cleanly, registered her
intention and gone to the medic as anyone would? I didn't
understand.

There was a good deal I didn't understand, and nineteen
years pretending to be human hadn't taught me as much as I'd
thought.